Book of JUDAS

Richard Hollands

AN M-Y BOOKS PAPERBACK

© Copyright 2015
Richard Hollands

A CIP catalogue record for this title is
available from the British Library

ISBN– 9781517188061

For Alexander, Henry, Max and Tilly
and especially Issie for all her help....

Chapter One

Sutton Dean, Oxfordshire

Philip Trenchard looked solemnly at the ground as the pallbearers began lowering the wooden coffin into the freshly dug hole. It was mid-May and the earth was soft from the seasonal spring showers. Philip glanced across at his brother Simon, while the Vicar, dressed in his black and white cassock, solemnly intoned the final prayers for their departed grandfather. Having known the deceased and the family for many years, Father George Wells was almost as grief-stricken as those gathered around him.

After days of seemingly ceaseless drizzle the weather had changed dramatically for the better as if to mark this sombre occasion. Now, just after twelve o'clock, the sun had emerged to bless the graveyard of the ancient St. Peter's church, which dated back to the twelfth century. Beyond its waist-high, stone wall perimeter, it was surrounded by green fields in any direction you cared to look and only a loose gravel path running between two fenced fields connected the House of Worship to its Parish, the small Oxfordshire village of Sutton Dean.

"Ashes to ashes, dust to dust," murmured the priest, holding a bible close to his chest with one hand whilst sprinkling earth onto the coffin below with his other.

As Father Wells' recitation moved from the Committal to the Dismissal and final blessing for the departed, Philip watched the dirt spatter harshly onto the wooden coffin lid, partially covering the shiny brass plaque engraved with the name of his grandfather, Sir Lawrence Trenchard.

Bowing his head, Philip closed his eyes and took a moment to pay his last respects to the man who had been responsible for his upbringing. Father Wells' even monologue blended into the background as he cast his mind back to the tragic circumstances that had led to their grandfather becoming their guardian at such an early age.

Although Philip was only eight at the time, fourteen months older than his brother Simon, he had a slightly clearer recollection of that terrifying night in October 1974. Recalling the events was always difficult; his mind would replay the tape the same way it had done on countless occasions in the past. It would begin with happy images of their family home and the brothers playing in the garden... only for the scene to be shattered as he moved to the next frame. It was dark – in the early hours of the morning. Simon sitting bolt upright on his bed, paralysed by the bloodcurdling shrieks from downstairs that pierced the silence for what felt like an age but in truth was probably a matter of minutes. Frozen with fear, Philip remembered the gut-wrenching panic that welled up as the screams became muffled and again an eerie silence returned. Several moments later their grandfather Sir Lawrence burst into the room, roughly seized both boys and lurched down the stairs with them clinging to his neck.

For both boys it was the same. From the moment they reached the foot of the stairs in their grandfather's arms, the memory ceased. The next thing that he could recall was Simon crying and screaming "Mummy" as they were hurled into the back of a car and driven off at high speed. The very next morning their grandfather came to them with tears in his eyes and told them the tragic news. Neither Philip nor Simon would ever forget his ashen, haunted face as he tenderly drew them both to him and told them that their mother and father, his own son, had been killed in

2

a fatal road accident. He never offered any further explanation for the events of that night – not then, nor in later years – but continued to hold them tightly, repeating, "You'll be safe now, I'll look after you". From that day onwards, the brothers lived with Sir Lawrence in his stately mansion, Tudor Hall, in the small Oxfordshire hamlet.

That was over twenty-six years ago, and Philip was now thirty-five and Simon, thirty-four. On many occasions they had tried to recreate the memory from the moment they had reached the bottom of the stairs but always came up against an implacable inner defensive wall that was not prepared to let them endure the insufferable pain of the truth. Something frightening had taken place; something the mind of a seven- or eight-year-old could not cope with and no amount of mental pressure could bring the barrier down. Philip's mind skipped to the scene with his brother screaming for their mother and his eyes burst open, startled, as if waking from a bad dream.

In the bright sunshine, he quickly took stock of his surroundings again. In line with Sir Lawrence's wishes there was only a small gathering present to see him lowered into his final resting place. Apart from Simon, Father Wells and the four pallbearers, there were only four other members of the congregation – and Philip knew everyone present save one, an older-looking gentleman with an academic appearance about him, which was not at all surprising, thought Philip, given the history and nature of their deceased grandfather's career.

Standing next to him was Mrs Vines, who leant stiffly forward and carefully dropped the bunch of white lilies she was holding into the open grave, scattering their white, trumpet flowers and green stalks spread evenly over the casket. She sniffled and covered her face with a tissue. Mrs Vines knew the brothers well. In her sixties now, she had been the cook, housemaid and secretary to Sir Lawrence for more than twenty-five years, living in her own annex attached to Tudor Hall.

Standing to her left was Felix Bairstow, the family solicitor. He shook his head in grim acknowledgement as he caught Philip's glance in his direction. Bairstow, also in his sixties, was a very old friend of Sir Lawrence. Their relationship had begun in earnest in the early 1970s when Sir Lawrence had returned from his well-documented travels abroad. Finally, the gentleman standing next to Simon was Dr. James Gifford who had become a close friend of Sir Lawrence over the last few years of his life. In his mid-forties, he worked for the local practice and had taken a sabbatical from the role of family doctor to look after him full time at his request. The thought of entering a private or NHS hospital had filled Sir Lawrence with terror.

Father Wells was reaching the end of the service.

Two days earlier, Father Wells himself had attended the memorial service that had been held in Westminster Abbey in Victoria for the late Sir Lawrence Trenchard. The service was conducted according to precise instructions he had left with Felix Bairstow and both Philip and Simon were requested to make selected readings. In total there were over four hundred friends, colleagues and distant relatives present to celebrate the life of Britain's most eminent archaeologist of modern times. The service was attended by various dignitaries, including members of the royal family who had befriended him over the years and who were familiar with his work and discoveries in the Holy Lands of the Near East – he had been knighted in 1971 in recognition of the advancements he had made to our understanding of ancient times and photographs of the occasion were proudly displayed on the wall of his study at Tudor Hall. After Sir Lawrence had completed his archaeological tours through Judea and the surrounding Arab states in the fifties and sixties, he was offered the position of Curator at one of Oxford University's most famous landmarks, the Ashmolean Museum. With its instantly recognisable domed façade, it was established in the late seventeenth century and internationally renowned for its archaeological exhibitions. The role allowed him the freedom to complete his chronicles and at the same time to accept public engagements to speak and lecture on the archaeological discoveries he had made.

"...In the name of the Lord, our Father..." intoned Father Wells solemnly, holding up his free hand and making the sign of the cross above the trench. "...Amen."

The vicar paused, looking up at the gathering around him.

"Thank you, Father Wells," said Simon Trenchard respectfully. "My grandfather would have appreciated your kind words."

The Vicar cast his gaze from Simon to Philip, who smiled and nodded his agreement. In turn, Father Wells dismissed the pallbearers with a discreet signal and two of them headed back towards the church. The remaining two picked up their tools and started shovelling the neat pile of earth back over the coffin, the first shovelful covering some of Mrs Vines' white lilies.

Father Wells, conscious of the brother's desire for privacy, started to make his way over to join Mrs Vines, Dr. Gifford and Felix Bairstow who were huddled in conversation.

Slightly bemused, Philip looked around for the elderly-looking gentleman wearing the black overcoat but he had disappeared. He heard a car engine starting and glanced beyond the stone wall to catch a glimpse of the figure at the wheel of a car steadily crunching down the gravel path towards the village and the main roads.

"Who was that?" asked Philip, touching the vicar's arm as he was passing and nodding towards the departing vehicle.

"I'm afraid I'm not sure of his name – David I think. He told me he was a very old friend of your grandfather's and Felix expected him."

"Thanks," said Philip curiously as he watched the car disappear from view. He knew Bairstow well enough to know that none of those present would have been there without his late grandfather's express permission.

The vicar joined the others and gently ushered them towards the path leading to the church. Simon approached Philip, carefully skirting the grave and the two gravediggers.

"Come on," he said, putting a hand on Philip's shoulder and gently pushing for him to follow.

The graveyard was grassy and uneven and the variously shaped headstones broke through randomly scattered bushes; the recent ones proud and upright, and weathered, ancient ones protruding at all angles from the greenery. Philip followed his brother past a flowering magnolia towards two headstones planted side by side against the perimeter wall.

Usually unaccompanied, they each visited this plot whenever they were back in the country.

The inscription on the first headstone read:

John Trenchard
Loving husband of Valerie and
Beloved father of Philip and Simon
1942-1974

Next to their father was their mother's headstone with matching engraving. The brothers stood in silence for a few minutes. Before the service they had arrived with flowers and, thanks to Mrs Vines' assistance, the flowerpots in front of the headstones were now a splash of spring colours.

"It's good to see you again, Philip," said Simon, still focusing on the headstones.

"You too," he replied. This was the first time they had seen each other for over two years.

"I had a phone call from grandfather three weeks ago asking me to come back to Tudor Hall as soon as I could... I was due to be here now to see him," said Philip.

"I know," replied Simon. "He called me afterwards and agreed the dates with me. Said he wasn't feeling well... but I could tell he was excited about telling us something… I guess we'll never know what now."

"Do you think it was something to do with our Mum and Dad?" asked Philip inquisitively.

"Too late… We'll never know," murmured his brother.

Philip looked over his shoulder, sensing someone coming. It was their grandfather's trusted solicitor, Felix Bairstow.

"I'm sorry to intrude," he said, as he got closer. "But it was your grandfather's wish that I read the will back at Tudor Hall after the service. He was adamant that he only wanted me to proceed if both of you could attend. Is that convenient for you?"

Philip exchanged a quizzical glance with Simon before nodding his confirmation.

"We'll be along in a few minutes," he replied, and Bairstow turned around and made his way back along the grass track to the others, still milling around the ivy-wreathed lych gate.

They stood quietly with their heads lowered, shoulder-to-shoulder, both absorbed in their own thoughts. At six feet three, Philip was marginally taller than his younger brother and everything about his appearance spoke of style and success. He was well groomed with dark hair, cut short at the sides and wore an expensive black suit that fitted his lean frame perfectly. Although they were alike in physical stature, that was where the similarity ended. In contrast, Simon's persona was much more relaxed and laid back – in faded jeans and an open-neck, checked shirt, he stood casually with his hands in his pockets.

"Ready?" said Simon, taking a step backwards. Philip bent down and pulled a single flower from the arrangement in front of each headstone and turned to accompany him along the path to join the others. As they reached their grandfather's half-filled grave, Philip halted.

"Hopefully he's finally gone to join them," he said and gently tossed the two flowers onto the fresh soil as the diggers continued shovelling the earth.

At the gate, Bairstow was organising who would travel in which car.

The brothers had walked together from the village in the morning and accepted his offer of a lift. On the other side of the swing gate, the gravel path swept around a grassy mound in a turning arc for the three cars that were parked along the verge.

Philip held the front door open for Mrs. Vines to get in and then clambered next to Simon into the back of Bairstow's Jaguar. They were the second car to depart and Philip gazed out of the window to his left through the wooden fence and out across the horse paddocks and the green fields that gently sloped up to the woods just over a quarter of a mile away. As he gazed into the bright sunlight along the line of trees with the blue skies in the background his mind wandered to the reading of the will that was to take place later that day. *At least it should be relatively short,* he thought – there were no skeletons in his grandfather's closet that he was aware of.

A few moments later the car left the driveway and joined a country lane that wound its way through the village for the short journey to Tudor Hall Estate, whose grand entrance was opposite the village green's central stone obelisk; a monument inscribed with the names of the local sons and fathers who had died during the Second World War.

"Felix, who was that man at the service wearing the long black overcoat?" asked Philip as the Jaguar turned in to face the high wrought-iron gates. Automatically they parted slowly to reveal the tree-lined drive through the magnificent grounds, whose every inch the brothers knew, towards Sir Lawrence Trenchard's splendid residence.

"I'm not sure exactly," he replied, catching Philip's eye in the rear view mirror. "I believe he was a friend of your grandfather's, connected with Oxford University or the Ashmolean Museum in some way. Anyway, he satisfied your grandfather's written instructions as to who could attend."

Philip nodded thoughtfully as the car drove through the gates.

Chapter Two

Vatican City, Rome

Cardinal Giacoma walked briskly across St. Peter's Square, the hub of the Vatican City. The mild evening temperature notwithstanding, he felt uncomfortable and very apprehensive with the news he carried. Giacoma knew, as would those he was about to meet, that the implications of his imminent disclosure, would go to the very heart of their religion. It was highly unusual to call a consistory, or papal, meeting at such short notice but this revelation required immediate attention. Cardinal Giacoma considered the priests he was about to face. *They all knew this day would was coming,* he thought, shaking his head.

As was usual at soon before dusk fell, the Square was quiet and empty as Cardinal Giacoma hurried with his robes flurrying behind him to the top of the steps leading into St. Peter's Basilica. A relatively young Cardinal at only fifty-two years of age, he reverently wore the traditional and distinctive scarlet cassock that announced his importance and high office within the Holy See. On his head was the traditional red cap, or "biretta", that was placed there by the Pope after reading the Holy Oath of Obedience at his inauguration ceremony.

At the grand portal he paused for a beat to acknowledge the Swiss Guard sentry who stood smartly to attention as he approached. Inside, he walked decorously through the atrium towards the central door, one of five leading into the magnificent Basilica itself. Despite having been a permanent resident of the Vatican for many years, he still marvelled at the opulence of its treasures and rich religious history. Giacoma passed through the door decorated with fifteenth century bronze panels by Filarete and made his way towards the aisle leading into the right arcade. Its vast emptiness gave the impression to many that the Basilica was a cold place – but no one could deny the imperious beauty and majesty its architecture. Built over the ancient tomb of St. Peter, the magnificent edifice was home to countless works of art by great artists such as Raphael, Della Porta and Michelangelo. The indescribable beauty of the religious frescoes and the statues' intricate, ornate detailing made the heart of the Vatican one of the greatest treasure chambers in the modern world.

Cardinal Giacoma scurried down the aisle, passing the magnificent Chapel of the Confession and the statue of Pius VI where day and night, ninety-five lamps burn before the tall "Baldachinno" marking the burial site of St. Peter the Apostle. He came to a sudden halt outside the entrance to the Chapel of the Sacrament. Inside, the elderly Cardinal Alphonso peered up from his meditation as he heard the steps on the stone floor come to an abrupt stop outside and the two men's eyes met through the Baroque iron grille wrought on the gates by Borromini centuries before. Without uttering a sound, Cardinal Alphonso nodded his head in acknowledgement, then closed his eyes to pray. As the sign at the gate proclaimed, the Chapel of the Sacrament was "only for those who wish to pray" – an edict reverently observed by who enter at all times. Cardinal Giacoma was no exception and he lowered his head in deference to the more senior Cardinal and continued on his way, striding down the aisle towards the Sistine Chapel on his way to the Sala Regia.

Cardinal Camerlengo Fiore was already waiting in the Sala Regia, an antechamber next door to the Sistine Chapel that houses the papal throne. Solemn singing could be heard in the background as the conclave in the Cappella Paolina next door recited the mass entitled *De*

Spiritu Santo. Cardinal Fiore was the second most powerful cleric in the Vatican. In his trusted and coveted role, he bore that additional title of "Camerlengo" because he was the Pope's Chamberlain, the papal official responsible for all the church's administrative and fiscal matters. In the event that the Pope died it was he who would temporarily assume the mantle of control until an elected successor was crowned. Cardinal Fiore was forty-five years of age and a tall man with jet-black hair crowned by the distinctive red biretta. Dressed in the same scarlet robes as Cardinal Giacoma and Alphonso, he was an imposing and commanding presence.

The door to the Sala Regia swung open and Cardinal Giacoma entered. Without turning around, Fiore continued to hum in time with the harmonic singing next door while examining a fresco by Giorgio Vasari. The scene depicted a momentous turning point in the life of the Roman Catholic Church; one which unknown to him, would pale into insignificance compared with the events that were about to unfold.

The door opened again and closed behind Cardinal Alphonso as he followed Giacoma across the centre of the broad room to where Cardinal Fiore was standing. At seventy-three, Alphonso was the oldest amongst them and the only one to have been a Cardinal at the time the original episode of crisis had first been debated over thirty-five years ago. Age had caught up with the hunched, silver-haired priest and with the help of a cane he approached in a lop-sided shuffle. Appearances, in his case, were deceptive – his intellectual prowess and ability to dispense even-handed wisdom had gained a substantial following amongst his fellow priests who had learnt the sagacity of his ways. Contrary to the impression he gave of a stumbling old man, his mental faculties were as sharp as the day he first took up the cloth.

Fiore turned around and welcomed his fellow priests.

"What's so important that we have to convene so urgently, Brother Giacoma?" he asked, slightly put out by the disturbance to his official duties.

11

"Will His Holiness be in attendance?" he replied, looking slightly flushed.

"I will meet with His Holiness once I've determined the nature of the emergency," said Fiore sternly, fixing his steely gaze on Giacoma.

This is outside what's been agreed, thought Giacoma ruefully. He had anticipated a direct meeting with the Supreme Pontiff, Pope Paul XII.

"His Holiness should be party to the news immediately," he hissed abrasively, flustered by the unannounced change of plan. "This is important – I need an audience now," he continued sharply.

Cardinal Fiore, the Chamberlain for the Pope, raised a reassuring palm to Giacoma.

"Calm yourself, Cardinal Giacoma, your concern is understood, but I'll be the judge of what's relevant to the official office of His Holiness."

Standing by the Sala Regia's double doors, Cardinal Alphonso shuffled his weight to his other foot before speaking softly.

"I can sense that you're worried, Brother Giacoma, but I believe I know the source of your troubles – you're quite at liberty to speak freely in this room."

Cardinal Giacoma stared deeply into Cardinal Alphonso's eyes before arriving at his decision. Since his elevation to the highest ranks of priesthood, the elderly Alphonso had become his close friend and mentor and he trusted him implicitly.

"Lawrence Trenchard's dead," he blurted out. "He's died at his home in England."

Cardinal Fiore's expression remained blank as he considered the implications of what they were being told. With his back to them, deep in thought, he walked towards the elaborate fresco depicting the mighty Battle of Lepanto. The gentle melodies of the choral singing floated into the room from the chapel next door.

"So the day has finally arrived!" Alphonso sighed.

"It's all going to come back... Everything will re-surface," he murmured softly, contemplating the menace that had lain dormant for so long.

"You'll have to tell His Holiness," Cardinal Giacoma insisted anxiously.

"Thank you," said Fiore dismissively spinning around to face them. "Your work here is done Brother Giacoma. I'll ensure that Pontiff's made aware of your news – you may return to your formal duties but I would request that such information's kept between the three of us for the time being until His Holiness decrees otherwise."

Giacoma regained his composure.

"I'll wait to hear from you, Brother Fiore," he said obsequiously and with that he lifted the crucifix that hung just above his waist on a thick, gold chain and kissed it. Turning to Cardinal Alphonso, he bowed his head respectfully.

"Brother Alphonso," he whispered before setting off towards the doors to the Cappella Paolina.

"This moment was destined from the time the Ruling Ecumenical Council last convened to close this chapter," said Cardinal Fiore with a good deal of resentment and cynicism. "Maybe a more forward-thinking, pragmatic decision all those years ago could have saved us from this day!" he chided scornfully. Fiore knew that Alphonso and the Council had eventually voted to defer their decision, thereby leaving the dilemma to the Vatican's next generation. Fiore shook his head as he weighed up the potential magnitude of the crisis.

"Make no mistake about it," he went on, "the threat to our faith and even the continued existence of the Roman Catholic Church itself is colossal. The consequences of Sir Lawrence Trenchard's death could change the face of the Christian world."

"I understand your concern, Brother Fiore – you know perfectly well that I sat on the Council… If there'd been any other way for us to go, we'd have done so."

"All I know is that you simply deferred a difficult decision thirty years," Fiore argued. "You and your fellow Council members took the easy way out and now we no longer have that luxury – there's no easy way out of this now!"

He walked over to where Cardinal Alphonso was standing and extended his arm.

"Come, Brother, we have much to consider," muttered Fiore. There was no point holding a grudge or pressing home his opinions. He had said his piece with regard to the past and now it was time to think of the future.

Cardinal Alphonso gratefully took his arm and, with the aid of his cane, they walked together towards the Eastern Wing of the Vatican Palace, which housed the residential quarters of Pope Paul XII.

Chapter Three

Sutton Dean, Oxfordshire

The interior of Tudor Hall was as grand as its façade. Philip entered the main reception room off the hallway and sank into a comfortable floral paisley-covered armchair while waiting for Bairstow to make his final preparations. His brother, following closely behind, stood with his hands clasped behind his back before the magnificent stone fireplace admiring the original lithograph of ancient Jerusalem by David Roberts that took pride of place above the mantelpiece.

It was a bright airy room with high corniced ceilings, exposed beams and two sets of glass double doors leading out on to the terraced patio beyond. Both brothers had followed careers that took them overseas and returning to the childhood house where time had stood still felt very peculiar – at every turn an object or a room would bring memories flooding back. The two of them had been totally inseparable during their formative and early teenage years, which was hardly surprising given the intensity of the trauma they had suffered after the tragic loss of their parents. In the early years, the emotional attachment to, and dependency on, Sir Lawrence was incalculable but as time moved on, their grandfather derived great pleasure as he watched the strength of their bond grow before him. Simon grinned as he caught sight of one of the early pictures high up on the mantelpiece depicting the young boys struggling to keep pace with their grandfather.

"Do you remember this one? He was enormous!" he said, pointing with a nod of the head as he recalled the amusing anecdote.

Philip focused on the picture in the silver frame and smiled.

"You still owe me for that," he said laughing at the fond memory although it had been far from funny at the time.

It was not a typical family picture. It depicted a visibly annoyed Sir Lawrence dragging the brothers by their arms on a cold winter's day with their primary school in the background. On closer inspection you could make out bruising around Simon's face. The year six school bully had made the elementary mistake of picking a fight with the younger Trenchard, who was half his size. Alerted by the commotion, Philip, who was not known for his aggression, dashed to the rescue and felled the giant tormentor with one powerful blow. Hearing the report from the playground attendant, the misguided headmaster had been furious at this shameful behaviour called their grandfather to come and remove the brothers from the battle scene. His initial annoyance soon faded to respect for young Philip when he grasped the truth behind the events and the photo was installed as a memento to his brave deed.

The close bond between them continued until they reached early adolescence. After that it didn't come to an abrupt end but rather gradually transformed as their personalities and mutual dependency evolved and the dependency. Watching proudly from the wings, their grandfather was as surprised at the growing difference in their characters as he had been impressed by the strength of their union in their formative years. The elder Philip was extremely clever and his academically prowess enabled him to sail through exams without too much difficulty. By contrast, Simon was intellectually "middle of the road", constantly striving to join the band of the elite although he didn't get too upset about not making the grade. From his side there was no envy because he had strong attributes of his own, excelling on the sports field not just by representing the school in rugby, swimming, hockey and athletics but also by being selected to represent the county and achieving "local" fame and recognition by touring with junior England teams. Again, mirroring Simon's intellectual capabilities, Philip played and enjoyed sport but his skill and ability were outclassed by his younger brother's innate flair.

Their grandfather often wondered how his son had managed to produce offspring with such abundant yet starkly different talents. Always looking to find new ways of encouraging them, he observed how their abilities affected the development of their personalities. Competing in two alien environments, Philip in his world of academia and Simon in his sporting arena, meant that they grew up in two very separate social worlds.

When they reached "A level" age, their day to day lives went their separate ways. Philip passed his Oxbridge exams with flying colours and accepted the invitation from St. Edmund's Hall to enter Cambridge University. The following year Simon achieved the grades necessary to accept a place at Loughborough University, which was renowned for its development of sporting talent. The notion of his taking the Oxbridge exam had been dismissed out of hand by the teaching staff at St. Edward's.

As they embarked on their differing paths, Sir Lawrence watched as the nature and intensity of communication and interaction between them changed. He was pleased that neither had lost his confident, outgoing personality – nevertheless, the social circles and peer groups in which they moved were radically different and the ease and comfort they once felt with each other's friends steadily diminished.

Throughout his university career, Philip's academic results continued to flourish and impress his grandfather. Not only did he graduate with a first class honours degree – he also received the distinction of becoming head of the Cambridge Debating Society attracting many gratifying plaudits from eminent professors along the way. As the time approached to leave, Philip devoted a lot of thinking time to his future career. He considered politics but felt that he would prefer a more well-defined and structured environment. As consequence he settled on the more lucrative and glamorous choice of Investment Banking. Cambridge University, being what it is, one of the top producers of executive talent in the world, attracted the biggest and best "City" firms to its hallowed halls, jostling to recruit the pick of the crop. Philip, at the top of their hit lists, was seduced by the financial rewards and responsibilities that were thrust upon him by one of the Big Five American investment houses. He accepted the offer and after completing the management training program and three years' work experience in London, he returned to Tudor Hall to make an announcement. His grandfather was delighted to hear the news that he had been promoted to Vice President but his enthusiasm was dampened when he learnt that the position also required his relocation to their Wall Street office. Accustomed to his regular trips back to Tudor Hall, his grandfather realised he couldn't stand in his way and gave the move his blessing.

Simon on the other hand, continued to excel in the world of sport but only bordered on a level where he began to toy with the idea of turning professional. After much deliberation and soul-searching, his head finally overruled his heart and he decided that he should embark on a structured career path. In the end, he too followed a career in the City of London but not in the privileged, high profile footsteps of his brother. Instead he started on the bottom rung with a gently declining, middle-of-the-road stockbroking firm. Simon's progress was rapid. He was friendly and go-getting and, more importantly, he started to make lots of money for the firm. His grandfather suspected that he felt slightly aggrieved by the differential in status and remuneration compared with his older brother so he went out of his way to applaud Simon's efforts.

In reality, though, his concern was unfounded because the goals and targets they set themselves were very different. If Simon had wanted to succeed in the City, if he had been motivated by others' perceptions or the trappings of success he could have made it, but the truth was that he didn't care. Philip only realised as much when Simon suddenly handed in his notice to his employer who was disappointed to learn of his departure after such an auspicious start to his career. Simon felt that he was following too closely in his older brother's shoes without really stopping to consider the alternatives. On top of everything else he felt stifled and bored in the job; it was not what he wanted. His next move was impulsive but still received his grandfather's full backing. He decided to join the army and obtained a commission with the Royal Duke of Edinburgh Regiment stationed in Berkshire. Enjoying the camaraderie, Simon passed through Sandhurst with flying colours and as a young captain he was posted on various peace-keeping assignments including tours of duty in Cyprus and Northern Ireland. After two years, just as his promotion to Major was announced, his command was sent into the Kosovo war zone. The death, the poverty and the barbaric conditions in which the local population lived and survived shocked him. Simon struggled to come to terms with the absurd futility of the "ethnic cleansing" as he watched innocent bystanders getting caught in the crossfire day after day. He saw friends killed in cold blood a few feet from where he stood and in turn he shot the enemy, justifying his actions as self-defence. It was insufficient – the senselessness of war distressed him and he found it harder and harder to live with his actions. In the end he saw out the tour but immediately on arriving back in England he bought his way out of the regiment. His grandfather was disappointed but understood his principles. He was also slightly concerned that Simon would be unable to find his true vocation.

After taking stock of his life and reassessing his own values, Simon discovered where his true calling lay and he conveyed his views to his grandfather over lunch in Oxford. Unsure how the news would be received, he was pleasantly surprised by Sir Lawrence's friendly and enthusiastic support and guidance. About a month later, while staying with Philip in his apartment off Sloane Square, Simon informed him of his decision to leave England. He told him that with the help of their grandfather, he had been offered a position within an international volunteer organisation affiliated to the United Nations that dispensed medical and teaching aid to the poorest communities in Africa and South-East Asia. Initially Philip was stunned and argued vehemently against it, but eventually he realised that further discussion on the subject was fruitless. Simon's mind was made up.

Just a week later, he boarded a plane for Namibia and the brotherly inter-dependence that had been so strong in their early years was formally broken. As each day passed, the ties that had once bound them so tightly together began to loosen, but not entirely to unravel – and over the years that followed and the thousands of miles that separated them, they gradually grew further apart.

In Tudor Hall's main reception lounge, Simon moved away from the impressive, stone fireplace to look at other memorabilia of a bygone age around the room. He stepped towards a circular mahogany George III table covered with more framed photographs surrounding an elaborate dried flower arrangement in the centre.

"Do you remember how happy he was that day?" asked Simon, holding up another picture.

The photograph showed the brothers beaming at the camera with grandfather, also grinning broadly, standing between them with his hands clapped around their shoulders. They were standing on the lawns of St. Edmund's Hall, Cambridge and Philip gave the impression of being very learned at his graduation ceremony in his black gown, mortarboard balanced on his head and clutching his degree certificate.

"I remember it well," recalled Philip fondly.

"He looks so well and full of life... Good times!" he added wistfully.

Now at the tender age of thirty-five, Philip had carved out an enviable reputation within New York's indiscreet, scandal-ridden banking community. Since embarking on his career, he had become the doyen of the senior management who had lavished the rich trappings of success upon him to pre-empt counter offers from rival firms. If he managed to avoid the many pitfalls, partnership status was on the horizon.

Simon looked at the picture one last time before replacing it on the table.

"Have you made any plans yet?" asked Philip.

Simon had already told Philip on arrival at Tudor Hall that we wouldn't be staying long – in his United Nations relief agency role he was constantly in demand, co-ordinating projects to alleviate the suffering in various war-torn, famine-infested third world countries, none of which could be put on hold for a family bereavement.

"I've booked a flight for tomorrow evening," he replied. "What about you? – I guess Heather must be keen to get you back."

Heather Adams was Philip's beautiful fiancée. They had met in Manhattan while working on a project of mutual interest to both their prestigious firms. She was a highly successful, highly-respected lawyer in her own right and would have gladly attended the funeral service herself if it had not been for an unprecedented multi-million dollar deal that would have stalled without her presence.

"She's really busy at the moment so I'm going to stay back a couple of days longer to sort his affairs out – if you're leaving that quickly we'll have to make a few joint decisions tonight and tomorrow morning," said Philip.

"What decisions?" asked Simon quizzically, having assumed that Bairstow could handle most of the outstanding matters.

"Well, for a start, what are we going to do with this place?" said Philip, casting his arm around the room to indicate the house and its belongings. "You might need to give me your Power of Attorney."

At that moment, Felix Bairstow entered the room.

"If you're both ready, we can begin the reading?"

Simon nodded towards his brother.

"Ok, let's hear what has to be said and then we'll sit down and go through the details – I don't suppose there are any major surprises in the will are there, Felix?" he asked flippantly.

Bairstow, in his long-term capacity as Sir Lawrence's confidant, knew the drama of what was about to unfold. Normally calm and assured, he suddenly seemed slightly and uncharacteristically – anxious. He fidgeted apprehensively, contemplating his answer to Simon's question before giving them a bewildering response.

"I think you'll find that the contents of the will the least of your concerns when you learn your grandfather's real legacy," he stated ominously from the doorway.

Simon and Philip were momentarily stunned by the reply; surprise registering across their faces.

"What do you mean, Felix?" asked Philip curiously.

"All will be revealed very shortly…" he replied slowly and mysteriously, before tapering off deep in thought. Suddenly, he jerked back to life. "Why don't we begin in the study? It's much more private in there."

Philip and Simon followed Bairstow down a wood-panelled corridor off the main hallway that led to Sir Lawrence's private study. Inside, it was like an exhibit room in a museum, every available space packed with ancient artefacts and relics from a bygone age displayed in glass presentation cases. It was an archaeological treasure trove; a testament to his life's work. Simon shuddered as he passed through the creaking wooden door – he still felt as if he were trespassing whenever he entered the study. As young children capable of getting up to all kinds of mischief, the brothers had been expressly forbidden from ever entering his sacred domain. From floor to ceiling, the walls were clad in bookcases and shelves and any space that did remain uncovered was filled with a mosaic of mostly monochrome and sepia framed photographs – pictures of excavation sites, ancient ruins and other interesting places he had visited on his archaeological tours. One particular picture always caught

Felix Bairstow's eye – a photograph of Sir Lawrence as a youth, standing in front of the Winter Palace Hotel in Luxor. Next to him was a solitary, distant-looking gentleman in his mid-sixties. As Sir Lawrence had recounted to Bairstow on more than one occasion, this aloof-looking gentleman was none other than Howard Carter, probably the most famous Egyptologist of all time. His most notable achievement and the one for which he received extensive international acclaim along with the Fifth Earl of Carnarvon, was the discovery of King Tutankhamen's tomb in 1922,

Outside, the evening was drawing in and Mrs Vines was busying herself drawing the long velvet curtains across the latticed window to replace the sun's fading light with that of two table lamps and a reading lamp that stood on their grandfather's antique leather-inlaid desk. Bairstow, anxious to commence proceedings, promptly walked around the desk and sat down on the old swivel chair. Bending down to his left, he clicked open a case and produced a carefully sealed package, which he laid out in front of him. Looking up, he politely ushered the brothers into the two armchairs he had arranged in a slight arc facing the desk. The brothers, still looking perplexed, dropped themselves down into the amply cushioned seats.

Behind Bairstow, Mrs Vines gave the room more light by pulling the dangling cord of a tall standard lamp.

"Thank you, Emily," said Bairstow and she smiled warmly before leaving the room.

Using an ivory-handled letter opener, Bairstow slit the envelope across the top. He pulled out the contents, which included a few bound sheets of paper and a plastic case the size of a thick paperback book. Putting on his half-moon reading glasses, he glanced at his audience before focusing on the will's italic writing and commencing his administrative role.

"In my capacity as Executor to the will of the late Sir Lawrence Trenchard, I am bound to carry out his specific wishes. In fact, as you will understand later, the reading of the will is only one of my duties this evening."

He glanced up, checking that he had the brothers' undivided attention.

"Fine, let's make a start. Firstly, I'll deal with the capital distributions of the estate before moving on to the real reasons why your grandfather was so adamant that both of you, and you alone, should attend this meeting."

Bairstow peered over the top of his glasses as the brothers traded confused glances.

What on earth does he mean? thought Simon.

"In no particular order, I'll run through the major contents of the will. The house and its possessions, save for your grandfather's private archaeological pieces, are bequeathed jointly to you both," said Bairstow, looking up.

"Your grandfather left a comprehensive list as you can see," he said, holding up a thick file containing a computer print-out of Sir Lawrence's private collection.

"Over the next few days, the artefacts will be carefully transported to the basement of the Ashmolean Museum where they'll eventually go on display. About two years ago, the Dean of Oxford University and Sir Lawrence reached a confidential agreement regarding the donation of his personal collection. The University wanted to commemorate the work of their most famous archaeologist and have made financial provisions to refurbish an exhibit hall to be named after him. That hall will become the permanent home to his artefacts and a testament to his life's work."

That's exactly what he would have wanted, thought Philip, nodding his approval. Up until that point, the question of a final resting place for his private collection had preyed on his mind.

"Your grandfather was a wealthy man," continued Bairstow, "and he has made some generous monetary gifts to me and to Mrs Emily Vines. He also consulted with Doctor Gifford and agreed to pledge a sum towards the appeal for a new ward at the John Radcliffe Hospital in Oxford. Am I right in understanding that you were familiar with these arrangements?"

Philip and Simon nodded.

"In total about three hundred thousand pounds, isn't it?" queried Philip. He then went on to tell Bairstow his understanding of how the generous bequest was broken up.

"That's correct Philip, but I suspect you may not be aware of the following," he continued raising his eyebrows. "Sir Lawrence has divided the balance of the estate three ways."

"What do you mean?" said Philip with a puzzled expression. He was not unduly concerned about the size of his inheritance now that it would be split by an additional fraction but he was genuinely taken aback by the revelation of a new third party.

"After government taxes have been paid and allowing for some fluctuation on his market investments, your grandfather's estate amounts to approximately one million eight hundred thousand pounds and is to be divided evenly between yourself, Philip… Simon… and… Anna Nikolaidis."

"And who is she exactly?" Simon asked sarcastically. He was genuinely startled by the news but as he thought about it a bemused smile spread across his face.

Well, well, well, there must be a skeleton in the closet after all that we don't know about, he thought. Like Philip, he started imagining the revelation of a love child from some illicit, extra-marital affair.

"I'm going to let your grandfather explain that," replied Bairstow dispassionately. His words took a few seconds to sink in.

The amused look on Simon's face was replaced by one of astonishment.

"What are you saying, Felix?" asked Philip, the irritated inflexion in his tone creeping up to reflect his increasing annoyance with Bairstow's games.

"You are both aware that over the two-week period before your grandfather passed away that he was very extremely keen to see you…"

Bairstow looked up, waiting for their acknowledgements. They both gave one nod of the head; it was not something they cared to be reminded about.

"Well your grandfather knew he didn't have long to live and he desperately wanted to have one final conversation with you both. His anxiety that you wouldn't reach him in time increased with each passing day and, with the help of Doctor Gifford and myself, he decided to make a back-up plan."

The brothers sat frozen, absorbed by what Bairstow was saying and fascinated to hear what would come next. Each of them suddenly sensed that somehow their deceased grandfather was going to speak to them – but how?

Is this woman, Anna Nikolaidis somehow connected? thought Simon.

Confused, they clung to every word the loyal and dutiful family solicitor had to say

"This…" said Bairstow, picking up the package in front of him, "… contains the real reason why Sir Lawrence was so anxious to see you. He knew he didn't have much time left and asked us to help him set up a video camera so that he could record himself. Your grandfather was adamant that his written word was not sufficient… He wanted to address you both in person."

Philip and Simon watched Felix Bairstow take off his glasses and open the sealed package to produce a video case.

"This is the only copy… It's your legacy – Are you ready to watch it?" he asked, holding up the black case.

Surprised, this is not what they expected and after a moment's contemplation, Simon was the first to speak.

"I don't have any problems, do you Philip?" he asked, sighing out loud.

At that particular moment in time, Simon couldn't possibly imagine what it was that their grandfather wanted to speak to them about.

What on earth is your secret? What have you got in store for us? he wondered, pondering the various possibilities. *Maybe it's something to do with his guilt about leaving a third of his estate to somebody else that we've never heard of – or maybe he wants to make amends, or at least get us to understand...*

The same myriad thoughts ran through the mind of his elder brother.

"No... I've no objections," Philip replied slowly with a hint of reluctance. His enthusiasm was not tempered by worry about what the truth might hold, but from a fear of seeing his surrogate father dying before them in his last few days. His concern only escalated as Bairstow issued the following words of caution.

"I'm afraid I must warn you that this film was made two days before your grandfather died... You must be prepared for that... His condition deteriorated considerably over the last week."

"Ok, we understand," said Simon, "I'm sure whatever he has to say must be extremely important for him to go to these lengths."

Bairstow stood up and walked over towards the large wooden wall cabinet and pulled open the double doors to reveal a television screen. Previously, the cabinet had been used to house some of the larger items in Sir Lawrence's collection and the modern flat screen appeared completely out of place.

"I had this unit installed specially for this purpose," he said, pulling out the cassette and leaning down to install it. The brothers jumped up and shifted their chairs around to get a better view. Bairstow, with a finger on the play button, turned his head to face them.

"Ready?" he asked, quizzically raising his eyebrows.

They nodded and the screen lit up as he pressed the button. Bairstow immediately stood up and walked slowly backwards, perching himself with his arms crossed, on the edge of the desk. The opening frames on the screen were slightly distorted as the picture showed the novice camera operator going in and out of focus until he reached the true definition.

Philip was shocked. He automatically reached out and put his hand on Simon's shoulder as they both recoiled from the painful, harrowing sight of their dying grandfather. They were used to seeing him buoyant and full of life but this was distressing. With sunken cheeks, his face looked drained and sallow. It was immediately apparent that any movement, no matter how small, required a substantial concerted effort. Motionless, he lay in his four-poster bed upstairs in the master bedroom. At that moment, the figure of Doctor Gifford entered the screen as he leant across the bed, locking his arm under Sir Lawrence's so that he could pull him up and place an additional pillow behind him.

"Is that better?" they heard the doctor ask his patient softly. Their grandfather mumbled something inaudible, which was promptly followed by the familiar voice of Bairstow confirming that everything was okay from behind the camera. He zoomed in so that the picture focused on their grandfather's face whilst his head rested on the pillows. Ready to begin, the dying old man looked up towards the lens.

"Philip, Simon," he spoke softly. "If you are watching this tape, I'm sorry I wasn't able to stay around long enough to see you in person. I bitterly regret the fact that I didn't try to contact you earlier but there's nothing I can do about it now…"

Despite his frail and ghostly appearance he spoke lucidly. Occasionally, the extended length of his pauses between words made it clear how much effort the act was taking. Seeing the horror on the brother's faces as they stared at the screen, Bairstow interrupted and reminded them that he was on very strong medication at this stage.

"I have a story to tell you that will now change both of your lives…" he paused and grimaced at the camera. "I'm angry with myself that I have left it so long; I thought the truth could stay buried in the past, but a recent event has changed any hope of that…" he said, blinking rapidly.

"Are you alright?" they heard Doctor Gifford ask and they watched their grandfather nod his head slowly and lift a handkerchief to remove the tears of anguish that were welling up in his eyes.

"I am so very sorry that I am not there to help, or answer your questions… I hope you'll be able to forgive me…" He looked away sorrowfully for a second. As if in a trance, he paused for an instant, deep in thought, before looking back to the camera and summoning up what little energy that he had to complete the arduous task in hand. Having steeled himself, he spoke clearly into the microphone attached to the lapel of his pyjamas. The sheets were tucked up across his chest.

"Let me start at the beginning," he said and stretched out a hand towards a glass of water sitting on the bedside cabinet. Doctor Gifford promptly returned into the frame to help before stepping back again.

"In 1947, a young Arab goat herder was walking through the rocky mountains along the North West Bank of the Dead Sea. To pass the time, he threw stones into the caves along the rock face and listened to them echoing as they ricocheted against the inside walls. However on this one occasion, he cast a stone and it made a dull thud… It had pierced a two-thousand-year-old ceramic pot…" Pausing, his eyes seemed to light up with the memory. "This was the first discovery ever made of the Dead Sea Scrolls at Qumran."

Engrossed, the brothers stared at the screen as they listened to their grandfather's voice speaking to them from the grave.

"This was over half a century ago, and since then eleven caves have been discovered with ancient artefacts and over eight hundred scrolls. In 1953, when I was in my mid-thirties, I travelled to Qumran, to head the excavation of a newly found cave. Other caves were being excavated at the same time but there was a particular sense of urgency in this project. Roland De Vaux, the Catholic administrator in charge of the entire project was keen to complete the excavation work at the earliest opportunity…" Sir Lawrence sighed, "…In hindsight, I now understand why De Vaux was so eager but nevertheless he was not to know how many more caves would subsequently be found."

Philip racked his brains to remember any mention of the Dead Sea Scrolls. He recalled all the pleasurable and animated conversations he had with his grandfather about his life's work but nothing jumped out at him. Slowly shaking his head, he concluded that this was the first time he had mentioned the Scrolls.

"My assistant on the excavation was a Greek called "Demetri" – an experienced and highly educated man who'd run archaeological projects for Greek government. And although it was the first time we'd met, we immediately became good friends – because we were both driven by the same passion for our work, I suppose. Many times we worked away in the close confines of the cave into the early hours of the next day as we catalogued and recorded our findings."

The brothers sensed his fondness and respect for the man. The glimmer of a smile and the warm tone he used to describe their comradeship left them in no doubt about the obvious affection in which he held Demetri.

"At the time," he continued, "the site and the finds were a major topic of world news. The Scrolls dated back to the time of the Bible and everywhere the religious community was waiting to hear the impact of the translations on the Old Testament. Theologians around the world were anxious to understand whether the writings would confirm or deny the words attributed to the Apostles in the New Testament. In the circumstances, given the eagerness with which the news was awaited by the followers of Christianity, it was not surprising that rumours and stories began to flow abundantly. The principal complaint or rumour was one of suppression. The accusation was levelled at the Vatican, which through their appointee, De Vaux, was allegedly deliberately stifling and withholding information that contradicted the teachings of the bible – and therefore the Roman Catholic faith."

Sir Lawrence suddenly coughed repeatedly and pressed a handkerchief to his mouth while he tried to regain his composure. For a moment his head fell so that his chin rested on his chest before Doctor Gifford appeared and hurriedly fed him some tablets along with a sip of water. Gradually the medicine took effect and, slightly reinvigorated, he continued with his intriguing story.

"We heard the rumours and to begin with we dismissed them but then things kept happening to make us reconsider. We began to get the feeling we were being watched – we were not unduly surprised that our work was being carefully screened but we soon became aware that De Vaux was actually making changes to our written records. Up to that point the contents of the deciphered Scrolls could be considered relatively harmless from the perspective of being anti-religious, but then Demetri and I made an amazing discovery. It was dark, just after midnight and we were working by the light of our gas lamps. At the back of the cave, Demetri noticed a soft lining in the wall. When we began to scrape what we thought was rock, to our astonishment it started to crumble, revealing a second but smaller inner cave. You had to crawl through the narrow hole in the rock on all fours to enter and once we were both inside we found that it was not big enough to stand upright. Inside, the contents were very different from those of the main cave. Demetri held up the gas lamp to reveal two ancient clay vessels sitting in the centre of a polished floor. We opened the pots and took out the papyrus scrolls that were folded inside. Their feel and fabric was different from the ones we had discovered earlier – they were flexible with a rubbery texture. I opened the first and was astounded to find that it was in perfect condition, unlike so many of the others – it was amazing; it was an intricately detailed map of Judea at the time of Christ. The second was even larger and we unravelled it on the floor. It was full of Hebrew text and we slowly started to decipher and read the ancient scriptures."

Philip and Simon watched, riveted to the screen, as he continued.

"The translation was shocking..." said Sir Lawrence, coughing

31

hoarsely. He stopped and stared intensely into the camera lens. "The scroll confirmed the existence of the Book of Judas…" he coughed again, struggling to get out the words, *"…the bible of the antichrist."*

Simon cast a sideways glance at his brother, checking the revelation's impact. Philip looked puzzled, confirming that he was just as confused as Simon about the import of the discovery. He turned back to the image of his grandfather as he croakily continued.

"Up until this point the book was considered a myth… Nothing, no evidence of any kind had ever been found to support its presence in the real world."

He stopped to contemplate his own words; the ramifications of this event had clearly filled him with dismay.

"The truth was potentially explosive. We had found the map and instructions to get to the biggest religious discovery of all time… Not only that, but if the Book of Judas really existed it was prophesised that its unearthing would destroy the pillars upon which the entire Christian religion had grown… *It had the power to unlock the devil himself."*

Sir Lawrence's face contorted as he recalled the moment when he and Demetri stood in the cave trying to decide what to do next. After sharing the initial euphoria of the breakthrough he remembered the excitement fading as their heightened senses gave way to anxiety and fear.

"We both knew that if these scrolls were passed on to De Vaux the discovery would be covered up immediately. His Roman Catholic administration team would escort the artefacts back to the Vatican where they'd never be seen again… The truth of their existence would never be acknowledged. The only people who could testify to finding the scrolls were Demetri and myself… And we knew this knowledge would put our own lives in danger."

Philip and Simon could see the effort being made by their grandfather to complete the remarkable story. Sir Lawrence stopped to draw breath before again summing up the energy to continue and recount the final chapter.

"It was the early hours of the morning and we decided that our only option was to escape with the scrolls and try and smuggle them out of the country. With Demetri leading the way, we left the cave using our gas lamp to light the path. We tried to act normally but one of De Vaux's henchmen must have been watching the whole thing and in our haste to get away we were taken by surprise when he jumped into our path. He asked Demetri aggressively to show him the contents of the cloth sack he was carrying – he was pointing a gun at us... At first Demetri refused..." said Sir Lawrence, struggling to remain calm as the memory came flooding back and the tone of his voice became bitter with rage.

"But then the guard leant out and smashed the bag from his hands. The sack hit the ground spilling out its contents. In the light of the guard's torch, we watched as the scroll slowly unravelled itself sufficiently for him to make out the first few lines. It transpired that he was more than just an agent; he was educated... And he looked up aghast, mouthing the words 'Book of Judas' with look of sheer terror on his face..."

The emotion of recalling the moment stopped Sir Lawrence in mid-flow. He dabbed the handkerchief he was holding against his eyes.

"If I could turn back the clock to this moment then I would – I have dreamed of being able to do just that on several occasions," he mumbled sadly. "Demetri lunged at the stunned guard, who fell back towards the edge of the rock face. As they wrestled, I dropped to the ground and pushed the contents back into the sack. Turning around, I just had time to stretch out my hand to Demetri as they both careered over the edge into the crevice below. He managed to grab my hand and I held on as long as I could but I just couldn't hold him... The guard's fall was broken by a ledge below but Demetri wasn't so lucky. I watched him fall to his death."

Their grandfather stopped to rub his eyes and Doctor Gifford came back into view, leaning down to whisper something inaudible. Philip and Simon watched their grandfather confirm to the doctor that he was happy to continue. Sir Lawrence, his spirit undiminished, refocused on the camera in front of him and continued to pour out his legacy.

"I stayed there a few moments wondering what to do, listening to the Catholic guard groaning on the rock jutting out below me. After I came back to my senses, I picked up the bag containing the scrolls and set off north towards Jericho. I covered the nine miles or so under cover of darkness before making my way to the Mediterranean Sea to the west. I knew they'd come looking for me so I travelled as fast as I could, smuggling my way onto a fishing boat before disembarking on the east coast of Cyprus. From there I managed to secure the help of the British Embassy to return me home. Once I made it back to England, I set up an elaborate scheme to preserve my own life... That's when I first met James Bairstow, who helped me carry out my survival plan..."

Philip and Simon turned to look at Felix. His expression remained unchanged except for the perceptible traces of sadness that lined his eyes as he stared at the screen. It was only then that they fully realised the depth of their grandfather's long-standing friendship with the Bairstow family. Sir Lawrence continued with the story.

"My good friend Felix will explain to you what happened in the week following my return to England. He, like his father before him, also knows the current whereabouts of the Judas Scrolls."

Simon glanced across at Felix Bairstow who nodded his acknowledgement.

"Incredibly, something happened two weeks ago that made it imperative that I see you as soon as possible..." said Sir Lawrence, trailing off miserably. The brothers sensed their grandfather's sadness; he knew he wasn't going to survive until their planned arrival and now they knew it too.

"The Judas Scroll writings tell of a labyrinth buried below the ground that leads to a temple where the Book of Judas itself is protected. When the labyrinth was sealed, three messengers were each given fragments of bone that resembled narrow, crooked needles just over a foot long. When assembled, the ancient script refers to them as the *"arkheynia"* or the bone necklace. The fragments are clearly identifiable and at one end of each piece of bone is a sculptured, smooth, round head dyed blood red. The scroll states that when the three fragments of bone are connected and placed over the map the path to the labyrinth will become clear…"

Philip shook his head in amazement at the story he was hearing. If it were anyone other than his grandfather narrating the episode, he would struggle to believe it.

The whole thing's incredible, he thought, *simply incredible.*

"The guardians of the labyrinth then entrusted the fragments of bone to the three messengers were who were told to travel as far away as they could in different directions – of course, I would have continued to search for the labyrinth containing the Book of Judas but without those fragments of bone the map's utterly useless. In the beginning, I naively thought it was going to be possible and I spent years researching the whereabouts of the *"arkheynia"* by tracking every single artefact and cataloguing every single relic contained in the archaeological museums around the world. After five years, my hopes were building when found two of the bone fragments. Unfortunately my hopes were short-lived and since that success I've devoted a large part of my life to finding the third key but to no avail… In fact I'd given up any hope of ever finding it until a few weeks ago."

Sir Lawrence was clearly excited by the developments. He became more animated and there was an added vigour to his speech.

"As part of my regular research, I obtained a copy of the *South China Morning Post.* I opened it up and there were colour photos of divers on the deck of a ship displaying the relics they'd brought to the surface from a shipwreck off the coast of Surithani in Thailand. Imagine my surprise, when I investigated their findings closely and saw that in the centre of the display was the final bone fragment with the smooth, red sculpture at the head. Unbeknown to these divers the implications of their discovery were enormous."

Sir Lawrence lay back against the pillows behind him. He was clearly exhausted but desperate to finish the story and tell the brothers all he could.

"Simon, Philip… you must understand that my death will trigger off a renewed attempt to reclaim the scrolls by the Vatican," he warned. "Both of you will find your lives in grave danger until the myth surrounding the Book of Judas is resolved. Until then, you will never be safe… Be warned that those seeking the truth will not just be from the Vatican but from other more sinister quarters. You must think hard and do what you consider to be right – but I truly believe that to save yourselves, the only course of action is to solve the mystery… You must think about it. If you decide to go ahead, I want you to go and see a friend of mine – Professor David Palanski. He'll give you the full facts behind the Book of Judas and tell you about those who'll stop at nothing to get their hands on it."

Sir Lawrence realised he was approaching the end and peered mournfully into the camera lens.

"I am sorry… So very sorry that I have left you in this situation. Since your parents died I've done my best to look after you and I thought I could handle this myself… And now, only when it's too late, I realise that I was wrong."

He turned away from the camera.

Simon sat staring at the screen. He was deep in thought. The palms of his hands were pressed together as if in prayer and contemplation of life itself. His chin rested tiredly on the points of his fingers as he listened to his grandfather's final words. Simon already sensed that what they were hearing would change his and Philip's life, possibly forever. He loved his grandfather but at that moment all he could feel was frustration borne from the fact that he hadn't felt able to trust or confide in them earlier. Resentfully, he listened to the last few minutes of his grandfather's speech.

"Whatever you decide, I want you to do one thing for me... Anna Nikolaidis is my friend Demetri' granddaughter. Unknown to her, I set up a trust fund with her as the sole beneficiary and, so far, I have managed secretly to sponsor her career... She has followed in Demetri's footsteps and has the makings of a fine archaeologist," he informed them proudly. "Please take great care of her... If you decide to solve the mystery then take her along with you... Her knowledge will be invaluable to you."

That explains the unknown beneficiary, thought Philip sardonically, recalling Bairstow's earlier reading.

Sir Lawrence looked at the camera one last time.

"I love you both dearly, never forget that... I have tremendous faith that you will choose the right path... And remember," he said, offering some final advice, "from now on trust no one. They *will* be watching you..."

They watched Doctor Gifford enter the screen before it suddenly went blank. Speechless, Simon and Philip stared at each other.

"Your grandfather was a very clever man," said Bairstow, breaking the silence. "I know he was devastated to be leaving you alone with his legacy. He desperately wanted to be here to help you."

"What I don't understand," asked Philip candidly, "is that if he has been in possession of these secret scrolls for so many years, why was my grandfather safe? Why wasn't his life in constant danger?"

"I agree. It doesn't make sense," added Simon, looking puzzled.

"Let me explain," said Bairstow, who had resumed his seat behind the desk.

"My father met your grandfather for the first time in the week after he returned to England, having smuggled himself and the Judas Scrolls from Qumran. Your grandfather explained the story that you've just heard to my father, James Bairstow, who believed him entirely. As you can imagine, at that time, Sir Lawrence was clearly very distraught, not only for his own safety but also for the safety of the scrolls. Together, your grandfather and my father sat down and devised a plan that would prevent the Roman Catholic hierarchy within the Vatican from threatening his life."

Bairstow stood up and walked over to another cabinet, pulling open its wooden shutters.

"Would you like a drink?" he asked, holding up a decanter and pausing momentarily for their response. He poured three tumblers while continuing his narration. Simon and Philip listened attentively.

"Almost immediately, my father helped him store the Scrolls in a secure place offshore and then they set about writing certain letters," he said, handing over the whisky tumblers to the brothers before resuming his seat.

"Together they wrote three duplicate letters fully explaining what had taken place one week earlier at Qumran. Each letter contained pictures of the Judas Scrolls with details of how to recover the originals. The three letters were then deposited with three prominent firms of London solicitors with express instructions that if Sir Lawrence failed to materialise on certain dates, or if he failed to call at certain times, then the letters were to be delivered immediately by a senior partner to the listed addressees. The recipients included one eminent politician and two businessmen running large independent media empires."

Bairstow paused looking thoughtfully at the drink in front him as he recalled the memory of his father telling him the story. It was shortly afterwards that he took over the reins of the family business and the duties towards Sir Lawrence Trenchard that went with it.

"Shortly afterwards, your grandfather received a notification from a Cardinal Deacon in the Vatican requesting a meeting in Rome. After some debate, Sir Lawrence agreed and in a private meeting at a church in Rome he met with two Cardinals. As you would expect, they asked for the Judas Scrolls and your grandfather told them of the arrangements he had put in place to safeguard his life. Your grandfather was under no illusions. He knew that he would still be in grave danger even if he handed them over."

Bairstow took a sip of his drink and Simon looked up quizzically at him.

"So what happened next?"

"The Cardinals wanted to see what was in the scrolls. They were very keen to know whether the Book of Judas really existed, and whether or not their discovery threw any light on its final resting place. Your grandfather told them what the scribes had written and gave them a picture of the Judas Scroll showing the ancient Hebrew text. Sir Lawrence even assisted them in translating parts so that they understood that no one could seek out the labyrinth without first obtaining the *"arkheynia"* that were, purportedly, scattered around the globe."

Bairstow drained the rest of the whisky from his cut glass tumbler.

"After that your grandfather returned to England and, to the best of my knowledge, he had no further direct contact with the Vatican."

"I don't understand," said Simon. "How would he be able to protect us?"

"Ultimately," replied Bairstow, "I think he felt that if you were honestly unaware of the scrolls he could keep you both hidden from the danger. I am not sure what he had in mind, but I believe he considered some kind of deal with the Vatican whereby the original scrolls would be offered up in return for a guarantee of your safety."

A momentary silence descended while the brothers thought about what Bairstow had said, and how that translated now their grandfather was dead.

"I'll leave you to discuss what you've seen and heard," said Bairstow, standing up and making to leave. He collected up the documents concerning the will but left the video where it was.

Philip stood up and extended his arm.

"Thank you Felix… You, like your father before you, have been a good friend to our family – I'm very grateful."

"We're both very grateful," said Simon, also shaking his hand firmly.

"If you want to ask more questions just call me, otherwise I'll be here tomorrow morning," he said, reaching the door. "You must also let me know whether you want the contact details for Professor David Palanski and Anna Nikolaidis... Please think about how we're going to tell her about her inheritance."

The brothers nodded, thanking him again. Philip followed him through the door to see him out of the main entrance. When he returned to the room, Simon was rewinding the videotape back to the start.

"This changes everything for me," said Simon, watching Philip take both their glasses and refresh them from the drinks cabinet. As usual, Mrs Vines had been very thoughtful. She had even been kind enough to fill the ice bucket.

"I'm cancelling my flight tomorrow – we have to solve this mystery... I'm going to tell them I can't resume my assignment till I've completed some important family business."

"Have you thought this through?" asked Philip quizzically, recognising his younger brother's impetuous streak. "Do you realise what's involved?"

"Ok, Philip," replied Simon, noting his brother's concerned tone. "You've seen it and heard it. Whether it's strange circumstances or fate, who knows, but I believe the discovery of the third fragment of the bone necklace means that it's our duty to find this labyrinth."

"Duty?" asked Philip, pointedly. He was tired and rubbed his eyes.

"Listen, we don't even know anything about this Book of Judas. Finding it could have far greater repercussions than just being a relic hunter's trophy, Simon... You heard the Vatican's response. They're prepared to kill to prevent knowledge of the book from escaping – we're not talking about some everyday artefact that's going to end up in some display cabinet in a museum. Do you not see that?" he said crossly.

Simon had not considered this.

"Do you understand what I'm saying?" Philip repeated. "It's possible that the world will better off if these scrolls are just handed back to the Vatican and the information in them buried for ever – maybe it's best if they are destroyed."

"Ok, maybe you're right," replied Simon thoughtfully. "We need to understand more about the Book of Judas before we know what we're embarking on… Why don't we go and see this Professor Palanski and see what we can learn from him?"

After a moment's consideration, Philip agreed that they would fix up an appointment with the Professor in the next couple of days.

Simon leant down to the machine and pressed the start button on the video. They sat back again to watch their grandfather's story for a second time. Philip put out his hand to touch his brother's shoulder.

"Whatever we decide, it's good to see you for a few more days," said Philip, holding out his glass and smiling.

"You too," said Simon. Their glasses clinked before their eyes reverted to the television screen.

Chapter Four

Sutton Dean, Oxfordshire

Two days later, Philip and Simon walked out of Tudor Hall's main entrance and across the gravel drive to where the grey Mercedes that had belonged to their grandfather was parked. Bairstow had originally intended to sell it but had been temporarily persuaded otherwise by the brothers.

"How long will it take to get there?" asked Simon, walking around to the passenger door as Philip de-activated the central locking.

"About twenty-five minutes," he replied. "It's not far; he lives just the other side of Oxford."

The day after they watched the videotape of their recently deceased grandfather the brothers had met with Felix Bairstow again. He had asked them what their intentions were, and they explained that they had decided to discover a bit more about the Book of Judas before rushing into a decision. Bairstow had fully supported the idea and readily agreed to give them Professor David Palanski's contact details as specified in their grandfather's will. Later that evening, Simon had duly called the professor and set up an appointment for eleven-thirty the following morning.

On the way over, Simon told his brother about the professor's nervous, short attitude on the phone. Oddly, he had declined to meet with them at first but when Simon mentioned it was to do with the Book of Judas and that their grandfather had suggested they meet in his will, he abruptly changed his mind. On the drive across town they discussed the questions they would put to him.

"We just don't know enough about him – do we?" said Philip, listening to his brother's final remarks.

"Anyway what kind of professor is he? What's his chosen subject?" he said with a smile on his face.

"I've no idea, maybe we can ask him – we do know that grandfather must have trusted him implicitly," replied Simon. "I don't think he'd have given us his name unless he was entirely familiar with the story."

"Makes sense," commented Philip as he spotted a sign saying *Moorcroft Drive*. "This is it – keep your eyes open for number twenty-eight," he added.

The property was a three-storey semi-detached house constructed around the 1930s and identical to every other residence in the street. The third floor was really no more than two attic bedrooms but with the steep steps leading up to the tiled porch and its pointed roof, its façade gave a flattering impression of its size. Simon pressed the bell and looked down over the metal rail guarding the steps. Down below at the base of the house he noticed an elongated glass window that provided the cellars with an element of natural light. Looking back along the front garden, he observed that it was small and overgrown. There was an old ash tree surrounded by creepers and bushes near the front wall that had lost its shape through a combination of age and neglect.

The door opened and Professor David Palanski appeared.

"Please come in," he said, gesturing for them to come inside.

"We have met before haven't we, Professor?" asked Philip with a bemused smile as he recalled the hasty departure of the man wearing the long black overcoat at their grandfather's funeral.

"That's right. Now please come through," he said, ushering them through the hall. Passing a staircase on their left they continued along the narrow corridor until they entered a large kitchen with a tiled floor and a square wooden table in the middle.

The professor walked over towards the cupboards around the sink leaving the brothers standing around the table observing their surroundings.

"You were at our grandfather's funeral weren't you?" quizzed Philip.

"That's right, I'm a very old friend of Sir Lawrence and against my better judgement I decided to attend the service," he said ruefully. "It was important to me after all we'd been through together; I had to pay my last respects to the great man even though I knew it could be tempting fate."

With his back to them, the professor stopped what he was doing and stood rigidly for a moment staring up at the ceiling. The brothers watched him curiously; he was evidently very troubled by something. Pensively, he turned around and rubbed his forehead with his hand before suddenly regaining his senses.

"Sorry," he apologised shaking his head, "can I get you a cup of tea or coffee?"

"Coffee for me," said Simon and Philip nodded his agreement.

"What did you mean by 'tempting fate'?" asked Philip inquisitively.

"Sorry," Palanski apologised again. "That must sound quite melodramatic to you but there's a lot you don't know – when you learn the truth you'll understand the incredible danger that's facing us out there!"

The answer was very disconcerting. The brothers glanced at each other with the same confused thoughts running through their heads – *What's he mean "us"? And why are we involved?*

"What danger?" blurted out Simon, his irritation growing by the second. Privately he cursed his grandfather for not having had the faith to confide in them.

"Professor?" added Philip inquisitively when no answer was forthcoming to Simon's question. *He's a strange man, he must be in his mid-sixties and a bit absent minded, even eccentric,* he thought, looking at his dishevelled grey hair and unkempt beard.

"Look, I think you're both owed some explanations. Why don't you make yourselves comfortable in the drawing room – that's the door to the left when you go back in the hall – I'll bring your coffee through in a minute."

"Ok," replied Philip more warmly. There was no point getting confrontational and he could see his brother's temper rising. They turned and made their way back through the gloomy hallway. Entering the front room with its large bay window overlooking the front lawn, Philip stepped over, pulled the grubby net curtain to one side and peered out at the elevated view of the residential street beyond.

"He must live alone," said Philip, looking around the room in dismay.

The air was musty and on the floor at the foot of the sofa lay an old food tray with the remains of a recent meal. Once upon a time the room must have looked quite regal with its ornate cornicing around the ceiling and the oil paintings hanging by drawstrings from the picture rail but now it just looked neglected. All the furniture, bookcases and open surfaces were gathering a layer of dust. As Simon scoured the room in bewilderment, his eyes fixed on a sight that made him gasp with amazement.

"Are you seeing what I am?" said Simon incredulously, staring at the end of the room where the dining table stood.

Philip followed his gaze and nodded slowly.

Everywhere you looked there were open books and newspaper cuttings. Piles and piles of them sat around the far end of the room covering the table, the chairs and any available floor space. The wall beyond the dining table was covered from top to bottom in fading old press clippings. To Philip, the mosaic of newspaper articles cast a sinister shadow on the room. They were obviously dealing with someone who was totally obsessed. All across the floor, there were discarded copies of old books and manuscripts, many of them half open, completely hiding the beige carpet that lived beneath them.

Philip walked across to the table and started to leaf through the scrapbook at the top of the pile. It fell open at a cutting taken from the *Sunday Times* in 1982. The article was yellowing and crinkled with age. The headline read:

Death of God's Banker Shrouded in Mystery

Below it, the article told the story of how Roberto Calvi, purportedly the banker to God and the Vatican, was found hanging under Blackfriars Bridge across the River Thames in the early hours of the morning. Philip skim-read the article. Very succinctly, the journalist put forward the case for a possible verdict of suicide on the one hand, but on the other suggested it was probably more likely the work of some sinister evil cult that had infiltrated the higher echelons of the Vatican. As he finished reading, Philip noticed something unusual: the initials "*MM*" had been written with a black marker pen in large letters just below the article.

At that moment, the door was pushed open and Professor Palanski entered balancing three mugs of coffee on a tray. Philip let the scrapbook close took a seat in one of the lounge chairs.

"Sorry about the state of the room," said the professor; he had noticed Philip's interest with the books on the dining table. "But the mess you see around you's my life's work."

"May I ask what you're a professor of?" said Philip directly.

Professor Palanski smiled.

"You may. I was expecting your visit even if I wasn't totally happy about it," he confessed.

He handed over the mugs of coffee before reclining into a cushioned sofa.

"You see that book there…" the Professor continued, pointing at an old, well-thumbed volume sitting on the floor near the fireplace. They could see that it was entitled *The Rituals of the Holy Lands*.

"Well that was my first published research over twenty-five years ago and the principle reason why I met your grandfather in the first place."

He took a sip from his mug of coffee before replacing it on the side table.

"I'm a Professor of Ancient Theology specialising in the biblical lands and I lecture here at Oxford University. Your grandfather read that book and when some of the theories contained in it immediately struck a chord with him he got in touch. We met professionally on several occasions before he felt comfortable enough to tell me his whole incredible story to me," said Palanski, looking up. "And now he's related the entire story to you – isn't that right?" he asked rhetorically.

The brothers nodded.

"Our grandfather also mentioned that you could tell us the myth behind the Book of Judas," remarked Simon.

"The myth?" the Professor replied abruptly with a sharp intake of breath. "It's more than a myth; it's the key to our future – to everyone's future."

The words flew out quickly in his excitement.

Obviously, myths and non-believers are not welcome here, thought Simon. He made a mental note to listen and not contradict or pull holes in his version of events.

Momentarily taken aback by the Professor's shortness, Philip held up his hand to restore the peace.

"Please Professor, tell us what you know," he said calmly.

The professor stared intently at him for a second and nodded. The sudden agitation had surprised the brothers.

He's uptight and apprehensive about something, thought Philip with a sense of foreboding for what he was about to hear.

"I promised your grandfather that I would tell you, and I will," he replied matter-of-factly with order restored.

The brothers exchanged knowing glances waiting for him to begin.

"How well do you know your Bible?" the Professor asked.

Simon shrugged.

"Just what we were taught at school."

"Well, let me begin by giving you a scripture lesson," he replied.

"Well, I'm sure you've heard of Judas Iscariot. He was one of the twelve Disciples of Jesus Christ, the Son of God. His background and his origins were distinctly different from all the other eleven chosen Apostles. As you'll recall, it was he who betrayed Jesus after the last supper by kissing him on the cheek in front of the Roman escort. It was his treachery that ultimately led to the crucifixion – do you not find it remarkable that this mysterious and unintelligible act of total betrayal should come from someone chosen by Christ himself as loyal and faithful disciple? Someone who shared his intimate company and followed him closely throughout his travels?"

Simon and Philip didn't answer but waited for him to continue.

"The Bible actually answers this question but many modern day theologians refuse to accept its explanation, or worse, they choose simply to deny its existence. The actual truth is in the pages of the scriptures themselves but they are ignored or misinterpreted. In the Book of John, chapter six, verse seventy-one, Jesus says, *'Have I not chosen you twelve; and one of you is a devil?'* and in Luke, chapter twenty-two, verse three, he says, *'and Satan entered into Judas, who was named Iscariot, one of the twelve.'* Now that is what the bible says but the teachings of the Christian Church put a different story and meaning behind the words. The truth is…"

He stopped and rubbed his face with his hand. He could see that they were listening avidly to his every word.

"The truth is that Judas Iscariot really was the mortal incarnation of

Satan himself – in the same way Jesus Christ was the flesh and blood of God, Judas Iscariot was the Devil's own son!"

Surprised, Philip rocked back in his chair; he was unsure where this conversation was leading.

"I've devoted my life to researching this theory and that's what it was, just a theory with plenty of circumstantial evidence until I met your grandfather and heard the remarkable truth of what he'd discovered in Qumran. As I learnt more about his findings all the pieces began to fall into place. Throughout the ages and the centuries since the crucifixion itself, the Book of Judas has been shrouded in mystery. The first written records of it dated from around the fifth century but I wouldn't be surprised if the Vatican archives hold documents that go back even earlier. The book of Judas has always been inextricably linked to the Roman Catholic Church and I think you need to appreciate how the Vatican has played its part…"

He took another sip of his coffee and observed that the brothers were fascinated, hanging on to his every word.

"In the beginning, those that were possessed by demons were taken to see the Head of Exorcism at the Vatican and he'd try and cast the demons out. The bodies and minds of these hapless souls would not be their own. They'd writhe on the floor in a grotesque fashion, screaming obscenities and incoherent gibberish in a multitude of different or unknown languages. On one occasion, His Holiness Pope Sixtus heard the screaming and visited the chamber where the exorcism was being carried out. The story says that when he entered the room the demon inside the victim's soul suddenly went quiet. Then, as the Pope moved towards the possessed spirit, his voice changed to a deep, resonating snarl as he kept repeating the words, *'Liber Liborum Loudas'* – 'Judas, the Book of Books'.

"Listening to the words, the Pope stepped forward and placed his hand on the wretched soul, the demon left his body but the words have lived on. After this incident there came many more similar cases over the centuries that followed. The demons possessing their bodies would repeat the same phrase and others such as *'Loudas Satanica'*, – 'Judas, the Black Lord of Satan'. In medieval times, the number of exorcisms reached their peak. The number reached epidemic proportions and the Vatican in its apparently less than infinite wisdom didn't know what to do to stop or stem the flow. They were in a quandary and took the fateful decision to try and hold a dialogue with one of the possessed souls. The Head of Exorcism at the time was Monsignor Angelo Montella and it was his idea to probe and interrogate the possessed spirit. Pope Gregory was the Supreme Pontiff at the time and when he entered the room, as before, the tormented soul went quiet for a few moments before starting to repeat *'Liber Liborum Loudas'* over and over again. This time, Monsignor Montella spoke back to the demon, asking him where the Book of Judas came from and what did it mean? The demon's rage flared up and through his ranting and snarling they could make out the words that translated as 'the Bible of Satan'. Pope Gregory, kissing his crucifix, went forward and placed it on his disfigured head of the possessed soul… That single event is said to have given birth to the macabre sect of devil worshippers known as the 'Satanica'."

Professor Palanski paused to gauge the reaction he was getting from his audience. He smiled as he saw the brothers sitting riveted to his every word. They wanted to interrupt and ask questions but both understood it made sense to wait until the end.

"History says that when the Pope's cross touched the victim's face, the beast flew from his body into that of Monsignor Montella who in turn became possessed by the same evil spirit. The Vatican did what it could for their Head of Exorcism but it was hopeless. They were forced to imprison him as every day he began acting more and more like a wild animal, striking out at anything that came near him. In between these bouts of savagery, Montella could have lucid moments that could last days and give hope of revival but they'd always come to an abrupt end. The last straw came when he killed one of his guards by biting out his throat – the General Ecumenical Council didn't know what to do and took the simple option of casting him out from the walls of the Vatican. From there, it is said, Monsignor Montella disappeared – the reality is that the origins of evil sect known as the 'Satanica' grew around Montella and it exists and lives amongst us today."

"What do you mean?" interrupted Simon curtly.

"I mean you can debate how they arrived but believe me they are here…" he glared back at Simon.

"I don't understand," said Philip, "who exactly are *they*?"

Professor Palanski slowly nodded his head, registering the question.

"After your grandfather shared his findings with me I've made a life's study of the Book of Judas… During the course of my work I have found substantial evidence to support my theory that the Satanica have created a highly motivated and clandestine underground organisation that has its tentacles in all the major centres of the globe. It's a highly secretive movement, obsessed by the imminent coming of the devil and whose members include prominent politicians, diplomats, businessmen and high-ranking members of the military establishment. They've pledged their allegiance to their controllers – the ruthless High Council of the Zoroastrian Priests who are the ultimate, all-powerful rulers of the Satanica."

"What do they want?" asked Simon curiously.

"They're united by their Church…" replied the Professor. "The Church of Satan – they believe that when the Book of Judas is found the 'Black Lord' – 'Satan' – will be unlocked from his resting place and that he will return to rule the world and when he does, they'll be his chosen ones."

"Incredible," said Philip, amazed by what he was hearing. "What do we know about these priests – what did you call them, Zoroastrian priests?" he asked uncertainly.

"The High Priests of Zorastri are the leaders of the Satanica and they mastermind their eternal quest to find the Book of Judas. They represent pure evil; I can't tell you who they are or where they reside but whenever they appear they're associated with death – I've found examples of brutal mutilations and obscene atrocities that have been put down to their dark and ritualistic practices. In their ceremonies they praise and invoke the name of Satan through incantations and human sacrifice… They believe in a grotesque form of 'animism' – worshipping the souls of the dead."

Professor Palanski suddenly stood up and walked towards the window and, pulling back the curtain, he peered outside into the street.

"The Satanica want the Book of Judas and believe me they'll stop at nothing – *nothing*," he repeated coldly, "to achieve this aim."

"Do they know about our grandfather's discovery?" asked Philip suddenly contemplating their own position. *If they do, surely our lives are in grave danger now*, he thought ominously.

"I don't know. I can't answer that – you know from what I've told you that the 'Satanica' used to have strong links with the Vatican. Well, it's believed that this unholy union has persisted through the ages and still exists now. If it does then it's only a matter of time until they find out. Your grandfather's death will have shaken up a hornet's nest amongst the powerbrokers inside the upper echelons of the Vatican."

"These cuttings," said Simon pointing towards the table and the floor. "Are they all to do with the Satanica and the Book of Judas?"

"Nearly all of them, and I should also mention," said the Professor, remembering another detail, "that there's one common trait that identifies the horrendous acts carried out by the Satanica."

"And what is that?" asked Philip.

"They like to brand their acts of atrocity but usually you have to look very closely to find it – they use a symbol, it's two M's, one written over the top of the other. It was taken, I believe, from the initials of Monsignor Montella."

That explains the initials 'MM' written in black marker pen next to the article on the death of God's banker in the scrapbook, recalled Philip.

"What about the book itself? Do you believe it exists?" asked Philip.

"You've heard what your grandfather discovered at Qumran– what do *you* think?" replied Professor Palanski impatiently.

"Yes, but how did the Book of Judas get to Qumran in the first place?" contested Philip, "I mean do we know who wrote it?"

Professor Palanski paused as he realised what Philip was driving at. *He wants a better understanding of the history behind the actual book itself.*

"You must understand that my theory's been compiled by piecing together fragments of ancient texts," Palanski continued. "Just as there's doubt about events that happened in the Bible you should also remember that what I'm saying can't be proven to our total satisfaction…"

Both Simon and Philip concurred by nodding their understanding. The professor walked back from the bay window and paced back and forth in front of the mantelpiece as he elaborated on the book's origins.

"As the Acts of the Apostles were written by the disciples of Jesus, so the Book of Judas was written by his followers and disciples. If you like they were disciples of Satan because as Jesus represented the human form of God, so Judas Iscariot was the living incarnation of the Devil. Having betrayed Jesus and after watching his crucifixion, he instructed his own disciples, six of them, to write the 'Satanic Torah', the testament of evil and immorality according to the Devil. Judas told his disciples that the time would come when people would worship the Black Lord above all else. With his work completed in the human body of a mortal soul, and in front of all his six disciples, he killed himself in a ceremony known as the 'Fields of Blood'. After that, the disciples carried out his final instructions. Three of them went to supervise the building of a labyrinth that would become a tomb for their finished work while the rest went undercover to complete the scriptures that would become the 'Satanic Torah'… And that is where Qumran offered sanctuary. It was the perfect place for them to carry out the wishes of Judas. Qumran was inhabited by an extraordinary Jewish sect called the Essenes. They were smaller than other Jewish sects like the Pharisees and the Sadducees but far more extreme in their beliefs and behaviour. They were reclusive and obsessed by secrecy, believing in a kind of Gnosticism; a covert knowledge only known to privileged insiders. Only males were tolerated in the sect, which loathed the presence of women and children, and they were totally fanatical about their ideas of cleanliness and fidelity. Many theologians and historians recognise today that it was this Jewish sect that was responsible for the Isaiah Scroll, the Temple Scroll, the Copper Scroll and other notable manuscripts that collectively make up the Dead Sea Scrolls. The three disciples of Judas infiltrated this sect and worked day and night as scribes to put down all the teachings and practices that Judas had taught them."

"So that explains why the map and Judas Scroll were discovered in an antechamber to the main cave built by the Essenes," remarked Simon.

"That's right," said Professor Palanski. "It's also said that the bone necklace – the key to the 'Book's' whereabouts – was crafted according to precise instructions from the bones of Judas himself."

"It's an incredible story, Professor," said Philip shaking his head.

Standing in front of the mantelpiece, the professor smiled back and added, "I am afraid the real story is just beginning, Philip – your story. Yours and Simon's story."

"What do you mean?" asked Simon.

"I mean, with the death of your grandfather and the apparent whereabouts of the final bone fragment… at last the truth can finally be established," said the professor, who sounded excited at the prospect.

"You're right," enthused Simon. "I can't explain why but it does feel like it's our destiny find the book."

Philip didn't share the emotion. He sat stony-faced, looking sideways through the net curtains into the street beyond. Lost in thought he sat with his hands clasped in front of him. Professor Palanski read the signs and chose that moment to articulate Philip's thoughts.

"Simon, you must stop to think; you must have your wits about you – your lives will be in grave danger from the start. On the one hand, you'll face the threat from the agents of the Vatican who'll stop at nothing to suppress or destroy the Book of Judas – on the other hand, you'll have to face the dark, evil forces of the 'Satanica'. Once they learn of the discovery they'll most likely search you out and kill you regardless of whether you decide to answer your grandfather's legacy or not. The Book of Judas is their golden prize, it's what they have been waiting centuries to claim, they will…"

"But what does it mean…" Philip interrupted him abruptly in mid-flow. "What happens when the Book is found?"

The room fell silent for a few seconds before the Professor spoke. His voice was slow and deliberate.

"That's the question only you can answer, Philip."

Chapter Five

Sutton Dean, Oxfordshire

That same evening back in the comfort of Tudor Hall, Simon marched down the hallway and into the main kitchen. Although the house had been extended on several occasions, the core, including the spacious kitchen with its exposed brick and wooden beams, dated back to the mid-eighteenth century. In the olden days there had been a staff of over twenty servants working below stairs in the mansion itself and on the estate outside. Simon crossed the cobbled stone floor and entered the large adjoining room that doubled as a cloakroom-cum-laundry. Picking up his stout hiking boots and leather jacket, he sat down at the kitchen table to pull them on.

"You should take the path through the orchard," remarked Mrs. Vines cheerfully without looking up. She was busying herself cleaning around the cooking range on the other side of the kitchen.

"Good idea," he replied.

"Are you ready?" Philip called impatiently from the front door.

"On my way," Simon yelled back loudly. He stood up and pulled on his brown leather jacket, patting his pockets for his wallet.

"Will you be back for supper?" she asked.

Watching the brothers growing up had been one of the joys of Mrs. Emily Vines's life. Regrettably, she had never been able to have children of her own and the failure to produce a family had been the main contributory factor to her divorce. She had joined the household shortly after her separation when the boys had arrived to stay with their grandfather. They took to her straight away and she revelled in their affections, rapidly becoming the mother figure they had lost.

"No thanks! Don't worry about us tonight. We've made plans to eat out – we'll be back around ten'ish," he called as he hurried out of the room to catch up with his brother.

Mrs. Vines chuckled as she watched him dash up the steps in to the hallway.

He never changes, she thought. *Always the last one to get ready*.

She had a big soft spot for Simon. As far as she was concerned he was the most caring and charming young man anyone could hope to meet. With his handsome good looks and confident personality, he had attracted the attention of many beautiful women but, surprisingly, he had entered very few long-term relationships. She smiled as she remembered how he often joked that he could never find anyone that could cook like her.

Yes, he'll make a perfect catch for some lucky girl one day, she sighed and continued preparing the breakfast table for the next day's meal.

Philip, wearing his green Barbour jacket, jeans and a white Aran jumper, was still holding the front door open, waiting for him.

It was approaching six-thirty as the brothers stepped out into the fresh air of a typical clear May evening with the light just beginning to fade.

The long evenings make all the difference, thought Simon as they set off.

Around them, the flowerbeds were blooming with spring colour as they strode down the gravel drive between the well-manicured lawns. As they reached the halfway point, instead of continuing down the drive towards the metal gates they suddenly took a detour, crossing the lawn to their right past a rickety old trellis barely holding up under the strain of the blossoming wisteria. Beyond, was the path through the vegetable garden that led towards a wooden doorway built into the twelve-foot high outer perimeter wall. Simon fished the key out of his pocket and they stepped through into the apple orchard with rows of blossom filled trees spreading out ahead of them.

On the drive back from Professor Palanski's they had agreed to follow a path they had trodden many times before to one of their old drinking haunts in the pleasant Oxfordshire countryside. The walk would give them the opportunity to talk and think things through after all his revelations. One way or another they were going to have to decide what to do.

"It must be over three years since we last did this journey," said Simon, recalling those carefree days when they both used the route on a more regular basis. Friends, girlfriends and even their grandfather had joined them on many occasions for the pleasant walk through the countryside.

"Yes, we had some great times didn't we?" replied Philip, grinning at some of the happy memories that came flooding back.

"Do you think it will be open?" asked Simon as they passed some run-down old beehives at the end of the orchard.

"It should be by the time we get there," responded Philip, marching on with hands pushed down into his Barbour pockets.

The journey through the orchard and the field beyond was quiet except for the gentle sounds of the countryside. There were very few houses and the only contact with the occasional traffic was when the path criss-crossed over one of the surrounding country lanes. As they strolled along, they reminisced about their grandfather and some of their earliest childhood memories.

The picturesque walk took around twenty-five minutes. Towards the end was a hill from which they could see their final destination – a relatively unknown country pub and restaurant that survived through its excellent reputation with the locals for good country fare. Apart from the food, it was also admired for its glorious location, particularly in the summer. As the brothers wound their way down public footpath, they could see the gardens and outbuildings at the rear of the main house that bordered the River Isis, a tributary of the Thames. In the slower months the owners would simply shut their doors but now the place was open – Simon could see people sitting down to eat at the wooden benches in the garden.

After ducking to enter the old pub, Philip went up to the bar and ordered their drinks, which they carried out to a riverside table along with a menu.

"I've thought it through," said Simon sipping his drink. "I've made up my mind to try and find the book – I hope you'll join me?"

Philip didn't look up but stared down at the menu.

"I won't be joining you," he replied after a few seconds. "I've thought about it a lot and I just can't see what there is to achieve. How can bringing this book, the Bible of the Antichrist, into the world be a good thing?"

"Don't you think there's a responsibility, Philip?" countered Simon. "If the book's going to be found, and if it's going to be revealed to the world, then don't you think it's better if the good guys find it first and not these Satan worshippers?"

"If we believe what Professor Palanski's telling us, finding the Book of Judas can only bring harm and chaos to the world as we know it," said Philip pragmatically. "Think about it Simon! It's been lying dormant since the time of Christ and this 'evil' cult is poised, waiting for the day they find the manuscript - the whole thing's absurd and destructive… We should stay as far away from it as possible - even if there *is* an element of truth why should we risk our lives?" he continued forcefully.

"What about our grandfather – wouldn't you do it for him?" queried Simon.

"I…" Philip stopped in mid-flow as a young girl with long hair wearing an apron, approached the table to take their order. They ordered just a main course and she promptly span on her heels and headed for the restaurant's kitchens.

"No, I wouldn't," said Philip, starting again. "Don't you see? This decision's far bigger than me, you or our grandfather. Besides I've got Heather to think about!"

They both fell quiet, looking at their drinks.

"I see…" said Simon at length. "What *are* your plans then?"

"I'm going back to New York tomorrow evening and I want you to come back and stay with us for a while."

Simon looked up sharply, and read the genuine expression of concern on the face of his older brother.

"It's not going to be safe here and I think it's best if we stay together. Come back to New York with me and after I've made a few arrangements we'll travel… The three of us can take a little sabbatical for a while – what do you think?"

Philip's so stubborn, thought Simon. He had made up his mind and Simon knew there was no way he could change it. The heartfelt fear Philip sensed for his brother's safety was real and if there was anything he could do or say to make him change his mind then he would have done it immediately. However, he was equally stubborn.

"I can't do that," he said finally. "I've made my decision; I'm going to find this book with or without you."

Simon paused before looking directly into his brother's eyes.

"You've always been there for me in the past… If you won't do it because it's right, and you won't do it for grandfather, will you do it for me?"

Philip shook his head.

"I can't," he said sadly, "What you're doing is wrong and I'm not prepared to risk everything, including Heather. I'm sorry I can't convince you of that."

He found it difficult to hold his brother's penetrating stare.

"How are you planning on getting started?" Philip asked, moving the subject on.

"Well… I hoped we'd be talking about this together," replied Simon cynically, but Philip didn't respond to the jibe.

"Well, we know the third fragment's been found off the coast of Thailand so that's where I'm heading but before that I've got some things that need to be taken care of."

"Such as?" said Philip.

"Well, speaking to Bairstow, it seems the scrolls are kept overseas in some international bank's security deposit box. I'll need to open it to get the scrolls out along with the map of Judea and the secret location of the two bone fragments that he discovered earlier. I also need to go back and speak to the Professor; there are a few questions that have been playing on my mind since our first meeting. I spoke to him and fixed a time for tomorrow morning."

"I see," said Philip.

Despite being adamant that he was making the right decision, he also felt guilty at the thought of not being there to support his younger brother. Simon could sense the way he was feeling.

"Don't feel bad, Philip… I fully understand your reasoning. I wasn't so sure myself to begin with."

"I feel like I'm letting you down," said Philip, looking up at his brother.

"I understand," replied Simon smiling. "Look, I'll keep you informed where I am all the time and if you want to join me at any stage then you can."

Philip looked away towards a white swan that was gliding elegantly with the current of the river.

"There's one other thing," he said, continuing to gaze out over the reeds on the riverbank.

"What's that?" asked Simon.

"What about the new heiress? Who's going to meet with Anna Nikolaidis and tell her of her 'new-found' fortune?

"Yes, I'd already thought about that… I'm going to try and meet up with her on my way to the East," said Simon. "After all, you heard grandfather… Maybe, if she wants to, she could help me find the book."

He looked up and smiled at Philip with the thinly veiled remark.

Behind them they heard the footsteps as the same long-haired girl appeared with their meals. She laid the tray in front of them and as they thanked her and helped themselves to the plates and cutlery she favoured Simon with a lingering smile before turning daintily and departing.

"I think you've got a fan," remarked Philip, looking amused as he pulled open his serviette.

"You've either got it or you haven't," said Simon grinning.

After a moment, Philips smile faded.

"I know I can't stop you going – I just hope to God that it works out for you," he said seriously.

"Thanks," said Simon. "Listen, what time are you going tomorrow – if I can I'll try and get back in time to take you to the airport."

"The flight's at four-thirty from Heathrow."

"Fine, let's leave our goodbyes to the airport then," said Simon, as he began tucking in to the plate of food in front of him.

Chapter Six

Vatican City, Rome

Cardinal Camerlengo Fiore clicked shut the door to Pope Paul's residential quarters and stood there for a few moments quietly contemplating the decisions they had reached together. Since the earlier meeting in the Sala Regia with Cardinal Giacoma and Cardinal Alphonso it was his third audience with His Holiness on the subject of Sir Lawrence Trenchard and the Book of Judas. The Pope himself was entirely familiar with the book's history. He had sat on the same General Ecumenical Council as Cardinal Alphonso thirty years ago when they had debated how to deal with Trenchard and his startling discovery.

It was seven o'clock in the evening as Cardinal Fiore turned and set off in the direction of the Sala Consistoriale, and the gentlemen he knew would be waiting for him there. Each step echoed on the stone floor of the great hall as he walked towards the rendezvous. He replayed the words of the Pope over in his mind and smiled with satisfaction to himself.

I've got what I want, he thought.

Cardinal Fiore had specially chosen the Sala Consistoriale, or Consistorial Hall, for the meeting. It was used specifically for secret gatherings, occasionally official, when headed by the Presidency of the Pope. Fiore, striding purposefully, entered the Sala Clementina, which served as a waiting room for the Great Hall. Opening the large wooden door he walked down the high but narrow chamber to where they were gathered, sitting on wooden stalls that lined the room. The light in the hall was poor and the dimness was exaggerated by the enormous dark red tapestries that clung to the walls.

As the tall, imposing figure of Fiore strode towards them, they rose as one to their feet. As before, Cardinal Alphonso and Cardinal Giacoma were in attendance but this time they were not alone. Colonel Renauld, the commanding officer of the Swiss Guards took two steps forward. Behind him in the gloom stood a sinister man in black civilian clothes. In the abstract darkness, only the random shadows cast by the flickering candlelight made his menacing form fleetingly visible. Standing completely motionless, his demeanour was typical of someone used to being in control.

On the other side of the two scarlet-robed Cardinals were two more clergy from the top echelons of the Roman Catholic Church. Cardinal Alphonso, standing with the aid of a walking stick, was resentfully cognisant of the fact that the circle of those privy to the secret knowledge was ever widening. He had made his views felt and Fiore had noted his disdain for the decision when their inclusion in the secret conclave had first been proposed. Unsurprisingly however, his condemnation of the appointments fell on deaf ears. The new members, Cardinal Deacon Weiss and Cardinal Bishop Lefebvre were known loyal and dedicated supporters of Fiore. Besides, considered Cardinal Alphonso, Fiore had delivered their submission as a 'fait accompli'. He had approached His Holiness and made sure he had his approval before breaking the news to himself and Giacoma.

As the noise of Fiore's footsteps came to a halt, Cardinal Alphonso spoke first.

"How is His Holiness?" he asked with concern.

"I am afraid his condition is still showing little signs of improvement, Brother Alphonso, we must pray for his recovery."

Cardinal Alphonso nodded his agreement.

The Supreme Pontiff, Pope Paul XII, was in his eighty-sixth year and the passage of time was catching up with him. Over the past six years he had been intermittently and increasingly bedridden as he suffered from the gradual failure of his vital organs. The deterioration of his kidneys and the increased requirement for dialysis took their toll and although occasionally the medication made it seem as though his health was improving, the setbacks would always follow shortly afterwards.

The on-going condition of His Holiness brought a new dimension to their dealings and it was a situation that the elderly Alphonso was acutely aware of, namely "succession". It was widely known within the Vatican Walls that Cardinal Fiore coveted the role of heir to the Supreme Pontiff. The determination of the successor was a complex and highly secretive affair. In the unhappy event that Pope Paul VII died, all the Cardinals from around the world would convene in Rome to vote in secret and determine who would step into his shoes. Although there were just over one hundred and fifty Cardinals, only those below the age of eighty could vote, reducing the total of those eligible to one hundred and twenty-four.

In the unofficial whisperings that resonated through the Vatican's dark corridors, it was widely accepted that there were only three Cardinals capable of attaining the number of votes required. Firstly, Cardinal Fiore, who as the Pope's incumbent Chamberlain would automatically hold the supreme position in the transitory period before the votes were cast and the result of the ballot known. Secondly, there was Cardinal Gregory whose credentials for the role were outstanding. He commanded a tremendous amount of respect amongst his peers and despite being the oldest, he was seen as the safe option for those opposed to change even if he was not a long-term appointment. In the previous election twelve years ago, he had come second to Pope Paul in the concluding vote. Finally, there was the frail Cardinal Alphonso himself. His wisdom and

65

influence over the General Council was as strong as ever although he knew, especially given Pope Paul's predicament, that there could be a consensus for a younger, healthier successor.

Cardinal Alphonso eyed Fiore with suspicion. He knew it was imperative that decisions taken at this meeting must put the future of their religious faith and church before any gain to themselves as individuals. How this matter was handled would set the stage for any future vote on succession, and with Fiore's new appointments, he had guaranteed that his own decisions would be undertaken by this forum.

"I welcome Brothers Lefebvre and Weiss…" continued Fiore, who nodded their acknowledgements before turning to Colonel Renauld. "…And thank you, Colonel, for making the arrangements so quickly. We are indeed indebted to your loyalty at this time."

It was the Colonel's job to protect the Vatican and that included all security matters pertaining to the Roman Catholic religion. During the ages since 1506, the Swiss Guards had been responsible for preserving the religious integrity of the Catholic faith and this included conducting undercover operations when necessary. In fact, Cardinal Fiore was referring to such undercover arrangements when commending the Colonel's actions.

"Thank you, Your Eminence," returned Renauld humbly, bowing his head in acceptance of the compliment.

Cardinal Alphonso resumed his seat on the wooden bench and, resting his hands on his upright cane in front of him, looked up at Fiore to continue his briefing.

"As you know, I've come straight from an audience with His Holiness. He's deeply troubled by these developments. He fears that the death of the British Knight will have unimaginable consequences for our Church unless we can obtain the scrolls and destroy any path that lies ahead to the Book of Judas… His Holiness has asked me to impart the following instructions – our agent must travel to England immediately to recover the scrolls and any knowledge supporting their existence. Colonel Renauld, you have our authority to use whatever action is required to achieve this objective… Is this understood?"

Behind the Colonel, the tall sinister figure in black answered the question.

"I understand fully," he said in a deep, low growl from the shadows. The Cardinals turned to look at the source but still could not make out his face. His foreboding, motionless presence, however, was almost tangible.

Cardinals Alphonso and Giacoma closed their eyes. They knew this decision had been likely but it didn't relieve them of the guilt. The man in the shadows was infamous amongst the clergy in the Vatican. It was difficult to conceive that he was truly a part of them, a part of their darker heritage. He represented everything that was bad about their work and they detested his deeds – nevertheless this man was a necessary evil.

"You will report everything you find to Colonel Renauld immediately!" replied Fiore. "Any change in our instructions will be communicated through him and he will make sure that all your requirements are at your disposal."

There was a pause before the deep voice came back.

"Your Eminences," he replied brusquely.

Stepping out of the shadows, he walked back down the stone path of the Sala Consistoriale to make his exit through the double doors. The gathering remained silent until the large wooden doors echoed shut behind him.

"I think we all knew what was required, brothers – if there any that would cast doubt on the decision we've taken…" Fiore challenged, "… let them speak now."

His voice reverberated in the silence that followed. Cardinal Alphonso kept his eyes shut.

"In which case I accept your reticence to speak as confirmation of your unanimous support and I will report accordingly to His Holiness," concluded Fiore. "Are there any questions?"

Again there was a momentary silence, although this time it was broken by Cardinal Alphonso, who looked up from his seat.

"Yes, Brother Fiore, I have one question."

Cardinals Alphonso was held in tremendous respect by his peers and they waited eagerly for his wise words.

"Are we not ignoring what we fear the most? We must be prepared and ready for the truth."

All of those present knew to what Alphonso was alluding. Their histories were entwined and well catalogued since the exorcism attempted by Monsignor Montella had failed and the demon purportedly entered his spirit.

"If the 'Satanica' find out about the scrolls and the existence of the Book of Judas, we face our greatest battle. It won't be sufficient merely to secure the scrolls; we must follow this through to the conclusion and locate the book itself."

Cardinal Fiore bristled at the mention of the evil "Satanica" and Cardinal Weiss crossed himself.

"How can they know anything?" replied Fiore sharply.

"In the same way they've surprised us in the past," retorted Alphonso, with equal abruptness. "Say what you will, Brother Fiore, but they have their tentacles in the Vatican… They've infiltrated this church in the past."

"I think maybe you're overreacting, Brother Alphonso – am I not right in saying there's been no mention of their evil cult for many years now," responded Fiore.

"Do you really think they've gone away? Just because we were successful in burying the truth from them when the discovery was made, it doesn't mean we can do it so easily again."

"Brother Alphonso makes a good point," said Cardinal Lefebvre, turning to gauge the reaction of his fellow Cardinals.

Colonel Renauld. Cardinal's Weiss and Giacoma nodded their agreement.

"What are you proposing, Brother Alphonso?" asked Fiore irritably.

A little too irritably, thought Alphonso. *Why does he want to avoid this issue?*

"We must be prepared… If it's God's will, we'll never have to face the 'Satanica' but if they find out we must be prepared to do all in our power to defeat their quest for the prize they so openly crave."

"Brother Alphonso speaks wisely," said Cardinal Weiss.

"Am I right in saying that only those at this meeting and His Holiness are aware of our decision to take possession of the scrolls?" questioned Alphonso rhetorically, clearly addressing Cardinal Fiore.

"Let all speak," he replied and thrust his hand in an arc towards the others.

Colonel Renauld went first. He stepped forward and looked straight into the face of Cardinal Fiore. In front of him and the forum, he confirmed out loud that he had not spoken to anyone about the scrolls or the Book of Judas.

"Your Eminence," he concluded and leant down to kiss the papal sapphire ring on Fiore's hand.

One by one they followed Renauld's lead. Cardinal Alphonso went last and like the others he testified to the sanctity of their inner knowledge and he swore his holy oath of obedience to keep the knowledge sacred. Finally, Cardinal Fiore lowered his head as sign of reverence and began reciting his own allegiance to their sworn code of secrecy.

"Then so be it," Fiore concluded, raising his head, and surveying those in front of him. "The truth resides with us… We must now see this through to its conclusion."

Giacoma approached Cardinal Alphonso and helped him to his feet.

"Let us pray that your agent meets with quick success, Colonel Renauld," said Fiore.

"Yes, Your Eminence," he responded.

Cardinal Fiore made his farewells. He lowered his head but levelled his piercing gaze at Cardinals Alphonso and Giacoma before walking briskly down the hall's main aisle. Cardinals Weiss and Lefebvre followed on his heels, their scarlet robes flowing behind them as they rushed to keep up.

Chapter Seven

Sutton Dean, Oxfordshire

It was late morning as Simon finished his coffee and grabbed his jacket from the hook behind the door in the cloakroom.

It's time to go, he thought.

In the background he could hear his brother reconfirming his ticket over the phone in the hall. Leaving through the back door, he immediately sensed the change in the weather. The past week had seen glorious sunshine with the odd intermittent shower but today the sky was grey and overcast. He pulled up the sliding door to the garage and jumped into the Mercedes. Twenty minutes later he was approaching the first of several roundabouts on the outskirts of Oxford.

As he drove, he contemplated some of the questions that were running through his mind. His priority was to find out more about the "Satanica". If they were going to come looking for him then he had to know all about them.

He turned into the leafy avenue of Moorcroft Drive and parked the car outside number twenty-eight. The traffic had been relatively quiet on the way over and he'd made good time – a couple of minutes early for his twelve o'clock appointment. He walked up the stone steps to the front porch and, pressing the doorbell, heard its muffled buzz inside.

It was getting cold, he thought, pulling up the collar on his brown leather jacket. He stood there fidgeting from foot to foot waiting for the door to be opened but nothing happened. He pressed the doorbell again and turned around looking back down into the street. Again he waited but the professor didn't appear. *How strange,* he thought, mentally checking the time that they had agreed to meet. He tried to lean over and peer into the bay window on his right but the grubby net curtains preserved the house's privacy. Pressing the bell again, he leaned over the railing on the other side and looked down. Something instantly caught his eye – long fanlight window that supplied natural light to the basement was broken at one end. *That's odd,* he thought. *That's happened since yesterday.*

Another minute passed and it was clear that no one was going to open the door. He backed down the steps peering up at the façade of the house for any tell-tale sign of life at the windows. *This is strange,* he thought. It was the agreed time, and the professor had been quite insistent that he should arrive promptly. He stood on the garden path at the foot of the steps wondering what to do. *Should I sit in the car and wait? Should I go home and try and arrange another appointment tomorrow?*

He was about to turn around and leave when his eyes caught sight of the broken windowpane again. Following the path of broken concrete slabs that ran around the overgrown, knee-high grass in the front lawn, he crossed over to get a better look. On closer inspection, he could see that the hole in the window had been made near the metal catch that opened it from the inside.

It looks like someone's broken the glass on purpose, he thought. Simon considered whether the professor might have done for some reason. He wondered whether he might have managed to lock himself out but he didn't feel at all comfortable with the logic. The professor was an old man and he would have really struggled to get through such a narrow gap. Simon estimated that the window was only about twelve inches high by about five feet wide.

Curiosity got the better of him and, putting his weight on his knees, he tilted forward, pushed his hand through the gap and started feeling around inside. Keeping his arm fixed so that he didn't touch the shards of glass around the edge, he released the catch and the window fell open.

"*Shit,*" he hissed sharply, wincing with pain.

The window was hinged at the top and the weight of the frame made it swing inwards. As the window fell, he tried to move his hand in time but it was too late. He cut the back of his hand on the glass shards and blood gushed from the wounds. Quickly, he pulled out a handkerchief from his jacket pocket and wrapped it around his hand, using his teeth to hold one end and pull it into a tight knot. The cuts were quite deep but the cloth did the job and stemmed the bleeding for the time being.

Lying down flat, he quickly pushed the window open and slid his body through the small gap and onto the narrow ledge beyond. In one motion he then swung in his legs and dropped about seven feet to the stone floor. He cursed as he heard the window slam shut behind him. He stood motionless for a few seconds, listening for any unusual sounds but there was nothing. It was dark in the cellar and as his eyes became more accustomed to the light he saw that the room was empty apart from some wooden packing crates in the corner. Moving forward towards the door he noticed a rock on the ground. He assumed it must have been the one used to smash the window in the first place.

Simon cautiously walked through the cellar towards the stairs, trying to get his bearings. *The steps must lead up to a door in the kitchen*, he thought, trying to remember the upstairs layout. He grimaced with the sharp pain from his hand. It was aching like mad and, glancing down, he saw the blood was beginning to soak through the handkerchief

Ignoring the throbbing, he climbed the staircase in the dark, until he reached the wooden door. Light filtered in from the gaps around the doorframe. Slowly, he turned the handle and pushed the door open. Nothing – he could hear nothing at all as he pushed his head out. There were no lights on in the house and bearing in mind how grey and overcast it was outside, the house felt eerie and deserted.

This could be called breaking and entering, he thought to himself. He was about to call out Professor Palanski's name when something stopped him – an eerie, morbid sensation that he recognised immediately from his days working for the UN in the poorest parts of Africa. It was the smell of death.

Quickly but quietly he entered the corridor, stepping closer to the door of the drawing room where they had been served coffee only the day before. The disturbing sense of trepidation grew stronger as he slowly pushed the door open and stepped in.

Terror shot through him like an electric shock. Convulsing, clutching his stomach, he felt as if he was about to pass out. He had found Professor Palanski and the cause of his alarm. High above him was his rotting body nailed to the wall and splayed in the shape of a crucifix. The sight was gruesome and macabre. Palanski had been mutilated almost beyond recognition.

Am I alone? Is the killer still here? His immediate thoughts were for his own safety as he tried to steady himself. His eyes frantically swept the room. He was alone. His heart pounding, Simon went closer and saw that the body had been attached using large masonry nails through the neck, feet and hands. Blood was smeared over the walls and dripping from the points where the nails had entered. The professor's arms were outstretched, his clothes had been removed and a single nail pierced both feet, completing the image of Christ's crucifixion. *Whoever did this was sick,* thought Simon, barely able to keep his eyes on the disgusting spectacle. Fighting the urge to just turn and run from the building, he forced himself to look again. "Whoever did this knew no limits," he muttered to himself. The professor's tongue had been cut out and his head lolled forward, the eyes bulged and Simon just couldn't imagine the pain he must have suffered in his final living moments.

What should I do next? he contemplated? *Should I phone the police?* He knew that would be a mistake and, besides, how on earth would he be able to explain this? They would never believe him and he quickly decided against it. His thoughts turned to escape and he wondered whether the killer could still be watching the building. He felt the panic rise as he suddenly sensed the danger he might still be in. He tweaked aside one of the net curtains and peeked furtively, trying to make up his mind what to do. *I've got to get away,* was his overriding thought. Reaching the door, he stopped to look around one last time – and noticed two tell-tale signs that confirmed his worst fears. Firstly, although the room had been ransacked, it was comparatively empty… all of the professor's books, papers and research documents had been removed and secondly, on the back of the door, were daubed the initials *"MM"* in blood.

Simon wasted no time. Scared he'd been seen coming through the front door, he rushed towards the back door to see if there was another avenue of escape. He was in luck. The path through the back garden led to a gate into an alleyway beyond. The walls of the garden were high enough for him to dart unseen past a timber garden shed and slip out of the garden gate.

What do I look like? he thought, suddenly very conscious of his own appearance. Apart from feeling hot and sweaty, his bandaged and bloody hand was sure to make him stand out from the crowd and attract the gaze of any innocent bystanders. Furtively, he looked over his shoulder before hurrying down the alley towards the path that would take back to the main road.

As he got to the corner, three youths in their mid-teens came around the bend laughing and chattering and faltered into shocked silence as their eyes fixed on the Simon. They abruptly sidestepped him as they noticed the blood soaked handkerchief. Averting his eyes from their curious gazes, he hastened past them, painfully aware of them watching him until he was out of sight. .

Out in the street, he crouched low and walked as quickly as possible to avoid anyone getting a good picture of who he was. He already had the keys in his hands as he reached the Mercedes. Jumping in as fast as he could, he turned on the ignition and pulled away.

"*Damn* those boys," he muttered under his breath.

Driving slowly so as not to raise any undue attention, his mind raced. What the hell could he do next?

The body will be found sooner or later and when it is the police will come looking for me. He looked down at the central console and saw his mobile phone. *There's no choice,* he thought.

He dialled Felix Bairstow and waited for him to answer.

"Felix, it's me, Simon," he said urgently, as he heard his familiar voice.

"What is it Simon? You sound as if there's a problem."

"There is, Felix, a big problem but I can't talk about it now. I need you to do something for me."

"Go ahead; I'll do whatever I can."

"I am going to be leaving the country today – so can you organise cash and any documentation I may need?"

"Where are you now?" Bairstow responded sharply.

"About twenty minutes from Tudor Hall."

"Ok, I'll be there within the hour," he replied and signed off.

Simon drove through Oxford city centre and into the country lanes beyond that wound their way to the village of Sutton Dean. His mind kept replaying the horrific image of Professor Palanski's desecrated carcass; his mutilated body crucified to the wall.

He turned the Mercedes into Tudor Hall's drive and tried to focus on the present. He wasn't sure what his next move should be but one thing was for sure: he had to get the hell out of the country.

Where should I go? he wondered. The professor' death had not deterred him from fulfilling the mission of his grandfather's legacy but now he really knew what he was up against. *Maybe I should try and meet up with the girl first,* he thought. *Philip, please be here,* he implored to himself, as the car pulled to a halt.

Marching quickly through the back door to the kitchen, he found Mrs. Vines.

"Where's Philip?" he asked, not stopping to wait for an answer.

"What's happened to your hand?" she replied, seeing the blood stained hankie.

"It's Ok," he said, continuing through the door to the corridor and the tiled hallway beyond.

"If you see Philip, can you tell him I need to see him now. It's urgent," he shouted over his shoulder. Reaching the hall, he swung round the banister, and raced up the imposing staircase two at a time.

"Philip!" he yelled, as he got near the top but there was no response. He rushed into his brother's bedroom but he wasn't there – only his packed suitcases sitting alongside his bed. Simon turned on his heels and entered his own bedroom to haul out his own suitcase from the depths of the wardrobe. Wincing at the sharp stab of pain in his hand, he realised he could ignore gash no longer – so he paused in the en suite bathroom to gingerly peel away the gore-encrusted cloth and douse the wounded area in cold running water.

Downstairs, Philip put his head round the back door. He'd been out in the garden when Simon had arrived. *Strange,* he thought as he saw the Mercedes speed up the gravel path. *There's something wrong.* Although some distance away, he watched as his brother dashed inside the house quickly started hurrying back to investigate what was going on.

Philip briskly entered the kitchen.

"He's upstairs," said Mrs. Vines not waiting to be asked. "Something's wrong. Philip. He's cut his hand somehow."

She had just been preparing to go out into the garden herself and try and find him.

"Ok, thanks," said Philip firmly, and quickly, he traced his brother's footsteps down the corridor and up the stairs.

"What's happened?" asked Philip, marching into his brother's bathroom.

"Palanski's dead," replied Simon, eyes wide in the mirror. "Murdered… His body had been nailed the wall in a crucifix… The letters *'MM'* were scrawled on the wall."

"*Christ!*" said Philip, shocked by the revelation he was hearing. He looked down at the running water in the basin. "What happened to your hand?"

"I cut it on some broken glass breaking in to the basement," he replied, taking his hand out from under the tap and patting it dry with a towel. Philip could see that the gash really needed a few stitches. Briefly leaving the room, he was about to shout down to Mrs. Vines for some bandages when she appeared on the landing holding a medical box. She looked worried.

"Perfect timing," said Philip, holding the door open for her.

She entered and immediately set to work on Simon's wound. After cleaning it with some cotton wool and iodine, she wrapped it in gauze before covering it with a bandage.

"Thank you," said Simon gratefully, rubbing his hand over the dressing. "That's much better."

With a taut smile, the elderly Mrs. Vines left the room. She sensed the tension in the air and knew the brothers were keen to be left alone.

"I have to leave immediately," said Simon. "I was seen leaving the house by some kids."

He threw his suitcase on the bed and lifted the top.

The events conspired against Philip's better judgement. Seeing his brother's plight, he couldn't just walk away. At that moment, Philip made a split second decision.

"I'm coming with you."

Simon looked up and saw his brother's smile.

"Thank God – at last," he replied smiling broadly back at him.

"Someone's got to look after you," quipped Philip reassuringly. He put his hand on his shoulder as Simon returned in earnest to the task bundling his clothes into the case.

"It was incredible… They'd cut his tongue out and cleared the room of all his research," he said, shaking his head.

"Do you think they'd have interrogated Palanski before they killed him? Do you think he's told them about us? About what we're doing?" asked Philip.

This was a thought that Simon forced to the back of his mind. Reluctantly, he knew he had to accept the fact that there was a strong possibility that the "Satanica" were on their trail.

"I think we have to assume they know," said Simon.

"In which case we need to get going now!" replied Philip. The doorbell sounded in the background and he glanced out of the window overlooking the front drive.

"That should be Felix, I called him on the way back," said Simon.

"It is," confirmed Philip, seeing his Jaguar parked at the front.

Simon swung his case off the bed and they hastened downstairs to meet him, Philip making a brief detour to collect his own things.

Felix was waiting in the drawing room holding a dossier under his arm.

"Philip will be coming with me," said Simon, entering the room.

"That's good news– your grandfather would be delighted… It's got to help your chances of success," he said, nodding at Philip.

"For reasons I can't explain now, we need to leave right now," stated Philip curtly.

"I understand. I'll be quick," said Bairstow, sitting down and opening the folder on the coffee table in front of him. "In here is everything you'll need. You have details on the whereabouts of Anna Nikolaidis, information pertaining to the fragment of 'arkheynia' discovered off the coast of Thailand, and of course, access to the actual hidden Judas Scrolls themselves. I'd suggest you think about regaining possession of these first."

"That's exactly what I was thinking," interrupted Simon. "Am I right in saying that the whereabouts of the other bone fragments are stored with the scrolls?"

"That's right – they're in a safe deposit box at a bank in Switzerland… You'll need to travel to Basle first – all the instructions are in here but I need your signatures on certain formalities that need to be processed." He lifted some forms from the folder, which they duly signed and handed back to him.

"That takes care of it…" Bairstow stated with heroic understatement, closing the file and handing it over to Philip. "Oh, one last thing I failed to mention… I've organised a joint bank account in both your names with a large credit balance – the details are inside."

He nodded at the file.

"It sounds like you've thought of everything," replied Simon gratefully. He looked up at his brother. "Time we were going."

"Felix, your life could be in danger as well," said Philip, stretching out his hand to say goodbye.

"I know," he replied. "I've put notes on the file in case you need to contact me."

He shook their hands and left. Minutes later, the brothers said their farewells to Mrs. Vines, loaded their cases into the back of the Mercedes and sped out of the drive. Fifteen minutes later they were on the M40 motorway, heading for Heathrow Airport.

While Philip drove, Simon used his phone to make enquiries about the next departures to Basle.

"Find out if there are any direct flights to Athens as well?" asked Philip.

Simon looked back at him curiously while speaking into the phone.

They were in luck. There was a direct evening Swissair flight to Basle that departed at five-thirty and another flight leaving from the same terminal to Athens an hour and half later.

"I think we should split up," said Philip. "I'll go to Basle and you go and find Anna Nikolaidis in Greece. I'll give you the information on her whereabouts when we get to the airport. Anyway, I'm pretty sure that getting the scrolls will only take a day."

Although Simon was reluctant to separate from his brother so soon, he knew that in the circumstances it was the wisest decision – it would mean getting to Thailand all the sooner. Nodding in agreement, he checked his watch and confirmed their reservations with a credit card over the phone.

The journey to Heathrow took just under an hour. They parked the car in the long-term car park and twenty minutes later they had both checked in and were sitting in the Business Class lounge waiting for their flights to be called.

An hour later the last call for Philip's flight to Basle was announced over the loudspeaker.

"Are we doing the right thing?" he asked as he stood up and collected his bag.

"Yes," replied Simon emphatically. "Remember, it doesn't matter what decision we make, they'll be coming after us now!"

"I guess you're right," said Philip.

"Call me when you get to your hotel."

His brother nodded.

A short time later Philip was staring out the window, thumbing absently through a picture brochure of recommended hotels in Basle town centre as the plane climbed up over the Surrey countryside. *What on earth have I let myself in for?*

A little over an hour later, Simon's flight took off for Athens. He tried to force himself to think of the job that lay ahead but it wasn't easy. Again he visualised the terrifying scene that had greeted him in the Professor's drawing room. The whole episode had left him feeling exhausted and emotionally drained. Just one thought gave him some comfort – that he was not embarking on this quest alone. For better or worse they were in this together.

Chapter Eight

Basle, Switzerland

It was approaching eight in the evening when the plane touched down on the runway at Basle Airport. Twenty minutes later Philip was walking through the exit gate in the terminal building in the direction of the taxi rank. The driver in the cab at the front of the queue jumped out to help him with the suitcases and together they loaded them into the back of the estate car.

"Can you take me to Hotel Central?" asked Philip tiredly, sitting in the passenger seat alongside the driver, who grunted acknowledgement as they nosed into the traffic.

The hotel he had selected was in the Kuchengasse District, between the main railway station and the city centre. The hotel itself was comparatively inexpensive and functional but the location was perfect for his next day's work. On the flight, Philip had absorbed some of the contents of Bairstow's folder and he knew which part of town would best suit them. At that time of the evening, the journey from the airport was quick and on arrival, the courteous reception staff guided him to his room. Philip went straight to the window and pulled the curtain to one side. His room was on the eighth floor at the front of the hotel and looking out beyond the flower basket on the ledge, he could see down into the dimly lit square below. Letting go of the curtain, he checked his watch and decided to go down and find the hotel bar. *It's too early to go to bed,* he thought, *and besides I can use the time to go through all Bairstow's information.*

He picked up the folder and, ignoring the lift, took a spiralling staircase to the ground floor lobby. The hotel bar, which was not very large but truly continental in style, was in a front room off the reception. Philip immediately noticed the plush velvet carpet chintzy, pink-washed walls and dainty tables topped with chequered tablecloths to match, each adorned with a white lace centrepiece. The bar itself corralled off a corner in an arc lined by cushioned stools, while the shelves on every wall were densely adorned by painted porcelain ornaments, mainly dancing figurines. *It's more like a doll's house than a boozer!* he thought.

It was quiet, though. Just a few lone drinkers absorbed in their business papers and airport novels – so the black-waistcoated bartender jumped to attention as Philip approached. Taking his drink, he sat at the table in the corner where he had the most privacy.

Philip placed the folder down on the table and began to examine Bairstow's documents and the other contents. On the flight he had already ascertained that the two scrolls were housed in a safe deposit box at Bank Ehinger in Freie Strasse. In order to access the safe deposit box a key was required – and the ever-efficient Felix had not neglected to include it. Philip held up the transparent plastic bag and peered at the long metal key inside.

Bairstow's notes were succinct and comprehensive. He had been very thorough arranging every detail, as Philip discovered as he read on.

Bank Ehinger had already been notified that he and Simon were the registered holders of the safe deposit key. All that was required was to establish his identity beyond question and access would be granted. Philip made a mental note that he would call the bank as soon as they opened in the morning to get the first available appointment.

Philip flicked through the sheets of paper occasionally stopping to register one of Bairstow's salient details. *Apparently, the scrolls are kept in two vacuum-sealed metal tubes about three feet long.* He looked up, considering the implications. *If I end up flying tomorrow night I'm going to need to repack them somehow,* he thought. *They mustn't attract the attention of Customs.*

Continuing down the page, he noted that the safe deposit box also contained an old worn notebook that his grandfather had used when tracking down the locations of the bone fragments. Philip paused to imagine the lengths to which the "Satanica" would go for such information. *They could possibly be tracing our movements now,* he thought anxiously. The prospect filled him with dread and he silently wished for the next day to come as soon as possible so he could finish with the bank and fly out. The more complicated the trail he left for them to follow the better, he considered.

Philip took a sip of his drink and read on. They had both photocopied the next section earlier at London Airport so they could glance through it on their journeys. Flicking through the sheets, he found that they dealt mainly with the whereabouts of Anna Nikolaidis in Greece. According to the notes she was based in a village just north of Athens where she was working on an archaeological site.

Below the details of her location Bairstow had included a brief description of her. *Shame there's no photo attached,* he thought as he read the paragraph in the notes: *"Twenty-nine years old, single, dedicated to her profession, already considered to be an expert in her field and well educated".*

Philip checked his watch; his brother should have landed in Athens by now.

He recalled his discussion with Simon before leaving Heathrow on the subject of what they should tell Anna and how they should phrase the news. "Don't waste unnecessary time," he had repeated to Simon.

"Tell her everything but do it quickly… We'll both feel a lot safer once we're out of Europe," he had added, a little unnecessarily.

Simon had agreed. He would tell her the truth about her own grandfather, Demetri, as well as the story of the Book of Judas. After that she could make up her own mind whether or not she was willing to go with them.

On the photocopied notes that Simon had taken, there were details of some confidential phone numbers that Bairstow had provided. If Anna didn't want to play a part in their search for the Book – *and who could blame her,* thought Philip – the telephone numbers were organised so that she could access her share of the inheritance without too much difficulty.

Philip put the notes down and scanned the bar – the pink room was now virtually empty. Exhaustion suddenly catching up with him, he drained the dregs of his glass and headed for his room, where he dialled his brother's mobile phone. Simon picked up after a couple of rings and after swapping details of where they were staying they agreed to talk again the next day when they knew how their plans would develop. Signing off with his brother, Philip hesitated before calling his fiancée Heather in New York. He had no idea how to break the news of his decision to her. She would be annoyed and disappointed at first – of that he was certain. But he also knew he could persuade her it was the right thing to do. In the end he was saved the trouble. The answering machine clicked in and as calmly as he could he relayed the news of his decision to help his brother and finished by promising to call soon.

Before getting ready for bed, he picked up the phone one more time and spoke to the young girl on Reception. She repeated the time of his early morning call in her singsong French accent. *Eight o'clock for breakfast should be fine,* he thought.

The next morning, Philip arose with the alarm and showered before descending the stairs for breakfast. On the way, he wandered up to the reception desk and asked the man on duty for the banks' usual opening times. He smiled at Bairstow's unfailing thoroughness as the attendant confirmed it was nine o'clock, and then ambled across the lobby to where the buffet breakfast was being served.

Pouring himself a coffee, he scanned the faces in the room. He recognised an elderly couple from the night before but saw no one sinister or out of the ordinary. Over *pains au chocolat*, he stopped browsing through a Swiss newspaper to check his watch. *At last,* he thought, standing up and making for the telephone kiosk in the lobby. He was impatient to make the call to the bank. *What if for some reason beyond the bank's closed? The sooner I find out the better,* he thought to himself.

Philip looked at the section of Bairstow's notes with the bank's telephone number and the person to contact – Bertrand Mendy, the manager in charge of the bank's security deposit boxes.

A few minutes after nine o'clock, Philip put through the call to Bank Ehinger and the receptionist put him straight through to Bernard Mendy. In his competent, if unpolished French, Philip confirmed an appointment time and the documentation required by the bank to establish his identity. *Excellent,* he thought, exhilarated with the news as he strolled back to the breakfast lounge. Taking a second cup of coffee, he sat at a table out of earshot and called Simon to give him the good news.

The reception on the line was poor, mainly because Simon was travelling in a poorly connected area but Philip still managed to get his points across. He told him the meeting had been set for three-thirty that afternoon at their head office in Freie Strasse. Unfortunately, he couldn't get an earlier time – the manager had informed him that for security purposes only one appointment was allowed at a time, so everyone had to wait their turn. In return, he heard that Simon was already on his way to meet Anna Nikolaidis before the line crackled and went dead.

Philip decided to use the time he had in the morning to go for a walk and organise his onward flight schedule. Picking up his blazer, he walked out of the hotel's front door into the bright, crisp morning. The first thing he noticed was how clean and fresh the air was. Taking the directions given to him by the porter, he found the travel agency and checked the timetables to Athens. There was a flight leaving that evening and he reserved a seat before heading back to the hotel.

Shortly before two o'clock, Philip again left the hotel and walked to the nearby taxi rank. Settling into the taxi, he asked the driver to take him to the street where the bank was located. He knew they would be early and once they had found the building, he jumped out, paid the driver and picked a street café whose tables and chairs spread across the pavement under an expansive red and white canopy. From here, he had a perfect view across the busy road of the bank's impressive-looking entrance.

At the appropriate time, he crossed the road and ambled into the bank's very imperious, traditional lobby where a smart young lady executive looked up at him, smiling, as he approached her desk. She listened intently as Philip told her his appointment time and whom he had come to see. As he finished, she asked for his passport and disappeared around the back to make the necessary authentication. A few minutes later, Bertrand Mendy crossed the marble-tiled reception hall to greet him with a broad, welcoming smile.

"Philip, I'm Bertrand Mendy," he said, offering his hand. After a handshake and the usual courtesies, Mendy returned Philip's passport, confirming that everything was in order.

"Please follow me," he said, gesturing the way with his hand. "I trust you've brought the key?"

Philip held up the key and Mendy nodded. He led the way to a sturdy-looking lift, which descended slowly into the basement of the building. Stepping out, the change in surroundings was so extreme it felt as if they were in a totally different building, the old traditional wood panelling replaced by a functional, hospital-like corridor. Philip matched Mendy's purposeful stride as the bare, immaculate white walls turned to the right and they approached an enormous safe door extending from floor to ceiling. From where Philip was standing, he could see that all the angles were covered by close circuit televisions that fed the information back to Security and recorded their every movement.

Mendy secretively entered the safe's code on a touch-screen panel on the wall and the heavy door slowly revolved open. Inside, a metal staircase led down to the security deposit room floor, which was the height and size of a squash court. As Philip followed down the steps, Bertrand Mendy delighted in detailing the safety features they had incorporated in the room, making it impregnable even from a heavy artillery attack. The concrete reinforcement surrounding the chamber was over thirty feet thick in places and fitted with electronic sensors that provided an early warning system for any underground tremors.

"This way," said Mendy, as he led him down the outer, right-hand aisle. Below their feet, as an extra security precaution was a see-through metal grille elevated a couple of feet above the true floor level. On either side of the aisle were the deposit boxes. Like the front of an apothecary chest, the wall was covered in square metal drawers. Locating the identification number belonging to Sir Lawrence Trenchard, Mendy inserted his key, and Philip's, into the outer flap. The metal shutter opened and he pulled out a long metal box over three feet in length, which Mendy carried to a small box-like chamber that served as a viewing room.

"Take your time," he said, placing the box on the table. "I'll be waiting outside the door."

Philip lifted the lid to reveal two long metal tubes and a box at one end. Opening the latter first, he discovered his grandfather's brown paper-covered notebook, presumably containing information on the whereabouts of the missing "arkheynia". He flicked the pages and saw that it was indeed full of his grandfather's handwriting.

Philip picked up one of the cylinders, checking each end to see where it opened. Carefully, he twisted what seemed to be a screw-top. At first it didn't budge, but with steadily applied pressure something yielded with a sudden pop and hiss… Air invading the vacuum canister as he broke the seal. He tipped the tube and then stared, mesmerised, as the ancient papyrus parchment fell on to the table.

This is what it's all about, thought Philip, as he unrolled the ancient scroll. *This is what he found all those years ago.* It was the scroll containing the map of Judea and the bible lands. The detail was incredible but the written names and references in early Hebrew meant nothing to him. *I wonder how the "arkheynia" point to the location of the labyrinth,* wondered Philip, as he traced his finger across the map; it had a "Hessian-cloth" feel about it. Alongside him was the other tube, which hissed again as he punctured the seal and the rolled up parchment flopped on top the map. As he had imagined this one was the scroll telling the story of the Book of Judas, and how to negotiate the final steps of the labyrinth. He unrolled it over the top of the map and, though conscious of the need to be quick, he paused to look at it in silence and wonder for a moment. There was something ominous and darkly foreboding about the unintelligible black script.

Time to go, he thought, snapping out of the trance. He rolled up the scrolls together and placed them in a single tube. Pushing the worn brown notebook into the inside pocket of his jacket, he turned to leave.

"Thank you for your help, Monsieur Mendy," said Philip, stepping outside. "I have all I need. The metal tube on the table's no longer required."

Mendy nodded and entered the room. It took the bank executive a few moments to replace the empty security box and then lead the way back through the safe door. Once they were back upstairs in the more conventional environs of the reception hall he thanked him for his help and walked out into the street. Philip, carrying the metal cylinder under one arm, hailed the next taxi that passed.

Back in the hotel, Philip walked into his room and put the tube on the bed. On the way back in the taxi, he had been contemplating ways to store the parchments for the onward journey. There were very few options. The scrolls had to travel with him and there was no way he could use the metal tube – it would attract far too much attention from the Customs officials.

This is no way to treat such ancient relics, he thought, as he folded the parchment, *but what choice do I have?* His concern was that the creases could easily become tears but he was pleasantly surprised to find out how malleable the material was. Pressed flat, the ancient manuscripts fitted neatly into the pocket lining of the suitcase.

That'll have to do for now, Philip looked down at his handiwork. *I'll have to find something more suitable when I get to Greece,* he thought… *Maybe Anna will have some ideas.*

It was approaching late afternoon as he settled his hotel bill. The flight was not for a few hours but he decided it would be better to get to the airport early.

Marching across the airport concourse, he felt pleased with his work and glad to be leaving Basle so soon. *We may have a head start now but for how long?* he thought. *They'll be on our trail soon.* He knew it wasn't always going to be this easy. Three hours later he was flying over the Adriatic Sea on the way to Athens.

Chapter Nine

Amsterdam

The side street was full of people pushing in opposite directions as the man steered a course through the crowd. He walked out onto the narrow lane that ran alongside the bank of the Singel Canal. Amsterdam, known as the "Venice of the North", was built on over ninety islands, separated by over 100 kilometres of canals and linked by over 1,000 bridges. It was late spring and much of the hustle and bustle stemmed from the holidaymakers who flocked in from around Europe to admire the sights and sounds of the city.

The man, walking alone, paid little attention to the people or the "picture postcard" scenes that accompanied him on his journey. Striding purposefully along the bank of the canal, he passed the floating flower market on his right and looked up at the building about 100 metres ahead of him on the opposite bank. He was nearing the end of his journey.

Amsterdam was once the trading capital of the world and during the seventeenth century, when land was at a premium, the city grew upwards. In order to maximise the limited amount of space available, tall narrow buildings were erected. They were tightly packed together but each was unique, with a distinctive character of its own.

The man, turning right across the bridge, could not be mistaken for a tourist. Over six feet tall with an athletic physique in black jean-style trousers, a navy T-shirt and an open brown leather jacket, he carried himself like someone who had once served in the forces. Arriving at his destination he pressed the doorbell on his right, which was just above a discoloured brass plaque with the words *Khandos Charity Foundation* engraved on it. The green front door was at the bottom of a narrow five-storey dwelling sandwiched between other similar buildings overlooking the canal. A few doors further along was a busy café with a beer-branded green awning hanging out over the street with shoppers and tourists alike settling for lunch on the tables below.

Standing patiently, he heard the whirring of a CCTV camera rotating to focus on him. He stared up at the lens. In truth, this was the least sophisticated part of the surveillance system that operated from the Khandos Charity Foundation, registered in Greece. From behind these closed doors, his movements had been monitored since he had landed at Schiphol airport that morning.

He heard a lock opening and the green door sprang open automatically. Pushing the door further ajar, he walked into the narrow hallway and marched past a staircase into a room beyond, which was used as the Foundation's main offices.

First created by a wealthy Greek shipping tycoon, the Foundation had operated from these premises for decades as a plausible charity. Visitors to the building were strongly discouraged. In the rare case that a genuine "civilian" entered through the green door, the scene was set for the well-rehearsed "charity" office charade in which administrators and "charity officials" busied themselves around the building to create a semblance of normal office life. The illusion worked and the callers always left satisfied with the authenticity of the good works carried out in the name of the Khandos charity every year. To reinforce the impression, the walls were covered with mementos and memorabilia of their outstanding contribution to society alongside dated photographs of the Greek founder shaking hands with various smiling dignitaries, grateful to receive their financial pledge.

93

The "do-gooding" bogus charity was the very antithesis of the real occupants' nature and purpose. – the building served as a well-disguised front for the devil worshipping, demonic sect known as the Satanica.

The man wasted no time in pressing a button to reveal a long spiral staircase that ran down into the building's basement. Over a hundred years ago, in the adjacent streets behind and on either side of the green door, the sect had acquired neighbouring properties. The handful of original workers who had helped construct and merge the large underground vaults into one had all died in mysterious circumstances shortly afterwards. The lengths to which the Satanica was prepared to go to maintain total secrecy were as astounding as they were morbid. Only in extremely rare circumstances were members allowed to live beyond the age of fifty, and even then such deferment could only be bequeathed by the sect's "High Council". During the cult ritualism of their induction ceremony, they pledged to sacrifice their lives to the Black Lord, the Devil himself.

The Satanica's roots could be traced to the time of Christ although the clandestine sect was really galvanised during the era when the disgraced Monsignor Montella was cast out of the Vatican. Although its widespread tentacles pervaded most modern-day societies and cultures, fewer than thirty members of the senior hierarchy were familiar with their headquarters in downtown Amsterdam. Of course this was not the only such sect – he notion and ideology of the Devil had spawned many other cults over the years, all of them transient, typically spurred on by one or more personalities who delighted in the demonic symbolism as a means of hiding their multi-dysfunctional personality disorders. Similarly, they generated followers, mainly from the world's lowlife, who believed in the supernatural worship of the occult. These cults were never really feared by mainstream family life and indeed were all but accepted as part of life's human make-up. Society recognised that they all had their day at one time or another – their demise would normally be the result of some misdemeanour or act of public outrage that would warrant brief but frenzied media attention. Eventually, the cult's appeal would dwindle away as the figurehead's power burnt out and the next generation of followers moved on. The Satanica was not such a cult.

Steeped in the history of demonic ideology, the Satanica craved secrecy for its membership. Only acts of barbaric sadism that were sanctioned by the High Council were allowed to be identified publicly to the world through the initials "MM".

This High Council coordinated the religious rites practised by the malevolent and immoral Satanica priests, known as the Zorasti. The Zorasti name had its beginnings in the Avesta, the sacred manuscript of the Mazdean religion, which condoned the evil transgressions of the Zorasti High Priests throughout Assyria and the Biblical lands – and it was translations of these early teachings that first referred to Judas as the dark disciple. The Zorasti religion centred on the internecine war between light and darkness; between good and evil. They worshipped the coming of the Devil with the same kind of religious fanaticism as the Jewish sect, the Essenes, whose infiltrators were credited with writing the Book of Judas.

During the era of the cruel and deranged Monsignor Montella, the sect was given new life. Throughout his times, as Head Priest of the Zorasti, he was given to extreme but relatively short bouts of twisted, sadistic madness that would culminate in some human atrocity. His normal, rational persona was replaced by an evil, snarling beast that would contort with an insane rage. The quiet period during which the madness subsided could last days, or it could last weeks and it was during these sober times that he breathed his form of death into the sect he named Satanica.

As Monsignor Montella set about building the sect, his work mirrored his own experiences and the sect's organisational structure became based on the Vatican. The Cardinals were replaced by the historical Zorasti

95

who dressed themselves in identical fashion to the Roman Catholic clergy except that their robes and birettas, or skullcaps, were black. His followers knew him to be possessed. What else could explain the carnage and violence that shook through his body leaving death and mayhem in its wake? It was therefore of little surprise to them when, as Overlord of the Satanica, he gave himself the title *"Contra Daimones Sade",* the "Demonic Pope". Ever since the passing of Monsignor Montella many centuries earlier, the title "Daimones", the Demon Lord was bestowed upon each new leader of the High Council of the Zorasti.

The man descending the spiral stairs was one of the elite; one of the chosen few to serve the elders of the Zoroastrian Council. He had shown early promise and had been hand-picked to reach the higher echelons of the Satanica during his formative years. His apprenticeship had been long and hard, testing his skills and training to the limit, but he now stood on the threshold of their greatest quest. The dark underground corridor ran for several metres before a sharp corner took him to an arched doorway.

Although this was not the first or second occasion on which he was to address the High Council the spectacle that awaited him beyond the arch still filled him with a sense of awe. In a small antechamber, he donned his black robe before stepping forward.

Barely able to squeeze through the narrowing corridor, he entered the unholy church of the Satanica. Above him was a domed roof and below were row upon row of flickering, white candles illuminating a cavernous hall. The candles offered the only lighting in the dark, musty vestibule as he descended the curved, wide stone steps to the chequered marble floor below. The size and depth of the chamber seemed incomprehensible compared with the square, boxed-in rooms above ground level.

At the opposite end of the chamber was a shrine. It was not like a shrine you would find in a Christian church with an altar table and a depiction of Jesus on a cross but instead it was a huge tablet of stone, twenty to thirty feet high and tapering to a point. It was obviously old, chiselled with worn writing in an ancient alphabet. It was about fifteen feet wide, standing in the centre of a circular marble platform with three steps down to the main atrium floor. The ancient hieroglyphic-style writing pre-dated Christ and told of the wonders of the Black Kingdom that would burst forth when evil triumphed over good. Worshipped as if the words came from Lucifer himself – it was the icon of the Satanica and the inscriptions foretold the future and gave guidance in the worship of the Dark Lord. Until only a week earlier the last prophecy had made no sense to the few Satanica brethren who had been allowed to see the tablet, but now the message rang clear and true.

In the shimmering darkness, five tall, cloaked figures stood equidistantly apart, facing the tablet. Upon their envoy's entrance they moved silently to the perimeter of the platform facing the main hall. Out of a need for secrecy their long, black robes had become hooded. They stood motionless, as he walked the length of the hall to face them.

"Your work is unfinished," the voice of the middle figure commanded, his imposing voice resonating around the great stone hall. He was Daimones, the Lord High Priest of the Satanica. His attire was almost identical to that of the Zoroastrian Priests standing to each side except that around his neck was a large gold chain necklace that held an amulet containing a lock of hair that once belonged to Judas, the Devil's disciple himself.

The man stood with his head bowed before them. He knew that the five elders of the Satanica Council had ordered the deaths of many of his brethren in the past for their failure to carrying out their wishes.

"His house held many records; he had obviously devoted his life to finding out as much about our organisation as possible – before I killed him, he told me that the Trenchard brothers had called to see him. We can assume he told them all he knew."

"Understood, Conchos," replied Daimones. He then took a step to his right and whispered privately to the statuesque figure.

The envoy had a name. He was called "Conchos", which was not a name given to him at birth but one bestowed upon him when he entered the Satanica as a young, pre-selected boy. He was thirty-fours years old now and he had no knowledge of any parents or any close relatives; to him the Satanica were his family. Conchos embodied all that was black and evil about the sect and Daimones and the four Zorasti High Priests were well aware of his special talents. They knew that when Conchos spoke about extracting information from Professor Palanski, that this would have meant remorseless and savage acts of torture. His fondness for mutilating his victims was well known to the High Priests.

Conchos worked alone but with the Satanica network' full support. Never was his loyalty questioned, and rare were the days when his callous, sadistic skills were not being put to use. The men who had helped to train Conchos had been staggered by his ability to handle pressure. No matter how dangerous the physical task, or how difficult the intellectual puzzle, even when his life depended on it, his heartbeat remained steady, fluctuating between sixty and eighty beats per minute. Such was his devotion to his family, the High Priests of the Satanica, that he had surgically removed any distinguishing features from his body and made himself as plain as possible. Beneath the dark hooded robe was the blank, expressionless face of a killing machine.

Daimones glided back to his position at the foot of the tablet of stone before speaking in a low voice that echoed around the hall, amplified by the domed ceiling above him.

"This is the final test, Conchos – the Book of Judas lays within our grasp. You must follow the Trenchards in their quest to recover the keys of arkheynia. They have the knowledge and the scrolls to unlock the sacred labyrinth of our Lord – follow them and learn the wisdom that will let us enter the dark kingdom. Once you have it and only when you are sure you hold all the secrets… then kill them and anyone else that shares the information."

Conchos, his arms folded in the wide sleeved robe, bowed his head in deference and acknowledgement to the High Priest.

In the constant strife between good and evil, the Satanica could sense that their time was approaching. The moment that they had waited centuries to arrive was finally coming.

They accepted that the Black Lord had been cast down into the depths by Christ during his time on earth. To the Satanica, it was as if he were being kept locked in a prison and it was the Book of Judas that would provide the key to his release. Their goal was to resurrect the Black Lord so that he could wage the final battle against humanity and the law according to God. Their faith throughout the years that the book would be found had never wavered. The Zorasti knew that the book was not just a text of the Antichrist but an actual manual to the rites that could unleash and conjure up the devil. If they, the Zorasti, performed the macabre ceremony as rendered on the pages of the manuscript the world would see the human form of Lucifer and feel the power of the devil as it descended into the abyss.

"When you have the knowledge bring it to us," repeated Daimones.

Suspicions had always existed within the higher echelons of the Vatican and the High Council of the Zorasti that their destinies were some how inextricably entwined. Both sides, despite putting secrecy above all else, feared the unwelcome intrusion of the other. During the past week, since learning of Sir Lawrence Trenchard's death they had marshalled all their resources to begin their last campaign.

The source of the Satanica's information was revealed with the next breath. Only a member of the Vatican's inner sanctum could know the following, as the man with whom Daimones had been whispering, offered to speak.

"Beware, Conchos, the Vatican has ordered its senior agent to stop at nothing to recover the Book of Judas. They will use anything at their disposal to make sure that you fail in your task." His voice was that of an older, cold-hearted man.

"This agent," the High Priest continued, "is the best in the Vatican's service – it is likely he will follow the brothers until they've gathered all the keys of arkheynia before he makes his move and it will be his duty to shield them from danger until this time."

"I understand," replied Conchos. "It will be a pleasure killing him!"

"Go now," said Daimones and with that Conchos bowed, turned on his heels and marched down the hall to the stone steps that would take him back to the exit.

When he left the hall, the High Priests turned to face each other and Daimones again addressed the hooded figure on his right.

"Is it safe for you to go back into the Vatican? Is anyone suspicious?"

"No one suspects," replied the robed figure promptly in little more than a whisper.

"The Pope does not have long to live and the foolish, shallow Cardinals are vying for position. They are too preoccupied with improving their popularity and gathering supporters – they all sense that the papal election may come soon!"

"Good, very good," muttered Daimones. "Having you inside the Vatican gives us a great advantage. All of us here appreciate the years of work you have invested in making ready for this time's arrival."

The robed figure bowed his head as Diamones turned his thoughts to the Pope's poor state of health.

"Yes," he mused. "It's amazing how the prophecies have come true!"

He was referring to the old myth that had circulated in the cloisters of the Vatican for many centuries. Circumstances had arisen in recent years that gave the myth added substance. In the papal chambers there was a gallery where the portrait of every deceased Pope was hung on the wall – after each Pope passed away his portrait would then be hung alongside his predecessor. The prophecy said when there was no longer a space to hang the next portrait the final battle between heaven and hell would commence and that the war would rage until one of them emerged victorious. In the gallery there was now only room for one more portrait – and the Pope was dying.

Daimones broke away from his own thoughts to turn back to the High Priest that had infiltrated the innermost circle of the Catholic Church.

"Go back to the Vatican and find out whatever you can – we should not meet again until the Book of Judas is with us."

He turned to address the three High Priests who had remained silent up to this point and raised his arms.

"Priests of the Zorastri, we know that Conchos has been a loyal servant and has never failed us in the past. Even for him, though, this is no ordinary labour – he must succeed in finding the Book of Judas!"

Daimones turned and looked upwards at the pinnacle of the stone tablet. The glowing flames from the candles flickered across the ancient writing, a language he had learned to decipher. He smiled to himself before turning towards a side doors beyond the tablet of stone and clapping his hands.

"It is time!" he called.

The gathered brethren of Zoroastrian priests were the controllers; the enforcers of Daimones' revered Satanica. Hearing the sound of his clapping hands, they instinctively knew what would happen next.

Two men dressed in black entered through the side door carrying a young, naked girl who had not even reached her teens. She had black lines painted across her chest and face that formed markings similar to those on the stone tablet.

The girl was heavily drugged and made no effort to struggle as they laid her body across the altar table around which Daimones and the priests assumed their positions and watched as her head lolled from side to side as she desperately tried to focus on the figures encircling her.

One of the henchmen handed Daimones the ritual dagger before quickly bowing and leaving the dark, cavernous hall. For several minutes, the High Priest of the Satanica continued his recitation in a strange language, beseeching the Black Lord to accept their gift.

Just as her eyes began to take in her surroundings it was too late. The knife ripped into her body and she shook violently as her lifeblood began to drain away.

Chapter Ten

Athens

Simon's flight had landed twenty minutes late but the airport wasn't busy and he cleared Customs quickly. His plan was simple. It was late evening in Greece and all he wanted to do was find a cheap local hotel and get a good night's rest before locating Anna the next day. This was easier said than done, as his mind was preoccupied with the frightening and macabre escape from Professor Palanski's house and the pain that still throbbed through his injured hand.

Athens was to be a short stopover. His brother would arrive tomorrow afternoon and together they would make their way to Thailand, with or without this mystery lady whom their grandfather had so passionately supported. He convinced himself to think ahead and found a place to stay near the airport. Simon smiled to himself – he had always been known as the "thinker" in the family. Whereas Philip was confident to the extreme, never afraid to get up and make a speech, or act the lead part in a school play, Simon had always been held back by fear of failure. Whether it was of letting someone down, or making a fool out of himself, he always felt reticent about standing up and being the "real" Simon Trenchard. His older brother recognised his lack of confidence and did all he could to help. On many occasions it would have been easy for Philip to bask in the limelight but he was not that way inclined. He felt protective of Simon and, through a genuine willingness to help, Philip pushed him in a direction that would force him to grow in confidence.

Simon admired Philip's attitude and the way he calmly reacted to difficult or unusual situations. He always seemed to have an answer or know what to do next.

As Simon grew older, he gained in self-confidence, thanks to Philip's help. He still felt more comfortable in small groups of his own friends rather than grand occasions where he was expected to circulate and engage in "small-talk" with strangers.

The small yellow taxi dropped him outside the hotel and he checked in for one night. Once in his room, he took out the map that Bairstow had drafted for them detailing the archaeological site north-west of Athens where they could find Anna Nikolaidis. It was recent, thought Simon, spotting the date pencilled in the corner. It should take about an hour to get there, he surmised after getting some help from the girl on the reception desk downstairs. It was getting late. He spoke to his brother in Switzerland briefly on the mobile and scheduled a rendezvous for the following morning before settling down for the night.

The next day he rose early. He had breakfast in the room and packed his belongings back into his carrier bag to check out. The weather was great at this time of year and wearing just chinos and a polo shirt he made his way to the taxi rank. He was pleased to learn that the driver spoke reasonable English as he asked whether or not he could take him to the ancient settlement of Eleusis. The driver looked puzzled for a moment before he realised Simon was referring to the ruins that dated back to the second millennium BC.

The journey took him through the crowded suburbs of Athens before stretching out onto a dual carriageway towards the coast to the west. From the main road they followed the signs for Eleusis and as they edged closer Simon began to really consider for the first time the practicalities of the meeting ahead. He had no clue what she looked like and she would not know him from Adam. *There's every chance this will end in disaster*, he thought. *At least she'll be richer for the experience,* he concluded, remembering his grandfather's bequest. *That should at least break the ice when I pass on the good news.*

Greek "B Roads" were not known for their driving pleasure and the taxi lurched its way along the winding hillside roads to their destination in the Peloponnesus.

As Simon looked out the window, he could see the beginnings of the ruins high up on the hilltops in the distance. The driver confirmed their imminent arrival by leaning over into the back seat and waving at the small village ahead of them. They passed a few yellowy sun-bleached houses on either side of a narrow old high street before the taxi driver pulled up in the town's main square, which was fronted by an old church with a few shops down each side. Simon dropped his bag on the ground and then handed the cash back through the window to the grateful driver. He paused to watch the taxi leave, dust trailing in the air as the car sped back down the road

Simon threw his bag over his shoulder and made his way to a small shop to ask directions to the archaeological dig that Anna was supposedly managing nearby. With a lot of pointing and gesticulation from the shopkeeper, he gleaned that the path leading up over the hill past the church would take him to what he was looking for. He thanked the man and set off up the dusty track in the blazing midday sun, consoling himself with the fact that at least the ache from his hand was beginning to wear off.

At the top of the hill the view was wonderful. He could see for miles in every direction with the lush, green hills in the distance to the north and the deep blue bay of Eleusis stretching out into the Mediterranean to the west. Simon had always kept himself in good physical shape but the incline of the track was steep and hard going in parts. Panting, he took a swig from his water bottle, happy to pause for a moment and catch his breath. He studied the landscape around him and tried to get his bearings and as his eyes followed the path down the other side of the hill, he spied the ancient Mycenaean ruins that he was looking for. Although a long way off in the distance, he could just make out the leaning Doric columns amongst the latticework of carved out, low level walls. Parts of the remnants appeared to be in good order where the pillars still carried the arches that once made up the impressive colonnade. The journey down the other side was much easier and as he got closer he could make out members of the archaeological team, filling the excavation of the Eleusinian sanctuary like worker ants busying themselves at various corners of the fortification walls.

The remainder of the journey didn't take long and as he got closer to the settlement he tried to guess which one of the archaeologists could be Anna Nikolaidis. His arrival went largely unnoticed. They were so engrossed with their work that no one had put their head up to see him coming.

"Hello there," he smiled broadly at a middle aged woman, looking hot and clammy under a grubby, white bandana. "I'm looking for Anna Nikolaidis."

The woman smiled back.

"Over there," she said, wiping her forehead and pointing with a trowel in the direction of a crouched figure, enthusiastically brushing earth from the ground at the other end of a channel in the ancient arcade.

Intrigued to meet her at last, he studied her closely as he walked in the shade of a line of pillars. Standing alone, unobserved, he watched her kneeling on the floor of the excavation trying to delicately unearth a fragment of a hidden relic. She worked with passion and minute attention to detail.

He stepped out from the shelter into the blazing heat and moved towards her.

"Anna?"

She sat back on her knees.

"Yes," she replied, matter-of-factly staring down at her handiwork before looking up at him.

Simon was surprised. The vision he saw in front of him was entirely different from that which he imagined. She was stunningly beautiful despite the dirt and the dust she was working in.

"My name is Simon – Simon Trenchard and I've come a long way to see you!"

He suddenly felt slightly tongue-tied by her captivating beauty.

"Oh, sounds important" she said smiling teasingly.

She had been working hard and the unexpected visitor gave her a chance to have a break. She stood up and shook the dirt from her clothes before pulling out a bottle of water that was buried in the backpack alongside her.

Simon put her at about five feet eight. She had shoulder length black hair, a smooth, honey complexion and a figure full of curves and symmetry. Wearing a white sleeveless blouse, she gazed up at him with her large blue eyes.

"Anna I know I'm a stranger and this request sounds unusual but I need to talk to you about something important and I don't have a lot of time!"

She studied Simon's face for a couple of seconds, staring at him quizzically.

"Look, I don't know who you are and I don't know what you want but if it's all the same to you I'll pass on this one."

She looked up at him with slight suspicion before taking another gulp from her water bottle. Simon realised that he was staring at her. She had deep, penetrating eyes and the olive complexion that was common to the pretty girls that came from this region.

"Look if it's still important tonight, I'm staying at the Hotel Delphi in the local village," and with that she knelt back down and resumed the work on the fragment of pottery.

Simon was not prepared to give up so easily.

"I can understand your concern – it's true that you don't know me at all but in a strange kind of way we're related!"

The comment worked. Without looking at Simon, she stopped what she was doing and rocked back resting her hands on her knees.

"What do you mean *related*?" she said inquisitively.

The word always struck a chord with Anna Nikolaidis. Being an only child had had its difficulties.

She really is beautiful, thought Simon again. His focus had changed. In the morning the meeting set up by Bairstow had been a chore on his way to re-uniting with Philip. In a matter of moments his emotions had been stood on their head. He now considered it his duty to tell her the whole, unadulterated truth and persuade her that their quest was really part of her destiny too.

"I have a story to tell you about a man called 'Demetri Nikolaidis' – like yourself an eminent archaeologist in his time…"

The mention of her grandfather's name brought a frown to her face. Curious now, she stood up and dusted the dirt from the front of her trousers. Hardly any of her relatives remembered her grandfather let alone complete strangers. All she had been told was that he had died, tragically young, in strange circumstances connected with his work.

"Ok, what are you proposing?"

The frown and the look in her eyes made him realise her poise and self-assurance had momentarily slipped and he was briefly exposed to the vulnerability beneath her brittle veneer. This only made her seem more attractive. What she didn't realise was just how much more Simon knew about her than she of him.

"I have to catch a flight from Athens later on this evening when my brother lands; I only have a few hours – can we go back to the village and talk?"

They stared at each other in the momentary silence. This was the defining moment. If she could not be persuaded then he knew that he must catch up with his brother in Athens. Simon sensed the emotions going on behind the sparkling azure of her eyes. She frowned as she wondered what to do and her look of confusion made him feel like reaching out to protect her. There was no mistaking her beauty, he thought as he studied her pretty, tanned face with her black hair brushed back in a bow.

"Ok," she nodded finally, and offered her hand to be pulled up from the hole she was working in. She too had a good feeling about him, about this young, handsome Englishman. In fact the same magnetic attraction that was affecting Simon was also playing with the emotions of Anna herself.

Simon watched as she went off to speak to an old bearded man on the other side of the excavation site. *How old is she?* pondered Simon. He couldn't recall Bairstow telling him. Transfixed, like most people meeting her for the first time, he stared unashamedly as she walked away with a feminine grace that seemed alien to the working conditions of an excavation site.

A few minutes later she had collected her things and they walked back together up the track to the village on the outskirts of Eleusis. He noticed the disappointed expressions on their faces as they waved goodbye to her. *Dedicated historians? Probably,* he mused, but he wouldn't be surprised if many of them were really there because of her energy and allure.

Anna refused Simon's offer to carry her rucksack. She had noticed the bandage on his hand earlier and enquired about the cause. He quickly passed it off as a silly accident from the day before.

As they strode up the hill, matching one another step for step, they both agreed that they would not discuss the reason for his surprise visit until they were having lunch in the local taverna. Instead on the way back she did most of the talking. The quality of her English was no different from his own and he listened to her tell the story of her childhood.

Her father had died young and she had grown up with her mother in a village close to the Macedonian border in Northern Greece. He listened intently to her life's tale, wishing he could interrupt and tell her of the bond that existed between them. He too shared the same pain of parents who had died tragically when he was too young to remember them. He winced privately at the memory and let her go on talking.

Anna talked about her schooldays; she had obviously excelled and achieved a great deal in her twenty-nine years. Simon smiled a knowing smile when she mentioned how her luck had changed. Against the odds, she won a place in High School and then became the beneficiary of a full scholarship to the University of Santa Barbara in California to read "History of the Biblical Lands".

Amazing, he thought. His grandfather, Sir Lawrence, had managed to keep himself behind the scenes for all those years. Later, he would enjoy revealing this part of the story when they discussed why he had come to see her but he knew that not all their conversation would be this easy. *How will she react when I tell her how her grandfather died?*

Back in the quaint village outside the ruins of Eleusis where the modern world had failed to intrude, Anna asked Simon to follow her as she led the way down a narrow alley off the main square to the local taverna. It had a few wicker tables and chairs protected from the sun by an awning that stretched out from the wall of the white building.

"Inside or out?" asked Simon.

He wanted a private location that was discrete enough to talk without fear of being overheard. However, there was no cause for concern; the taverna was practically empty save for a few staff working behind the long wooden bar.

"Let's stay out," she said with a smile.

As they settled, a moustached waiter appeared to take their order. She spoke hurriedly in Greek and the waiter left without showing them the two menus he had been carrying.

"They do great sandwiches here and I think you could do with a beer – am I right?"

"Sounds good," said Simon smiling back.

"Well, it's a long way from England to take someone out for lunch – I guess you'd better tell me what you're doing here, Simon Trenchard," she said, taking a seat.

The story began. She listened intently as Simon started by telling her about his grandfather's death and the funeral service. He introduced his older brother Philip and told how they had first learned about her existence at the reading of the will. She learnt about the financial inheritance left to her by their grandfather. Then, having placed their drinks and sandwiches on the table, the waiter departed and he began to describe the legacy that had been left to them, including Anna, in the dying words of his grandfather, Anna's secret benefactor.

Spellbound, she sat mesmerised as he slowly explained everything. The relationship between their grandfathers unfolded as he recounted how they had worked together for Roland De Vaux, the Catholic Vatican representative who had masterminded the excavation of the scrolls at Qumran. He narrated clearly, leaving out no details. He described the antechamber in the cave they were excavating that revealed the Judas Scroll – the manuscript that confirmed the existence of the Book of Judas – and finally the way they could locate its alleged hidden resting place in the secret labyrinth. Inevitably, he reached the part he was going to find difficult to explain. The part where her grandfather, Demetri, had been needlessly killed falling over the ledge in his efforts to escape the clutches of the Vatican agent.

"Are you Ok?" he asked, watching her sorrowful expression. He suddenly remembered the wrinkled photograph of Sir Lawrence and Demetri with their arms around each other's shoulders outside one of the caves at Qumran. He reached inside his pack and pulled it out, handing it over to Anna.

"Yes, I'm fine," she said, looking down at the black and white picture. Both men looked happy.

"I knew very little about him… I knew he was an archaeologist and that my mother could not understand why he had just disappeared. She always hoped he would come back one day – but he never did!"

Simon put his good hand on hers. She looked up.

"I'm Ok – really, please go on," she whispered in a small voice.

He continued, telling her about his grandfather's escape back to England and how he began his research into locating the three keys of arkheynia that would ultimately solve the riddle of the scrolls. He watched her face as he explained how the answers would ultimately lead to the entrance to the underground labyrinth where the Book of Judas was allegedly preserved. She sat silently, fascinated as he recounted the tragic tale of how his grandfather had given up his lifelong quest after failing to discover the whereabouts of the final key of arkheynia. Anna shook her head as she heard how its resting place came to light only weeks before his grandfather passed away.

"My brother Philip's on his way here from Switzerland where he's been retrieving the Judas Scroll and maps from a bank vault – in fact I'm going to try and call him shortly and find out which flight he's on."

He was conscious of the fact that so far he had made the whole affair sound like a swashbuckling romantic escapade. He had a sudden pang of guilt that he was putting a rosy gloss on the adventure because he liked her and he was keen to persuade her to travel with them. In reality he had seen what had happened to the professor and nothing could be further from the truth. He privately scolded himself and determined to paint a more honest picture of the quest ahead.

"You know when I met you at the ruins I told you there was not much time…"

"Yes," she nodded. His expression had changed.

"It's not just us who are searching for the Book of Judas."

He then proceeded to tell the events of the previous day when he had visited Professor Palanski's house for the second time.

She looked visibly shaken when he described the sight of the Professor nailed to the wall in the shape of a dark angel, his skin peeled and spread out like wings. Simon himself had still not come to terms with the sort of person who could do this. Insane, possessed, demented? Who could do such a thing?

"Whoever did this will now be looking for us and they'll be tracing our journey. We…" he paused and looked into her eyes. *"I…* would love you to join us but if you decide not to, then you must at the very least disappear for a while because the very fact we've met could put your life in danger."

"What do you mean?" she asked nervously.

Simon decided to reveal all he knew about the Satanica and their deadly desire to capture the Book of Judas.

"The book is no ordinary manuscript – it's alleged to contain the commandments and the ritual that will enable the Satanica to release the Devil – once he's been unlocked then it's believed that he'll take his place on earth in the body of a mortal human being and the final battle between good and evil will take place!"

He continued with some of the facts that he had learnt from Professor Palanski and made sure that Anna was left in no doubt as to the deadly nature and mandate of the underground sect. Having explained all he knew about the Satanica, he began to describe the equally sinister and convoluted involvement of the Vatican.

"They'll also be searching for us – and the book – with the same ruthless passion as the Satanica and they'll stop at nothing to prevent it from falling into the wrong hands. They know its contents would destroy the very foundations on which the church has been built – imagine the reaction of Christians around the world once they know and understand that the Pope and the Vatican have deliberately suppressed evidence for centuries that contradicts the teachings of the bible!"

Ashen-faced, she gulped the rest of her drink and stared out over the hills beyond the village. She had listened silently through most of Simon's narration as she contemplated the incredible story she was hearing. She sensed that this meeting had just changed the direction of her life. She allowed herself a wry smile, as she remembered getting up that morning and beginning another normal day commanding her team on the archaeological site before this stranger had walked into her midst.

"Anna, I'm sorry to give you so little time – " he took her hand and looked deeply into her eyes, "but you have to decide whether you want to come with us or not!"

Before she could respond Simon's mobile phone rang.

"It's Philip," he said, standing up to take the call. He wandered away from the table to talk freely to his brother and left her to reflect on what he had just said.

She sat there trying to rationalise everything but it was impossible. With her skills and experience of the Biblical Lands, the search for the Book of Judas would be the challenge of a lifetime, the pinnacle of any career that one could only dream of. However the terrifying machinations of the Satanica and the Vatican, who would do all in their power to prevent them from succeeding were real and deadly. She had never encountered a situation where her life was in threat before and the thought horrified her.

As Simon walked back to their table, winding up the call with Philip, she looked up at him.

"I've made a decision – for better or worse, I'm coming with you!" she said and smiled.

"Anna's decided to join us," announced Simon into the mouthpiece as he broke into a broad grin. She could sense from the conversation that his brother had also been pleased to hear the news.

Simon reached out and squeezed Anna's hand while he listened to Philip's meeting arrangements. A couple of minutes passed before they finally signed off.

"Ok, Philip, we'll both see you at the airport later on," said Simon, putting the phone down on the table. She looked up at him expectantly.

"That's great news, Anna," he said smiling, "but we're going to have to get moving. We're travelling to Thailand tonight."

Chapter Eleven

The Vatican, Rome

Colonel Renauld sat behind a large ornate wooden desk in his office. There can be few senior-ranking positions in any army that command such a grand and prestigious setting. His office was on the third floor of a tower, close to the public entrance of the Vatican. The bare stone walls were bedecked with coats of arms and weaponry from medieval times.

The week's events had been testing. Even for him, the regimental leader of the Swiss Guards who was renowned for his unquestioned loyalty to the Cardinals and the Vatican, the latest news on the Book of Judas had been a revelation. He contemplated again the significance of such a book's existence. He had known about the Satanica and their ruthless ambitions for years but that was more hearsay and story-telling than sensible, hard facts. Never had all the parts of the jigsaw clicked together as quickly as they had since the meeting called by Cardinal Camerlengo Fiore in the Sala Consistoriale.

Colonel Renauld's allegiance and devotion to the Supreme Pontiff, Pope Paul XII was absolute. A religious man who saw himself as a "protector of the faith", his job safeguarding the Pope himself had been relatively easy over the past few years because ill health had deterred the Pontiff from travelling and attending public occasions. Instead, he had watched from the sidelines as the senior cardinals jostled for position to fill his shoes. His own appointment as Head of the Swiss Guard was decreed by the new Pope so he had a vested interest in making sure that he supported the right candidate. He had placed the full weight of his influence behind Cardinal Fiore since he saw him as the natural successor.

There was a knock on the door.

"The Cardinals are here to see you, Colonel."

"Show them in, Major," he barked without looking up.

As the Major held the door, Cardinal Deacon Weiss and Cardinal Bishop Lefebvre stepped in, fully clad in the velvet robes of office. Immediately, the Colonel jumped up to welcome them.

"Your Eminences," he said, stooping to kiss the rings on their outstretched hands. "That will be all, Major," he added and the large panelled door swung closed.

The Cardinals were staunch allies of Fiore and part of the select few who were privy to the secret knowledge of the Book of Judas. With the exception of the Pope and Lefebvre and Weiss, who worked directly for Camerlengo Fiore, only three other Cardinals, namely Alphonso, Giacoma and Gregory were party to the truth. In the Swiss Guard, it was just himself and the Vatican's Head of Special Projects who had been briefed for this special assignment. Colonel Renauld knew that to do his job effectively he would have to enlarge the circle that was privy to the details of the Book of Judas. He had it in mind to brief Major Dupont, his loyal number two in the Swiss Guards, over the next twenty-four hours.

"What is it, Colonel? Why the urgent call to your office?" asked Cardinal Weiss.

"Have you seen this, Your Grace?"

The Colonel picked up a folded newspaper from the corner of his desk and handed it over to Cardinal Weiss who proceeded to unfold the pages.

The headline on the front page stood out in bold letters alongside a photograph of a stern-looking police superintendent for Oxfordshire:

RITUAL KILLING TERRIFIES LOCAL RESIDENTS

The article had top billing, covering half a page in the English national broadsheet.

Cardinal Weiss read on. The article spared nothing as it told of the brutal and sadistic death of an Oxford Professor, disfigured beyond recognition. *The Satanica – it had to be.* His thoughts were confirmed a few lines later.

> *"The police found the body spread-eagled, staked to the wall in the shape of a crucifix. His skin had been peeled from his chest and pulled taut to his arms to form 'wings'. The Police found the victim's blood had been used to daub the initials 'MM' behind the door. The Superintendent admitted they were lost for a motive or reason for such a ritual slaying."*

"Well, if we didn't know before, we know now – the Satanica know about the book and they will be, like us, trying to trace the scrolls Trenchard's kept hidden for so many years."

Cardinal Weiss was in his late fifties with greying hair, a craggy face and large bushy eyebrows. He was well known amongst his peers for his wisdom and his hard line attitude to the scriptures and despite the secularisation of the Catholic Church caused by the Vatican's unyielding stance on modern day matters, he firmly believed in the values of the old school.

Cardinal Weiss handed the paper to Cardinal Bishop Lefebvre.

"Have you informed Goran?" enquired Cardinal Weiss.

"No not yet – I'm scheduled to speak with him again in two hours."

"What are your views, Colonel?" asked Cardinal Lefebvre, putting down the newspaper.

Renauld had a sharp mind that paid great attention to detail. He was mildly curious at the scant attention Lefebvre had seemed to give to the article.

"My proposal is as follows – the paper has included a short biography of this Professor Palanski. Apparently he worked at the Ashmolean Museum where Sir Lawrence Trenchard was the Curator. Although I don't think the local police will ever put this connection together, I think we can safely assume from the work of the Satanica that this professor must have been knowledgeable about the Judas Scrolls – he must have had a close association with Sir Lawrence and indeed he may even have known the scrolls' whereabouts!"

Cardinal Weiss nodded,

"I think that's a reasonable assumption."

"The Satanica have tortured him – anything that he knew will now be passed on to them, which means they have a head-start on us."

"Maybe he didn't know too much," ventured Cardinal Lefebvre.

Colonel Renauld glared at him. He didn't care much for this cleric but he had to go through the motions, after all he was one of Cardinal Fiore's closest aides. To him he looked like a weasel with his black goatee beard covering a pointed chin and those beady eyes, too close together behind round metal-framed spectacles. On several occasions he had found the Cardinal prying into affairs of the Pontiff that were not in his domain.

"My proposal is this…" he continued, directing his attention back to Cardinal Weiss.

"I'll speak to Goran. I imagine he's probably already seen the papers and put together the same thoughts as we have – the most important task right now is to locate the two Trenchard brothers. We know they returned for the funeral and that their grandfather will have passed everything on to them. And since the Satanica will also know this – their lives are now in grave danger!"

Renauld paused for their approval before continuing. He could see that he had their undivided attention.

"Our objective must be to claim the book before the Satanica – if necessary we must destroy it, or bring it back to the Vatican where its contents can be buried forever. The brothers will either be carrying out their grandfather's legacy or they'll have been scared into hiding – either way we must find them. If they're searching for the book and have the means to find it, we must order Goran to shadow them. They'll be in constant, grave danger from the Satanica and unbeknown to them, he must monitor their progress until the time comes when the book is found – that's when he must strike."

Cardinal Weiss was the first to speak.

"Your plan is a good one Colonel – he must locate them with God's speed. The future of our Church depends on it. Inform Goran of this message."

"Yes, and we shall inform Cardinal Fiore immediately," replied the beady-eyed Lefebvre.

The meeting was closed. The Cardinals turned and made their way back down the winding staircase to the courtyard below and Colonel Renauld watched them cross the Piazza in the direction of Cardinal Fiore's private quarters.

Two hours later he made a call to England.

Chapter Twelve

Athens Airport

Anna and Simon watched from the balcony as the flight from Basle landed. They had stopped briefly at Anna's lodgings where she had collected a few personal things and written a lengthy note to her deputy on the excavation. She had taken Simon's advice and explained that she would be travelling for an indefinite period due to the death of a close relative. She made sure there were no clues to her whereabouts and didn't leave any contact details just in case someone came looking.

Simon had spent the last forty minutes at the sales desk sorting out the tickets to Bangkok. He already knew the flight details – they would have a three-hour wait before the departure of the flight via Delhi.

They watched as the passengers swarmed down the steps to the waiting buses that would carry them to the airport terminal.

"C'mon," said Simon, "let's go downstairs."

As they descended the staircase towards the Arrivals exit, he began to wonder how his brother had packed the ancient manuscripts. He saw the puzzled look on Anna's face – she was obviously thinking the same thing.

"Philip's carrying the scrolls with him, somehow…" explained Simon.

"This is madness," replied Anna scornfully. "If there's one thing that's guaranteed to make the Customs and Immigration people go mad, it's the mere thought that someone's smuggling ancient antiquities – it's been the pastime of villains round here for years! He could be carrying ten times the normal duty allowances and he'd be safer..."

They waited behind the barrier as passengers from Philip's flight, mainly holidaymakers, began to drift through, pushing old trolleys laden with luggage. As the double exit doors swung open Simon's heart jumped – a Customs official was poking around in Philip's open suitcase, while apparently firing questions at his brother.

Anna saw what was going on.

"That's it – they've got him," she whispered. "What do we do?"

"Just wait a minute," Simon's voice held out a small glimmer of hope. The case was being closed and a second guard seemed to be approaching them. *This is it*, he thought, *either Philip's about to be taken away or he's free to leave.*

The doors closed again and nervously they stood there, fearing the worst. *What's happening?*

The automatic doors sprung open once more and Philip emerged smiling and pushing his luggage trolley.

"What happened?" said the exasperated Simon, hugging his brother.

"If you've got the manuscripts with you, you've just had one of the greatest escapes of all time," said Anna, looking up at him. Her heart had been in her mouth for the last few seconds.

"And you must be Anna," said Philip grinning broadly. "Don't worry – there's no cause for alarm."

How alike they look! she thought. Philip was definitely the elder brother. Not because of the difference in age was obvious, after all it was only fourteen months, but there was something more commanding about his presence and she could sense this in the way Simon greeted him.

"What happened?" she quizzed.

"Just a routine check – that's all."

"And found nothing?" said Simon, looking confused.

"Don't worry, they'd never have found anything – c'mon, I'll explain," said Philip, and he lifted their bags onto the trolley and started pushing it towards a small café on the concourse.

Anna felt a surge of confidence with Philip's arrival. He was charming, intelligent and full of self-assurance. If Simon was the adventurer, the dashing risk-taker, Philip was the very model of control, a natural leader whom people looked up to. Her whole impression was cemented by the appearance and stature of the brothers. Looks counted for a lot when it came to making the right first impression and Anna noticed that Phillip was a shade taller than Simon. She placed him at about six foot four.

Simon stayed at the café table as Phillip and Anna walked to the counter and ordered three coffees.

"Well? Where did you hide them?" asked Simon curiously when they came back.

"I didn't hide them at all – in the beginning I packed them in the luggage the best way I could but it didn't matter. I knew if the luggage was opened then the manuscripts would be found so in the end I had second thoughts on the way to Basle airport – I didn't feel I could risk Customs at this end of the journey."

"Ok, so what have you done with them?" asked Simon.

"I got the taxi to turn around and I went to a shop selling posters – I then carefully rolled them up between two large prints of impressionist paintings and gave them back to the shop assistant who put them put them in a sealed cardboard tube – that tube's now travelling by international courier to a hotel address in Bangkok. We'll pick it up when we get there."

Philip smiled broadly and produced a courier's airway bill.

Both Anna and Simon smiled back.

"I can't say I'm that happy to be letting them go so soon after recovering them but I think it's the safest thing we can do – if everything goes according to plan the package should be arriving at around the same time as we do. I've called the Century Hotel and made our reservations – I've asked them to hold onto a package addressed to me if it does arrive before we do."

"What did the scrolls look like?" enquired Anna, excited by the prospect of seeing them.

"I can guarantee you'll find them fascinating and intriguing, Anna – forget finding the keys of arkheynia," he joked. "We'll need all your skills to understand the map – it's clearly of the Biblical lands but that's where my understanding ends. The names and references are written in a script that's not a language I recognise."

"I wish I could see it," Anna said eagerly.

Philip looked at her. Simon had been right when he spoke to him at Delphi. She was stunningly beautiful, her pretty face beaming warmth and sincerity as she grinned up towards him. Suddenly his thoughts jumped back towards his fiancée, Heather, and a wave of sadness came over him. He recalled her trembling voice after he had explained why he would not be coming home. *"Then take me with you,"* she had pleaded tearfully but Philip had been adamant. He deliberately hadn't revealed the true extent of the danger and he promised to call her whenever he could.

Sipping his coffee, Simon explained the travel arrangements for the night ahead and Phillip confirmed his approval of the plan.

"Ok, so we can check-in shortly – I take it you haven't seen this yet?" said Phillip, standing up and throwing the rolled up newspaper onto the table in front of them. Anna picked it up and unfolded it to reveal the shocking headlines on the front page. They both pored over the story while Philip made his way down the concourse to buy some provisions for the long journey ahead.

The imagery that Simon had conjured up that afternoon in the taverna at Eleusis became stark reality as Anna read on. If she had any doubts about the story or the horrendous danger they were in then they were now dispelled.

Philip saw the startled look on their faces as he returned.

"Anna, can I buy you dinner in Bangkok tonight?" said Phillip, trying to inject a bit of light humour into the atmosphere.

Anna grinned.

"That sounds very nice. I accept!"

The smiles returned as they proceeded towards the first class check-in desk.

"Oh, I've also got some reading for you," he added, revealing a brown leather book from the inside pocket of his jacket as they strode down the concourse. It was the notebook that had accompanied the scrolls in the safe deposit box at Bank Ehinger. He pulled it out and handed it over to Anna.

She nodded and flicked through a couple of pages before carefully returning it into her hand luggage.

The plane from Athens airport departed twenty minutes late on its eleven-hour crossing to Bangkok and the Far East.

Chapter Thirteen

Bangkok

The flight across Iran and the northern part of India to Delhi had been calm but for some reason the second leg across the Bay of Bengal towards Malaysia had been excessively turbulent. Philip had flown the route on several business trips in the past and had noticed how the same area always seemed to be the worst affected. *Must be something to do with the changing temperatures over the sea,* he considered. Anna was not a good flyer and genuinely looked terrified as the plane bumped along with passengers and cabin crew alike strapped to their seats. The experience made her contemplate how fragile life was really. *It's fate*, she thought. *You have to live your life for the moment because who knows what's around the corner.* She looked around at the other passengers. It amazed and comforted her to see how some of them were managing to sleep through the constant jolts shuddering through the plane. Smiling she looked down at Simon's head as it slipped onto her shoulder. He was sound asleep, oblivious to the commotion around them. She pulled the flashlight attached to the head rest and re-immersed herself in the contents of the notebook and Bairstow's folder, which Phillip had given to her on take-off. They were nearly at their destination.

It was mid-afternoon and the sun was shining brightly as the plane landed, half an hour behind schedule. They cleared the airport quickly and jumped into a taxi, which clattered and hooted its way through streets that were teeming with life in the smog and haze. The journey to the Century Hotel took forty minutes through the congestion as the yellow "tuk-tuk" three-wheelers weaved noisily in and out of the traffic.

The hotel itself was nothing exceptional, a typical middle of the road – and suitably anonymous – European tourist selection that found in a travel guide in Basle. They checked into two rooms.

Simon dumped his bags on one of the single beds in the room he was sharing with his brother and unbolted the interconnecting door. Seconds later he heard the lock clicking on the other side and Anna pulled it open.

"Well it looks like you've got the master suite," said Simon, looking enviously over her shoulder at the double bed.

"Yes, thank you," she smiled, "and with you two here to protect me I should get a decent night's sleep after that ghastly flight!"

Simon looked at Phillip who was lying on the bed, hands behind his head, looking at the ceiling.

"What's the plan?"

"It's four-thirty now – let's grab some rest and then go down and get something to eat about seven. We can discuss our plans for tomorrow."

"Ok – that sounds good," said Anna, "I've still got some reading to finish off. Your grandfather's notebook is captivating – such attention to detail. I should be able to brief you on the contents over dinner – see you in a couple of hours."

And with that she went back into her room, leaving the door slightly ajar.

The sun was beginning to fade outside their window as Simon reached over to check the time on his watch on the bedside table. He still felt tired but forced himself up and walked out onto the balcony, stretching his arms. They were on the sixth floor overlooking the swimming pool and he looked down at the figure gracefully swimming up and down. Once she stepped out of the water, he recognised the deeply tanned figure immediately. Anna reached for a towel and started drying her shoulder length black hair.

"She's wonderful, isn't she?" the voice came from behind him.

Simon twisted round and grinned at his brother.

"Yes, I think you could be right for once."

He waved down to Anna below after she spotted him on the balcony. Thirty minutes later, they were all dressed and showered, and ready to go down to one of the hotel restaurants. They had debated whether to eat out but on closer inspection, Anna had persuaded them that the local Thai menu looked good and the alcoves in the dining room gave them a decent amount of privacy.

The smartly dressed waiter took them to the table below the cave-like recess at the far end of the room. They were eating early by normal Thai standards so the remainder of the tables were deserted.

"The service should be good," joked Simon as they were seated and as if to reinforce the point another waiter sprang towards them clutching three menus.

They ordered a bottle of wine and selected items from the à la carte menu that they could share in the middle of the table.

Phillip pulled a piece of newspaper out of his pocket, unfolded it and smoothed it out on the table in front of them. It was the cutting from the *South China Morning Post* that had first alerted Sir Lawrence to the whereabouts of the missing third arkheynia. The article had several photographs of divers on the deck of a boat crouching down around some of the relics they pulled up from sea floor. There in the middle picture, was a large bearded man, smiling as he held up the third fragment of the bone necklace across the palms of his hands. *He has absolutely no idea what he's discovered,* thought Simon, staring at the crooked piece of bone. It was about twelve inches long and the tip was unmistakeable – it was round and bright "blood" red.

The rest of the article told of the salvage team, headed by Hans Friedel, that had discovered the remains of a ship believed to date back to circa 100BC. The team had been looking for a merchant vessel that had sunk in these parts carrying gold at the turn of the century when their sensitive underwater camera equipment had discovered the ancient wreck under layers of silt and sand. Only the original mast had been protruding from its final resting place.

The journalist writing the piece had done so under the headline *"Extraordinary, experts hold no answers"*. He was not referring to the discovery of the wreck itself because similar ships had been uncovered before. What he was referring to was the actual location of the find. Here was a ship, previously only found in waters around the Mediterranean and in descriptions and drawings from Biblical times sunk in the sea off Thailand. *"How could this be?"* asked the author without offering any theories of his own.

The date on the newspaper showed that the article was only a couple of weeks old. The story went on to interview the leader of the salvage team, who dismissed the findings as having negligible monetary value but significant historical interest.

Philip knew the next sentence was critical. It was a quote from Hans Friedel: *"Once we've completed our search for the Spanish merchant ship 'El Garrido' in the waters east of Koh Samui, we'll donate the historic relics to a recognised national museum for further investigation"*.

"How do you plan on getting the arkheynia back?" asked Anna, looking across the table at Philip.

"It's a good question – I've been thinking about nothing else for a while now and I'm still not sure. All I know is that if we were to turn up out of the blue and just ask them for the bone relic they've just discovered two weeks earlier their curiosity will be aroused – they're highly unlikely to give it away to strangers and if we offer money they'll probably think they have something they can auction to the highest bidder!"

"I agree," said Simon, taking a sip from his glass of white wine. "Any approaches of friendly nature will only raise their interest in a item that they currently don't perceive as having any value – the problem is we don't have time; we have to assume that it won't take the Satanica long to locate our trail and try to catch up with us."

"You're right, we haven't got time to wait for them to sail back to dry land before we talk to them – we're going to have to go out there and capture it, steal it, do whatever's necessary to get it and leave… What do you think?"

Anna nodded her agreement. It was the only way.

"Yes, we'll need to find out where they are on the high seas – once we've found them we'll need to come up with a plan for how we board their ship and steal the arkheynia…"

"How can we be sure they still have the artefacts on board?" Simon queried.

"Aah, we can thank your grandfather for that," replied Anna, "I am not sure how he managed it but somehow he contacted the salvage team to register the keenness of the Ashmolean Museum to house their findings – in doing so he discovered that Hans Friedel had decided to keep the remnants aboard their ship until they finally called into the port of Singapore at the end of their project."

Two waiters arrived with a host of authentic local dishes and placed them in the middle of the table. They helped themselves to the sticky rice, chicken wrapped in banana leaves and hot green curry sauce as they continued pondering the pursuit of the third key.

"I have the beginnings of an idea," stated Philip calmly, offering one of the dishes to Anna.

"We need to get aboard their salvage ship and secure the arkheynia without arousing too much suspicion – why don't we get in touch with them and convince them that we're journalists and tell them we've come a long way to do a piece on their discovery? The fact that this Hans

Friedel's done this article shows that he doesn't mind the limelight – the key is that we have to be a big enough journal to capture his interest."

"Ok, this sounds good – we could introduce ourselves as journalists from the *National Geographic?* We could even offer a reasonable financial incentive for their granting us an exclusive?" pitched in Simon.

"You know it could actually work," said Anna. "Why don't we buy a camera? I've had to become a bit of a photographer over the years – I could join you as the journal's official photographer."

"Great idea," Simon grinned. "I guess that leaves me in charge of the transport and fake IDs! There's a business centre on the first floor. I could log onto the *National Geographic* site and see what information I can download – I might be able to pick up some logos and create some passes but I'll need passport photos."

"Ok, that's settled," said Philip. "We're going to need to make a very early start in the morning, so do whatever you can tonight – the flight to Koh Samui takes off at seven-thirty so we'll need to be at the airport an hour or so before that."

He reached over and topped up Anna's wine glass.

"Well, here's to our success!" toasted Philip and held his glass out. As the others chinked glasses his mobile phone rang. He looked at the screen – it was Heather calling from the east coast of America.

"I'll see you in a moment," Philip whispered to them, and he sidled out from behind the table, pressing the connect button to speak to his fiancée.

"Who's that?" asked Anna and she listened intently as Simon told her their story since they had left university. He told her how he had decided to work for the United Nations helping the third world after his career in the City didn't work out – and how Philip had made a huge success in investment banking in the city, as evidenced by his palatial houses in London and New York.

"It was in Manhattan where he first met Heather," he remarked. "In fact I've actually only met her a couple of times but they must have been together now for about five years or so – true love I'd say. She's very attractive and also has a pretty high-profile city career."

Philip returned to the table.

"Everything Ok?" asked Simon.

"Yes, fine – pretty early her time but all's Ok."

Seconds later Philip's mobile rang again.

"Funny," he shrugged. "I wasn't expecting her to call back."

No name was registered on the flashing digital display. Frowning, he clicked the receive button.

"Hallo!" A couple of seconds skirted past.

"Hallo! Who's calling?" he repeated, slightly louder.

Anna and Simon sat and watched in anxiety as the colour started to drain from Philip's cheeks.

"What do you want?" Philip exclaimed hurriedly into the receiver.

He sat there rigid as if in a trance. His arm fell onto the table clutching the mobile.

"What is it?" cried Simon, grabbing the phone from his hand and listening. It was disconnected. Whoever had been there had gone.

Philip took a deep breath and exhaled slowly and deliberately.

"Why have we not thought about this before?" He looked at Simon. Whatever it was it had shaken him, he looked ghostly pale.

"What happened?" blurted Anna, reaching out and touching his hand. She also looked fragile.

"A low voice, a man's voice, said he knew where we were! He said he was coming to find us – when I asked him what he wanted, he said us, *he wanted us!*"

Simon was playing with the mobile.

"The only thing I can establish is that it was an international call – whoever it was couldn't be calling from this country!"

The call had clearly rattled Philip but he also felt cross with himself that he hadn't considered such a possibility.

132

"We need to get rid of everything that gives away our movements – that means mobiles, credit cards and any other bank cards." He paused. "And somehow we need to get new passports."

The restaurant was approaching capacity and the ambience had changed completely. The waiters were busily rushing between tables and, above the noise and mêlée, they suddenly heard it at the same time.

"Trenchard – Philip Trenchard!"

A bell rang and the Thai voice called out again.

"Trenchard – Philip Trenchard – Room 612?"

Following on from the call, Philip's heart was in his mouth. Round the corner came a young Thai boy smartly dressed in the attire of the hotel concierge. He carried a bell and rang it again.

"Message for Philip Trenchard – Room 612."

"Over here," he beckoned the boy with a wave.

The boy approached and handed over an envelope. Opening it warily, Philip's expression gradually softened and, smiling at the boy, he place a few Thai baht notes on his silver plate as a tip.

Simon and Anna wondered what it could be this time.

"Please tell them I'll be along shortly to collect it."

The boy in the blue uniform nodded and left.

"Our package?" asked Anna.

"I believe so," he replied. "Why don't you order some coffee and I'll sort the delivery out, it shouldn't take long."

And with that, Philip got up and made in the direction of the hotel lobby.

"They know we're here now, so we can't hide that fact but if we're quick and everything works out tomorrow we can be on our way before they find us," Simon said, looking to calm Anna.

"We need to get to a bank and take out enough cash to survive on for a few weeks – no more traceable bank payments!"

The coffee arrived and Anna added some milk and sugar. She sat stirring her cup.

"They know we're in this hotel?" she moaned.

At that moment Philip returned clutching the cardboard tube that held the scrolls. Anna's demeanour changed immediately when she saw it – her face lit up in anticipation. Since reading the notebook, she had been coming to terms the enormity of finally seeing and reading the Judas Scroll. *This is probably the most significant archaeological find of all time,* she thought.

"Here you are – I know you've been longing to see it," said Philip, handing over the long cylinder to Anna. Her face glowed.

"If it's Ok, I'm going to take it up to the room?"

They nodded and watched as she disappeared excitedly in the direction of the lift.

Philip lifted his cup and took a long drink of coffee.

"We're leaving tonight," he said, staring across at Simon.

"I used my credit card to make the reservations – anyone who gets hold of that information will be able to trace us immediately. We're not safe while we stay here!"

"Ok – what's the plan?" asked Simon.

"There's a train that leaves tonight, a sleeper from Bangkok station – it departs at ten-thirty and arrives shortly after seven tomorrow morning."

Simon looked at his watch.

"Just coming up to nine o'clock, that doesn't give us very long."

"I've already organised and paid for the tickets through the concierge – they've told me the main station will take between ten and fifteen minutes in a taxi at this time of night."

"Ok, you break the news to Anna – I'm going to see if I can quickly put those passes together in the business centre."

Simon departed, leaving Philip to sign the bill. Before going up in the lift to see Anna, he stopped at Reception and used his card one final time to settle the entire bill.

Upstairs, he found Anna in her room poring over the scrolls, which were sprawled over the floor and held down by makeshift weights at each end.

"They're incredible," she murmured, oblivious to Philip's entrance through the interconnecting door.

"Aren't they?"

He startled her for a moment. Apologising for making her jump, he then proceeded to tell her of the new travel plans as she regained her composure.

"If we're successful tomorrow, where will we go next?" enquired Anna as they both started throwing their few belongings in their carrier bag.

"What do you mean?"

"Well we'll have to secure all three keys of the bone necklace before this scroll will help us," she said, pointing at the map on the floor. "The other two keys of arkheynia are going to be much harder to obtain – one's kept in the sacred relics chamber of the Egyptian Museum in Cairo and the other, according your grandfather's notes, is in the hands of a rich, reclusive private collector in New York."

"I see," remarked Philip. "I guess you're right. We'll head for New York first – does that make sense to you?"

"Yes, that makes perfect sense – our final destination, the entrance to the labyrinth, is somewhere on that map and that's got to be closer to Cairo!"

Anna rolled up the scrolls and put them back in the tube while Philip packed for his brother. Not long later Simon entered.

"What do you think?" he asked, holding up two laminated passes with photos that depicted Anna and Philip as bone fide reporters for the *National Geographic.*

"Very good – not sure you got my best side though," smiled Anna, screwing up her face as she pretended to look a bit closer.

"Good job, Simon – let's go," Philip said as he slung his carrier bag over his shoulder and headed towards the door.

"You know, seriously, there's one thing we need to talk about?" Anna's voice took on a more stern tone.

Philip stopped in his tracks and turned around.

"What's the matter, Anna?"

"At some point we have to talk about the consequences of finding the book! What do we do if we do find it first? What does it mean if we find it? We've done nothing but discuss the details of getting to the book since we met, which is right but…" she paused and saw both brothers were listening, captivated.

"Look, I'm just saying we need to discuss the bigger picture – right?"

"Yes, you're right, Anna," said Philip slowly. "I think we all need to give it some serious thought – we'll talk it through when we have the first part of the arkheynia in our hands."

"Ok," said Anna cheerfully. "Let's go – we've got a train to catch."

Chapter Fourteen

London

With the right connections and for the right price almost any information you wanted on a person residing in the UK could be discovered in London. Whether accessing police records, bank or credit card details or simply using the internet, there was always a host of person-specific data that could be uncovered.

In this case the records being sought belonged to two mobile phone companies and the subjects of the investigations were Simon and Philip Trenchard. The private investigation company had a long-established mole within their corporate structures who was more than happy to supply details on these anonymous names for a bit of extra cash.

Conchos had agreed to meet the private investigator in a public house called The Coal Hole on the same side of the Strand as the Savoy Hotel in Central London. It was early evening and the famous old pub was busy – it had been the rendezvous site for countless clandestine and romantic liaisons over the years. Both parties were punctual and the transaction didn't take very long. He stood at the end of the bar drinking a pint of bitter to blend in with his surroundings although privately he detested alcohol. Wearing his brown leather jacket and reading a copy of *The Times* as agreed, he waited patiently for the man to arrive.

It wasn't long before the private eye walked in, pushing his way through the dense mass of bodies to reach a standing place next to him at the crowded bar. He placed a half-folded newspaper on the bar and, pulling out a cigarette, he stretched over and asked Conchos for a light. A few seconds later the hired private eye left but this time he was several thousand pounds richer. After a reasonable length of time, Conchos nonchalantly drained his glass, picked up the newspaper and walked outside into the busy thoroughfare as the dusky evening light began to fade.

Passing Charing Cross Station, he marched towards the north end of Trafalgar Square accompanied by the sound of irate drivers beeping their car horns. The centre of London had lost the ability to cope with its traffic volumes years earlier and the "gridlock" congestion was now commonplace. He stepped through the throng of idling black cabs and entered the church of St. Martin in the Fields. Once inside, he walked down the aisle and sat in the third pew from the front of the altar. Lowering his head, he smiled to himself. It was the smug, manic grin of someone bordering on insanity. Here he was, the Satanica's "brutal slayer", used to carrying out macabre executions for the Zoroastrian High Priests, sitting shamelessly, blasphemously in a church pew challenging the very sanctity of the Christian religion.

In the other wooden pews around him sat a handful of local worshippers facing the altar while a youthful-looking member of the church's clergy edged his way around the perimeter lighting the tall wax candles.

He opened the brown envelope and began to study the reports. The pages detailed all the phone calls made to and from Philip and Simon Trenchard's mobile phones over the past few days since he had viciously murdered his latest victim – Professor Palanski.

He ran down the list and noted the location and number of the calls. There weren't many and most of them were between the brothers themselves. He saw the calls from Basle and Athens and then picked up on the last call made by Philip to a number in Bangkok. He made a mental note that he would investigate this number in more detail a bit later on.

As he folded the sheet, his mind homed in on one interesting aspect of Philip's mobile communication list. Why were there so many inbound calls from this same number in America? Who was it that was communicating so persistently with him? This aspect was puzzling. The information he had on the brothers was limited and put together at very short notice by the Satanica's own researchers. Before he had set off to England, Conchos had been given a dossier that contained as much as they had on Simon and Philip Trenchard. Nothing signalled such a strong link with this residential number in New York. He knew it was not related to his firm's office and the dossier confirmed that he was not married. Again, he made a mental note to investigate the number carefully – if he could establish any close ties or relationships they could be useful later on.

As he stood up to leave, the young clergyman stood at the end of his pew holding the long pole used to light the candles.

"Go in peace, brother," he smiled as he saw the "worshipper" stand up in the pew – and then his expression crumpled as he stared into the executioner's cold, emotionless face. Never before had he encountered such vindictive wickedness burning with so much intensity: the foreboding sense of death behind those callous eyes.

Cowering, he coughed and spluttered as the menacing Conchos covered the few steps towards him with terrifyingly silent speed. Sharply, he turned away and cast his eyes to the ground as he drew level, no longer able to bear that maniacal gaze. As he passed he felt a strange sensation that felt like a gust of pure and intoxicating evil whistling around him. Seconds later, he had passed, leaving the young cleric gasping to catch his breath.

Shaken, he leaned on the wooden pew as he turned to watch the back of the black figure exiting the church, his footsteps echoing loudly on the grey stone floor.

Chapter Fifteen

Vatican City, Rome

"Colonel, I have a code seven international call from England – can I put it through?"

Colonel Renauld stared at the console on his desk for a moment, wondering what could be the reason for his agent making such an unscheduled communication. Their last conversation had been to discuss strategy earlier that afternoon and they had agreed to speak again tomorrow night.

"Yes, go ahead put the call through and then you can go, Major; we'll sort out the rest of the regiment business in the morning."

"Very good, Sir," he replied.

It was early evening and although he trusted his assistant implicitly, he had no intention of leaving any opportunity for any misinformation leaks.

"Colonel, are you there?" Goran inquired.

"Yes, go ahead, Goran, is there a problem?"

"Not exactly Colonel… but there have been some more developments that I need to make you aware of."

"Ok, what is it?" he answered gruffly.

"My contacts have been very useful – it would appear the brothers have both left England. One travelled to Basle and the other took a flight to Athens – I also know that they visited Professor Palanski's house the day before he died. It would appear that this Professor was a close colleague of their grandfather's – further checks confirm that they booked themselves on a later flight to Bangkok."

Colonel Renauld listening intently shook his head slowly.

"Ok, at this point in time it would seem that they've decided to step into their grandfather's shoes – I'm surprised you've found it so easy to trace them!"

"It's been too easy Colonel – they've even been communicating on their mobiles and the computer print-out backs up all their movements – one brother's been to Bank Ehinger in Basle while the other's contacted a young archaeologist lady in Athens, called Anna Nikolaidis."

The Colonel cursed at the news. It was one thing having the information but it was another thing altogether when it was so readily and easily available.

"So we can safely assume that any information that's with us will also be in the hands of the Satanica?" he questioned dryly.

"Yes," responded a disgruntled Goran. "But I have taken deliberate counter measures – I called Philip Trenchard directly on his mobile in Bangkok and I'm confident that they won't be using them again!"

"Good," replied the Colonel thankfully.

The line went quiet for a moment before Goran spoke again in his deep low voice.

"Colonel, I don't want to go into details on the line but I believe we have a leak directly to the Satanica and it's someone within our inner sanctum."

The Colonel froze for a second, taking in the comment. He had worked with Goran on many difficult and life-threatening assignments in the past when trust and integrity between them was stretched to the limit. Renauld knew him well enough to give serious credence to the damaging remarks. Although he was a man of few words he would not have offered such a statement without real facts to back it up.

"Ok," the Colonel muttered quietly, almost inaudibly.

"Can you tell me more about any indications or information from your end?" requested Renauld cautiously. He was well aware of the need for secrecy.

Goran pondered the best way forward.

"Colonel, the Supreme Pontiff's dying and that leaves only five within the Vatican walls who could know the real facts, all potential successors to the Catholic throne – maybe we should release some, er, 'news'…. to flush the infiltrator out or potentially put the enemy on the wrong track!"

He knew straight away what Goran was implying. If there was someone with links to the Satanica in their midst they could find the source of the leak by giving them snippets of incorrect information.

"Ok Goran, I'll give this some thought – you've done a good job!"

The Colonel signed off and stared at the picture of his regiment on the wall contemplating the latest developments. *Who can the traitor possibly be?* he thought as he considered each of the Vatican's five most senior Cardinals one by one and weighed up the implications for the successful completion of his assignment.

Chapter Sixteen

Surithani, Thailand

There had only been daylight for the last hour as the wide-gauged, large-bodied silver train ran parallel to the coast down the final length of track into the small southern harbour of Surithani.

The journey was obviously a popular one as the concierge had only managed to secure second-class tickets, which translated into rotating fans on the ceiling of the carriage and hard, short beds that unfolded from the luggage rack and the seating below. Thai trains operated three classes of travel and they were at least thankful for securing some degree of comfort in the second-class coaches. Bleary-eyed from a sleepless night, they had taken it in turns to use the small washroom at the end of the carriage.

"It's going to make life a lot harder without our phones," moaned Simon as they discussed their plans for when they arrived at their final destination.

The previous evening they had ceremonially destroyed their SIM cards and thrown their mobile phones into a rubbish skip on a side road outside Bangkok station.

"Forget the phones – a few more changes of clothing would be nice," replied Anna tiredly. She was still wearing jeans and her sleeveless white blouse that was cut in a V-shape revealing more than a suggestion of her youthful, tanned cleavage.

"I think you look great," smiled Simon.

"When we're finished down here, we'll go back through Bangkok do some shopping on the way," said Philip, throwing a few personal belongings back in his carrier bag.

The train slowed down as it pulled into Surithani. It was not really a station as such but there was an open-air platform on one side with a small car park full of trailers, motorbikes and the odd tourist bus. Carrying their few possessions, they climbed off the train and made their way towards the exit.

The temperature was already approaching the mid-thirties and the sun was blazing down from the perfect blue skies. For Thailand this was the start of the holiday season and the town was flooded with families heading for the islands and scruffy backpackers on the Asian leg of their intrepid expedition.

"Ok, it looks like we'll be going this way," Simon said indicating to what looked like the main street in the town.

They had agreed that Philip would contact the salvage vessel while Simon and Anna would visit the bank and purchase any articles that could make their disguise as National Geographic reporters more plausible.

"Ok, I'm following the signs down to the harbour – I'll meet you down there at the jetty for Koh Samui when you're finished."

Anna and Simon set off towards the main shopping area. Their first port of call had to be a bank. Amidst the hustle and bustle of street traders they spotted a couple of banks and money exchange shops. None of them bore western international names but the usual Visa and American Express signs were posted to their facades.

"This one will do," said Simon, grabbing Anna's shoulder and steering her in the direction of an open door. There were CCTV cameras inside but apart from this the security seemed almost non-existent. The interior reminded him of those scenes from old western movies where the robbers broke in to rob the bank. There was a long counter with metal-framed glass screens behind which the tellers sat. As if to complete the setting, there was a large, sturdy-looking black safe beyond them at the back of the room.

Simon walked over towards the Chinese-looking girl behind the nearest window. Privately, he thanked Bairstow again as he produced a plastic wallet full of traveller's cheques. Each one had a thousand-dollar denomination and there were forty of them.

The girl looked at the wallet, smiled up at them as she recognised the commission potential, and shouted something to a colleague in Thai. Not long later, after he had produced his passport and signed all the cheques, the safe door was opened and they departed into the sunshine pushing the new bills into their pockets.

"Now to do some spending – I bet you're good at that aren't you?" he joked.

"Not bad," she smiled, and yanked his arm playfully as they crossed the road towards a camera shop. Inside, Simon did not waste much time, he bought a pair of binoculars and a sophisticated camera with two detachable long lenses similar to those used by goal-line photographers. The square metal case filled with cut out foam to house the lenses completed the paraphernalia of a professional photojournalist.

At a store a few doors further down the street, he bought a jacket to complete the outfit. Khaki-coloured and similar to a safari suit in style, it had a plethora of pockets sewn on the outside and plenty of padding. The pockets were what attracted him; they could be filled with rolls of films and camera lenses to render the look of the roving photographer even more plausible.

"Well, try it on then!" said Simon smirking.

"What me?" exclaimed Anna.

"Yes you – if anybody can assure us of a warm welcome when we arrive on the boat, I think I can safely say that a beautiful young woman carrying a camera could do the trick! Anyway, you did say you were a bit of a photographer!"

Anna cupped her hands over her face for a second and took a deep breath.

"Yes – Ok," she responded slowly. "I guess I'd better try it on."

By the time they'd finished she really did look the part. For added authenticity, Simon had punctured the edge of the laminated passes and attached them to lanyards so that they could be hung around the neck. Anna's pass reached down to her navel and could be tucked inside her new jacket.

On the way back to the harbour to meet Philip they picked up some local Thai snacks and a couple of bottles of water.

They spotted him easily, leaning nonchalantly against a post.

He looks pleased with himself, thought Anna.

"How did you get on?" Philip asked as they drew closer.

"Pretty good," said Simon. "We've got a present for you." He tossed a bag towards him. It contained notebooks, pens and a pair of dark sunglasses – the kind of items no self-respecting journalist would ever be without.

"Great – what do you think Anna?" said Philip, trying on the glasses and striking a mock film star pose.

"Could be worse," she giggled, holding up her new khaki tunic. "You could have to wear my jacket."

Her laugh was infectious and, smiling broadly. Philip led them along the jetty to a rundown outside café with white plastic tables and chairs littered around.

"So far so good," said Philip, settling into one of the chairs. "We have an appointment with Hans Friedel, leader of the salvage team at any time after three this afternoon – they're going to be anchored two kilometres off the Chaweng beach on the east coast of Koh Samui."

"How did you find him?" Simon quizzed.

"Apparently, he calls into Surithani to pick up provisions now and then – the harbour master put me straight through on the radio when he knew who I was looking for. I told him we were from the *National Geographic* and that we'd like to do a lead article on his team's exploits."

"How did he react?" asked Anna.

"He was delighted – I think he can see that a bit of international fame and celebrity status might boost his ability to raise sponsors for the rest of his project! The harbour master was helpful as well, if we're going to get there for three this afternoon he advised us to get the ferry to Koh Samui and a taxi to Chaweng beach – apparently there are plenty of opportunities to charter a boat from there. The ferry should be pulling up there in twenty minutes," Philip pointed back down the jetty.

They had something to eat and embarked on the small, motorised ferry. It was crowded with just one small room below deck so Anna did not need to try too hard to persuade them to sit outside. The cool breeze was pleasant but the noise of the engines, and the occasional splash that hit them as the boat bisected another rising wave, made it difficult to hold a conversation.

Once on dry land, they commandeered the first available taxi and sped off towards Chaweng. The island was idyllic, the winding narrow roads almost overgrown by the tree-high, tropical vegetation and they occasionally passed local islanders making their wobbling way along on rickety old bicycles. The road followed the coastline and not long later they paid the driver and walked past an arcade of shops towards the beach. The harbour master had been right; it was easy to hire a boat and Simon negotiated a good one, a twenty-foot speedboat with two powerful outboard motors that could propel them along at a fair rate of knots if required.

"I guess this is where you acknowledge my glory days as a water skiing champion," Simon goaded as he started to unravel the mooring rope from the capstan on the wooden jetty.

"Aaah yes, that's right, I can't quite remember whether you made the Olympics or not!" he smiled, and gestured to Anna to get in.

"Right, here we go," said Simon and, turning in an arc from the beach, he opened up the engines and the boat's prow lifted up as it roared out to sea. As the beach faded in the background, Philip and Anna put themselves in their journalist attire. Anna conscious of the part she had to play, started getting herself in the right frame of mind by taking some shots of the wooden squid-fishing boats whose crews waved to them as they sped past.

The salvage ship was easy to recognise; it was huge compared with other craft in the area. At the front was a large crane; the sides were painted a dingy orange and a craft like a bathyscaphe hung from two thick steel cables. Pinned along the side of the vessel were old rubber tyres to protect it against minor collisions. *It must be over sixty feet long,* thought Philip as he stared at some of the crew beginning to appear on the deck. The side of the hull itself was a good ten feet above sea level.

The reality of what they were doing suddenly came home to Anna. It no longer felt like a children's adventure where everything always worked out in the end – they were about to lie and impersonate people they were not. She looked up at Philip who showed no such signs of nerves and was busily trying to make an assessment of the ship and the number of crew members on board. Spotting Anna's worried face he leant down.

"We'll be fine, trust me," he said and squeezed her hand tightly.

"There's someone shouting over there," yelled Simon above the engines.

Leaning over the railing running along the deck, they could see a man waving them towards the metal ladder that was attached to the side of the hull.

Simon altered course and headed for the ladder. The sea was perfectly calm; the only noticeable waves were the wash kicked up by the outboard motors.

Peering down over the side, the water was crystal clear. Anna could see for about ten feet or so before the water became murky and dark.

When they were within fifty feet of the ship, Simon turned the engines down and the boat crested towards the ladder at idling speed. Pulling alongside, he reached out and grabbed the metal rungs, holding them steady while Philip and Anna began to pull themselves up. Anna went first with her camera swinging at the front and her leather-strapped lens case slung over her shoulder.

"Welcome," beamed the ship's captain, stretching out his hand to help them over the side. "It's a pleasure to have you on board."

Their arrival had certainly generated interest and any crew members not at their post had come on deck to greet them as the captain helped Philip aboard and shook his hand. Down below they heard the engines roar again as Simon pulled his little craft away to rest a safe distance from the ship.

"Welcome on board, I'm Hans Friedel." A tall man stepped past the captain to introduce himself. He stood out immediately in the heat of the midday sun; he was wearing long beige trousers and sporting a navy blue blazer. The rest of the crew were in shorts and T-shirts.

Apart from the newly introduced Hans Friedel and the captain there were four other men of European descent. Going by the prominent creases on their weathered faces they had obviously spent a lot of time in the sun – Philip guessed that these were the salvage team's divers. A couple of local Thai members had joined the party but the captain barked a few orders and they trudged back reluctantly towards their new assignments. It was not every day that such a beautiful woman stepped on board this ship and the news travelled fast.

"It's a pleasure to meet you, Hans. My colleague Anna and I have been looking forward to this exciting opportunity."

Anna was crouched next to her open case detaching and re-attaching a new lens in the most professional manner she could. Philip smiled to himself. *I wonder if she feels the pressure of eight or so pairs of eyes that have been glued to her since she clambered over the rail.*

"How would you like to proceed?" asked Hans in a friendly manner. He had glimpsed the *National Geographic* tags around their necks. The thought of their being impostors never entered his mind for a second. After all, who on earth would want to do such a thing! And for what reason!

"We could go down to my cabin and start from there if you like?" he suggested with a polite smile.

"That sounds a perfect idea – but would it be possible for Anna to get some shots of the relics while we do the interview? Unfortunately we don't have as much time as we would like and…"

Before he had finished one of the European men stepped forward.

"I could show her the relics," he suggested eagerly to Hans.

The captain looked momentarily upset. He too liked the idea of being the centre of attention in the company of such a beautiful lady.

"Yes, I guess that'd be Ok," he replied sullenly, his German accent slipping slightly and reinforcing the fact that he was not entirely overjoyed with the arrangement.

Anna noticed his dismay and quickly came to his rescue.

"Maybe I could come on to your cabin afterwards and take some pictures of you in your 'natural habitat'?" Anna suggested with a broad smile.

Hans's reserve melted. In his mid-forties with blond hair and matching trimmed beard, the thought of appearing in such a distinguished journal with worldwide distribution excited him.

"Very good," he nodded, and turned to lead Philip along the deck to the stairs leading down to his cabin. Philip sent a knowing glance to Anna before following on his heels.

Anna turned to face her guide.

"My name is Biscan – can I carry your case for you?" he asked keenly. He had never seen anyone so beautiful before.

He was probably the youngest member of the greeting party. Wearing white knee-length shorts, deck shoes and with a youthful, tanned chest, he had a thick East European accent, or maybe even Russian, she thought.

"Thanks," she replied kindly. "Do you mind if we go and see the relics now?"

She did not want to spend any more time on board than they had to.

"Come this way," he said, picking up the case. He led her to a ladder that ran down into the hull and the deck below. Biscan went first and waited for her at the bottom. *I'm sure there must be stairs to this level,* she thought as she felt his hands on her waist, helping her down the last few rungs. Hiding the urge to push his hands away, she reached the bottom and brushed her waist before turning to thanked him with a polite smile.

They seemed to traipse the whole length of the wooden deck until they reached a set of double doors in the bow of the ship. He turned the round doorknob and pushed through into a cabin that matched the V-shape at the ship's bow.

She hadn't expected this. She had imagined that the treasures would be held somewhere on board wrapped up in cloth in a safe storage space. Instead she gasped in amazement; this was like an exhibit room in a national museum. Items were neatly laid out in flat, glass-cases at table-height that ran down the length of ship wall and then again in the middle of the room. The space between showcases had been carpeted to form a walkway. To Anna this was like Aladdin's cave – she slowly edged along the worn red carpet marvelling at the treasures on show. Occasionally she looked up at the wooden cabinets attached to the wall holding fragments of ancient pottery

"Amazing," she murmured, and leant over to see if she could lift the glass case.

Just then she heard the cough and realised that Biscan was standing a few feet behind her watching her every move. *I should be taking pictures,* she thought and reached down for her camera.

"Do the glass cases open?" she enquired. "I'd like to get some shots with more natural light closer to the windows."

"Sure, no problem," he said, showing her how the glass cabinet simply lifted from the front on hinges fastened at the back.

"Thank you," she replied and placed what looked like a stone carving of an animal onto the table near one of the large portholes. It had been worn down by centuries of tides at the bottom of the sea. *I must look like I know what I'm doing,* she thought, peering through the viewfinder and turning the camera ninety degrees before snapping a shot.

As she played with the focus, she saw it. The blood red tip glinted as she stared through the lens. Slowly she lowered the camera. *I've found it!* It was a thin crooked fragment of bone, about seven or eight inches long, with a round polished end. The blood-red colour was so bright it did not look natural.

He followed her gaze as she moved automatically towards it.

"Unusual isn't it," came the thick accent. *Must be Russian,* she decided.

"Sorry," she replied rapidly pretending not to hear and quickly turned her attention and lens on another ancient relic in the cabinet opposite. She cursed herself. She didn't want to give the impression she was overly interested in the arkheynia.

Suddenly standing up straight, she winced, pinching the bridge of her nose for added effect.

"I've got a bad headache, maybe too much sun – do you have any tablets?"

Biscan was mesmerised by her every move. At that moment he nodded his head. He would have done anything to gain favour and if there were tablets to be found on board the ship he would surely find them as quickly as he could.

"We've got a medical kit down below; I'll be back in two minutes."

She waited till he'd left the room then moved to the double doors to make sure it was shut; she could hear him running down the ship's deck ahead. *I could do without him being so keen,* she thought. *I haven't got much time.* She raced back to the cabinet housing the missing arkheynia and tried to pull up the glass top as she'd seen Biscan doing earlier. It was sticking but with an extra effort it jerked up and she grabbed the needle-like fragment of bone. *Where can I put it?* she thought. It was too awkward a shape to fit in any pockets. *I haven't got much time.* She imagined the young Biscan hurrying back, taking the rungs of the ladder, three at a time.

There's only one place I can put it, she judged and pulled out a white handkerchief from one of khaki tunic pockets. She wrapped up the fragment of bone not only to protect it but also to protect herself from some of the spikes and serrated edges. Once it was rolled up, she lifted the back of her jacket and pushed it into the waistband of her jeans. She made sure her shirt covered the part that ran up her back.

Quickly she started arranging the other artefacts in the cabinet to make sure the space left by the arkheynia was camouflaged. Dropping the lid carefully to make sure there was no noise, she picked up her case and darted to the other side of the room. Lifting the camera, she started rattling off some shots just as eager Biscan entered the room looking slightly out of breath.

"Here," he stretched out his hand with two oval Solpadine capsules.

"Thanks," she smiled, taking them off his palm. Pulling a small bottle of water out of her pocket, she popped them in her mouth and took a swig.

"You know I think I've got enough pictures of the artefacts now. Would it be possible to go upstairs so I can get some shots of Hans and maybe a few of the other crew members?" she asked.

Biscan's face dropped, he looked upset. *Is it because I've been so quick doing the photo shoot or because he wants to be down here with me a bit longer on his own? Probably the latter,* she thought wryly.

She lifted the camera case over her shoulder and walked along the tired old carpet towards the exit. Biscan held back and she sensed him looking across the room to where the arkheynia had stored. Turning back sharply, she smiled at him and put her hand on his forearm.

"You know you've been incredibly helpful – do you ever get much shore leave?"

His face lit up and he followed her like an obedient dog as they walked along the deck of the ship. In his deep Russian accent he eagerly explained all the dates when he could be expected to be on dry land over the forthcoming weeks. Anna pretended to be interested until they reached the captain's cabin.

Philip was sitting the other side of Hans's desk looking serious and earnestly taking notes on the questions he had prepared earlier. He looked into the face of Anna and received a glance that told him immediately that she had been successful.

"That'll be all," Hans said to Biscan, who trudged out slovenly with his shoulders slumped.

"Sorry to interrupt – all I need is some shots of Hans himself," said Anna, trying to muster as much excitement for the task as possible. "In fact behind the desk would probably be the best. When we publish this article the editor normally likes the headlines to be accompanied by a head and shoulder shot of the main character," she added as she adjusted her camera lens.

Philip smiled. She was certainly playing the part.

Twenty minutes later after several re-arrangements of backdrops and two rolls of film, Anna announced that she was satisfied with her collection.

"Would you mind sending me some copies directly?" asked Hans as he handed out a business card with a company address in Hanover.

"No problem," said Philip getting to his feet. "I think we've got a great piece and I imagine the article will be run in June."

The sun was still beating down as they walked along the deck thanking their hosts for their gracious hospitality. The same crew members who had gathered on their arrival, congregated to wave them off. Biscan handed over the camera case he had been carrying for Anna and received what he thought was a knowing smile in return. Philip looked down from the side and waved to Simon, who saw him immediately and sprang into action, firing up the engines with a roar and navigating the boat back towards the ladder.

We're nearly there; we're going to make it, thought Anna.

The captain reached out and gave her his hand as she clambered over the railing onto the ladder running down the side of the craft. She began the descent as Simon steered the boat over the wake caused by the ship's hull of the ship as it rose and fell in the water. Simon looked up at Anna as she descended the ladder rung by rung with her back to him. *What's that sticking out from her waistband?* he thought as he pulled closer and then the realisation suddenly dawned on him. Unbeknown to the crew members on the top deck, she had hidden the artefact by stuffing it in her back pocket, still partially wrapped in her white handkerchief. Her khaki tunic had hidden the eight-inch bone fragment from sight when they were on board the ship but totally failed to cover it as she descended. Slipping from side to side, it looked very precarious as she edged her way down the side of the boat. Trying to keep the boat steady, he watched as it began to work its way loose from the back of her waistband. *Oh my god, it's falling out!* he thought in a moment of panic. The same thing must have been going through Anna's mind for in the next second, she let go of one side of the ladder and pushed her arm behind her back to try and push it more securely into place. Disaster! Clumsily her hand only managed to loosen the ancient relic further from her waistband; she wanted to shout as she felt it slipping.

"Simon!" she whispered anxiously but it was too late.

The fragment, unravelling from the white cloth, fell towards the swelling sea. In that split second Simon, pushed the boat into neutral and launched himself fully clothed towards the spot where the arkheynia was falling. She felt hopeless with everything around her happening in slow motion as she turned and watched the little bundle falling through the air towards the waves. The sight of Simon diving in brought her a glimmer of hope as she stared helplessly after it. He was still a long way from where the arkheynia hit the water, maybe twenty feet or so but if he was lucky the white handkerchief might give it a second or two's added buoyancy, she thought, before it slipped into the murky depths below.

Anna gritted her teeth sharply as she saw the fragment beginning to nose-dive through the clear water on the surface. *He doesn't have long,* she thought. Simon didn't resurface but with the momentum of the dive he kept swimming underwater towards the area where it would be sinking. Eyes wide open, stinging in the salty seawater, he caught sight of the bright red end as the needle-like bone fragment began its descent. Desperate to get there in time, he pushed harder and deeper with his arms. Just a little bit closer he thought and then he lunged out with his outstretched arm. He had made it – he had managed to grab the arkheynia but his lungs were bursting and how on earth was he going to explain this strange event to the ships crew when he surfaced?

The men on deck leaned forward over the railing wondering what was going on. They had heard Simon dive in but couldn't understand why. Philip sensed what had happened as soon as Anna had turned around and looked back up the ladder towards him.

Simon broke through the surface of the water gasping for air. Anna stared down wondering whether he had reached it in time. Her sense of relief was enormous as she realised from his look that he had made it.

"Are you Ok down there?" shouted one of the crew, ready throw him a lifebelt. "What happened?"

"Sorry," he cried amidst the splutters. "Anna dropped one of camera lenses as she was climbing down the ladder. I tried to save it but unfortunately I was too late – I'm afraid you've lost it!" he added sympathetically, looking at Anna.

"*Damn!*" she called angrily as she purveyed their concerned faces. "That lens cost me a fortune."

"What happened?" asked Philip.

"Sorry, I slipped on the wet rung, I thought I was going to fall – it just slipped out the case," she moaned belatedly.

Meanwhile, Simon had secretly tucked the fragment into his shirt and was swimming back to the motorboat that was bobbing up and down listlessly as it drifted further away from the side. He finally caught up and scrambled up on the stern next to the engines and pulled himself up into the boat. Rolling over, in the same motion, he pushed the fragment on to the floor.

"I think you have some good men looking after you," said the captain, shaking his head and smiling at Anna. Visibly shaken at almost losing the treasure, her demeanour made the episode seem more plausible.

"We'll be covered under insurance, don't worry," added Philip sympathetically before turning to face the captain. "Apologies for all the dramatics!" he said, smiling and raising his eyebrows.

"Don't be silly," he responded in his German accent. "We don't often get such eventful days," he said grinning.

Drenched, Simon pulled off his shirt and began towelling himself as he steered the boat one-handed back under the ladder. As he got closer he threw the towel he was holding over the arkheynia on the floor just in case anyone should catch a glimpse. As he approached, Anna carried on descending the ladder followed closely by Philip. Helped on board by Simon, they looked up to wave goodbye to Hans, the captain, Biscan and the rest of the crew leaning over the side of the salvage vessel.

"Thanks again and good luck with the rest of your search," shouted back Philip as the motorboat's engine wound up and Simon steered them in a large arc away from the ship's hull. The crew waved goodbye as Simon opened up the throttle and they sped off towards Koh Samui and Chaweng beach.

"What the hell happened?" bellowed Philip above the roar of the engines as they put some distance between them and the boat. He didn't feel annoyed just curious to understand how his brother had ended up in the water.

"It's my fault – thank God for Simon," shouted back Anna smiling. "He's our hero!"

Simon grinned and lifted the towel to reveal the missing key of arkheynia.

"We've done it," cried Philip and put his arm around Anna shoulders and squeezed her tightly. "You were brilliant," he whispered loudly in her ear.

She felt elated with the praise and proud of her performance.

Philip opened his sports bag and took a pair of dry shorts up to Simon in the cockpit.

"I think you might be needing a pair of these?" he said, throwing them up to him.

"Thanks," replied Simon and, pleased with their work, they exchanged knowing glances.

"What on earth are we doing?" murmured Philip philosophically to himself in the breeze as he took stock of what they had just done. Only a month earlier he had been negotiating high level corporate mergers on Wall Street and now he was embroiled in an adventure miles from home and the woman he was due to marry.

"We'll need to get going," shouted Anna as they reached the wooden pier where the boat had been originally moored. "They know this relic well," she continued, "and if they go back down to inspect their collection they'll soon see that it's missing."

"Don't worry, we're going straight to the airport now – we'll be in Bangkok in time for dinner this evening," answered Philip, returning sharply to the present.

Koh Samui airport, if you could call it such, consisted of a runway with a wooden shelter at one end with an office inside where you could buy tickets. There were three flights that landed each day and they all came from Bangkok. They were in luck – the ATR propeller aircraft parked at the end of the runway was due to take off in the next thirty minutes. No luggage checks, no baggage handlers – they just walked across the across the tarmac and up the deteriorating metal staircase onto the plane.

It was early evening and the light was beginning to fade. The propellers buzzed noisily as the nose pulled up into the sky. Exhausted, they watched as the picturesque tropical island disappeared from view.

Chapter Seventeen

London, England

Conchos sipped a glass of water as he listened intently into the receiver. He was staying at a small, innocuous hotel close to Kings Cross station in Central London. This small, run-down establishment would not be found in any of the usual tourist guides – the area around Caledonian Road was renowned as the habitat of some of London's most notorious lowlife and the grubby hotel survived on the back of the prolific prostitution business. It was a tall three-storey terraced building with peeling white plasterwork on the façade. Just outside the front porch was a skewed sign advertising a massage parlour inside and the red light in the hallway along with the middle-aged woman on Reception with the cigarette clenched between her teeth added to the illicit, seedy atmosphere.

Without uttering a word, Conchos replaced the handset and smiled wryly to himself. He had the news he was looking for.

Earlier that morning he had sent the telephone data to Amsterdam to help him identify the source of the mystery American caller that was trying so hard to contact Philip Trenchard. The Satanica's omnipresent tentacles had reached out and the information had flown back urgently from its underground network. Checking his watch, he noted it was now approaching ten-thirty at night. He lay on the well-used bed and stared out into the darkness outside as he contemplated the news once again.

So the American caller was identified as none other than Heather Adams, the long-term girlfriend of the elder Trenchard brother, he pondered, flicking through the pencilled notes he had made during the long telephone call. *That's not quite right,* he thought correcting himself. *She's not his girlfriend – she's his fiancée!* And the glimmer of an idea began to form in his mind.

Conchos continued pensively leafing through the pages of scribbled facts. He had a critical decision to make and he wanted to make sure he had considered all the options available. A seemingly high profile person, he thought, reading on about the well-respected career woman in a renowned Wall Street legal firm working mainly in the field of legal due diligence for corporate mergers and acquisitions. Despite being Philip's fiancée, she had not moved into his penthouse apartment but kept her own in a tower block overlooking Central Park. *Useful, very useful indeed,* he thought, looking at the address of that apartment block.

Suddenly, he heard a clanking noise outside and he jumped up to peer through the net curtain of his second floor room. He smiled ruefully; it was only a drunken tramp tottering along the pavement, scraping his empty bottle against the metal railings. When it came to observing the terms of engagement for such an important mission Conchos was not about to take any chances. No matter what the situation, he took nothing for granted and never stayed in the same location for two nights running. Reassured, he returned to lie down on the bed.

It was getting late and he knew he had to make a decision. Should he travel to Thailand and pick up the Trenchards' trail or should he obtain some leverage to bring them to him? The private investigator he had employed to recover the data on their phone bills had informed him earlier that day that the phones were no longer being used. This wouldn't make it impossible to locate them but it would mean a lot more local fieldwork and could take time that he could ill afford. *I'd prefer it if they found me,* he thought candidly.

As he mulled over the idea, the bathroom door suddenly burst open and out stepped a partially clad hooker. She was past her prime. She must have been about forty years old – overweight and with far too much glossy make-up on, she attempted to look alluring by standing provocatively with only a see-through negligée covering her ample frame. Conchos paid little attention to her entrance. Earlier that evening he had enticed her back to his room from under one of the many railway arches with the lure of money and a place to stay.

She nearly lost her footing as she stepped towards the bed; he was not surprised, he had seen her swigging from a bottle hidden in a brown paper bag and imagined that she was feeding a regular habit. Undeterred, she pressed on, attempting to arouse his interest by mustering what feminine grace she had left. She knew this was potentially a good earner, which was in itself an event that was rare for her these days. Fumbling forward she collapsed on one side of the double bed and leered up at him through her long false eyelashes and heavy mascara. Conchos smiled at her and reached in his pocket, drawing out a roll of twenty-pound notes, which he teasingly waved in front of her eyes. The excitement at the sight of the money was etched all over her face.

"There must be over five hundred pounds here," he goaded. "This will be yours if you perform for me."

"Kinky are you," she smirked. He could smell the alcohol fumes when she spoke.

"This will be yours," he repeated waving the money before putting it on the table top next to his chair.

Her eyes followed the money to its resting point as she lay next to him, her head resting in her hand propped up by one elbow.

"Go on then – what is it?" she said with a drawl, lurching for a second before regaining her composure. She propped herself up on one elbow again as her breasts sagged down to her waist.

"This," he said rolling over and producing four leather straps that had been lying under the bed.

"You want to tie me to the bed do you," she laughed grinning inanely. *She really is disgusting,* thought Conchos to himself. She obviously had an advanced drug problem as well.

Speedily, with murmurings of encouragement from the prostitute, he strapped her wrists and ankles to the corners of the bed. She put up no resistance; five hundred pounds would see her right for a few days.

"Now I'm yours, what are you going to do me?" she japed, her eyes were glazing over.

"This is what I'm going to do," he replied coldly, and undid his trouser belt. She stared up but struggled to focus as he straddled her.

"Come on then," she said, trying to hiss enticingly as she imagined going through the motions again although nothing could ever have prepared her for what was about to come.

As Conchos entered her body, he pulled out a long switch knife and scored the blade down her torso from the base of her neck to her navel. It took her a few seconds to realise what he had done, as suddenly the bright red blood began to flow and the excruciating pain began to shake through her body. The look of disbelief in her eyes changed to sheer terror in an instant as the realisation set in. She stared up at the knife, opening her mouth to scream but it was too late. He stuffed in a sheet, pressing it harder and harder so that she choked. Her body writhed with every last ounce of effort she could muster but it was hopeless. Pausing with despair, she looked up into his face, realising the final truth: she was going to die. Her eyes welled as she stared at his vicious, twisted smile. He was enjoying every second as he penetrated her harder and harder. Blood was seeping faster from the wound in her chest as he took the knife in one hand again and thrust it deeper into the incision he had already created. She made one last effort to lash out with her arms and legs but it was useless with the straps holding her taut across the bed.

The pain was unbearable, and her eyes bulged as if they were about to burst out of her head, but she couldn't make any noise, just muffled sobs. Smiling down into her eyes he rested the point of the knife above her heart and started putting more and more weight on his two hands gripping the handle. The blade sunk deep into her heart as he reached his orgasm. Her petrified face was set like a death mask as the blood spewed out from her chest, splattering Conchos in the process. She was dead. He pulled himself away, dripping with blood and calmly began to complete the rest of his macabre handiwork as he surgically plunged the knife into another part of her lifeless anatomy.

Ten minutes later, he had finished. He had removed any tangible bodily evidence that could be linked to his evil presence, including severing the section of her lower torso with which he'd had direct physical contact. He placed these body parts in the bathroom sink, which he had filled with concentrated sulphuric acid and watched the liquid turn red as they dissolved. Finished with his masterpiece, he destroyed or bagged the evidence before entering the bathroom cubicle himself for a shower.

An hour later, totally relaxed, he picked up the telephone and called the sales office at Heathrow Airport. As he had suspected the flights were frequent and regular – plus there was a ticket office open twenty-four hours a day. He quickly got his belongings together and went down the stairs to the chain-smoking lady sitting behind the small counter that served as the hotel Reception. He had paid for the room up front and so checking out close to midnight wasn't a problem. The lady looked unsurprised as he informed her that he would be back later and he had remembered to put out a *Do-Not-Disturb* sign on his door handle. For good measure he also gave the woman on Reception a note that requested his room was not to be cleaned until at least eleven o'clock.

Walking into the midnight air, he stopped a black cab, which he directed towards Piccadilly. From there he walked a couple of streets towards St. James's Place and caught another local mini cab direct to

Heathrow. Four hours later he sat back comfortably in his seat on flight path that took him over Ireland and down the east coast of Canada towards JFK airport and Manhattan Island.

Chapter Eighteen

Bangkok, Thailand

The flight from Koh Samui was a short one and it was still early evening as they cleared Bangkok immigration. Before heading for the taxi rank, they checked on the flight schedules for the next leg of their journey. Cathay Pacific flew direct to San Francisco via Tokyo and they could pick up a connecting flight to New York shortly afterwards.

As they paid for the tickets with cash, Philip allowed himself to picture his reunion with Heather. She had found the distance between them much harder to deal with than she had imagined, especially once she had found out about the late Sir Lawrence Trenchard's legacy. Philip had been staying in her apartment when he had heard the news of his grandfather's death and when he left they both assumed that he would be away for a week only. He couldn't wait to see her.

"Right, we need to find a new hotel," said Simon, turning back from the sales counter holding the tickets. He had paid for them with cash.

"Ok, I've found one." Anna was reading a brochure she had obtained from one of the tourist information kiosks.

"It's called the Bangkok Plaza and it looks fantastic," she smiled, holding up the glossy pictures for them to see.

"It should be it's one of the world's top hotels," replied Simon grinning back. "What do you think Philip?"

"Let's go for it – we're only here for a short time and anyway, we'll need the facilities of a good hotel for some of the arrangements we'll need to make."

"What have you got in mind?" asked Anna as she followed just behind the brothers as they headed down the shiny white marble concourse towards the sliding doors and the taxi rank.

"Well, I've been thinking, how are we going to deal with the scrolls? – we can't risk running them through customs. Am I right in saying that we don't need them until we've secured the third key Anna?"

"That's right – they're our passport to finding the entrance to the labyrinth once we have all the arkheynia."

"In which case, I think the best thing to do would be to forward the scrolls straight to Cairo – my firm has an office in Heliopolis in the centre of the city. It makes sense for me to call them and send them the package direct by courier. I can tell them to keep the package safe until I arrive to collect it."

In the modern age, courier companies consolidated their many deliveries and sent them on their own jets. Gone were the days where express package deliveries travelled on national carriers accompanied by the courier firm's representatives. Once the planes landed with their cargo, Customs officials would review the manifest – the list of all designated items in the cargo – and only if the description looked unusual would they ask to see the packet. Items described as documents were rarely questioned.

The eager driver from the yellow taxi at the front of the queue jumped out of his car to open the boot.

"It makes sense," said Anna and Simon nodded.

"Can you take us to the Plaza?" said Anna as the last door slammed shut. The driver pulled out immediately, on the scent of a greater reward.

Fifteen minutes later, having battled through the downtown traffic, they reached the luxurious Bangkok Plaza. Philip approached the Reception desk to sort out the arrangements whilst Anna and Simon wandered around the expansive lobby looking at the shops and restaurants.

In the time-honoured spirit of Thai hospitality, the uniformed staff were cordial and willing to go to extreme lengths to please their guests. Instead of organising an interconnecting room as before, Philip took a suite on the top floor that had two bedrooms, a large central lounge and its own dining area. He informed the desk that they would be checking out after breakfast and that they should prepare his bill promptly for his departure. He had one sticky moment when they required his credit card to authorise payment but he gave them a sufficient amount of dollars to pay for the suite in advance and give them additional credit.

"I'm feeling exhausted," said Anna as they reconvened at the front desk whilst the bellboy collected their bags and their room key from the front desk.

"I think that goes for all of us," replied Philip. "It's coming up to seven thirty – why don't we sort out the jobs we've got to get done and at the same time order dinner in the room. After that let's get an early night."

"Ok sounds great," replied Anna enthusiastically as they entered the lift. "I'm really looking forward to soaking in hot bath."

"Well you can soak in it with the room menu because I'm putting you in charge of ordering the meal for all of us," he said, grinning back at her.

The double doors to the suite were at the end of the corridor. The bellboy opened them and they stepped into a lavishly decorated hall that led to an even more ornate and luxurious lounge with huge cushioned sofas, glass side tables and a stunning view of the city below. The walls were adorned with large framed prints of historical Thai art and embroidered local tapestries to create an ambience redolent of their romantic Asian location.

Anna gleefully entered one of the bedrooms and was thrilled at the sight of the deep sunken bath – the prospect of a relaxing soak was overwhelming. She returned to the hall announcing her room's menu selections with a smile as the bellboy placed their bags in their rooms before dutifully nodding as he closed the double doors behind him.

"It's even got a kitchenette," said Simon, pointing beyond a couple of bar stools next to a breakfast counter.

"I think we'll manage here – good work, Philip," said Anna jokingly putting on a deep army voice. He smiled at her, pleased that she was looking so contented.

"Right I've got a few calls to make and, Simon – I think we should go ahead with our plan to withdraw more cash!"

"Ok, I'll get on to it now," he replied eagerly.

They had agreed that if they were to avoid the use of their credit cards they would have to obtain access to a lot more cash in the future. Simon was tasked with cashing further books of the traveller's cheques that Felix Bairstow had so obligingly provided. Without pausing, he grabbed the necessary documentation and after promising to return before dinner was served, he promptly walked out of the luxurious suite.

Anna went to her room to sort out her belongings. She had also spotted some boutique shops in the lobby that could add to her meagre wardrobe. If she managed to clean her current outfits and add a few extra items she knew she would feel much better.

"I'll organise the room service for eight thirty – is that Ok?" she asked Philip as she too headed towards the door and the shopping mall downstairs.

"That's fine," he replied as she disappeared to complete her shopping list.

With the apartment to himself, Philip went to the mini bar and helped himself to a cold bottled beer before settling down in one of the comfortable armchairs next to the phone. The first call he made was to his firm's office in Cairo. He'd had a few dealings with one of the partners there in the past two years over various cross-border investment deals and he hoped the same man would still be in charge. It was late afternoon in Cairo as the operator put his call through.

"Hallo can I speak to Sami Hussain?" Philip asked as he connected to his secretary.

"Who can I say is calling?" she answered politely.

He introduced himself and waited a few seconds while she went through the normal set of protocols for an unknown caller.

"Philip, this is an unexpected pleasure!" came the deep, jovial tones of Sami Hussain.

They traded pleasantries before Sami enquired about the purpose of the call. He then listened intently as Philip asked if he could dispatch a valuable package to his office for safe keeping until he arrived to collect it within the next week or so.

Philip knew from his business dealings with Hussain that he was a straightforward, reliable man who had developed a reputation for honesty in a region where this was not always taken for granted. Hussain enquired about the nature of the package and Philip knew it would be rude not to give his friend an answer and that it could provoke unnecessary curiosity later on. He decided to take a bit of time to explain that his recently deceased grandfather was an archaeologist and that he needed the contents in Cairo. Hussain thought for a moment before agreeing to Philip's request.

"Ok Philip, you've done favours for me in the past so it's the least I can do – don't worry, we'll keep it safe – I look forward to seeing you in a week or so."

"Thanks Sami, I appreciate it," said Philip, signing off. He took a few moments to double check the scrolls' packaging before feeling comfortable that he had completed his task.

Lying back in his chair, he took another swig of his beer and tried to work out what time it would be on the East Coast of America. He was excited at the prospect of his next call. With the events of the past few days it seemed like ages since they'd had a chance to speak. The time difference was twelve hours so he figured it had just passed eight o'clock in the morning. Probably the best time to catch her in the office, he thought.

Philip was right. Heather had a reputation for being an early starter at the swish offices of the prestigious Wall Street law firm. The call was put through directly.

"Philip, what on earth's going on? I'm scared!" demanded Heather as she heard Philip's voice. She sounded strained and fretful.

"Listen, I'm on my way back to New York," replied Philip, hearing the audible sighs of relief from the other end as he quickly passed on the details of their flight booking. He did his best to placate her as he sensed her worry and concern changing to anger that she had been left in such a desperate position. She was a strong woman who was used to dealing in a man's world but none of this prepared her for what she was undertaking. She loved Philip with a passion and simply couldn't imagine life without him – and the distance from what was going on in his life hurt her.

"I'll be there at the airport to meet you when you get in – call me if there's any delay," she said, consoling herself with the thought that they would be together again tomorrow.

Philip told her in the gentlest possible way that he could that they would only be in New York for a week or so before having to leave again.

"I'm coming with you this time Philip!" she insisted in her uncompromising lawyer's tone. He knew she was a determined woman but this was dangerous. *How can I jeopardise the life of the woman I love?* He made uncompromising noises of his own.

"But you've got this Anna woman with you," she argued vehemently.

"Look, we'll talk about it when I get back," he promised and she reluctantly agreed, imagining taking up the gauntlet on his arrival.

Philip heard the door to the apartment opening.

"I've got to go," he whispered quickly. "I love you," he added, before putting the receiver down.

Anna entered with an assortment of shopping bags from downstairs and headed for the privacy of her luxurious bedroom.

"I'll get room service ordered," she shouted to Philip as she pulled the door closed behind her.

Mulling over the conversation with Heather and wondering whether he could let her travel with them, Philip set off to finalise arrangements with the concierge. It was important that they fully understood their instructions for delivering the scrolls to his firm's office in Cairo.

Shortly before nine o'clock the doorbell to the suite signalled the arrival of their supper. Anna let them in and two waiters pushed in a metal trolley and began laying the dining room table for dinner. They were quick and proficient in their task and finally a few minutes later, they placed the bowls of Thai cuisine in the middle before bowing their heads respectfully as they retreated from the apartment leaving the sumptuous feast behind them. Sitting down at the round table they needed no second invitation to begin.

"You've ordered well," said Simon, smiling at Anna and staring at the assortment of dishes before them.

"Thanks – you know we need to discuss the book at some point… Is this a good time?" said Anna, helping herself to some chicken curry and sticky rice.

Philip looked up.

"What did you make of the scrolls? Can you translate the language?" asked Philip.

"Yes I can. It talks about how to find the entrance to the labyrinth and then once inside, when you navigate the passages and find the Book of Judas, it literally tells you how you can summon the dark forces of the Devil who'll come to take over mankind!"

"What do you mean?" inquired Philip curiously, also helping himself to the dishes in front of him.

"If you like, it says the book's a tool, an instrument, through which the Devil can be conjured up into his human form… just as Jesus was the human incarnation of God – that's why the Satanica are so desperate to get it at any cost. It's their calling, it's the ritual they've been waiting to perform throughout the centuries since the time of Judas himself."

The brothers listened, absorbed by what she had to say. They both knew in the back of their minds that the book had the power to challenge the religious beliefs of Christianity but actually to re-incarnate the Devil himself was frightening and almost beyond belief.

"What does it say about the Devil?" asked Simon.

"It says that if the satanic ritual as instructed in the book is followed to the letter the birth of Lucifer will come forth among them – it's fairly macabre. The sacrifice of pure and virtuous human life is accompanied by the ancient ceremonial chanting of incantations to the Dark Lord."

"Does that mean he just appears?" Simon continued.

"Maybe… It's not clear – it could be that he takes over the soul of someone carrying out the ritual or someone else present at the ceremony," she replied nonchalantly as she saw their probing expressions.

"Wait a minute, I'll show you," she said and stood up to enter her room, returning with an A4 envelope.

"Look – see this writing?" said Anna, pulling out two enlarged photographs, twelve by eight, one of the Judas Scroll and the other the scroll of the map displaying the biblical lands.

"I didn't know you'd taken those," said Philip curiously.

"I managed it yesterday, when I was studying them," she replied matter-of-factly.

"You see these markings here," she said hurriedly pointing to the ancient script as she handed over one of the photographs to Philip.

"That tells how the Devil once he appears will devour all before him – that evil will reign in the heavens and darkness will control the souls of men."

"What shall we do, if and when we find this book?" uttered Simon. "Do we have any options?"

"Yes we do – we have to destroy it," said Anna who stopped eating and stared coldly across the table at the brothers.

Simon stared back at Anna seriousness. *She is really is beautiful,* he thought as he wondered if she had any feelings for him. Her black shoulder-length hair was tied at the back and her pretty features glowed after the sun of the day. She sensed him watching her and smiled back at him. There was a boyish charm that surrounded Simon and she couldn't help feeling aroused by his concerned and protective attention to her well-being. He was also physically attractive with his athletic and physically powerful build but there was much more underneath that she wanted to understand and get to know. She liked his sense of humour and watched as his eyes lit up with excitement as he smiled towards her.

"I want to get this whole affair finished as soon as possible," said Philip. "We're in intense danger – we're going to have to use all our ingenuity and combined resources to get to this Book of Judas before Satanica or the Vatican and they won't be far behind us by now. I must agree, I don't see how we can take the manuscript and give it to any authorities – I mean which authorities would we give it to? You're right, Anna – our best bet's to destroy it and let everyone following us know we've destroyed it!"

Simon reached out for the bottle of white wine chilling in the ice bucket and refilled their glasses.

"Do you think that's what Grandfather would have wanted?" he inquired, raising his eyebrows.

"I don't know – it was his life's quest – probably he'd have liked to have seen it and studied it but that's not a luxury we can afford. We have to put an end to it!"

"Anna?" quizzed Simon. He knew in his heart that his brother was right.

"I agree with Philip totally. Believe me I'd like nothing more than to have the chance of discovering the book and learning more about it but we can't afford it; we can't risk the possibilities – in the wrong hands it spells disaster and we just can't take the chance that it's anything other than what the Scrolls says it is. We'd be putting life and the Christian religion as we know it in mortal danger if there's any truth in it!"

Simon rubbed his hand against his forehead, he felt really tired after so much travelling and the exertions of the day.

"That's agreed then – we find it and we destroy it."

Philip and Anna nodded their heads.

Silent for a moment, Simon spoke again.

"We've still got to get to it first and that means we're going to have to pick up the remaining two arkheynia as quickly as possible!"

"Well we have the first one and all we need to do now is devise a plan to secure the second – we'll work it out on our way to America," said Anna optimistically.

"We're going to have to become international art burglars to secure the second," chipped in Simon.

"Have you read the report Bairstow put together on the location of the second arkheynia? – it sounds like it's housed in Fort Knox. What's the name of the owner again?"

"Theodore Grainger," said Philip, "an eccentric multi-millionaire with generous philanthropic tendencies towards museums and archaeologists that help reveal the secrets behind events in ancient history. It's just as well that our grandfather came to know him so well otherwise we'd never know he held the second key – he became one of his few friends, in fact only those that were allowed into the eccentric millionaire's inner circle ever gets to see his personal private collection – it must have been quite something when he realised his friend owned one of the three lost arkheynia!"

175

"What's this Theodore Grainger like? Do we know whereabouts he keeps the arkheynia?" Simon asked Philip.

"He's reclusive, shuns public attention – he's made his money in holding and trading silver reserves – the brief Bairstow put together also said that he has a very short temper. On the odd occasion when he does step out into the public domain his rage normally hits the inside pages of the tabloids!"

"Sounds like a real head case," said Simon grinning.

Anna stretched over and picked up the pot of coffee.

"Would anybody else like a cup?" she offered before offering a new and unexpected perspective on the conversation.

"You know there's actually something very sinister about him as well!" she added in a tone that implied she knew him personally.

"What?" the brothers were both taken aback.

"You know him?" questioned Simon.

She remained tight-lipped until she had filled both their cups with the fresh coffee.

"I've met him on two occasions," she answered with a wry, bemused smile as she registered the look of surprise spreading across their faces. "I was lucky – at the time I was going through University in America when he agreed with the course governors of our faculty to sponsor a one-off prize for the best thesis on the 'Life and Times of the Essenes' – I put hours of dedicated research into my thesis and to my amazement and surprise... I won the first prize!"

"What was it?" interrogated Simon.

"The prize was a personal tour around his private collection in his mansion based in Westchester just north of New York City."

"Does that mean that you've already seen the second arkheynia?" inquired Philip frowning. This revelation was unexpected.

"No, or at least I have no recollection of ever seeing it – the importance and value of the fragment was unknown to me then, and I think it was unknown to Theodore Grainger as well, he treasured it simply because of its uniqueness and age."

"You said you met him twice?" Philip queried, as he stretched over and ladled himself a second helping from the bowl of mixed fruit.

"Yes, funny really – he must have been in his sixties when he first showed me around his collection but for some reason he took a real liking to me – whilst he accompanied me around the artefacts he would ask me as many questions as I would ask him – he wanted to know about my background, my family, how I'd developed such a depth of knowledge in the biblical lands and of course on the Essenes. The questions just kept coming; it was almost as if he knew me or knew something about me and was testing me to see if he was giving him the right answers – I was so awestruck by his collection of ancient relics and the imposing mansion that I was roaming around that the full impact of his questioning didn't really sink in until much later. He was always very polite and made me feel welcome, offering me the chance to wander around his house and its treasures as freely as I wished. Anyway he caught a nervous young girl by surprise when he asked me later on if I would like to join him in a few days' time for a trip on his luxury boat."

"And you said yes?" answered Simon anxiously.

"I said no," replied Anna sharply.

"I was much younger at the time with no family in America and frankly the prospect of meeting him again just seemed to be too overwhelming – and anyway why me? Why should he, a multi-millionaire with access to anything he wanted, wish to take me on board his boat? The questions he had asked when he escorted me around his collection began to play over and over in my mind and I gradually began to worry that his interest in me was more than just platonic."

Simon's face looked horrified and she felt an urge to reach out and reassure him that all was Ok now.

"So what happened? Where did you meet him again?" he asked inquisitively.

"By chance – supposedly, only I don't believe it was by chance," replied Anna.

"About two weeks later, I was in the campus library working when I had the strange sensation that I was being watched, I kept looking around but I didn't see anything unusual… Later on when I'd finished it was early evening and I set off walking back to my student apartment a couple of blocks away (I shared it at that time with some girlfriends I'd made on my course). As I was walked through the dimming evening light I had the surprise of my life when he literally came around a corner and bumped straight into me. He offered his sincere apologies, helped pick up my books and remarked at what a remarkable coincidence it was that we should meet again like this so soon – I was scared and I think he sensed it, he tried to calm me and told me that he was visiting the university to make a donation for an archaeological expedition to Egypt organised by my faculty but there was something suspicious about him. I panicked and ran off swearing that if I ever saw him again I would tell the police."

"Sounds like he was stalking you," muttered Philip.

"A few days later I received a card – an apology for having caused me such distress and a promise that there was nothing threatening behind his interest. He said he could understand why I reacted as I did and that if I ever wanted help or needed to see him for any reason that I was welcome to call – he wrote some private numbers on the card where he could be contacted in an emergency."

"Maybe you were overly cautious; maybe he was genuinely interested in helping you," suggested Simon.

"Maybe," she said in a resigned fashion shrugging her shoulders. "Who knows… When you're alone and fending for yourself everything takes on a much bigger meaning!"

"There could be an opportunity here," recommended Philip.

"According to Bairstow's notes, Theodore Grainger will be holding his annual black tie soirée in a couple of days' time for all the authors, historians, lecturers and eminent archaeologists he has befriended over the years – why can't you call him and ask for an invitation?"

"After all these years?" she sounded unconvinced. "I never got in touch with him since that meeting you know?"

"Yes, I think that's a great idea," added Simon quickly. "We've to got into his mansion somehow and this could be our best chance – from what you've said I'm sure he'll remember you."

"I can understand your reticence, Anna," said Philip, "but when you do call him you can tell him you're married now and Simon can go along with you as your husband."

"I think I'll be able to manage that," said Simon, grinning and Anna smiled knowingly at him. *I think I'd like that,* she thought to herself as she imagined entering the ball room in his enormous mansion dressed in her party gown with the handsome, debonair Simon on her arm.

Philip noticed her look of contemplation and prodded her playfully. Her serious expression quickly returned as she woke up from her fanciful daydream.

"Ok, I'll call him when we get to America and let's see if we can get a last minute invitation."

"Great," said Philip, pulling back his cuff and looking at the time. It had just gone past ten. "I've had it," he said standing up and stretching. "I'll see you for breakfast in the morning," he called as he departed in the direction of the bedroom he was sharing with his younger brother.

"I feel exhausted as well," said Anna as she started to gather and stack a few of the empty plates.

"Don't worry, just leave it; they'll sort it out in the morning," said Simon.

He felt exhausted himself as he stood up and walked round the table offering his hand to help her up.

"C'mon, let's call it a day," and she nodded allowing herself to be pulled up from her seat. Comfortingly, he put his arm around her shoulder and led her in the direction of her bedroom.

"You know I never did thank you properly for saving me today," she said, looking up at him with a glint in her eye.

"What do you mean?" he asked, squeezing her shoulder.

"I mean I'd never have forgiven myself if I'd sent the arkheynia to the bottom of the sea."

Reaching the bedroom door, they paused for a moment before she turned towards him and slipped her arms around his waist. *She's so beautiful,* thought Simon as he looked down into her beautiful, smiling face, her eyes sparkling with tired happiness. She looked up with her back close to her bedroom door.

"I'm prepared to collect a small reward," he said, squeezing her again and pulling her closer to him. Impulsively he leaned down and kissed her and felt the passion tremble through her soft lips. Lingering for a moment, she pushed him back gently.

"Bedtime," she smiled. He leant down and kissed her one more time on the cheek before letting go and turning in the direction of his own room. She stood enticingly with her back against the bedroom door as she watched him step down the hall.

"I doubt you'll be able to get rid of your husband so easily in New York," he laughingly quipped over his shoulder.

She smiled broadly and disappeared into her room.

The next morning they woke early and organised breakfast in the suite. Their minds were on packing and getting ready for the long flight ahead. Their tiredness was not satisfied by one good night's sleep and they passed most of the journey from the hotel to the airport in silence. Walking down the white marble concourse again, they checked in for their flight and moved through to the departure lounge. The take-off was on schedule at ten o'clock as they bid farewell to Thailand as their plane took off on the first leg of its journey to America via Tokyo.

Chapter Nineteen

Vatican City, Rome

Alone, the tall figure of Cardinal Camerlengo Fiore stepped down the winding stairs leading away from the papal apartments in the heart of the Vatican. Although he strode purposefully he felt the weight of the heavy burden he carried. His loyal aides, Cardinal Deacon Weiss and Cardinal Bishop Lefebvre greeted his appearance with deference as they lowered their heads, aware of the duties that now rested on Fiore's broad shoulders.

"Are they present?" asked Cardinal Fiore sombrely as he weighed up the task ahead.

"They've all gathered and are waiting in the Consistorial Hall, Your Eminence," replied Lefebvre obediently.

"My brothers, we knew this time would arrive and now it has – come, we have much to do," he commanded.

His voice was firm and in control, belying the turmoil that played havoc with his inner emotions. He strode past them down the Scala Nobile into the Sala Clementina, an enormous, lavishly decorated chamber from the Renaissance period with a ceiling as high as two-storey house. Both Weiss and Lefebvre dutifully followed hard on his heels, their scarlet robes flowing behind them in their hasty passage across the chamber's marble floor.

The Sala Clementina was frequently used as waiting room for the Consistorial Hall. It was one of the many treasures within the Vatican; the walls had several repetitions of the arms of Clement VIII, the builder of the hall. In the past, Fiore had stopped on many occasions to admire the magnificent marble wainscoting and the bold ornamental frescoes but as he stepped beneath the colossal chandelier whose green patina combined beautifully with the harmony of colours, his mind focused solely on the important speech he had to make in a few moments' time. *Will they be prepared to accept changes to traditional Vatican protocols? Protocols that have existed for centuries?* wondered Fiore. He knew which path was the best for the Vatican and he would do all in his power to persuade them.

Cardinal Deacon Weiss reached the huge wooden double doors first – with an effort he pulled them open for Cardinal Fiore to pass through ahead of him. The Consistorial Hall, where they had met on earlier occasions, was darker than the Sala Clementina, although many lamps were lit around its perimeter as the early evening light began to fade outside.

Some were standing but those sitting on the hard, wooden benches rose immediately as the company of Cardinals entered the room. They had been waiting since mid-afternoon after receiving the urgent, handwritten message from Cardinal Fiore to meet in the Consistorial Hall. As they sprung to their feet and made towards the arriving delegation Fiore registered the distress and anxiety on their faces and raised his hand for silence.

"The Supreme Pontiff, Pope Paul XII is dead; he passed away very peacefully in his sleep just a over an hour ago!"

The news was greeted by a forlorn silence. Across the room the Cardinal Alphonso, crouched, resting his weight on his wooden cane. With sadness in his eyes he reached down and lifted the large golden crucifix hanging from a long chain around his neck and kissed the cross.

They had all suspected the worst ever since they had received the calling from the deputy Pope's office but nevertheless it still could not completely prepare them for the shock of hearing the final truth.

The wise old Cardinal Gregory stood next to Cardinal Alphonso. Both of them, along with Cardinal Fiore himself, were widely accepted as the Vatican's front runners to take over the mantle of the Supreme Pontiff and Ruler of the Holy See. Also present in the great hall was Colonel Renauld whose Swiss Guards would play such an important part in the religious and political ceremonies that would take place in St. Peter's Square and the inner sanctums of the Vatican over the next few days. Also in the room was Cardinal Giacoma, the trusted friend of Cardinal Alphonso whose intimate knowledge of their past and present predicament with the Book of Judas warranted his presence.

Apart from it being the end of an era it was also terrible timing. They all knew that the news of Pope Paul's death could not have come at a worse time for the preservation of their faith and their church. His long reign at the helm of the Catholic Church had been commanding and visionary although the impetus had began to wane in the last few years in line with his increasingly fragile state of health.

"My brothers – " said Fiore, opening his speech in a conciliatory tone.

"The death of Pope Paul XII is tragic but let us not be in any doubt that we face the greatest threat to our faith, and to our church, that has ever manifested itself. Not even since the time of the apostles have we… the Vatican, ever encountered such a potentially catastrophic threat." Fiore's voice boomed around the chamber, echoing in the stony silence as he paused to calmly observe their facial expressions.

"Unless we unite in this moment of crisis we face internal strife and friction that may cloud our judgements and allow our enemy to get the upper hand. If those dark forces seeking to overturn the minds and souls of those that are true Christian believers then we will be responsible for having let our own personal battles get in the way of defeating the

Satanica! We will have failed our people and we will have failed ourselves!"

His words crystallised their thoughts. They knew the impending danger that surrounded the uncovering of the Book of Judas. His conciliatory tone and sensible approach also struck a chord with Cardinal Alphonso who was not accustomed to being in the same corner as the self-promoting Cardinal Fiore. During his lengthy spell as deputy to the Supreme Pontiff, he had always given him an assured personal performance that sometimes bordered on arrogance.

Standing a respectful few paces behind the Cardinals, Colonel Renauld nodded his head in agreement with his chosen successor's words.

"We cannot afford division – we have to put our past differences to one side and agree a framework for the election of the new Pontiff that will confront the trial ahead."

The election of a new Pope was steeped in Catholic tradition. The news of his death would be made public by the Dean of the College of Cardinals later that evening and then throughout the world the message for all Cardinals to return to Rome would be communicated.

The rules for the election had not changed since their determination in the times of Alexander III in 1178. In those days men who had an insatiable itch for the irresistible power held by the head of the entire Christian church would try and grab the papal throne. Rival claims threatened to destroy the unity of the church and John De Struma, calling himself Calistus III, threatened Alexander's appointment. The pretender was besieged by Christian of Mainz and eventually succumbed to his rule. From that day, Alexander III determined that better rules for papal elections were needed. He created the first ecumenical council consisting of Cardinals, Prefects, Senators and Consuls of Rome, over which he himself presided from his elevated position on the throne of the Catholic Church.

In the council's first order of business they created a canon that set the regulations for future papal elections. They decided that only the

Cardinals of the church would have the right to elect a new Pope and that his accession would require the minimum consensus of two thirds of their combined votes plus one additional vote. Only Cardinals under the age of eighty were considered eligible to vote in a papal election. Therefore, in other words if the current number of eligible Cardinals in the Vatican was one hundred and twenty then eight-one votes, two thirds of this number plus one, would be required to elect the new Supreme Pontiff and Ruler of the Holy See. Since their declaration in the twelfth century, anyone challenging these laws faced exclusion from the ecclesiastical order and immediate excommunication from Rome.

The atmosphere in the hall was apprehensive as Cardinal Gregory, Alphonso and Giacoma waited for the proposal that they sensed was forthcoming from Cardinal Fiore. Cardinal Gregory, who had clashed metaphorical swords with Fiore on several occasions in the past, felt uneasy about the direction the dialogue was taking.

Cardinal Fiore knew he had their undivided attention and he reached in his pocket and pulled out a handwritten note, which he held up in the air for all to see.

"I would like to show you this!" he said, his voice booming out around the great hall.

"It is a brief letter addressed to us all written by the Supreme Pontiff Paul XII himself who I can vouch was in clear and total command of all his senses at the time."

Fiore promptly stepped a couple of paces forward and handed the note to Cardinal Alphonso. Stepping back, he folded his arms and waited patiently for the stooped Cardinal to read the short italic writing that had been crafted in black ink. The others watched on, observing Alphonso's facial expression for any sign that would give away his reaction to the note.

The wise Cardinal recognised the handwriting immediately; it was shaky but nevertheless he believed it was the authentic calligraphy of

Pope Paul XII. Reading it quickly one more time to make sure he had digested the "irregular" contents he stared up sharply at Fiore. Without saying anything he calmly handed the sheet to Cardinal Gregory standing on his left who peered at the writing through his round, metal rimmed spectacles.

"This is outrageous," Cardinal Gregory fumed as he reached the end and pulled off his spectacles to glare up at Fiore suspiciously.

"When was this written?" he demanded.

"Does that matter? It was the last thing the Supreme Pontiff wrote and the last request he made before leaving this Earth," replied Fiore abruptly.

The signed note was addressed to Cardinal Gregory and Cardinal Alphonso together and contained the last wish of the dying Pope. *For the sake of a united church*, he wrote, *I would like you to stand down from the papal election for my successor and put the full body of your support behind Cardinal Camerlengo Fiore.* It was clear from the deteriorating handwriting that he didn't have the stamina to put down all his thoughts as it became increasingly illegible as the note scrolled towards the end. Pope Paul XII finished his last missive by requesting that they pray for his soul as he himself would pray for their combined strength to take the path of righteousness in the face of a potent evil enemy.

Over the centuries the intrigue, the lobbying and the cunning politics that underscored the papal elections for the highest clerical position in the Christian world was as intense as it had become legendary. The bribes and false promises made to secure the hearts and votes of politicking, self-seeking Cardinals knew no bounds.

Cardinal Alphonso continued to remain composed and silent, contemplating the facts before him, as the elderly Cardinal Gregory vented his distrust of Fiore's dealings. The aura that surrounded the mantle of becoming the next Pope was the dream, the heartfelt desire of all Cardinals who, with the Pope's blessing, entered the inner sanctum of the ecumenical councils of the Vatican. This was no different for Cardinal Gregory. For over three quarters of his long life he had aspired to reaching the pinnacle office of their faith. Many decisions that would have brought substantial personal benefits and new pleasurable challenges in life had been rejected throughout his rigorous regime in favour of steps that would lead him up to the elevated papal throne. Normally a self-assured man, renown for dispensing even-handed wisdom with clarity and calmness, the spontaneity of his reaction to Fiore's note surprised those present. Cardinal Alphonso felt a degree of sympathy and understanding for Gregory's reaction. After all, hitherto it had been widely known throughout the cloisters of the Vatican that Pope Paul's preferred candidate was actually Cardinal Gregory.

"Is this how you manipulate your trusted position, Brother Fiore?" Cardinal Gregory hissed, the venom in his trembling voice filled with defiance that would not accept the despair of a fading dream.

"I will not answer that question and you will never raise this subject in my presence again," retorted Fiore angrily.

Colonel Renauld, a known loyal supporter of Cardinal Fiore, stood calmly a few yards behind the priests wearing his bright uniform of office. Motionless, he observed the proceedings with his arms clasped behind his back. He knew that in the race to become the heir to the Catholic throne Cardinal Gregory and Cardinal Fiore could expect to command around forty per cent of the vote each. The balance was made up of Cardinal Alphonso loyalists and pockets of uncommitted lobbyists running minor political sideshows on specific religious issues. Having already cast his support behind Cardinal Fiore, the Colonel watched the eagerly anticipated confrontation begin to unfold.

Suddenly Cardinal Gregory, still clutching the letter in his left hand, felt all of his eighty-six years. The exertion of the volcanic emotion that pumped through his body left him feeling weak and despondent. Tired or not, he primed himself to scold Cardinal Fiore again. *Who is he to issue such a diktat to me?* As the response came to his lips he felt the reassuring hand of Cardinal Alphonso gripping his arm and the tirade he was about to unleash was stopped midstream.

"Control yourself, Brother Gregory," Cardinal Fiore ordered in a quiet, controlled manner. He had anticipated such a reaction from both Cardinals so took some solace in Brother Alphonso's more favourable demeanour.

"We need to be responsible and pragmatic, Brother Gregory – this is a very serious matter, a unified leadership is essential," he continued.

Suddenly a new voice joined the debate.

"The position we find ourselves in calls for some personal sacrifices for the greater good of the church," contested the voice of Cardinal Deacon Weiss who was standing reverently behind Fiore's left shoulder. Cardinal Lefebvre dutifully nodded his agreement.

Cardinal Gregory felt the rage well up again as Cardinal Alphonso tightened his grip on his brother's arm. Restraining the urge to dismiss the junior and irreverent Cardinal by informing him of his place at this meeting, he glared angrily, his intense piercing expression forcing Cardinal Weiss to look away to the floor.

Cardinal Gregory shook his arm free from Brother Alphonso and put his hands up to his head to straighten his scarlet red biretta, which had began to fall out of place.

"I will not give you my support, now or ever," retorted Cardinal Gregory angrily; his mind could only contemplate the lost prize and the lifetime of work he had devoted to his one true vocation. The potential catastrophe for their church created by the Satanica and the Book of Judas had been misted over, its prominence relegated in his mind's eye.

"We need to work together," reiterated Fiore but it was no good.

"My work here is done," he exploded, deriding Fiore, and span around towards the exit of the Consistorial Hall. Taking a few brisk paces towards the double doors past Colonel Renauld, he paused momentarily and twisted back to look into the face of Cardinal Alphonso. He knew he needed his support. The day that the voting papers were cast in the secret ballot held in the Sistine chapel would soon be upon them. Cardinal Alphonso's backing for himself or Cardinal Fiore would decide the election. *How will he stand? Surely he can't be persuaded by that bogus letter from Pope Paul?* he thought to himself.

In a softer, much calmer tone Cardinal Gregory spoke to his friend before leaving.

"Brother Alphonso, we've been family for years, I trust you'll act wisely when it comes to it."

Leaning on his cane, Cardinal Alphonso nodded and Cardinal Gregory swung around and continued his march to the door that would take him to the Sala Regia and out towards his own private quarters. In the silence that accompanied his footsteps they could make out the sound of singing emanating from the Sistine Chapel – the harmonious *Miserere* for nine voices composed by the Italian Gregorio Allegri in the seventeenth century. The ethereal high notes resounded shrilly until the door swung shut behind Cardinal Gregory and Fiore's gaze swivelled back to Cardinal Alphonso.

"My Brother, we're also going to have to break with centuries of tradition – we don't have the luxury of waiting the normal fifteen-day period for the Cardinals to assemble in Rome for the elections. We must issue an urgent directive for all of them to be here in two days' time for voting to commence by midday on day three!"

Alphonso was extremely wary of Fiore and his intentions. He could have illicitly extracted the letter from Pope Paul XII but he also felt that the note could be real – after all it was in his handwriting and in the circumstances it would have been difficult to say the least to extort such a statement from a dying man. Besides which, Alphonso felt he could also justify the Pope's train of thought. In thinking of the best way to deal with the threat, who would be the man likely to take the arduous decisions to save their Christian faith? *Gregory or Fiore?* Despite the Deputy Pope's ambitious and sometimes narcissistic behaviour, Alphonso genuinely felt that Fiore would not shirk or falter from the responsibilities placed upon him by the office. *Will Cardinal Gregory be able to command the respect of those around him and focus on the problem in hand? Or is he too infatuated with the dream of being Pope to unite them against the Satanica? Colonel Renauld has made his views known to all – how important is it that his trust and chain of command are kept intact? After all, has Gregory not just left the Consistorial Hall without stopping to discuss or realise the situation we're in?* he wondered, pondering the outcome of the various scenarios.

Maybe he should listen to the words of his friend, the deceased Pope Paul XII who despite his reservations about Fiore becoming his true heir genuinely saw him as the Vatican's man for the moment – the man who could make the decisions and lead them through this time of crisis.

With the aid of his cane and Cardinal Giacoma, the hunched and lop-sided figure of Cardinal Alphonso hobbled to the wooden bench at the edge of the hall and sat down. The seat was hard and he tilted forward with his hands clasped, as if in prayer, over the silver top of his walking cane. The look of concentration left his face as he looked up at Fiore and nodded.

"We're in agreement on this point – we should bring the papal elections forward," Alphonso replied after a lengthy pause.

It was the support Fiore needed. He turned to the immaculately presented Commander of the Swiss Guards.

"Colonel, please dispatch the messages at once – demand confirmations and itineraries for all those that need to travel to Rome, let them be in no doubt of the urgency and the severity in which it will be held if for any reason the Cardinal does not meet the stipulated timetable – tell them that the business of Rome commands priority over all local or otherwise ecumenical matters. Am I understood?" asked Fiore, raising his dark eyebrows.

The Colonel stepped forward.

"Your Eminence, I will see to it right away," and he turned on his heels and set off towards the door through which Cardinal Gregory had departed moments earlier.

The walls of the Consistorial Hall could be considered priceless with the works of art that ordained them. Behind the bench on which Cardinal Alphonso was sitting was an enormous elaborate fresco painted by the widely revered and respected painter Vasari. It was one of the Vatican's great treasures and it depicted St. Bartholomew in what became known as the infamous Battle of the Huguenots. Fiore waved his hand towards the magnificent work of art.

"My friend… St. Bartholomew's great victory! You've made the right decision, time is not on our side – we'll need all our strength, guile and courage, as did one of our greatest saints, if we're to defeat the evil Satanica."

Had he still been present in the hall, the meticulous Colonel Renauld would have possibly noticed another piece of the jigsaw He had always believed in judging a man's character and emotions by his words and the bodily actions that accompanied them. If he had still been there he might have seen the slight shuffling from one of the Cardinals that followed Fiore's mention of the words "evil Satanica". In Renauld's mind, he was already beginning to delve deeper into the characters that could be behind the leaks to the Satanica. At this stage he had no hard facts – just a gut feeling.

"Brother Fiore, we need the virtues you describe… We also need unity, so please find it in your heart to make peace with Brother Gregory. I believe that the newly elected Pontiff can serve for a fixed length of time of his own volition before stepping to one side and making way for a successor… Maybe there's an opportunity for compromise?" he suggested.

Pushing down on his cane with both palms, Cardinal Alphonso raised his weary frame and stood up to leave. He had sown the seeds but he didn't really hold out any hope of Fiore bringing them to fruition. He was as keen to hold the church's top position as Cardinal Gregory and once he had hold of it he was unlikely to let go. *Anyway,* he thought, *I've planted the seed of an idea and maybe he is capable of delivering and honouring such a notion.* He would have to wait and see.

"We'll all meet again when we have more news on the Book of Judas from Colonel Renauld. And please remember…" added Fiore, looking around at their faces, "…everything that's uttered within our secret conclaves must remain strictly confidential!"

Alphonso nodded his agreement and slowly shuffled with the aid of his cane towards the exit. His good friend Cardinal Giacoma sprang forward to help, offering his arm as support

"Tonight I will pray for the soul of my friend Pope Paul XII – and I'll pray for you too, Brother Fiore," called Alphonso.

Cardinal Fiore smiled privately to himself.

The meeting had gone surprisingly well and the response he had received from Alphonso offered him great encouragement. The fires of emotion that burned deep inside Cardinal Fiore for the prestigious trappings and power that accompanied the Pope's high office wanted him to forge ahead with the newfound softening of his relationship with Alphonso. The skilful diplomat within him knew that it was best left until another day but the temptation was too great.

His booming voice called after Alphonso.

"And which way will you cast your votes, Brother Alphonso?" asked Fiore as the Cardinal lurched from side to side on Giacoma's arm.

"All in good time, Brother Fiore… All in good time," he boomed over his shoulder.

Chapter Twenty

New York City

The journey across the dateline from Bangkok was exhausting. Although they had flown comfortably in first class, their recent exertions combined with the length of time cooped up the aeroplane all added up to an overwhelming sense of fatigue. Their physical and mental states of mind were also not helped by the tedious hours of waiting in transit at Tokyo and then again in San Francisco Airport.

Now as the back wheels hit the tarmac and the plane's nose dropped to the runway, they shared a feeling of elation that their nineteen-hour crossing was coming to an end. For Philip the feeling was magnified tenfold – he was about to see his beautiful fiancée Heather. She had promised to be there to greet him and he recalled her squeal of delight when he called during the transit stop at San Francisco to tell her the time of their connecting flight to New York.

Standing up and stretching as the seat belt sign went off, they gathered up their belongings and walked up the aisle of the plane to the gangway that took them into JFK airport.

"Not long now!" said Simon with a friendly grin as he patted his brother on the shoulder.

Anna was also looking forward to meeting Heather. She had received her full life history from Philip on the plane and he'd been at pains to tell her how well he thought they would both get on together. Regardless of Philip's excited overtures, she sensed herself that Heather actually was the kind of person with whom she would get on well.

The baggage came through quickly and they joined the queues to proceed through Immigration. Security was strict as they watched armed officers escorting away fellow passengers for further random checks. Ten minutes later, they passed through the "Green Channel" in the Customs zone and onwards towards the exit. Philip went first, pushing the trolley in front of him while Simon and Anna followed a few steps behind. It was a busy time for the airport and the crowd behind the barriers to meet arriving passengers was five or more deep in parts.

Philip scanned the mass of faces all staring at him as he passed through the electronic sliding doors. He didn't need to wait long; he saw her frantic wave before she stooped below the waist-high tape and sprinted forward to greet him.

Jumping into his arms, they embraced and kissed in the same movement.

"It's so good to see you," she said, brushing away the tears welling up in her eyes. *She looks as beautiful as ever,* thought Philip. Her long, natural blonde hair gave away her Californian origins, where she had won her regional and hometown's beauty pageants with unassailable majorities.

There were many things that had attracted Philip and a host of other potential suitors to Heather. Apart from her stunning looks she also possessed the rare combination of being a brilliant academic with a great sense of humour. In her late teen years she had the option to embark on a glamorous career in modelling or continue studying to secure a place at an Ivy League university. In the end, her head ruled her heart, although the decision was helped when the offer letter arrived from Yale inviting her to read law.

When Philip finally let her down she turned to face Simon and Anna with her intense blue eyes.

"It's been a long time Simon – you haven't changed a bit," she said, trading kisses on the cheeks as she embraced him. Then, turning to Anna, she stretched out her hand.

"Welcome, Anna. Philip's told me all about you," she smiled as they quickly shook hands.

"Come on – we're blocking the walkway," said Philip, noticing fellow passengers struggling to get past their stationary trolley.

Heather led them off in the direction of her BMW saloon, which was parked across the road in the short-term Arrivals car park. At five feet nine inches tall, her slender physique was comparable to that of an Olympic swimmer and they followed, her arm interlinked with Philip's, she walked with an assurance and poise that harked back to the days when she was tempted by the lure of the catwalk.

With Philip taking the wheel, they headed out from the airport towards downtown New York. Speeding along the freeway, they passed the home of the Yankees baseball team before reaching the opening to the tunnel that would take them up across to Manhattan Island. As usual the traffic congestion increased as they reached the other side – *Every third car seems to be a bright yellow taxi!* thought Anna – but finally after another bumper-to-bumper twenty-five minutes they reached Heather's block with her luxury penthouse apartment on top.

Heather's rise as a lawyer in the competitive world of corporate finance had been meteoric. Since graduating from Yale with top honours she had joined one of the leading Wall Street firms, developing her relationships to the extent that she was now considered one of America's chief deal-making lawyers. To have achieved such success so quickly and at such an young age in a predominantly male environment was a testimony to the respect in which she was held by her partners and fellow professionals as well as the many hours of hard work and dedication she had put in.

From the car park in the basement, they caught the small lift up to her penthouse suite, which was on the tenth floor occupying the northwest corner of the building. Entering, Heather flicked the lights on and the spacious apartment, tastefully and lavishly decorated was revealed for all to see. For Philip it felt like being home again while Anna stood in awe at the elegance and lavishness of the plush décor. The room's golden and burgundy theme lent it a sumptuous, opulent feel. She cast her eyes around the lounge and admired the marble-topped side tables and the golden-stemmed lamps that matched perfectly the luxurious high-backed Burgundy suite with its gold cord detailing and long golden tassels. The floor was finished with white-flecked marble and several silk Persian carpets covered the open spaces. Heather was especially proud of these because she had chosen them herself on an extended business trip to Dubai in the Middle East. Anna was impressed: Heather's style and taste was evident everywhere you looked.

"This is fantastic!" said Anna, admiring the decoration on the walls. "If you ever wanted to go into interior design I think you'd be a natural!" she added with a broad smile.

Heather smiled back appreciatively as she watched Anna continue to scan the room.

On the emerald green walls hung large gilt-framed canvases, which showed her love for bright and bold colour arrangements. Most of the art in the room exhibited contemporary style but some were impressionist, more "Matisse-like" in their style.

Simon stepped past their luggage and a flamboyantly framed mirror resting above a Louis XIV side table as he wandered down the three marble steps that led you into the main body of the lounge. The gold, greens, burgundies and elaborate works of art combined magnificently to create a regal yet homely setting.

"I see everything seems to be going all right in the high-stakes, cut-throat world of corporate law," said Simon, grinning at Heather.

"Not sure about your taste though," he added with a cheeky smile as he stood in front of another oil canvas.

"That one was actually a present from your brother!" she said dryly, smiling back at him. Heather liked Simon. They had a similar sense of humour and she always found it easy to relax in his company.

"It seems such a long time since I was last here," he mused as he wandered towards the floor-to-ceiling sliding glass doors that opened onto the balcony and the panoramic view beyond. It was dark outside as he slid the glass door to one side and stepped into the evening air. The balcony was covered in an assortment of well-tended bushes and plants and spanned the entire corner of the apartment block. Anna left Philip and Heather talking inside and stepped out to join Simon who was staring out across the road below at Central Park and the dark silhouettes that wandered down below.

She reached out and put her arm across his shoulder as he leaned over the top of the barricade that protected them from the sheer drop to the sidewalk below. He turned to face her. A wisp of her black hair had broken free and fallen across her face. He raised his hand and tenderly pushed it from her face.

"You're very beautiful you know," he said, and she smiled up at him, squeezing his hand.

"Good, that's exactly the sort of practice you need if you are going to be my stand-in husband at Theodore Grainger's party," she teased.

Simon laughed.

"And what sort of practice will you be putting in as my stand-in wife?" he quizzed.

Anna, with an excited glint in her eye, leant forward and gave him a soft kiss on the cheek.

"That's good, maybe a touch longer," he joked coyly and she laughed.

Ever since their first meeting in Eleusis just outside Athens, she had felt the thrill of exhilaration that comes from being in the close proximity of someone you really like. He felt the same way, constantly wanting to impress her, wanting to show her how he truly felt towards her and, in return, to understand what she thought of him. Pulling her closer towards him around the waist, he looked into her eyes and saw all the signs he wanted to see.

At that moment, Philip stepped out onto the balcony and looked across at them embracing.

"Oh," he said, sounding surprised but he wasn't really. He had picked up all the vibes and the tell-tale signs ever since they had arrived back in Bangkok from the islands.

"I hope I'm not interrupting anything?" he said apologetically with mock sincerity.

Simon and Anna released their embrace quickly as if they had been caught in the act before relaxing and grinning back at Philip. For a fleeting moment they were ruffled by the elder brother's sudden appearance as if their display of affection would be considered in bad taste or in some way problematic for the completion of their quest. In truth, this was nonsense; Philip was happy for both of them and didn't foresee any problems in their completing the arduous job ahead as long as they kept their wits about them. However he did feel one "related" pang of concern and that was the additional pressure that would come from Heather to join their mission when she understood the developing relationship between Anna and Simon. The younger brother put his arm around Anna's shoulder as they turned to hear what Philip had to say.

"Look, I'm feeling really tired after the flight so I'm going to call it a night in an hour or so – if possible I'd really like to get this issue with Theodore Grainger out of the way before then. I think we need to know how the next few days will shape up."

"Yes, I agree," said Anna promptly. "I'll call him right away," she added and headed back into the apartment to find the numbers.

"She's really lovely and definitely your type!" said Philip genuinely as she disappeared out of earshot.

"I know," he replied with a knowing look and they both followed her in through the sliding glass doors.

Inside, Heather had disappeared to have an evening bath, leaving the wide, flat-screen TV on in the background with the CNN anchor-man relaying their network's version of world events for the day.

"I've got it!" exclaimed Anna as she walked out of her bedroom towards the side table in the hall. Just below the ornate mirror was a telephone and she lifted the roaming receiver off its stand. *What time is it?* she wondered as she dialled the local number. Checking her watch, she saw that it was approaching nine-thirty. *Not too late to make the call,* she thought.

Listening to the ringing tone, she walked back down the three steps into the lounge where Simon and Philip sat waiting on the couches. The shutters, which operated automatically to cover the penthouse doors at the flick of a switch, remained open. As she paced back and forth in front of the brothers she could see the amazing silhouette of the New York City skyline every time she turned around to face the windows. Concentrating hard, she put her hand up to rub her forehead as she wondered what she was going to say. She heard a voice at the other end.

"Hallo, can I speak to Mr. Theodore Grainger please?"

"Who can I say is calling?" asked the woman politely.

"Tell him it is Anna Nikolaidis; tell him we met several years ago when I was a student in California."

"Please hold on," the lady replied.

Anna felt herself becoming increasingly nervous as she waited for what felt like an eternity. Finally she heard the "clicking" of the exchange as the call was redirected at the other end.

"Anna, Anna Nikolaidis?" questioned the instantly recognisable tones of Theodore Grainger.

"Yes," replied Anna simply.

"I knew that I would hear from you again one day," he said with excitement.

Anna felt relieved to know that he still remembered her but also a degree of concern that he should be so confident that she would reappear again. What was this fascination in her that made her feel so uneasy? she wondered? *What is it? What does he know that he's not telling me?*

The brothers sat silently on the sofa watching her pace up and down. They scoured her expression for any sign that could tell them how the call was going. Simon wished he could do something to help as they noticed that she was more than a little anxious.

"I'm in New York at the moment," she continued. "As I was passing through I wondered if it would be possible to see your private collection of artefacts again? I've learnt a lot from working in the field since I last saw it and the pieces would have a whole new meaning to me," she implored.

"Anna," he laughed, "you're always very, very welcome to see my collection, you know that – you're also very welcome to see me if you'd like?" he asked poignantly. "I know I'm not quite as interesting as my collection!"

"Yes, I would like to see you as well," she heard herself reply. Although she was lying for a good cause it did not rest or sit with her very well. Simon noticed her grimace as she paced the floor, pressing the phone to her ear.

"Well then why don't you come to my party on Saturday?" he asked, clearly excited at the prospect of seeing her again. "The timing's perfect, it's my annual black tie ball this weekend. Maybe… " he paused. "… Maybe, you'd care to join me on the head table?"

"I'd love to come," replied Anna eagerly and looked animatedly towards the brothers. They smiled simultaneously; elated that they had achieved the breakthrough they were looking for.

"I'm holding it in the ballroom of my home in Westchester – starts at eight o'clock and you'll make it an occasion to remember, my dear," he added. He sounded thrilled.

"Great – I'll look forward to it," replied Anna, trying to match his evident enthusiasm.

Suddenly, out of the corner of her eye she noticed Simon gesticulating and she realised what was missing.

"Oh, just one thing more?" she added quickly.

"Yes, what is it?" he replied eagerly. Like all confident billionaires, he was used to getting what he wanted and in this case he was prepared to go to extraordinary lengths to ensure she could make it. However her response did raise an element of doubt and he wondered what it could be?

"Since we last met I've got married… Would it be Ok if I brought my husband along to the ball as well?" she asked, looking into Simon's face.

There was a brief pause as Theodore Grainger considered his reply.

"That's fine Anna – what's this gentlemen's name?" he asked in a curious tone that had lost some of its initial excitement.

"He's called Simon," she responded happily.

"Congratulations," he said but she knew that the sincerity was missing.

For a moment she became aware of the old, haunted feelings about his real intentions towards her – the feelings that had scared her so much in the early days.

"I look forward to meeting him on Saturday - you can both join me on the top table!"

Anna thanked him repeatedly before signing off. As she pressed the button to disconnect the call she sighed heavily and looked up to the heavens.

"How was he?" asked Simon.

"I just don't know what it is but there's something creepy about him," she replied, shuddering at the thought.

"I could sense it was difficult but you did it - that was a really great result, well done!" said Philip enthusiastically.

"Goodness knows how we would have tackled the problem of the second arkheynia without this foothold!"

"Thanks!" Anna was comforted by his confidence in her.

Heather felt more relaxed after her bath as she returned to the room wearing an old pair of jeans and a white polo top.

"You all look exhausted," she remarked, settling down on the sofa and snuggling up to Philip before stretching out her hand towards the TV remote control. Pointing it towards the screen she raised the volume of the CNN news broadcast.

"You're both going to have to go out and do some shopping tomorrow," said Philip directing his comment towards Anna and his brother. "You'll need to get new outfits for this ball on Saturday."

"Anna, I know just where to take you," said Heather, suddenly excited at the prospect of shopping with her new friend.

With her heavy work schedule she didn't often find the time to browse around some of the most famous shopping landmarks in the world that New York's Manhattan Island was famous for. However on this occasion she had made certain that her home life was put ahead of the long hours of commitment she clocked up for the time-hungry law firm. Besides she wanted to join Philip on his quest and knew she would have to be able to respond and act quickly. Earlier in the week she had laid the appropriate plans with the hierarchy in the office. Her first move was to hold a meeting with the Senior Partner and carefully explain, without giving cause for alarm, her unusual predicament to him. He was a friendly if sometimes unpredictable man who in this instance turned out to be very understanding with the firm's biggest fee earner and his own personal protégé. After a few moments deliberating the pros and cons they had agreed that she should take a month's sabbatical and if necessary they would be flexible and open to an extension providing she kept them regularly informed of her progress. She was delighted with the firm's attitude and the rest of the morning and afternoon had been taken up with a mad scramble of briefing in-house lawyers on the status of her on-going cases and then speaking to clients to enlist their concurrence for her short term plans. Most were supportive but, the timing and short notice of the decision ruffled a few lucrative feathers.

Anna's face also lit up with the prospect of shopping for clothes.

"Great," she replied, smiling at Heather. She was also excited by the opportunity to explore New York's famous shopping boulevards.

"We're going to need to work out a plan once we get to the party," said Simon wearily.

He felt exhausted from all the travelling and slouched on the sofa squinting at the TV.

"Simon, you and Anna are going to have to somehow find a way of locating the second arkheynia in his collection and devise a way of taking it during the party," instructed Philip. "Unless you can suggest otherwise I can't see a way of getting more intelligence on its exact whereabouts?"

Anna nodded in agreement.

"When you get to the ball, you'll need to see what security they've got covering the collection and artefact. You'll have to decide how best to proceed when you're on site – having said that there are some things we can do. Tomorrow, for my bit, I'll make sure that you have the tools with you to help you deal with any security system and secondly, I'll create, or have made, a close replica of the arkheynia so that you can substitute one for the other."

"That's fine," said Anna. "I can't remember whether I actually saw the arkheynia in his collection but I can recall most of the mansion's – if the artefact isn't on display tomorrow, I know where it might be kept."

"I want to come with you," said Heather stubbornly.

"No – no need," responded Philip calmly. He knew his fiancée's persistence and wanted to avoid a minor confrontation so he decided to play the whole thing down.

"I'm only going myself as the driver!" he added. "You know there isn't a third invite for the ball and there's no point in your waiting with me in the car."

Heather was about to argue when Philip gently put his finger up to her mouth.

"Look we'll talk about this later," he said with a reassuring smile.

"You're right, we will," replied Heather somewhat abrasively although she knew it wasn't the right moment. Besides she had not even told Philip of her agreement to take a month-long sabbatical from work.

"Ok, we've got tomorrow and until the following evening to get everything set up and put our plans in place," said Philip, stretching out his arms and yawning. "Right now, I think it's time we all caught up on some sleep!" he sighed, and playfully dug Heather below the ribs.

Suddenly, without warning, Simon sat bolt upright and started scrabbling around to find the TV remote control.

"Quiet, everyone quiet – what's this?" he exclaimed, pushing up the volume.

The broad American accent of the CNN newsreader filled the room.

"Today, in London, England, the police confirmed they are again investigating the horrifying and tragic murder of a lady believed to have been sacrificed as some sinister part of a bloody, ritualistic killing – the following is a report from our correspondent in London that was recorded earlier today, however we would advise that this report may contain language unsuitable for minors!"

Simon sat spellbound along with his brother as the story unfolded. What had made him realise the importance of this news item was the artist's hand drawn impression of the appalling carnage found at the terraced house in Oxfordshire when Professor Palanski's body had been discovered. The gruesome image had been used by most of the broadsheets and tabloids the following day and for some curious reason this report on a new crime scene was carrying the same impression.

Heather looked slightly confused as she watched their earnest expressions remain glued to the news coverage. The picture changed as the report switched to the microphone-holding correspondent in London who was standing on the pavement with Kings Cross Station in the background. Behind him there were crowds of people watching the spectacle while busy commuters flowed past on their way to catch their train. Out of the corner of the screen it was just possible to make out a police cordon blocking the entrance to a small side street.

"I'm standing here in Kings Cross after it was revealed that the lady killed in the Bedford Hotel was murdered in a similar fashion to the Ashmolean lecturer whose mutilated body was discovered recently. In fact the similarity has resulted in Scotland Yard calling in their Oxfordshire colleagues to establish whether the killer, or killers were in fact the same."

"So, what's this about?" asked Heather, blissfully ignorant of the relevance but nonetheless startled and more than a little worried by Simon and Philip's reaction to this macabre report. Philip had made a conscious decision not to tell Heather the truth behind their rapid escape from England for fear that it would cause unnecessary worry and stress that he could do nothing to resolve.

Simon flashed a knowing glance at Philip.

"Just wait a minute until the report's finished," he said softly, squeezing her arm for reassurance. Heather had already seen the same CNN coverage earlier on – she recalled thinking that these sick stories of twisted, demented individuals were more at home in America than they were in England. *What on earth has this got to do with Philip?* she wondered again and began fretting about the possibilities.

"…inside one of the hotel bedrooms the police discovered the body of an unidentified woman said to have been one of the many prostitutes that ply their trade around Kings Cross station. Unconfirmed reports that we have received from staff in the hotel who discovered the horrific murder state that the body had been staked out like a cross, the ankles and legs strapped together while the arms were pulled out sideways and pegged with nails through the hands. The skin had been peeled from the victim's chest and pulled taut between the outstretched arms. Her ribcage had been sprung open and the skin from her face removed in what is becoming known as the 'Death Angel'. The local population are terrified, living in fear that…"

"It's the same person; it's got to be," said Simon, shaking his head and reducing the volume on the TV set. The gruesome revelation that the act had been repeated again made him prickle as he recalled the shocking scene that confronted him when he entered the professor's front room.

"What's going on Philip? – I don't understand," asked Heather sharply.

Philip looked at pains to explain.

"She needs to know," added Simon calmly.

Philip nodded his head; he looked even more drained and tired than earlier on.

"We'll talk about this tomorrow," said Philip to Anna and Simon before standing up and reaching out his hand to Heather. "Come on, I'll tell you the whole story, let's go to the bedroom and talk – we'll see you in the morning," he said, and they departed up the lounge steps to the corridor leading to the master bedroom suite.

"Why would he go and kill this woman?" asked Anna once they had disappeared around the corner. "Do you think that there's relevance or anything that connects her with us?"

"I don't know," said Simon, rising to his feet. "What I do know though is that the person capable of doing these atrocities to human beings must be insane!"

He stood up and walked over to the glass doors that led onto the balcony. He felt like he could do with some air. *At least this maniac, this merciless monster doesn't seem to have caught our trail yet,* he thought thankfully.

Anna stepped through the gap and joined him.

"We're in grave danger aren't we?" she asked reluctantly.

She was scared, he could tell as soon as he saw her face. He put his arm around her shoulder to comfort her.

"We'll be Ok," he said gently, stroking her hair. "What's important though is that we keep moving, so the sooner we sort out this business with Theodore Grainger and secure the second arkheynia the better."

"Is Heather going to come with us?"

"I don't know – that's Philips decision," he answered tiredly. "Come on, we should make the most of this opportunity and get as much rest as possible."

"Just tell me we'll be safe," she repeated anxiously as they leaned against the balcony overlooking the park.

He smiled down at her.

"I'll look after you, have no fear of that," he said laughingly and pulled her towards him. She felt so much safer in his arms.

Down below, on the edge of Central Park, the solitary figure stepped out from the dark shadows of a tree and pensively replaced the miniature binocular set in his jacket pocket. A cruel, cynical smile spread across his face as he realised he had registered all the information he needed to know for now. *This is indeed an unexpected bonus,* he thought, sneering at his surprising good fortune. *All of them present together in New York City! This is going to make things even easier,* he concluded with a degree of satisfaction. Staring up one last time at the romantic couple leaning against the balcony, he silently walked alongside the metal railings making his way to the park's exit.

Tired but buoyed by their burgeoning feelings for each other, they pulled themselves away from the side and wandered hand in hand back into the apartment.

Earlier that evening Heather, as usual the exemplary host, had made a huge effort to set up their bedrooms so that they were as warm and as comfortable as possible.

Anna closed the glass doors behind them as Simon flicked off the light switches before leading her up towards the hallway.

"Goodnight, Anna – and don't worry, I won't let anything happen to you, I promise," said Simon as he kissed her softly on the lips.

She looked up and smiled.

"I know," she replied nodding.

Minutes later, she had changed into her pyjamas and hopped straight into the clean, luxurious sheets of her double bed, stretching out her toes in gleeful anticipation of a great night's sleep. Worn out, her mind blanked out the catalogue of thoughts constantly echoing through her mind and she fell asleep moments later as soon as her head reached the pillow.

Chapter Twenty-One

Vatican City, Rome

Colonel Renauld's phone rang in the medieval chamber overlooking Bernini's piazza that served as his office. He picked up the receiver and promptly agreed to take the call. He had been holding a meeting with his senior officers only a few minutes earlier when he had received a coded message informing him that Goran needed to speak him urgently. His initial assumption was that it about the recently released news from the Dean of the College of Cardinals informing the world of Pope Paul XII's sad demise.

"Hallo Goran, I take it you've heard the news?"

"This could not have come at a worse time, Colonel – who are we working for now? Who's running the show?" he asked brusquely.

"Will we have to remain on the sidelines until the new Pope is announced? This will give the Satanica an unprecedented advantage!" he continued impatiently. "It could be too late by then!"

"No – that can't be allowed to happen… We're working under the directions of Cardinal Camerlengo Fiore until the new Pope is elected – we'll take our orders from him, besides, you should be aware that Pope Paul XII blessed his candidacy shortly before he passed away."

"That's good, but remember strange things have happened during these elections in the past; the Cardinals hold their votes to ransom when those secret ballots take place!"

Colonel Renauld paused briefly for a moment. He knew there was element of truth in Goran's words and he, not his agent, would be held accountable if they made the wrong decision. However, he dismissed the possibility – this was a time of crisis and he realised that the crime of inactivity in such important circumstances would be treated with equal contempt. *Anyway,* he consoled himself, *the other Cardinals challenging for the Pope's High Office are being kept informed of their actions at all times… Aren't they?*

"Time is of the essence, Goran," he replied forcefully, barely disguising the irritation in his voice.

"Fiore has convinced them to break with tradition; they've brought the papal elections forward to this weekend… Already most of the eligible Cardinals have gathered in Rome! If all goes according to plan the world will have a new Pope by Sunday."

"That's positive news but the election of a new pope's not the reason I'm calling!" replied Goran pointedly. "You're going to need to inform Their Eminences that there's been a second bloody killing by the Satanica!"

Goran paused for a moment whilst the news registered with Colonel Renauld.

"Who was it? Give me the facts!" Renauld demanded. His initial thoughts suddenly went to the possibility that the Satanica's executioner had caught up with Anna Nikolaidis and the Trenchard brothers.

Goran then spent the next few minutes recounting the events as they had been announced in the media, on the TV networks and in the press.

"Can you be sure that this was the work of the Satanica? Are you sure it wasn't some kind of copycat murder?" he quizzed once he had digested all the relevant information. He was relieved that the Satanica still appeared on the face of it to be some way behind the brothers' trail.

"No I'm sure – I went to the murder site personally and found out from the people who discovered the body that they saw the initials 'MM' daubed in blood on the bathroom mirror – and these facts were never revealed to the public after Professor Palanski's death!"

"It doesn't make sense, what's the purpose or meaning of such a killing?" wondered the Colonel out loud. "If you're right, we don't suspect that the victim was in any way connected to the Book of Judas or the search for the scrolls."

"I don't know," said Goran lost for an answer. "It's difficult to see any rational logic for this act – in some demented way, he clearly enjoys what he's doing. I also suspect that he knows we're studying him, observing the media surrounding these murders. Maybe the sick bastard enjoys the fact that we're watching… Sees it as a kind of challenge!"

"Maybe," the Colonel mumbled, "I'm sure he loves what he does but in a way I'm also surprised he'd take these additional risks."

"In which case, Colonel, if the message is for us," Goran began surmising thoughtfully. "He's either trying to tell us he's still in London and is not following their trail or he's doing this to provoke more anxiety and unrest amongst the Cardinals – we know there's a leak here in the top echelons of the Vatican and maybe the Satanica feel if they can provoke more unrest and disunity amongst the Cardinals they can learn more intelligence about our plans through their insider!"

"You're right on that point," replied Colonel Renauld. "You can almost feel the suspicion and unrest hanging in the air here. Most of the Cardinals want to know why there's been such a dramatic change to the timing of the election – it's been held fifteen days after the death of the Pope for centuries so they're questioning such a fundamental break with tradition."

"I think these are dangerous times, Colonel – we have to find out how the Satanica's getting its information from the Vatican. Have you considered tapping the phones?" Goran queried.

"Yes, it's an unprecedented step in the history of the Vatican that would cause an internal revolution and a damaging international media incident if it was discovered," said Renauld, imagining the potential backlash against the Swiss Guard and against the internal system if the clergy became aware that their papal phone calls were being listened to. The thought of this knowledge extending into the public domain would give rise to an international incident that would damage the profile and standing of the church irreparably.

He knew the size of the stakes he was playing with but what other options did he have? He paused thoughtfully for a moment before answering.

"Yes… Yes, I think it's the right thing to do. I'll activate an internal cell of men whom I know can trust and from this point on I shall receive transcripts of all conversations going in and out of the Vatican."

"It makes sense," agreed Goran.

"I should obtain Cardinal Fiore's clearance," said Renauld, stroking his chin and thinking aloud.

"With due respect, I think that's a bad idea," retorted Goran sharply. "I think you should keep those who know to a minimum and besides, what if he says 'No'? We know that the leak comes from a small circle of Cardinals and we can't categorically rule out Fiore from that list!"

The point was not lost on Colonel Renauld and he murmured his agreement.

"Where are they at the moment?" continued the Colonel, referring to Anna and the Trenchard brothers.

"They're in New York," replied Goran swiftly. "Still travelling on their own passports."

"Are they safe?"

"Yes, I believe so."

"Ok Goran, let me know as soon as you have any more news, if everything works out this weekend we'll have a new Pope in place to guide us through the final chapters of this assignment! In the meantime the Satanica will be trying to use this time to their advantage; they'll try and get the upper hand while they feel we're headless!"

"Then let's hope the new Pope's elected soon!" replied Goran. "But remember Colonel, only we know that we still hold the upper hand!"

Chapter Twenty-Two

Greenwich Village, New York

"Right, time to go," announced Philip. "Is Anna nearly ready?"

"I'll go and check," said Heather, hopping up the steps from the lounge and heading for Anna's bedroom.

It was approaching seven-thirty on Saturday evening and they would be expected to arrive at Theodore Grainger's annual ball between eight and eight-thirty. The shopping trip the day before had been successful and both Simon and Anna, thanks to Heather's help, had found appropriate attire for the occasion. She had enthusiastically accompanied them, dragging them from store to store, in search of the perfect, stylish outfits. Anna had enjoyed trying on so many pretty ball dresses but Simon, in typical male fashion, managed to find ninety-nine per cent of his requirements in one store, Bloomingdales, and then promptly left to leave the girls happily shopping in earnest without him.

Back in Heather's apartment, Simon stood in front of the elaborate hall mirror and put the finishing touches to the knot on his black tie. He had nearly purchased a white tuxedo jacket but in the end decided to stick with tradition, and bought a black tie suit with a silver paisley-patterned waistcoat.

Philip looked anxiously at his watch again. There was no need for him to get dressed up; his role in the evening's events was decidedly more functional and he stood casually waiting for them in chinos and open-neck checked shirt.

"Time we were going," he repeated loudly enough that Anna could hear while holding Simon's jacket open for him.

"I'm ready!" announced Simon. "We're just missing the belle of the ball!"

The door behind them opened and out stepped Anna looking simply stunning in her white strapless dress, her black hair bunched, revealing her slim, pretty neck. The dress caught all her curves perfectly and was set off by an intricate gold and diamond necklace that had been lent to her by Heather with dangly earrings to match. Following just behind her, Heather stepped out, beaming with delight at the results of her handiwork. Both brothers stood there, speechless, genuinely in awe at the beauty of her transformation.

"You look amazing… Fantastic," mumbled Simon, shaking his head. Anna glanced up, her eyes sparkling. She smiled warmly as she saw the spellbound look on Simon's face.

"And you – " said Heather loudly, approaching Simon and reaching up to adjust his bow tie one last time, " – look very dashing, the perfect Prince for the perfect Princess!"

Simon leaned down and gave Heather a kiss on the cheek.

"Ok, have you got everything?" asked Philip.

Simon opened up his jacked and showed his brother where all the items were safely stored. Earlier that day they had decided what tools and implements might come in useful if they had to break through locked doors.

"Arkheynia?" asked Philip.

Simon patted the inside pocket where he was keeping the replica of the arkheynia.

"Good luck both of you and call me as soon as you have some news," demanded Heather, opening the front door for them.

The previous night, Philip had told Heather everything, from the events surrounding the funeral of his grandfather in Oxfordshire to picking up the scrolls and their exploits in Thailand. In the past twenty-four hours she had run through the whole gamut of emotions. From "astonishment and disbelief" at Sir Lawrence Trenchard's legacy as Philip told her the story of how his grandfather had found the Book of Judas to "fear and sheer unadulterated horror" as she learnt about Simon's experience in Professor Palanski's house. Philip left her in no doubt as to the danger they were all in. The revelations about the Vatican and the Satanica were equally as shocking and she began to truly understand the reason for Philip's reticence and uncharacteristic behaviour in some of their brief and peculiar telephone calls.

Despite the threat to their lives, once she had heard the whole story she knew immediately that she wanted to join Philip and the others. They had argued in private about the way forward. Philip was keen that she took the sabbatical from work but he wanted her to get away from New York and join her parents in California until the matter was closed. Heather was not amused with his pleas and stubbornly insisted that she could not sit thousands of miles away knowing that his life was in danger.

"Philip do you realise that I love you and that I would give up any part of my life to be with you," she had said. In the end after a great deal of soul-searching, he had succumbed and agreed that if they were successful in obtaining the second arkheynia from Theodore Grainger that night then she could join them on their forthcoming journey to Cairo. Her mood had picked up instantly once Philip agreed to her wish; she now felt part of the team even if she wasn't accompanying them on this evening's assignment.

They descended to the basement garage and Philip took the wheel of the BMW as they pulled out into the busy evening traffic and headed north in the direction of Westchester.

"It still seems an incredible coincidence," said Simon, referring to the constant media coverage they had endured throughout the day when the news broke about the death of Pope Paul XII.

"I know," replied Philip.

"What do you think this means? Do you think the Vatican's going to be too preoccupied with its own affairs?" quizzed Simon.

"Definitely not," replied Anna sharply from the back seat. To compliment his black tie, she was wearing a white shawl around her shoulders.

The speed and ferocity of her response surprised them.

"You seem very sure," replied Philip as they crossed from the west side of Manhattan on to the famous Henry Hudson Bridge with its two levels allowing for seven lanes of traffic.

"It just doesn't make sense otherwise," she replied, backtracking. She had not intended to sound so vehement and sure of herself. "Listen, think about it! If this book's discovered and it contains all the revelations that it's supposed to then doesn't it have the power to question, even topple the foundations of Christianity itself? Do you think the powerbrokers in the Vatican would sit by and do nothing?" Anna changed her tack, becoming rather more suggestive than so outwardly sure of herself.

Leaving the high-level, steel-arched bridge constructed just before the Second World War they joined the Saw Mill River Parkway, which proceeded north to the affluent suburb of Westchester.

"But who in the Vatican is driving this; who's controlling their day-to-day decisions?" asked Simon curiously.

"I don't know but they must have a central committee or something similar that's steering their progress," answered Philip stoically.

"We have to keep ahead of the Satanica, and that means we have to keep moving as fast as we can," said Anna. "Remember we're still travelling on our own passports – who knows what information they might have access to?"

The comment struck a chord.

"Anna's right," said Philip. "The sooner we're successful tonight the sooner we can leave and frankly I'll feel much happier when we're on the plane out of here."

After a further forty minutes on the road they arrived in Westchester and after following some instructions they saw the tall metal gates to Theodore Grainger's mansion looming before them. After showing their invitation to the security guard they were directed to a car park at the end of the tree-lined drive. The mansion was as enormous as it was spectacular. Built in the late 1880s, the house was an old Gothic masterpiece with several round towers soaring up to various heights above the parapet. The masonry around the roof was eerily striking with gargoyles at every corner and stone statues of griffins, dragons and other mythical medieval monsters. Driving past the front of the house they could see the dozen or so steps leading up to the high stone porch that covered the main entrance. It looked busy. The steps teemed with party guests in their evening frocks eager to be met by their esteemed host prior to making their grand entrance.

"Right this is it," said Philip, pulling the car to a stop on one of the lawns that was functioning as an overflow car park for the guests.

Simon stepped out and walked around to open Anna's door.

"Wish us luck – we'll be back just as soon as we can," he said, and hand-in-hand they walked off purposefully to join the other party revellers heading for the main entrance.

"Nervous," asked Simon, squeezing her hand.

"I'm Ok," she muttered unconvincingly.

"You look fantastic," said Simon, "like a dream!"

"I feel a lot better with you alongside me," she replied, squeezing his hand and smiling up at him.

The queue to meet their host Theodore Grainger was gradually shrinking. They could see him down the line shaking hands firmly with the men and bowing before the ladies as the guests proceeded into the house and its nineteenth century ballroom.

When the ebullient millionaire saw Anna patiently waiting in line, he stopped what he was doing and, ignoring guests ahead of them, came striding forward to greet her.

"Anna, it's been such a long time – you look lovelier than ever," he said, holding her fingertips and leaning back as if admiring a famous work of art.

"It's nice to see you too, Theodore," she replied, conscious of all the gazing eyes of the surrounding guests wondering who she was.

"And this is my husband, Simon," she said politely, indicating his arrival.

Grainger turned his attention to Simon just long enough to dispense with the greeting formalities before turning with ill-disguised haste back to Anna.

"You must sit next to me on the top table," he pronounced at the top of his voice and, taking her arm on his, he led them off through the main door towards the red-carpeted corridors that led to the grand ballroom.

Although slightly miffed at the insincerity of his slightly patronising welcome, Simon did not notice anything to suggest anything sinister underlying Grainger's behaviour and excitement at Anna's arrival.

Most of the guests had already taken their places at the round tables seating ten as they entered the room. The Grand Ballroom was rectangular with high chandeliers and ornate coving around the perimeter of the ceiling. Guests marvelled at the table settings and flower arrangements in a room that was used on just one occasion every year to entertain just over five hundred privileged guests.

"And you, Anna, can sit here," said Grainger enthusiastically, pulling out her chair from under the top table. They were positioned on an elevated stage at the head of the ballroom with a lectern alongside them from where Theodore Grainger would make his regular annual address later that evening.

The smart waiters in waistcoats and bow ties politely ushered standing groups of eminent historians and noted archaeological authors to their table. Moments later, Simon watched as the master of ceremonies approached the lectern to introduce their host. Echoing with the sound of chatter and laughter, the hall suddenly fell quiet as the microphone projected his voice.

"Ladies and gentlemen, I would like to introduce you to your host this evening – Mr. Theodore Grainger."

The rapturous applause reverberated around the room.

"Please excuse me for two minutes, my dear," said Grainger, patting Anna's arm as he stood up to make his welcome speech.

As he began, Simon leaned over to Anna to whisper in her ear.

"It's not going to be to easy to search through his private collection with all this attention he's giving us!"

She nodded.

"I know, we'll have to wait until after the meal's been served – the band starts after the speeches. Maybe we can escape for twenty minutes then."

"Where's the collection? Can you tell me how to get there from here?" he whispered.

She quickly explained before the applause went up again and Theodore Grainger, smiling and waving to the floor, walked back to his seat.

The meal was sumptuous and the service impeccable, although Anna only played with her food. She felt far too nervous with the impending task ahead to relax and enjoy the occasion. Throughout, Theodore Grainger was almost oppressively attentive to Anna, asking her about what had happened in her life since they had last met. He expressed delight at the fact she had become an accomplished archaeologist and listened avidly to her stories of excavations in Greece and the Holy lands of the Levant. Simon looked out across the hall, the laughter and chatter of the guests continuing to ring out. They were obviously enjoying the occasion and continued to do so for a further one and half hours until the time for speeches arrived.

During a brief interlude when Grainger wasn't deep in conversation with Anna he leant forward and told her that they would both slip away as soon as the speeches were over. Once the band struck up and guests left their seats to commence dancing it would be a lot easier to slip out unnoticed he whispered in her ear.

It's getting close to the speeches now, she thought and nodded her agreement.

Simon noticed her lingering gaze as she scrutinised him for a moment longer.

"What is it?" he asked with a curious smile.

"You," she replied with a grin. "Heather was right, you are a Prince and you do look very dashing tonight!"

Simon leaned over a kissed her quickly on the cheek. He wanted to say more but now was not the time.

"Let's hope the speeches aren't too long-winded!" he added, glancing around as the lights dimmed and the spotlight fell on the wooden lectern.

In the end they were thankful as the speeches did not take too long. They sat listening patiently until it was Theodore Grainger's turn to address his guests. He was a good and confident speaker and Simon wondered why he chose to be so reclusive in his private life. Anna could hardly bear the suspense; she was now at the stage where she just wanted to get on with it and escape to the sanctuary of Heather's apartment as soon as possible afterwards. After thirty minutes Theodore Grainger signed off to loud and spontaneous applause and the jazz band moved in and quickly took up their position on ready-made stage. The guests needed no second invitation and the dance floor soon filled up with party revellers. Just as Grainger was about to return to his seat and re-engage Anna in conversation, Simon saw his chance and jumped in.

"Would you like to dance?" he asked, getting to his feet and stretching out his hand.

"I'd love to," she replied, and Simon led her towards the dance floor.

They paused briefly as they bumped into Grainger walking back towards them. Initially Simon thought he looked upset but as they got closer he broke into a wide grin.

"Enjoy yourselves!" he said generously and flamboyantly waving his arm in the air towards the jazz band.

"We will," Anna shouted back as they pushed through the throng of people towards the middle of the dance floor.

As soon as they became an inconspicuous part of the crowd, Simon pointed towards the side exit and they both slipped off without giving rise to any unwanted interest.

Outside in the darkness of the estate grounds Philip looked at his watch; it was approaching eleven-thirty. He was bored and frustrated at being sat in the car for hours on end waiting for something to happen. Throughout his life, Philip had always liked to feel in control of the situation and this experience was firmly testing his resolve. Yawning as he checked his watch again, he decided to get some air and stretch his legs. Stepping out into the brisk evening air, he sauntered along the rows of cars nodding to some of the other chauffeurs in the car park who were leaning against their vehicles smoking and chatting to each other. The mansion, although impressive, had an eerie feel to it with the silhouettes of the towers and the stone statues etched out on the skyline carved by the battlements against the light of the full moon. Philip shuddered from the cold as he walked across the lawn with his hands in his pockets towards the house looking for tell-tale lights at the upstairs windows. The commotion from the lively party on the far side of the mansion could be heard in the background.

Inside the house, Anna tugged Simon's jacket.

"This way," she whispered. "Follow me, the exhibit rooms are on the third floor," and she set off down one of the narrow corridors leading to a stone spiral staircase at the bottom of one of the elevated towers.

"We have to be quick – I think we've got between fifteen and twenty minutes before he notices we're missing," said Simon.

Anna led the way, travelling as quickly as she could. Holding her shoes and hitching up her dress, she climbed up the circular stone staircase. Suddenly they both heard a noise that made them freeze on the spot. The sound came from above them; it was the slow, deliberate sound of footsteps echoing down from the winding staircase above them. Anna gasped and stared at Simon in horror.

Simon didn't have time to think, he had to react and he grabbed Anna's hand and pulled her up the stairs. He felt they were close to the tower's juncture with the second floor and if they could just get there in time they might have a chance to escape unnoticed. Anna followed instinctively despite Simon holding her arm so firmly that she almost fell over the last step.

They made it to the open arched doorway that led to another long corridor on the second floor of the mansion. Simon looked for somewhere to hide but there was no time, the steps were getting louder. *We'll have to take our chance*, he thought. Quickly, he pressed his back into the corner where the corridor met the jutting-out brick of the stone archway. The steps were almost upon them as he pulled Anna hard around the waist so that she fell back against him. Anna held her breath – if the owner of the footsteps decided to exit at the second level and pass through the archway then the game was up. The constant click of heeled shoe against stone sound got louder and louder until the person was on their level, within a metre of where they were standing. Simon was holding Anna so tightly that he felt the shiver of relief run through her as the footsteps continued down the spiral staircase.

Still holding her waist, Simon peered around the edge of the archway and spied the back of the uniformed security guard disappearing into the darkness. They waited a few more minutes until the sound had faded.

"That was close," Anna sighed as he released her from his grip.

"Come on, let's get going," whispered Simon and motioned to her to overtake him back up the spiral staircase.

"Don't worry, I'm right behind you," he added as she glanced back nervously at him.

They swiftly climbed one further storey before reaching the same stone archway leading into the pitch-black corridor of the third floor.

Simon reached into his pocket and pulled out two small but very powerful flashlights and handed one to her. The small windows in the tower had given them some natural light but once out into the passageway it was very difficult to see the way forward.

"This way," said Anna, using the doors and the contours of the hallway to gauge her bearings and determine the correct path. The day she had visited the house many years ago was still etched on her memory and she could remember the grand, double-door entrance to the exhibition room through a circular atrium with a domed ceiling. The walls were taken up with large canvas portraits and in the middle of the atrium was a podium with a life-size replica statue of Michelangelo's Venus.

"It must be this way," she said, beckoning Simon to follow her and they moved quickly and quietly down another passageway. Although everything was still and quiet, the low-level hum from the booming party below filtered up from down below.

"This is it," Anna whispered excitedly as she saw the shape of the atrium appear round the corner.

Moving around the statue, Simon reached for the handle of the door to the Exhibit Room. It was not locked and he pushed it open. He thanked his luck but at the same time was slightly suspicious. *This is easier than I expected… Maybe a bit too easy*, he thought privately to himself.

Once inside the exhibition chamber, Anna's memory came flooding back. She recalled its size, the high ceiling and the width spanning most of the front of the house.

"Where do we begin?" asked Simon, bewildered by the scale of their task.

He stood motionless as he panned the dimmed torchlight around the hall to reveal row upon row of different sized display cases and tables, full of ancient relics, running in parallel to each other across the length of the wooden panelled floor.

"You start at that end," she pointed, "and I'll start down here. Be quick – we haven't got much time left."

Simon rushed to his starting point and, pointing the flashlight down at the showcases, he moved slowly along the line looking for any trace of the second arkheynia.

Outside, Philip had completed his first circumnavigation of the mansion and he stood in the shadows of a tree in the middle of the front lawn staring up at the house. As he wondered how they were getting on he thought he saw a flicker of light coming from the window on the third floor. Keeping his eyes trained on the same location he spotted the glimmer again. His senses heightened as he realised they must be searching for the arkheynia in the Exhibit Room at that very moment.

On the third floor, in their excitement to find the chamber and locate the second arkheynia they had been totally oblivious to the mechanical whirring of the camera that had been watching their progress.

"Anything yet?" hissed Simon loudly with a hint of desperation.

"No nothing…" replied Anna who suddenly stopped unable to finish her sentence.

"Oh my God, Simon, do you hear that?" she called anxiously.

Outside the chamber doors was the unmistakeable sound of voices coming from the atrium and they were getting louder.

With the feeling of panic rising, she turned to Simon.

"They're coming in!" she cried in a hoarse whisper.

"Get down!" said Simon urgently, slipping behind a tall display cabinet for cover. *If they come in now we're done for,* he thought, hoping against hope he was wrong.

The voices outside got louder until suddenly both doors were swung open violently by Theodore Grainger who promptly turned on the central lights and stood with his hands on his hips in an expectant manner flanked by two armed security guards.

"I think you can both come out now," his voice boomed around the high ceiling of the exhibition chamber.

Outside Philip saw the light come on and immediately realised something must have gone dreadfully wrong. *Why else would the light suddenly come on?* Startled, he contemplated his options.

Inside the hall, Anna cautiously stood up from below the table under which she had been hiding and similarly Simon moved into view from behind the wooden cabinet. Despite the shock of being discovered, Simon maintained his wits and walked calmly to where Anna was standing. As he moved his eyes held the intense gaze of Theodore Grainger. Anna's acute embarrassment at having been caught red-handed caused her to start fiddling busily with her white ball dress in an effort to pull it straight.

"I suppose you both know that you could go to jail for a very long time don't you?" bellowed Grainger mercilessly, his face remaining deadpan. He reached into his jacket and pulled out a cheroot, which he began rolling in his fingers before lighting.

"About ten years for burglary, I believe," he continued, blowing a great plume of smoke in the air and staring at them with an emotionless disdain. Neither Simon nor Anna said anything.

Is this it? thought Simon with a grimace. *Has our quest for the Book of Judas already come to an end? There's no way we can make an escape past those armed security guards.* Anna stood alongside him like a cat caught in the headlights, her heart pounding in anticipation of what would happen next.

Outside in the shadows Philip had made up his mind. He was going to find out what was going on up on the third floor. Furtively, he moved towards a side entrance that was being used by the party caterers.

On the third floor Theodore Grainger, seemingly bristling with anger, took two steps towards them and subsequently, expecting the worse, they were caught totally by surprise. To their astonishment the hard craggy lines around Grainger's face softened and disappeared as he broke into a warm smile. At first Simon thought he must be mistaken but then Grainger walked across the hall to a locked cabinet, opened it with a key and pulled something out.

"Is this what you're looking for?" he asked and held up the second arkheynia with the distinctive, bright red tip shining at one end.

Confused, Anna stared at him. Grainger's anger seemed to have evaporated – he actually seemed amused – and somehow Simon felt sure his new demeanour was genuine rather than some maniacal pretence.

"How did you know?" asked Anna quietly, shaking her head.

"Actually I've known this day might come for quite some time now," he replied somewhat insouciantly, looking down at the artefact.

Suddenly, the doors behind them were flung open again and in came Philip, escorted by two burly security guards.

"We found him coming up the back staircase and…" said one of the guards before Grainger silenced him with an impatient wave of his hand.

"Leave him – and you can all go now," he commanded abruptly.

The senior security officer stared at him for a second making sure the order was real before turning around and instructing his men to leave. The large double doors were pulled closed behind them leaving Philip and Simon exchanging surprised glances while Anna's amazement was evident from her face.

"Hallo, Philip," said Grainger.

"I don't understand," he replied. "How do you know me?"

"I've known of all three of you for quite some time," he said smiling benignly. "Come with me. I'd like to show you something."

Theodore Grainger, carrying the second arkheynia in his hand, led them towards a narrow recess in the Exhibit Room. The walls were covered in photographs, many in black and white, depicting him with various dignitaries in a multitude of international settings.

"Do you see that picture there?" he asked invitingly, pointing at an old photograph hanging above their heads on the wall.

All three of them instantly looked up at the worn and frayed image, mounted in a thin black frame. It depicted two middle-aged men smiling at the camera. In the background there was what looked like a Bedouin camp with camels tethered together and the faces of the two men were partially obscured by the Arab headdresses they were both wearing to protect themselves from the heat and dust of the desert.

It took Philip and Simon a moment to identify their grandfather – he was obviously a lot younger at the time but closer scrutiny confirmed that it was definitely him.

"I don't believe it!" muttered Simon under his breath.

Standing on Sir Lawrence Trenchard's right hand side, Anna recognised the youthful, smiling face of Theodore Grainger himself.

"Yes, once upon a time I was very good friends with your grandfather," said Grainger looking nostalgically at the black and white picture. It had been taken some time after Sir Lawrence's discovery of the Judas Scrolls at Qumran.

"Once?" repeated Philip quizzically.

"Yes, once upon a time we were inseparable but then I'm afraid a terrible, terrible tragedy happened – a terrible accident from which there was no turning back!"

They noticed his face contort with the bitter agony of the distant memory. *What could it be?* thought Philip. *What could be so bad that it would completely destroy their relationship?*

"What happened?" asked Anna softly. As she listened to him relive the events as they unfolded many years ago her feelings towards Grainger began to thaw.

"There's no easy way to say this – I'm responsible for the death of your parents!" said Grainger remorsefully, looking directly into the faces of Philip and Simon.

Emotionless, the brothers stood there blankly staring back at him. They were stunned by the revelation. Anna, searching for their reaction, immediately stretched out her arm to clutch Simon's hand. The terrifying memories of the night their grandfather had pulled them from their beds when they were only seven and eight years old came flooding back.

"What do you mean?" asked Philip, shaking his head in bewilderment.

"I mean that your grandfather blamed me for their murder!" he said with regret.

"They were *murdered!*" stuttered Simon. *All our lives Grandfather had been shielding us from the truth,* he thought.

"You need to explain," said Philip angrily, the suppressed emotion rapidly welling up inside him.

In the faded, grey light of the Exhibit Room recess, Theodore Grainger suddenly appeared much older than his years. His shoulders slumped as he slowly and deliberately began to recount the events surrounding the death of their parents.

"Your grandfather trusted me..." he sighed. "He trusted me with his life and when he made that discovery in Qumran all those years ago, he let me in on the secret. I never actually saw the scrolls themselves although I do confess, I'd have loved to have done so."

"When your grandfather told me about the role of the Vatican and their sworn intention to recover the scrolls and destroy the Book of Judas I simply didn't believe him," he reminisced.

"In this modern age, I just could not believe that the Church, Christianity and the Catholic religion was capable of murderous, evil acts to support its continued existence – the church I was familiar with preached about family values, strong ethics and peaceful virtues but how wrong could I be!" he said, gritting his teeth with frustration and shaking his head in disbelief. Even now it still seemed absurd and ridiculous to suggest there could be so much immorality in the fabric of Christianity.

"At the time we were friends, your grandfather was fearful for his life – he hadn't been back in England long since the discovery and he knew that they'd eventually come looking for him. I should have believed him and I should have trusted him totally…" he muttered ruefully.

"As it happened," he continued, "through my own fieldwork work in Jordan, I'd built up a relationship with some senior members of the Vatican's archaeological team – I decided in my wisdom, and unbeknown to your grandfather, to call one of them and find out what was going on. When I called him and asked about the Judas Scrolls he became excited and gave me a number in Rome to call. I didn't attach any great importance to it, and called the number. I was put through to an officer in the Swiss Guard who asked me how I knew about the Judas Scrolls and I told him I was with Sir Lawrence in England. At this point I was foolishly insisting that I speak to someone senior in the Pope's administration, someone that could put an end to this nonsense that my good friend was suffering – they told me that one of the senior Cardinals would speak to me directly that evening and could I give them a telephone number that he could contact me on…"

Grainger looked up, the cigar he had been holding had gone out a long time ago but, agitated, he kept rolling it around his fingers while his other hand kept a tight grip of the second arkheynia. Riveted to his every word, Simon and Philip urged him to continue.

"Normally we'd have been staying at Tudor Hall but I knew we had plans to be at your parents' that evening so I gave the Vatican official their telephone number – the housemaid appeared not long after and told me that the engagement with your parents had been cancelled. Later, that night at Tudor Hall after your grandfather returned late from a meeting, he was very uptight – he was anxious for us both to leave the house and seek refuge somewhere else the very next morning."

Grainger snorted and gave an ironic shake of the head as he recalled the conversation.

"This is when I told Lawrence of the earlier conversation I'd had with the Vatican and that I'd soon sort out this ridiculous nightmare for him…"

Philip began to see the writing on the wall. He winced as Grainger revealed the final truth about their parents.

"Your grandfather went berserk; he couldn't understand why I didn't believe him – I just couldn't accept that the clergy and the Vatican were capable of ordering cold-blooded killings."

Grainger looked across at Anna and shook his head sadly.

"In his rage, Sir Lawrence told me what happened to your father – I'm very sorry."

Anna remained speechless although she thought he looked sincere with the remark.

"It must have been approaching midnight. Your grandfather grabbed his coat, raced to the car and set off for your parent's house – but as you know he was too late!"

"What happened?" demanded Simon.

"I wasn't there myself," replied Grainger, "but I understand that agents of the Vatican had broken in and murdered your parents before ransacking the house looking for the scrolls – maybe your grandfather's arrival scared them off, I don't know, but he returned later that night with both of you."

Philip turned around and paced back and forwards along the recess wall, thoughts running through his mind as the last pieces of the jigsaw from that unbearable night were finally put in place.

"Your grandfather was distraught," Grainger continued. "I thought he was going to kill me he was so mad but in the end he simply asked me to leave and never return – he told me that he never wanted to see me as long as I lived. It was a very difficult time for me. I was disgusted with myself for what I'd done – I understood… How could he ever forgive me or how could I ever expect to be forgiven. After that he obviously somehow managed to make a deal with the Vatican and as time went on I did attempt a reconciliation but it was totally futile – I think he hated me with a passion – he told me that every time he thought of me all he could see were the faces of his dead family!"

In the background outside the Exhibit Room, they could hear the bangs and whizzes as the fireworks display began in the garden for the guests' entertainment, the rockets' explosions illuminating the midnight sky and showering the alcove in flickering multi-coloured light. Outside, the revellers shrieked in delight as the party overflowed into the lawn.

Grainger ignored the noise.

"You know I even offered him this." Grainger held up the second arkheynia, the red tip extending from his fist on the spindly fragment of bone.

"It was me that found that it – I knew your grandfather wanted them and I too researched night and day to discover their location, hoping that this peace offering could be the key that could bring us together again… But it wasn't – he refused to accept anything from me!"

Simon and Philip now knew the real story. Their grandfather had tried to protect them with the story about the car crash. Philip's initial rush of anger had subsided; there was nothing to be gained by pushing Grainger any further, and there was nothing that he could do to bring their dead mother and father back.

"Take this," he said, handing the second arkheynia to Simon.

"Learn from me, there are centuries of fear that has built up behind the Book of Judas, and the power mongers at the Vatican will do anything to preserve their situation. Please don't do what I did; don't underestimate the danger your lives are in," he warned coldly.

"Now go!" he shouted and waved for them to leave. "The guards won't touch you."

They didn't need to be asked twice – and they quickly followed Simon towards the double doors with Grainger standing motionless with his back to them, his head lowered towards the ground.

Just as Simon turned the door handle, Grainger shouted.

"Anna!"

They all stopped in their tracks and looked back one last time.

"Anna!" he implored again.

"I just wanted to do what's right," he pleaded, seeking her forgiveness or belated exoneration for his unilateral act of stupidity that led to the death of Simon and Philip's parents.

For a few seconds, she gazed intently across the room searching out the emotion behind his expression.

"I know," she whispered softly. She felt pity for his tormented soul and granted him some comfort with a warm, meaningful smile.

"Come on, let's go," barked Philip and they rushed through the double doors, leaving Theodore Grainger alone with his thoughts in the exhibition chamber.

"Have you got it safe?" he asked Simon as they rushed down the main staircase.

"Yes, it's safe," he replied patting his jacket.

Anna felt relieved as she was being dragged along by Simon, her free hand clutching the straps of her shoes and drawing up the hem of her dress so she could run freely. At the foot of the steps they ran through the hall and passed surprised guests as they rushed out through the main entrance where the host had so graciously met them earlier on.

"That explains everything," said Philip, glancing at Simon as they broke into the midnight air. Learning the truth about their parents had come as one hell of a shock.

Outside, the firework display was still in full flow, and with the noise of rockets exploding into colour above them followed by the applause and cooing of the excited crowd, they raced past to the where the BMW was parked.

Wasting no time, Philip started the car and they sped down the drive and out into the rich metropolis of Westchester.

"Well we've got it," said Simon although his flat tone reflected the manner in which they had achieved it.

"We have got to leave; we've got to get the next flight out of here," stated Philip firmly.

"I believe we're in more danger now than ever before," he added.

"Absolutely, let's just go," agreed Anna.

It was just after midnight and the traffic on the roads had eased. Philip kept his foot down and they made good time back to the apartment block opposite Central Park.

"We need to find out what time the next flights to Europe and on to Cairo are," pointed out Simon as they exited the elevator on the top floor and walked down the corridor to Heather's penthouse suite.

"Let's hope Heather's ready to go," said Philip, pushing the key into the lock and opening the front door.

Immediately on stepping inside the apartment he sensed something was wrong.

"Heather," he shouted and Simon noticed the sound of panic in his voice. *The only light on's the one on the side table in the lounge – that's not like Heather at all!* thought Philip, stepping hurriedly inside.

"Heather," he yelled loudly again. But there was no reply.

As he rushed into the hall, he saw there was a note on the table below the lamp. Anna and Simon watched agonisingly as he raced over to get it.

"Oh my God!" he shrieked, his hands shaking.

"The Satanica – they've got Heather!" he cried.

Chapter Twenty-Three

Vatican City, Rome

Colonel Renauld stood, arms clasped behind his back, watching out of his office window the pious procession of Cardinals below crossing Bernini's piazza on their way to the Sistine Chapel. It was a unique time. Dressed in their deep scarlet robes of office, one hundred and twenty elder Cardinals strode purposefully towards the entrance of St. Paul's Basilica. The time had arrived to choose the new Pope and Ruler of the Holy See.

Just outside the Vatican walls thousands of people had gathered to observe the proceedings, some with religious passion to hail the new Pontiff, others realising the importance of the historic moment, excited to watch the ceremonial spectacle and be part of the moment.

The Cardinals' response to the break with tradition had been successful. Every elected Cardinal, from every part of the globe, had been prepared to forgo his plans and travel at short notice to the Vatican. This had not been achieved without considerable effort. In certain cases there had been an underlying reluctance from Cardinals who had made serious ecumenical commitments involving Royalty and ruling Heads of State in their representative countries. Some of the more senior clerics openly questioned the Rome's authority to break with tradition and pull the election date forward. In these cases, depending on the relationship with the Vatican, Colonel Renauld had called upon Cardinal Fiore to telephone them personally to explain the seriousness of the occasion.

It was eleven o'clock in the morning and, in this case, in keeping with time-honoured tradition, the conclave of Cardinals would remain within the walls of the Sistine Chapel until the successor was chosen.

"I've reviewed the transcripts," said Colonel Renauld dryly, continuing to gaze out of the window.

Behind him, standing to attention, was Major Claude Dupont, a dependable and trusted member of his elite inner cell. A cell he had selected personally and whose unquestioning loyalty he knew he could count on. Under his orders, they were recording all of the outgoing and incoming calls within the Vatican walls.

"Nothing – I've found nothing to raise suspicion," he continued with disdain.

Major Dupont, standing to attention in front of his Commanding Officer's desk, remained silent.

Following the call with Goran, Colonel Renauld had decided to set a trap. He was convinced that there was a top-level leak. This meant that one of the senior Cardinals who had been privy to the decisions of the deceased Pope had delivered the information into the hands of the Satanica. Indeed it was likely, he thought, that the deceitful Cardinal himself was a member of the evil organisation.

During the previous day, no matter how improbable their guilt in his view, he had sought appointments with those who were knowledgeable about the Vatican's inner decisions. This included only the most senior members of its top echelon who were fully informed and briefed on all matters relating to the scrolls and their quest to destroy the Book of Judas. Disturbingly, the list he had drawn up included the three most prominent and favoured Cardinals, namely Fiore, Gregory and Alphonso, from whom the deceased Pontiff's heir was likely to be chosen. In addition to them the list included Cardinals Weiss, Lefebvre and Giacoma, making a total of six suspects in all.

The engagements with most of the respected clergy had been arranged privately and in advance so as not arouse unnecessary interest. However, in the case of both Cardinal Gregory and Fiore who had onerous commitments, he had made it his business to find out their likely movements around the Vatican and had subsequently staged "accidental" meetings.

During the course of each separate meeting he had told each Cardinal that Goran had made an incredible breakthrough. As he had planned, their curiosity was aroused immediately. When pressed for further information, he told them in total confidence that he had discovered details that pointed to the labyrinth's entrance being close to a town called Hom in southern Syria.

All the Cardinals had expressed their dismay and surprise at the news. As a consequence the questions had poured out from the confused clergy. *Are you saying that the Trenchards have uncovered all the keys of arkheynia? How do you know this? Where are they now?* The questions had flooded out, with the Cardinals demanding immediate answers from Renauld but he had followed his carefully laid plans. By promising to give those answers as soon as possible in the right circumstances when he could address them together he had managed to deflect their spontaneous barrage of questions.

"We need to meet at the earliest possible opportunity," he had replied, knowing that this was not possible until the completion of the imminent papal elections – but the proposed meeting had not satisfied everyone. Cardinal Fiore himself had been outraged by Renauld's lack of response and made it clear to him that his position in the Swiss Guard would be reviewed at some point in the very near future.

It was a gamble and Colonel Renauld knew it. If the traitor in their midst was not exposed by the time the new Pope was chosen he would have to come clean at the first meeting with the senior clergy. How they would react to his unilateral action, he couldn't be sure, but he was certain that it was worth taking the risk.

Turning away from the scenes in the piazza below, he stepped back towards his desk, picked up the ream of transcripts he had studied in infinite detail earlier and threw them angrily in the bin.

"Nothing!" he repeated through gritted teeth. The Major flinched at his superior officer's irritation.

"Have we got every possible means of communication covered?" demanded the Colonel.

"Yes, Sir," replied Dupont sharply.

"Ok, Major," the Colonel's tone softened. He knew he was being unreasonable and that his trusted officer's performance was not really the source of his frustration.

"I want every report as soon as it's taken, do you understand?" he ordered.

"Yes, sir," he repeated.

The election may have started, he thought, but there would be recesses during the holding of the secret ballots in the Sistine Chapel. It was still possible, indeed likely, that one of the Cardinals could communicate with the outside world.

"Ok, Major, I appreciate that you'll be working around the clock. You and the team are doing a commendable job – just keep me informed of all communiqués no matter how irrelevant you think they may be. Do you understand?"

"Of course, Sir," responded the smartly presented officer to his superior.

"That's all, Major Dupont," said Renauld.

As the Major left his office he returned to the window and gazed pensively towards the final procession of Cardinals climbing the steps to St. Paul's Basilica.

Chapter Twenty-Four

Manhattan, New York

Philip, shaking with fear, clutched the note. He felt sick inside, distraught with the realisation that Heather's life was in impending danger from an insane, ruthless killer who cared nothing for his hapless victims.

Simon and Anna rushed down the steps of the barely lit lounge to join him. There hearts in their mouths as they tried to comprehend the news.

It just can't be possible! Please say it's not real!

Philip stood motionless, paralysed with morbid dread as he played the thoughts over and over in his mind.

Simon looked down at the table; apart from the note that Philip was holding there was another envelope and underneath that there were two carefully outlined newspaper cuttings. Both reproduced the artist's impression of the spread-eagled bodies found cruelly and savagely dismembered, once in Oxford and then again, only days earlier in Kings Cross, London. As the highlighted newspaper article confirmed, the media had heightened the local hysteria surrounding the deaths by dubbing the brutal slaying the work of the "Death Angel". The first cutting was taken from a UK tabloid and the second from the *New York Post*. Conchos had smiled, pleased with his own handiwork as he placed the articles on the table; he wanted to leave them in no doubt as to the fate that awaited Heather if they did not comply with his demands.

Simon grabbed the note out of Philip's hand as Anna clumsily tried to lead him to one of the high-backed chairs. Trying to focus on helping him gave her some short-lived respite from the untenable thought of Heather being held by a possessed, soulless killer.

"I'm Ok," he muttered, rubbing the side of his face with his palm and gently pushing Anna away with his other hand. Despite the nauseous feeling inside he turned back towards the side table and reached for the envelope that had been placed by the kidnapper next to the two newspaper cuttings.

Simon read the note he had snatched from his brother's hand. It was handwritten and signed with the initials "MM" at the bottom.

> *"Heather is with me now. You will follow the instructions in the envelope or I will enjoy torturing and cutting her in a manner you couldn't possibly conceive so that she dies slowly in painful agony. Any communication to the authorities, any deviance from my instructions – SHE DIES."*

The note was real and it filled him with dread. Simon had seen the killer's handiwork at first hand and now he feared the worst. *How could they possibly save Heather from the horror of this insane murderer?* He handed the distressing note to Anna. She looked stunned, her face like Philip's, drained of colour.

Simon heard the sound of paper ripping and turned to see Philip tearing open the sealed envelope and pulling out a neatly typed page of instructions. *He obviously prepared himself well in advance,* thought Simon as he watched his brother quickly scanning the contents.

"We get her back if we follow his directions," he blurted out. His despondency waned temporarily; he had found a small shred of hope to cling on to.

Philip handed over the typed sheet to Simon and paced around the room deep in thought. Saving Heather was all he could think about. Getting her back, alive and safe was now his primary objective – the Book of Judas and its consequences were no longer of any relevance to him. Marching up and down, he contemplated the contents of the sealed envelope and tried to fathom out the best options open to him.

Simon, with Anna peering over his shoulder, read the kidnapper's instructions.

"You will complete your task and recover all three keys of arkheynia and locate the entrance to the labyrinth within the next seven days. All three of you will remain together at all times. If you do not complete my demand within the time frame or if you separate for any reason then the girl will die.

I will be in touch with you from time to time to understand your progress and to give you new instructions. Do not try and locate your friend, she will be with me at all times and I will be close to you. If you obey my instructions without question I will grant you the opportunity to speak to her at a time of my choosing in the next few days.

Tomorrow morning, you will put a statement in the personal columns of the New York Post. The message will contain three words, the first will be Cyclops, the second will be a town or city representing your final airport destination and the third will be the number of keys of arkheynia that you currently hold.

When you arrive at that airport you will be given a note telling you which hotel you are to stay in. I will contact you again."

Finishing the last sentence, Simon looked up at Philip who was still pacing, deep in thought.

"We go through with the instructions – agreed?" demanded Philip.

"Of course," replied Simon. "Do we have any other option?"

Anna opened her mouth to speak and then closed it again.

"Agreed, Anna?" repeated Philip pointedly, he had noticed her vague expression, which did not sit well with the immediate and unconditional confirmation he was looking for.

Anna stared blankly at him for a moment. She had only known Heather a few days but had immediately formed a strong bond with her new friend. However there were other things playing on Anna's mind. Of course she would like her freed from the clutches of this insane murderer immediately but there was more to consider here. She knew that in any normal kidnap circumstances the obvious and only answer would be to rescue the victim at any cost because saving human life came above everything else. However, in normal kidnap circumstances the perpetrator's motivation was typically money, the release of prisoners or some other political goal where the equation balancing "cost" against "life" was indisputable. This situation was very different, and that gave her a severe problem. Fulfilling their obligations according to the instructions in the sealed envelope would give the Satanica direct and uninhibited access to the Book of Judas. If history was correct and the myth behind the book was real – and the more she delved into the facts the more she felt convinced it was – then the potential destruction to humanity that could be caused by giving the book away to the Satanica was exponential in its consequences.

"Anna?" said Simon, willing her to respond encouragingly to his brother's calling.

She was still dressed in the ballroom attire from earlier in the evening but it was no longer in the pristine state in which it had been when they left the apartment to go the party. Black wisps of her bunched hair now fell in a curl at the side of her face and her dress carried the marks of their earlier exertions. It didn't matter to Simon – for him she was the lady of his dreams and her beauty was beyond compare.

"Agreed!" said Anna, making a concerted effort to drum up a positive demeanour. Simon quietly sighed with relief. He could sense there was something on her mind but now was not the moment to discuss sensitive matters with his brother.

"We must work together to do all we can to get Heather back," she added and watched the relief spread across Philip's face. At that moment seeing his tearful expression, her heart yearned to make things right for him.

She also sensed Simon's concern and like him she knew that now was neither the time nor place to raise questions on such emotional issues. Whatever the outcome of such a debate, she knew that right now the main objective must be to obtain the keys of arkheynia and find the entrance to the labyrinth. There would be plenty of time to discuss matters later, she thought. Besides, she wanted to speak separately on the subject with Simon first.

"Good," said Philip, rubbing his eyes as he walked over to the drinks cabinet.

"Anybody else?" he asked as he poured a generous tumbler of Heather's malt whisky.

Both nodded their heads and he passed the glasses around.

"No point in getting the police involved?" asked Simon rhetorically. He already knew the answer but thought it worth mentioning in case anyone had something to say on the subject. Anna replied before Philip had a chance.

"We can't do that! Once the police become involved we're no longer in control of the situation or our destiny... Finding the book will no longer be an option!"

"Frankly you're right, Anna, I don't think we have an option," remarked Philip, adding his seal of approval although he would have preferred to hear more concern in her voice. *She makes it sound like recovering the book's more important than saving Heather!* he thought before continuing.

"I have no faith in the police being able to rescue Heather and I think we know enough about the Satanica to know that he'll go through with his threat if there's any deviation from the instructions – I'm just not prepared to take the risk."

"I agree, we haven't got a choice," said Simon. "I'll get the number for the airport and find out what the best schedule is to get us to Cairo."

"Good – in which case, we need to place the ad in the personals tomorrow morning before we set off," said Philip, anxious, exhausted and fearing the worst for Heather.

Taking a sip of Scotch, he felt marginally better knowing they had agreed a plan to get her back, albeit simply by following the Satanica's instructions. There was a small glimmer of hope and he kept repeating in his mind the line that mentioned he could be speaking to her in the next couple of days if they did as they were told. Taking another sip of Scotch, he winced inside as he pictured Heather bound and gagged in the hands of this monster and the thought made him grit his teeth. He loved her and he promised himself that nothing in the world would stop him from getting her back.

Chapter Twenty-Five

Vatican City, Rome

Cardinal Fiore paused for a moment before entering the cloisters surrounding Bernini's square. He watched the procession of Cardinals passing in front of him, their scarlet birettas covering the tops of their heads and their matching velvet robes flowing behind them as they paced across the piazza on their way to the portal of St. Paul's Basilica. It was mid-morning on an early summer's day and like the pageant in front of him, he was dressed in his full clerical regalia. The days leading up to this point had passed slowly but now the time had arrived to elect the new Pope.

Cardinal Fiore stepped through the doorway into the colonnade where his trusted allies, Cardinals Weiss and Lefebvre waited to join him. They both looked apprehensive at his arrival.

"Come, my friends," said Fiore reassuringly, "let us see what outcome awaits us."

He put his hand on their shoulders and steered them past the pillars and into the procession. They joined behind another group of Cardinal Priests who were marching purposefully across the square.

Cardinal Weiss, bolstered by his mentor's confidence, gave a sanguine nod of agreement before suddenly turning to look skywards. The noise of the media helicopter above them was getting louder, he thought, as they strode on. Over the past thirty-six hours it had seemed like there was no other news in the world such was the attention being paid by the multitude of international TV crews to the unfolding events in the Vatican. The ancient and ceremonial tradition of electing the new Pope had caught not just the religiously minded but also the general public's imagination.

The media crew manning the helicopter was swiftly informed by Vatican security that they were breaking the boundaries of acceptable behaviour. Moments later they diverted away from their hovering position on the perimeter of the Vatican City's outer walls. With tranquillity restored, Cardinal Fiore stared up, marvelling at the architectural masterpiece that loomed ahead of them. Commissioned by Pope Julius II in 1506, St. Peter's Basilica had taken over two hundred years to build with famed masters such as Bramante, Raphael and Michelangelo all taking time at the helm of the Cathedral's noble creation. At the top of the building, he could see the splendid hemispherical dome but he knew privately from personal experience that if you wished to capture the best view of the dome's architectural brilliance you needed to see it from the Papal gardens at the back.

Fiore studied the faces of his fellow Cardinals as they proceeded up the steps into the church. For many of them this was their first election to choose a new Pontiff. The deceased Pope Paul XII had reigned for a long time and the media had been rife with speculation about his successor. Many commentators propagated the view that as he had been responsible for selecting and swearing in so many of the new Cardinals there was a high probability that the new Pope would also share the same conservative outlook on pressing and contentious liturgical matters. However, Fiore knew this was unlikely to be the case with the frontrunners in this election.

Encouragingly for Camerlengo Fiore, many of the Cardinals who had travelled thousands of miles in the past few days recognized him as he climbed up the steps to the entrance. Before entering through the famous gateway, he paused and looked back nostalgically across the piazza. Once upon a time the square had been small and enclosed until Mussolini famously decided to change its appearance and made it much more open to the outside world. Fiore smiled to himself; he knew that once he entered St. Paul's these doors would remain closed until the new Supreme Pontiff was revealed to the world. As soon as it was closed behind them, the closed outer gates of the Vatican would be opened allowing thousands of people, from all walks of life, to flood into Bernini's Square to camp for the duration of the election, waiting and watching for the impending outcome.

Followed by Cardinal Weiss and Lefebvre, Fiore turned and walked into the Cathedral.

In the past, papal elections had taken days and sometimes weeks to decide, the whole process being filled with drama, intrigue and rumours were rife of bribes and promises to secure the votes of self-indulgent and self-motivated Cardinals. In modern times, the newspapers had reported, the election process had been subtly refined so that the final outcome could be reached within twenty-four hours and certainly should take no longer than two days. The rules stating who could be present during a papal election were very clear. Apart from the body of Cardinals eligible to participate and vote in the secret ballots the Constitution allowed for various outside personnel essential to control and manage the process. The secretary of the College of Cardinals was there to take on the secretarial duties of the electoral assembly. In addition, two medical doctors were there in case of emergency as well as chefs and housekeepers to meet the Cardinals' daily needs and assistants to help the Cardinal Dean with his onerous tasks. In accordance with the rules, all the external personnel had been vetted and approved beforehand by the office of the Camerlengo.

The noise of the great doors being slammed shut together by two members of the Swiss Guard reverberated through the colossal inner halls. Cardinal Fiore walked solemnly over to the tomb of St. Peter to pay his respects.

Although there were over one hundred and fifty Cardinals worldwide, only those aged below eighty years old were entitled to vote. This meant that only one hundred and twenty would pass beneath the dome and through the great halls into the Sistine Chapel where they would remain until the voting was over.

Outside the doorway to the Sistine Chapel stood Colonel Renauld accompanied by members of the Swiss Guard under his command. It was his duty to guarantee the security of the ceremony that gathered the most senior clerics in the Catholic Church. As Fiore approached, their eyes met and Colonel Renauld, maintaining eye contact, slowly bowed his head in deference, before he strode past him, the last Cardinal to enter the chamber.

As he entered the Sistine Chapel, the doors were closed behind him. The secret meeting was known as a conclave, translating literally to mean "under locked key". Inside, the Cardinals sat facing each other on either side of the great room below the celebrated fresco painted by Michelangelo on the ceiling shaped like a flattened barrel. The chapel, constructed in the fifteenth century, was rectangular in shape and built to the same specifications and dimensions as the Temple of Solomon as recounted in the Old Testament.

All the Cardinals began to take their seats on their individual thrones. The grand chairs were covered in violet cloth with a violet canopy above their heads. In addition there was a table in front of each throne, again covered in a violet cloth to be used by the Cardinal to record the results of the secret ballots as they were announced by the papal "scrutineers".

Cardinal Gregory sat with his band of faithful supporters at one end of the hall while Cardinals Alphonso and Giacoma settled in a neutral section towards the middle. Those who supported the tall figure of

Cardinal Camerlengo Fiore sat on the opposite side with the thrones between them filled by the many Cardinals whose intentions weren't known.

At the turn of the century most of the Cardinals came from within Europe but during the time of Pope Paul XII the demographics had changed substantially with many of those present coming from Africa, North and South America and the Far East of Asia.

The only non-voting member of the gathering was the Dean of the Vatican College whose responsibility it was to conduct the election. He sat upright in a throne placed in the middle of the room between the Cardinals with a microphone raised before him. As Cardinal Fiore finally took his seat next to Cardinals Weiss and Lefebvre, the Dean broke into the excited chatter and opened his address to the gathered conclave.

"Your Eminences, my brothers, we are gathered here today to elect the new Supreme Pontiff, the religious head of our Catholic Church – in order to do so the chosen Cardinal must achieve two thirds of the vote plus one. There are one hundred and twenty of us in this room which means that if you grant eighty-one votes to the same nomination, to the same Cardinal, then he shall be declared the new Supreme Pontiff."

Looking around the room, he paused to let his words take effect.

"The vote will be conducted through a secret ballot and if there is no outright decision at first, then the ballot will continue until the decision has been made."

With the rising sound of murmuring in the background, Cardinal Gregory looked calmly and confidently towards Cardinal Alphonso. Since their meeting with Fiore straight after the news of the Pope's death, he had urged Alphonso on several occasions and in no uncertain terms, to see Fiore for the man he was and throw his support behind him for the papal crown.

Cardinal Alphonso sat hunched on his hard wooden seat with his arms resting on top of his walking cane. His close friend, Cardinal Giacoma sat next to him. He had noticed that the past few days had really taken their toll on Cardinal Alphonso.

Alphonso knew that he would not win the secret ballot but he knew that he potentially controlled sufficient votes to give either Gregory or Fiore the prized number they were looking for.

The problem, thought Alphonso, *is which one of them can be called upon to make the big decisions against the Satanica in this pressurized time of crisis that threatens the very heart of our religion?* He still felt that the note left by the deceased Pope Paul XII supporting Fiore was genuine and was also slightly disenchanted by the way Cardinal Gregory had been conducting himself of late. He seemed more intent on grabbing the papal throne at any cost than on focusing on the calamity that would unfold once the Book of Judas was found. However, Alphonso drummed his fingers on the head of his cane, his anxieties were not automatically relieved when he considered the proposition of electing Fiore.

Cardinal Alphonso gave a wry smile as he contemplated the ironic timing of the election ceremony. Of the hundred and twenty cardinals present, only six were aware of the Book of Judas that endangered their existence. *How would they vote,* he wondered, *if they knew what was really happening?*

In the background, the Dean continued his opening address, explaining to the Cardinals the election procedure and informing them that anyone present could stand as a candidate. Finally, he approached the moment where he would ask that those who wished to be considered for the position of Supreme Pontiff should make themselves known.

Around the room, solitary Cardinals dressed in their fine scarlet robes stood up to signify that they wished to be accepted as contenders. The Dean asked them to introduce themselves and one by one they announced their names, their dioceses and a summary of the Catholic and Papal views for which they stood. This change to the charter for papal elections had been introduced by the recently deceased Supreme pontiff himself, adamant that the romantic traditions of the ages should be tempered by a more democratic and more informed procedure.

Six contenders entered the first secret ballot and Cardinal Gregory spoke first, followed by Alphonso and the other candidates. Cardinal Fiore elected to speak last. In silence the conclave, sat in their violet thrones, listened to their salutary words as they echoed around the chamber before the Dean informed them it was time for them to cast their first votes.

Many blank ballot papers had already been dispatched by the scrutineers, placed on the tables within easy reach of the Cardinals who were politely reminded that abstentions were not permitted. The ballot box was placed in the centre near the Dean, and the Cardinals took it in turn to walk across the chapel floor and swear the ritual oath before casting their vote. After completing the words, they placed their ballot paper in the receptacle before bowing towards the altar and returning to their throne.

Only ten minutes after the last Cardinal registered the final vote, the three chosen scrutineers began counting the papers. The rules of the election provided that each one of them had a specific task to do. The first scrutineer opened the folded ballot papers and noted the chosen Cardinal's name before passing it on the second. He too noted the contents before handing it over to the third scrutineer who read the name of the selected Cardinal out aloud to the gathered assembly. Each Cardinal, sat at his throne, recorded the announcement on the table in front of them thus keeping track of the votes as they were called. Finally, after the third scrutineer had called out the Cardinal's name he pierced the ballot paper with a needle and placed it on a thread, which was tied in a knot at one end.

Once the final name was read out, it was the job of the "revisers" who were tasked with checking the work of the scrutineers to move into place to verify the result.

As predicted by many the first secret ballot was indeterminate.

Cardinal Alphonso glanced around at Gregory and Fiore as the votes were being read out. Both were surreptitiously straining to see the third scrutineer while at the same time marking down the score on the table in front of them. *They look excited,* thought Alphonso as he watched them anxiously record each vote.

"And finally Cardinal Gregory," called the third scrutineer, enjoying the avid attention of his audience. Many of the new Cardinals who had not witnessed the election before were carried along by the magic and grandeur of the traditional occasion. Some of the older Cardinals, though, had seen it all before – they knew that the same process might be carried out many times before a final result would be known.

Cardinal Alphonso sat back in his throne and smiled dryly as he mulled over the consequences of the result he had penned for the first ballot.

The revisers did not take long and the Dean finally stood up in front of the microphone clutching a piece of paper to announce the outcome.

"Your Graces, the ballot papers have been counted and the result is as follows," he said, looking up at the eager faces around the room.

"His Eminence Cardinal Salvatore – five votes, His Eminence Cardinal Heath – two votes, His Eminence Cardinal Palermo – four votes…" He paused, savouring the anticipation around the room as he reached the names the whole chamber was waiting to hear.

"His Eminence Cardinal Alphonso – thirty-one votes," he said slowly.

Cardinal Alphonso was pleased; he had received more support than he had imagined.

"His Eminence Cardinal Gregory – thirty-nine votes," he called, his voice reaching a crescendo.

Around the chapel, the chatter grew louder.

"And finally, His Eminence Cardinal Fiore – also thirty-nine votes."

The sound suddenly increased as Cardinal Gregory and Cardinal

Fiore both received the joyous and vocal congratulations of their loyal supporters. For one bitter moment they stared coldly at each other across the magnificent chamber before turning back and gratefully accepting the plaudits of the surrounding Cardinals by respectfully bowing their heads in a gesture of appreciation.

"And now," continued the Dean, "we will proceed to a second ballot, which will commence with the two candidates who received the most votes – Cardinal Gregory and Cardinal Fiore. We shall take a short break for exactly one hour before commencing the second ballot."

Pope Paul XII's change to the constitution should speed things up, thought Alphonso as he watched the scrutineers, along with the secretary of the Conclave and the Master of Ceremonies, gather up the ballot papers and take them to be burned. Mixed with wet straw they would emit the black smoke that signalled to the expectant crowds and outside world that the first ballot had been unsuccessful.

Chapter Twenty-Six

Manhattan Island, New York

Philip had barely been able to sleep and had arisen early, his mind reeling with all the excitement and events of the night before. He checked his watch – it was now approaching eight-thirty and he was anxious to get started. Simon was also sat at the breakfast table and he poured them both some coffee while Anna finished showering in her room.

"I've worked out that the best flight to Cairo's via Paris," stated Philip matter-of-factly.

"What time does it depart?" asked Simon.

"One o'clock from JFK – do you think we can make it?" Philip queried. Privately he had worked out that catching this flight should not pose too much of a problem but he wanted his brother's confirmation.

"It won't take us long to pack and all we have to do is place the message in the personal column, which we can do over the phone, so if check-in's at eleven we should make it comfortably," replied his brother, suddenly turning his head to watch Anna approach the table.

"Any chance whatsoever that you can manage to pack within a couple of hours?" he asked Anna sarcastically with a grin. Despite the dreadful news of Heather's capture the night before he knew they had to keep their spirits up and the best way he knew how was to attempt some light-hearted humour.

She grinned back. Even his elder brother managed a fleeting smile before the frown returned to his face.

"Yes, I think with a strong wind behind me I should just about manage that," she replied, smiling.

Philip stood up and sipped his coffee before wandering over to the telephone that was attached to the wall in the kitchen. He dialled the number for the *New York Post* by pressing last number recall. He had tried several times in vain earlier that morning before the newspaper had opened but now, looking at his watch, he figured he should be able to get through to someone at the end.

He was in luck and with the help of the operator working on the reception board he was put through to the department responsible for collating the messages in the personal column.

Holding the kidnapper's instructions in his left hand, he followed them to the letter, relaying the coded message that he wanted placed in the next edition.

"Can you read the message back to me?" he asked the young girl on the other end of the line.

"Certainly, sir. Your message is three words long and says, **Cyclops, Cairo, Two**," she recounted.

"When does the next edition cone out? Are we in time for it?" asked Philip after he had given the girl his credit card details for the payment.

"Let me see, that will be published in the late morning edition," she replied cheerfully.

Philip thanked her for her help and put down the receiver.

"What did she say?" asked Anna.

"It's going to be in this morning's edition of the *Post*," he said, repeating the girl's response. "It comes out around lunchtime."

"Right – well we don't need to wait for it, do we?" said Simon. "We may as well pack and head over to JFK now so we can get our seats confirmed."

"Agreed," said Philip, springing into action. "Let's get moving."

An hour later, they packed their cases into the trunk of the taxi and headed off Manhattan in the direction of the airport. When they arrived well ahead of schedule they went straight to the check-in desk and Anna was pleased to find out that they would only be waiting an hour in transit at Charles De Gaulle Airport before starting their final leg to Cairo.

They all agreed there was little point in waiting at check-in and proceeded through to the departure lounge, looking to base themselves at a coffee shop table until it was time to board – and anyway, Simon was hungry. Just after the waiter had served them their order Philip, who wanted to be certain that his earlier instructions had been correctly followed, went in search of a *New York Post*. He found a newsagent along the concourse and allowed himself a relieved smile as he found what he was looking for. Returning, he showed them where he had highlighted the unusual three-word entry.

The loudspeaker announced the imminent departure of their flight to Paris. Twenty-five minutes later, the plane's nose pulled up in the air and they commenced their journey across the Atlantic Ocean in search of the third and final arkheynia; the key to saving Heather's life – and maybe the world as they knew it.

Chapter Twenty-Seven

Vatican City, Rome

Outside the Vatican, the noise of the excited crowd rose as they pointed at the black plumes of smoke issuing from the hallowed chimneys and drifting over the rooftops. For centuries, the scrutineers had ritually overseen the traditional burning of the ballot papers to signal the outcome of the secret elections. Mixed with straw, the paper produced a black smoke that informed all those watching that the ballot had been inconclusive. When the time would come to burn the papers without adding any straw this would signal to the mass of expectant onlookers that the new Pope had been chosen. The pure, white smoke arising from the chimneys above St. Peter's Square would confirm that the secret conclave had finally made their choice.

Inside the Sistine Chapel, the tension was high as both Cardinal Gregory and Fiore at first acknowledged their own supporters before moving on to address the Cardinals whose vote was uncertain or wavering. Out of the one hundred and twenty eligible to vote, seventy-eight had backed Fiore and Gregory. They both understood how important it was to gain the confidence and support of the "undecided" forty-two if they were to secure the ultimate prize and get past the finishing line. Cardinal Camerlengo Fiore pensively looked around the magnificent chapel; even the windows had been blocked out as part of the ritual to make sure the

257

Cardinals had no contact with the outside world. He considered his next steps. He had always suspected that Cardinal Alphonso would gain a reasonable amount of votes but it was evident that he and his supporters held the balance of power.

To Cardinal Gregory, the politics of the situation were clear. He felt sure that most of the thirty-one voters who had backed Alphonso would do so again if he personally instructed them where to cast their votes. In other words, convincing his lifetime friend to side with him would surely assure him of victory at the next ballot. Cardinal Gregory knew he was close to the final hurdle; it was almost within his reach and he walked almost triumphantly down the centre of the chamber to meet face-to-face with Cardinal Alphonso, his entourage of doting supporters eagerly following in his steps.

"Cardinal Alphonso, I trust I can count on your support for the next ballot?" inquired Gregory confidently.

Cardinal Alphonso, leaning on his silver-headed walking cane, looked searchingly into his old friend's eyes.

"Brother Gregory, may we speak alone?" asked Alphonso, nodding towards the posse of supporters over his shoulder, who were straining to eavesdrop.

"Of course we can," he replied, and quickly whispered something in the ear of his trusted lieutenant, who promptly ushered the growing crowd of intrigued clergy away to another corner of the Chapel.

"What's on your mind, my old friend?" asked Cardinal Gregory as they moved out of earshot.

"We need to finish this papal election as soon as possible! We need to concentrate on more important matters – while we're locked in here the Satanica could be getting closer to the Book of Judas… If they reach it first there might not even *be* another papal election! What if there are urgent new developments that require our attention – it's imperative that Colonel Renauld receives our guidance and direction at the earliest opportunity!" whispered Alphonso fervently into his ear.

"Remember, there are only six of us within this room who know the full truth – we have a responsibility that weighs more than personal edification!"

In truth, Cardinal Alphonso was not quite as anxious as he pretended. He simply wanted to hear his friend's response to his urgent plea. The result of the first ballot had given him confidence that he could sway the next election but he had to make the right decision. *Time is of the essence,* he thought to himself, *but if we can get a result in the next ballot we should be able to brief Colonel Renauld by nightfall.*

"You're correct – we can finish this election quickly. I know you'll put your support behind me, my friend, and when this is finished I'll make sure that you sit next to me... You'll be my Cardinal Camerlengo – together we..."

"Am I interrupting anything?"

Both Cardinals turned around immediately.

It was the tall, imposing figure of Cardinal Fiore approaching from behind them.

"Apologies, it's not my intention to disturb your private conversation," he continued.

As usual, he was flanked on either side by Cardinal Deacon Weiss and Cardinal Bishop Lefebvre, who was rubbing his goatee beard with his fingers.

"No, you're not interrupting anything," responded Cardinal Alphonso politely before Gregory had a chance to speak.

"Excellent – then may I remind you, Brother Gregory, of the crisis that faces us at the moment. Only we know what's truly going on and the threat that hangs over us! I have said this before and I repeat it... This is not the time for division!" said Fiore firmly.

Cardinal Alphonso glanced at Gregory. He could sense his aggravation rising with every word that Fiore spoke.

"Cardinal Alphonso," continued Fiore, "you've been a wise and well-respected member of Pope Paul XII's inner circle for many years – the Satanica, which history tells us sprang to life here in the Vatican itself, is now trying to secure the Book of Judas. We've known of its existence for years, decades, but we failed to do what we should have done – destroy it!" he said forcefully.

Although they were out of earshot, a nearby group of Cardinals huddled in deep conversation, immediately raised their heads with the vehemence of the Fiore's closing remark

"Hindsight is a marvellous thing," replied Alphonso cautiously, wondering what Fiore was building up to.

"But we can't afford to make another mistake, can we?" persisted Fiore. "The time has arrived for you to decide, you Brother Alphonso – who between us can lead our church through this crisis. When you contemplate your decision, I would ask that you bear two points in mind – firstly, that it was Pope Paul XII's last wish that I should take over his mantle of responsibility…"

"How can we…" interrupted Gregory before Alphonso sharply raised his hand from his cane, gesturing for his fellow Cardinal to remain silent.

"And secondly," continued Fiore, ignoring the outburst. "Because the guidance needed to protect our faith in this time of crisis will be beyond Brother Gregory's capabilities!"

"That is outrageous!" snorted Gregory, shaking with rage.

"Is it, Brother Alphonso?" asked Fiore calmly, before turning away and heading back towards his supporters with Cardinals Weiss and Lefebvre only a few paces behind him.

"He can't get away with this," rasped Gregory furiously. In his moment of rage he temporarily forgot where he was but quickly came back to his senses when he saw all the eyes suddenly trained on him. Silence was encouraged throughout the election and all the Cardinals in the immediate vicinity had noticed the commotion.

"Calm yourself, Brother Gregory," said Cardinal Giacoma, approaching them in the wake of Cardinal Fiore's exit.

Cardinal Gregory took out a handkerchief and patted his mouth as his followers flocked back towards him.

"Are you all right?" asked his faithful lieutenant, reaching out to clutch his arm in a gesture of support.

"I'm fine, I'm alright," he fumed, wheezing slightly.

Cardinal Giacoma checked his watch; it was approaching the time when they should reconvene for the second ballot.

"Brother Alphonso, your loyal followers are waiting to hear from you," he said, indicating the corner of the Chapel where they were congregated.

"I'm coming now," replied Alphonso softly, and he ushered Giacoma back to the corner.

"Brother Alphonso," said Gregory, his composure returning. "We've known each other a long time. You know what I stand for and indeed what I'm capable of – I will trust and pray that you do the right thing."

Cardinal Alphonso looked into his eyes and nodded before turning to walk away, his hunched frame supported by his wooden cane. In the background, he heard the Secretary of the College of Cardinals informing the assembly that they would resume in five minutes.

That's all the time I need, he thought as he lurched back towards Cardinal Giacoma and the expectant priests. *My mind is made up!*

Chapter Twenty-Eight

Teterboro Airport, New York

The immigration officer barely scrutinized the passport before handing it back over the counter to Conchos. He received it with a nod, and walked past the glass-faced counter and down towards swinging doors at the end of the corridor that led out to the private charter airfield at Teterboro airport in County Bergen. It was mid-afternoon and the blue skies above his head confirmed the perfect flying conditions.

Conchos was satisfied with the arrangements. From the moment he had received the telephone call earlier that morning corroborating his carefully laid plans, everything had proceeded like clockwork. The twelve-kilometre journey to Teterboro Airport from Manhattan Island, passing through the Lincoln Tunnel, had been relatively trouble-free and having negotiated the passport kiosk without any hitches he was through the hardest part of his plan.

Kidnapping Heather had been easier than he thought. After the brothers and the girl had left the apartment, he had entered the building from the basement posing as a courier. He knew its exact location and used the lift from the car park to gain access to her floor. Heather never even contemplated the fact that her life could be in danger when she heard the sound of the apartment bell ringing. Without stopping to think, she opened the door and came face to face with her assailant. As soon as she looked into his ruthless, piercing eyes, void of any emotion, she realized her mistake and tried to push the door shut but it was too late. Conchos struck her forehead with deadly speed, just hard enough to stun her long enough for him to press a drugged cloth over her mouth and nose until her body went limp. She wanted to scream in panic as she felt the terror and fear build up inside her but her eyes rolled back and she slipped into the unconscious. Seconds later, Conchos pushed the apartment door closed and laid her prostrate body on the cold tiles of the hallway floor.

Conchos wanted his presence in the apartment to be as brief as possible. He worked quickly, binding her feet and hands before stuffing her body into a large courier's wheeled collection box. After leaving the instructions on the side table for the brothers, he shoved the box onto the trolley with no concern for her contorted body and proceeded back to his van in the basement. The car park attendant didn't give the courier van a second thought and unwittingly raised the barrier. Minutes later, Conchos and his unconscious hostage were on the way to the first of his planned hideaways.

The next day he had picked up a copy of the *New York Post* and learned that the Trenchards' next destination was Cairo, Egypt. Using his own established contacts, he double-checked the passenger lists of the outbound flights from JFK, which soon confirmed which plane they had boarded.

With the details of their final destination to hand, he made one call to a trusted member of the Satanica in Cairo with whom he had worked before and on whom he believed he could safely rely to follow through with his meticulous arrangements.

He gave him the details of the passengers travelling and then recited the message he was to write down and give them upon their arrival. Conchos made it abundantly clear, in no uncertain terms, how important it was to get the job done properly. The Egyptian, who had been a member of the Satanica for over fifteen years, did not need to be told twice. He had a sense of fear and dread as he remembered his previous unsavoury encounters with Conchos. He had seen some of the abominations he had performed in the past. He was all too familiar with what he was capable of and knew that his own life would be in danger if he failed in the tasks he had been given.

Since then he had been in touch with Amsterdam. He needed their assistance for the next part of his elaborate strategy, namely to get both himself and his victim from New York to their next destination in the North of Africa.

With the help of trusted members of the Satanica based in New York, the preparations had been put into place quickly. Conchos knew that his options were limited. He couldn't take a less risky course such as driving up to Canada or, alternatively, stopping to examine the possibility of travelling overland, or across water because there just wasn't time. Instead, he had arranged to charter a plane from Teterboro Airport directly to Nassau in the Bahamas where the plane would refuel before crossing the Atlantic to Rabat in Morocco. The pilot, called Ed Lehman, was just completing the final formalities with the aviation authorities before making his way out to the plane. He had been recommended to Conchos by one of the High Priests of Zorastri in Amsterdam. He still had his doubts. Despite Lehman being known as a loyal and proven affiliate of the Satanica, Conchos still felt uncomfortable with a total stranger playing such an important role in his carefully laid plan. As he walked across the tarmac towards the light aircraft he quietly made up his mind to kill him when they arrived at their final destination.

"I've filed the flight plans – we're clear to take off in twenty minutes," called Lehman stepping on board moments after Conchos had arrived.

"Ok – let's get going," replied Conchos, pulling the cabin door closed behind him.

He watched Lehman going through the normal pre-flight ritual, checking the various switches above his head. Turning back towards the tail of the plane, he leant over and pulled back the dividing screen behind the cabin. Smiling as he held back the curtain, he revealed the six coffin-length boxes that had been added to the light aircraft's cargo manifest. Satisfied, he pushed back the screen.

The cabin had four seats facing each other, but Conchos elected to sit with the pilot as they taxied down the runway and buckled himself into the cockpit seat. He sneered as he listened to Lehman's southern drawl while he communicated with the traffic controller. He had taken an instant dislike to the overweight American – even if the senior echelons of the Satanica had recommended him.

The control tower gave them clearance for take-off and the plane banked sharply as it headed for an altitude of seventeen thousand feet. As soon as they began to level off, Conchos undid his belt and returned to the long wooden crates at the back of the plane. He knew immediately which one contained his valuable cargo and he prized open the sealed lid with metal wrench. Inside it was filled with pieces of miniature polystyrene. He put in his hand and scooped them aside side to reveal the face of Heather Adams. Lying awake, utter terror still pulsing through her veins, she stared up at him through the oxygen mask he had placed over her head. Bulging slightly from the after-effects of the drugs, her eyes pleaded with her captor to release her from the terror of this physical and mental torture.

"Are you going to be good?" he asked calmly, brushing away some more of the polystyrene pieces from around the glass face-mask.

She nodded, her eyes beginning to brim with tears of fear and anxiety.

Conchos slowly lifted the mask off and withdrew the oxygen canister. Then, plunging his arms into the container, he helped her into an upright position. Heather's legs and hands were bound tightly with masking tape so he lifted her out and dragged her forward onto one of the four cabin seats.

The pilot looked around the cockpit door and gave a big grin when he saw what Conchos was doing.

"Well, well, isn't she a pretty one?" cooed Lehman in his strong southern accent. "I can see we might have some fun with you, baby, before we land," he laughed.

Conchos stood up and stepped towards the pilot. Heather watched as Lehman's expression froze on his chubby features. Ed Lehman was not a stupid man; he had been a member of the Satanica for a long time and the stories that circulated about the ruthlessness of Conchos were legendary.

"You will concentrate on flying – do you understand me?" he said menacingly, holding the cockpit door.

Lehman, realizing the company he was in, shook his head vigorously.

"Sorry, I understand perfectly," he muttered meekly and reached out to pull the cockpit door.

For a moment Conchos contemplated the moment when he would kill him and decided it was going to be a special one… He would inflict pain on Lehman like he would never have experienced before. *Your time will come,* he thought, before turning back to Heather.

"Let's hope your boyfriend loves you a lot," he said, reaching inside his case and producing a bottle of water. Carefully, he poured some into a plastic cup and then leant over, placing it close to Heather's mouth so she could take a drink. She gulped the water hungrily – her throat was parched and sore from the mouthpiece of the oxygen mask.

"Now try and sit back and relax," he commanded. "We have a very long flight ahead of us."

Her body aching and her heart still pumping, she watched him put his head back and close his eyes.

Chapter Twenty-Nine

Vatican City, Rome

The Dean of the College of Cardinals spoke into the microphone and called the senior Catholic clerics back to their seats. It was time for the conclave to hold their second secret ballot for the election of a new Pope.

Just outside St. Paul's Basilica, in Bernini's piazza, the media, the Catholic faithful and the thousands of onlookers caught up in the historic moment waited cheerfully and patiently for the impending announcement to be made. Happily for the masses, it was a glorious late afternoon in June and the square was bathed in sunshine.

From his office window in the tower at the southern end of the square, Colonel Renauld peered at the crowds down below. Again, he contemplated his decision to feed the six Cardinals with bogus information in an attempt to flush out the traitor. He still sensed that his gut feeling was correct but time was rapidly running out. Clasping his hands behind his back in anguish, he considered the profiles of the six most senior clerics in the Catholic faith again. *One's doubling-up as a member of the Satanica, I'm sure of it,* he pondered, brooding over the facts. *But how are they communicating?* So far, none of the telephone transcripts that had been brought to him by Major Dupont had given him any clue to the identity of the conspirator in their midst.

He stopped watching the crowds below and looked up at the chimney silhouetted above the rooftops housing the Sistine Chapel. The wispy black smoke was still rising into the air, signalling that the conclave had yet to reach their momentous decision.

Earlier that morning he had spoken to Goran, who was still based in London. He informed the Colonel that the two Trenchard brothers and their female companion, Anna Nikolaidis, had taken off for Europe from JFK Airport. After they had discussed their latest movements, Goran listened patiently as Colonel Renauld outlined the plan he had laid to trap the perpetrator of the Vatican leaks.

"I've informed them all that the entrance to the labyrinth containing the Book of Judas is situated south of Damascus near a place called Hom," revealed Renauld.

Goran listened attentively occasionally muttering his approval for the cunning scheme.

"We need to be patient," he had told Renauld after he had learnt that nothing out of the ordinary had been discovered in their recent communications. However, privately Goran was surprised. He knew that the information Renauld had fed them would be of vital importance to the Satanica so he was confused by the absence of communication. *If nothing's been discovered yet,* he pondered, *it's unlikely to transpire until after the new Pope is elected because till then all the six Cardinals are locked away in the Sistine Chapel*

"Are you sure you reviewed every single potential mode of communication?" enquired Goran, looking for any new angle that may help them.

For a few seconds the Colonel was pensive, mulling over the various channels that Major Dupont and his team were monitoring. They had been careful to locate all the potential telephone and computer communication points for each Cardinal as well as those within the Vatican's public domain. As he looked down at his ornamental desk he spied a stamped sheet of paper on the edge of his in-tray and suddenly an idea flashed into his head.

"You know I'm not sure we have," he said slowly and deliberately as he considered the full impact of his brainwave. *It may not be the standard form of communication,* he pondered, *but it would serve as a cover for anyone thinking the phones were tapped.*

"I should have thought of it earlier," he said crossly, chastising himself for his lack of foresight.

The idea had at least offered another channel of hope and, after ending the call with Goran, he immediately called Major Dupont into his office to issue him with a fresh set of instructions.

Am I clutching at straws? If nothing develops now how am I going to explain my actions to the new Pope and the Senior Cardinals? How will they react? I've probably staked my command, my entire career on this? he reflected.

Let's wait and see what Major Dupont comes up with, he thought, anxiously wringing his hands tightly together.

Inside the Sistine Chapel, the atmosphere was electric. The strain showed on Cardinal Gregory's face as he peered through the semi-darkness. Around him the scarlet-robed priests sat in their high-backed thrones began crafting their votes on their ballot papers for the second round of the election. The tradition to hold the election away from the gaze of the world was centuries old. It was written in the very first ecumenical charter governing the rules for the appointment of a papal successor. In the olden days, it had been held behind closed doors so that the priests could be alone, without the pressures of the outside world to affect their thoughts. This monastic behaviour, it was believed, supported their divine quest to be enlightened by the Holy Spirit when making their choice.

Cardinal Alphonso felt the burden of holding the casting block of votes was no longer on his shoulders. For better or worse the decision was now made. His dependable supporters had listened patiently to his views and had faithfully concurred that they would follow his lead.

In silence, one by one they rose from their seats and proceeded across the chamber floor towards the three scrutineers who presided over the ballot box. It stood in front of the Chapel's altar where the celebrated work, *The Last Judgement* by Michelangelo, exquisite in its detail, added to the remarkable and historic aura of the occasion. For many of the Cardinals it was impossible not to be emotionally moved when reciting the oath before such a monumental work of art.

As Cardinal Alphonso returned to his seat with the aid of Cardinal Giacoma and his trusty cane he graciously acknowledged the plaudits from either side of the chamber. The esteem and respect in which he was held throughout the Catholic world was unprecedented.

One by one, the Cardinals took it in turn to approach the ballot box at the foot of the Chapel's altar. Again they recited their oath before posting their ballot paper and bowing before the altar's crucifix.

The last Cardinal to take the oath and register his vote was none other than Cardinal Fiore himself. As he walked down the centre of the dark Chapel, he paused briefly in front of Cardinal Alphonso's throne. All the votes at Alphonso's command had now been recorded. Fiore stared into his eyes looking for a sign that might tell him the outcome but his face revealed nothing. The entire chamber appreciated the show that they were witnessing. Fiore fuelled the intensity of the occasion by nodding respectfully to his Cardinal brother before casting the final vote.

"Please remain seated for a few minutes before the scrutineers begin declaring the result of the second ballot," decreed the Cardinal Dean as the scrutineers wasted no time in beginning to organise the lodged ballot papers.

"Is this it or will it go to a third ballot?" wondered many of the elderly priests collectively as they set up the table in front of them to record the votes as they were announced. Around the chapel, the air of anticipation and suspense surrounding the pending declaration of the new Pontiff was overwhelming.

Half a kilometre away in Colonel Renauld's office the door burst open. Major Dupont in his excitement and eagerness to see his commanding officer had dispensed with all manner of formalities.

"What is it, Major?" barked Renauld, irritated by his improper entrance. He had not been caught totally unawares. Through the latticed window of his office, he had observed the strange reaction of the crowd below as they stared at something going on beyond his window's view down the right-hand side of the Piazza.

"I think we have something!" he gasped.

Dupont had followed the Colonel's instructions to the letter and the resulting discovery had been startling. His efforts to maintain some decorum in front of the expectant crowds were lost. En masse, they wondered what could possibly be going on as they watched him dash the length of the colonnade to give Colonel Renauld the news.

"Look at this Colonel," said Dupont, holding out a sheet of paper. *Please let this be the breakthrough!* thought Renauld, as he grabbed the sheet and began reading through its contents.

In the Sistine Chapel, the Dean, stern-faced, approached the microphone.

"Your Graces," he called, his amplified voice echoing around the chamber.

The murmuring subsided. Cardinal Gregory, frowning on the edge of his seat, peered down the hallway towards the Dean.

"I would like it to be known that the chosen scrutineers are ready to commence with the declaration of the second ballot to elect the Supreme Pontiff of the Apostolic See, the head of the Roman Catholic Church – in the traditional manner they will announce the vote on each of the registered ballot papers."

The Cardinal Dean turned to the first scrutineer and nodded.

"You may begin."

Further down the chapel, Cardinal Bishop Lefebvre reached out and

271

put his hand onto Fiore's arm. He knew his own future career also hinged on the elected successor to the papal throne.

As before, the first scrutineer opened the ballot paper, noted the contents and passed it on to the second. Again he noted the contents before handing it to the third scrutineer who then leaned towards the microphone and announced the name of either Cardinal Fiore or Cardinal Gregory as written on the ballot paper. This chain-like process would be repeated until all the votes, all one hundred and twenty of them, were called out, echoing around the great chamber.

"Cardinal Gregory," called the third scrutineer.

The intensity of the charged atmosphere was heightened as the first five votes announced by the scrutineer went to Cardinal Gregory.

This is it, thought Gregory – the Sistine Chapel was totally shrouded in silence. He looked down the centre aisle and smiled broadly at Cardinal Alphonso.

The scrutineers continued calling the names regardless of the murmurings around them when either of the Cardinals seemed to make a significant step forward. In the early stages it was neck and neck but after eighty votes had been announced a definite pattern was beginning to appear.

The scrutineers continued to call out the votes. The leader's pattern was confirmed but was it sufficient to give him the required majority?

Cardinal Gregory stared across the dark hall at Cardinal Fiore. They both had tears in their eyes as they realised that a result had been achieved.

The third scrutineer holding the ballot papers on a thread turned to the Cardinal Dean to allow him to make the final announcement.

"Within the laws and traditions of our Catholic faith," the Dean called out aloud. "We can praise our Lord God that a new Supreme Pontiff and Ruler of the Holy See has been chosen for the world!"

The Dean of the College of Cardinals, the most senior of the Cardinal Bishops was relishing every word as he reached the moment of truth.

"His Eminence Cardinal Camerlengo Fiore – eighty-one votes!"

Immediately, a wave of commotion broke out around the chamber as the Cardinals, sitting on their thrones, absorbed the result.

The Dean appealed for quiet before stepping down from his raised platform and walking down the aisle to present himself before the throne of the new Pope. The murmurings and congratulations continued until he reached the Cardinal Fiore when the Chapel suddenly fell quiet. There were still some traditional election criteria to be observed.

"Will you, Cardinal Camerlengo Fiore accept the results of this election?"

With the attention of the entire room focused on him, Cardinal Fiore confidently surveyed the scenes around the chamber. He saw Cardinal Gregory slumped in his seat being attended to by his close aides. Further along the sea of faces in front of him he met the gaze of Cardinal Alphonso. In an unprecedented step, Fiore stood up, walked over to Cardinal Alphonso's throne and bowed before him – an historic gesture for a newly anointed Pontiff. The chamber burst into spontaneous applause and Fiore smiled broadly at the elderly priest. Alphonso respectfully bowed in return to the new Pope and Fiore, determined to keep the decorum of the moment, raised his arm above his head and silence was restored immediately. Kissing the crucifix hanging on a long gold chain around his neck, he turned and walked humbly back to his violet-coloured throne.

"Cardinal Camerlengo Fiore?" repeated the Dean earnestly.

"I do accept," he said loudly for all to hear.

"Under the full authority of the Vicar of Christ, you are now the Supreme Pontiff of the Catholic Church – by which name would you like to be called?"

"Pope Leo the fourteenth," replied Fiore, in the past months he had given much thought to the name he would take if he were ever elected. The choice had not been difficult; time after time during his formative years when he had been studying late at night for his theological classes he had identified himself in the actions and sayings of the celebrated Pope, "Leo the Great".

Asked to stand again, the new Pope Leo XIV was escorted by his joyful and trusted aides, Cardinal Deacon Weiss and Cardinal Bishop Lefebvre into the Sacristy where three sets of robes, one large, one medium and one small were waiting for him. The Cardinals helped him don the white cassock, the white stockings and then assisted putting on the red slippers, each embroidered with a golden cross. Minutes later, he returned to his throne, adorned in the vestments of his office and then one by one, in order of seniority, each Cardinal in the Sistine chapel advanced to kiss his hand and kneel before him.

Cardinal Gregory was one of the first to pay homage. He looked pale and drawn as he struggled to get down on one knee. It was a tragic scene. The room strained to watch as the defeated Cardinal mustered all the dignity he could manage to laud the new Pope.

"My prayers are with you," mumbled Gregory, although he couldn't bring himself to look into his face.

After the procession of Cardinals was completed, the Dean approached and placed the ring of the Fisherman on his finger. It was a symbolic gesture and the new Pope removed it immediately and handed it back to the Secretary of the College of Cardinals. The ring would then be taken to be engraved and used as the seal on all important documents despatched from the Papal offices of the Supreme Pontiff.

Outside in St. Peter's Square, there was great rejoicing as the white smoke could be seen rising from the chimneys above the Sistine Chapel. The three scrutineers had wasted no time in burning the ballot papers but without the straw this time. The Vatican radio was also quickly off the mark as they broadcasted the wonderful announcement through the many intermittent speakers spread around the colonnades and walls of the city.

Standing on their feet applauding and cheering, the excitement of the multitude reached fever pitch as the loudspeakers relayed the news, in numerous languages, that the new pope would appear on the balcony shortly. The crowd's excitement was unprecedented.

In the office of Colonel Renauld, alerted by the cheering both he and Major Dupont approached the lattice window that looked out over the Vatican and the throng in St Peter's Square below.

"The new Pope has been chosen," remarked Major Dupont, seeing the pale smoke rise into the air.

"Indeed!" replied the Colonel, reading the contents of the sheet of paper once again.

The message was typed and brief.

"The entrance to the labyrinth rests at a place called Hom in Southern Syria."

Only six Cardinals know this information, he thought happily. He sensed he was getting closer to his target. *I knew I was right; I've caught the traitor at last!* he mused as he watched the celebrations taking place outside.

"Ok, Major, who was it? Where did you discover it?" he barked at his subordinate above the noise.

Outside, the crowd was reaching fever pitch in anticipation of the balcony doors opening with the new pontiff. This is what they had come to see and Major Dupont was forced to raise his voice to be heard.

"As you suspected, Sir, the message was sent by fax – it went to a number in Amsterdam, which we subsequently traced to an office bureau company that normally takes unsolicited faxes on behalf of unnamed clients."

The Cardinal Deacon appeared on the balcony to a crescendo of waving hands and noise. In his traditional robes, he began his formal task of introducing the new Pope to the world.

"Annuntio vobis gaudium magnum. Habemus Papam," he called out loud into the microphone.

"Major, who was it? Where did you locate the communication?" shouted the Colonel.

"The fax was sent from the office of Cardinal Fiore!" replied the Major.

Cardinal Fiore! thought the Colonel, momentarily stunned.

In the square below, the cheering suddenly came to a halt and the broadcasts were terminated as the Cardinal Deacon issued his last words. He informed the gathering that the new Pontiff would take the name Pope Leo XIV.

As he turned and left the balcony, the entire mass of people sank to their knees like a wave across the square, in expectancy of the new Pope.

The whole square covered with thousands of people fell silent as the figure appeared on the balcony.

The Colonel and Major stared out of the window transfixed as the white robed figure appeared.

"Oh my God!" cried the Colonel as he recognised the face of Cardinal Fiore, the newly elected Pope Leo the fourteenth.

Chapter Thirty

Cairo Airport, Egypt

As the plane slowed to a final standstill Anna stood up, stretching her legs, and opened the locker above her head. The Air France flight to Cairo had been delayed leaving Paris. The pilot had done his best to make up for some of the lost time but nevertheless, the plane still managed to land about twenty minutes late.

Simon saw Anna struggling to reach her luggage above her and he quickly stepped in to help.

"What time is it?" asked Anna tiredly as Simon, jammed in amongst the other standing passengers in the narrow aisle, handed down her carry-on bag. Her limbs were aching and she silently promised herself that she wouldn't get on another aeroplane for at least a year once this was all over.

"Late. It must be around ten o'clock or so," replied Simon, staring out of the small oval window into the darkness. The only lights he could see outside were those from other taxiing planes heading for the end of the runway and the bright yellowy glow from the square rundown building that was the airport terminal.

The wait to exit from the plane always irritated her but finally, ten minutes later, she was following the brothers down the staircase to the tarmac and the waiting bus that would ferry them to Immigration. Despite the late hour, the first thing she noticed was the rise in temperature and the humidity.

As they stood in the bus, Philip noticed Anna taking one of the moisturising tissues out of the packet and wiping her face in an attempt to freshen up.

"It must be about twenty-five degrees," he remarked as they suddenly lurched around a bend to draw alongside the airport building.

"Yes," she shouted above the noise of the engine. "I think we'll really feel the difference in temperature tomorrow – a bit more like my native Greece!" she said, smiling.

The sliding doors of the passenger bus burst open and they joined the frenzied exodus of passengers hurrying along the gangway trying to be the first in line to get processed through Passport Control. They marched along trying to keep up with the pace. Simon and Anna went through first and then stood by patiently on the other side while Philip's was being stamped.

"This place hasn't changed much," commented Philip as they entered the tatty baggage hall. It was in desperate need of renovation. He had travelled to Cairo on a few business trips in the past and he often wondered why governments would not invest more in their country's gateway. After all it was the showpiece through which every visitor to the country would have to travel.

Simon heaved one case after another off the old rubber conveyor belt and onto the lopsided trolley.

"I think that's everything," he called and started pushing towards the baggage screening ahead of the exit.

"Well, aren't we supposed to be receiving our next set of instructions any second now?" asked Anna as they settled into another queue.

"That's right," replied Philip. "I'm sure he knows we're here, he'll have the information right down to the flight we've landed on so I'm sure he's thought of some way of communicating with us."

Philip caught Anna's look of surprise.

"Best keep your eyes open!" he added.

With a grunt, the scruffy Egyptian bag handler, wearing a stained, sweaty pair of overalls and a mouldy white vest, swung their bags onto the belt of the X-ray machine. Behind the apparatus, the security guard sat slouched in his seat laughing and chatting to fellow officers. He occasionally turned his head to study the TV monitor in front of him before happily re-joining the conversation.

Philip helped put the bags back on the trolley. Emotional and tired, he was still struggling to come to terms with the fact that Heather was out there somewhere being held by a fanatic that would think nothing of killing her in cold blood. Hope was all that was driving him on. In fact it was all that he could cling to and he prayed that there would come a moment when she would be returned to him. There was a chance that if he, if they, could fulfil all the "Death Angel's" instructions to the letter then maybe he would hand over Heather unscathed. It was a chance that offered hope even if it was a slim one. Besides that, the killer had indicated that if they did what they were told then he might be allowed to speak with her during the course of the next few days. *Yes, if I can just speak with him, there's a chance that I can negotiate with him… offer him something he wants*, he thought, feeling a little more upbeat.

With all of their luggage re-loaded onto the rickety trolley they set off towards the exit where the sliding doors revealed a sea of expectant faces watching for their friends or relatives to come through. Some of them were European but on the whole they were local Egyptians, hanging over the rails, three or four deep in places, anxiously trying to pick out a familiar face from the exiting passengers. Even the balconies around the hall were full of waiting onlookers. At that late hour the busyness of the airport took them by surprise. *Every single international flight must land at midnight,* thought Philip as the sliding doors closed behind him.

"Come on, this way!" shouted Simon, pushing the trolley around a couple who had stopped to greet relatives alongside the barrier.

Philip overtook him as they walked towards the excited crowd through the hustle and bustle of the passageway. As he looked over the top of the heads towards the end of the gangway he could see a mass of placards being waved in the air. They all had names on and some of the more up-market banners were being held by smartly dressed concierge attendants from some of the city's five-star properties.

"Well, what do we do now?" said Anna as they came towards the end of the gallery of spectators.

Philip was about to suggest that they wait for a while when he suddenly heard his name being called out above the commotion.

"…Trenchard, Simon Trenchard, Anna Nikolaidis…" the shrill voice repeated. This time Anna turned as she heard her name being called.

Philip saw the placard branded with the Hilton Hotel being waved above the heads of the crowd. Walking towards the sign he guessed that the standard bearer was probably a driver from the hotel. *So this is how he plans to keep in touch with us,* he mused. *He's organised our hotel for us to make sure he can observe and communicate with us whenever he wishes.* Anna and Simon were thinking the same thing as the Egyptian driver, smiling in recognition, lowered his sign and hurried towards them.

"Mr. Trenchard?" he asked, addressing Philip cordially as he got closer.

"That's right," he nodded.

"Please come with me. Everything has been arranged for you," he said politely in good English. "My car's parked just outside and I will be happy to take you straight to the hotel. You must be tired after your long flight?"

"Have rooms already been arranged for all of us?" asked Simon curiously.

"Of course, sir," replied the driver, a bit puzzled by the question.

Simon quickly realised that he wasn't going to get very far questioning the hotel driver about the source of his instructions. He made a mental note to try and question the hotel Reception when they arrived but he suspected that would also be a closed avenue.

"Ok," said Philip, raising his eyebrows, "it looks like these are the directions we're meant to follow – let's go!"

Unbeknown to them, the watchful man above them leaning against the balcony railing in the mêlée of the waiting crowd, observed every step they took. He watched, pleased with his evening's work as they followed the hotel driver out of the terminal and in to his waiting car. With the luggage loaded, the driver slammed the boot shut. As the car pulled out, he reached inside his jacket for his mobile phone out of his pocket as they sped off through the busy traffic in the direction of downtown Cairo.

Chapter Thirty-One

Vatican City, Rome

"Put him through," said Colonel Renauld irritably into the receiver.

Since the announcement had been made to the media, he had still not spoken to Cardinal Fiore who had now renamed himself to the world as Pope Leo XIV.

"Colonel?" said the voice at the other end.

"Goran, I was beginning to wonder if we had a problem."

"We do have a problem, Colonel," replied Goran, dryly getting straight to the point. It was late evening in England and he was also not in the mood for normal telephone pleasantries despite the fact that it was his commanding officer on the other end of the line.

"It would appear that the Satanica have moved much quicker than we thought they could!" he continued.

"What do you mean?" asked the Colonel, steeling himself for another setback. The progress and deception of the Satanica was deeply irritating. They had infiltrated the Vatican and were obviously closing in on their quest to reach the Book of Judas first.

"I mean, it looks like the Satanica's executioner, the same one that has carried out the publicised 'Death Angel' murders, has kidnapped Philip Trenchard's fiancée!"

Colonel Renauld rocked back in his chair as he tried to rationalise the repercussions of such a manoeuvre.

"It's clever, I'll give them that," admitted Goran reluctantly. "We've been concentrating on the wrong area – we thought he'd be on their trail, probably following them to the Far East but instead he's found a way of bringing them to him! He's probably controlling every move they make!"

"What does this mean?" asked Renauld.

"It means that the job of destroying the book is going to be much harder than we imagined..." The tone of his voice changed. "Are you absolutely convinced that no one else has access to our secret, Colonel?"

"Of course I'm sure," he replied indignantly. On this point he felt sure.

"So where are they now?"

"My information is that they're on the way to Cairo. It would appear that the Satanica want them to finish the job... They want them to obtain all the arkheynia before they step in!"

"I see," responded Renauld. This was an important development and they would need to come up with a solution.

"I'd like to hear your thoughts on this later!" he added.

"Can I take it that now Cardinal Fiore is the new Supreme Pontiff that we can expect the level of support we need?" Goran enquired.

The remark made Colonel Renauld revert his mind to the problems that were closer to home.

"We have a real problem here!" he muttered.

He then informed Goran of the new evidence that they had uncovered over the past few hours. He told him about the faxed communication that had gone through the office of Cardinal Camerlengo Fiore.

"This is just incredible!"

Goran shook his head in disbelief. He was amazed to find out that the discovery pointed to the newly crowned Supreme Pontiff himself. It was an absurd thought. The Head of the Catholic Church and Ruler of the Holy See, whom the world would watch being crowned the next day could, unbelievably, also be a High Priest of their sworn enemy, the Satanica. The concept was almost too ridiculous to contemplate.

"It's not straightforward; there is a glimmer of hope," the Colonel continued. "We checked the time of the fax and it was late at night – almost any one of the six priests could have sent it. Access wouldn't have been a problem because Fiore's office was not locked at that time."

"What are you proposing to do now?" enquired Goran.

"I've been considering all my options since I discovered the news. It confirms our hunch that we have a leak but it doesn't tell us who it is. I could try confrontation in the hope it might provoke a reaction but without categorical evidence it could backfire. The traitor is obviously a cool customer and if we show our hand too early it might allow him to retreat behind his false persona and we'll end up none the wiser! I need to work out a ruse that will expose him further – in the meantime I do know that our aim of destroying the Book of Judas is still our overriding objective and whatever else happens we must not let the Satanica get their hands on it!"

"What are you going to say to the Pope Leo XIV?"

"I won't be granted an audience until tomorrow morning. In my view the least likely suspect in this whole affair is Cardinal Alphonso – I am toying with the idea of informing him of developments and seeking his council."

There was a pause before Goran responded.

"I agree with you," he replied.

"But remember, time is not on our side here and we know that one of them is a High Priest of the Satanica hiding within our midst. If you reveal that you know that what do you think will happen?" he asked rhetorically.

"You will not be able to trust any of them… On the positive side you'll probably stop any flow of information back to their central command because the traitor's not going to risk exposing himself again but at what cost? I think you're right. Don't reveal your hand but work out a scheme to flush him out. You have to start somewhere and I agree Cardinal Alphonso is the least credible as our infiltrator; although I'd have said the same about Cardinal Fiore!"

"Yes," said Colonel Renauld, rubbing his chin as he considered his words. "I think I also need to make it clear that none of the Cardinals are allowed to leave the Vatican, although this will raise questions – if it *is* Fiore we'll know soon enough because he'll want to use the powers of his office to bring our mission to destroy the book to an end – in fact one of his first acts will probably be to remove me from office!"

As they continued speaking on the phone there was a knock on his office door.

"Hold on a moment," Renauld said irritably covering the mouthpiece before barking, "enter" towards the door.

Major Dupont marched in.

"Sorry to interrupt, Colonel, I have an urgent communication for you!"

Renauld opened the note. Frowning, he quickly read the contents.

"Confirm my receipt of the message and acknowledge I'll be there as requested," he commanded.

Major Dupont noted the response and looked up.

"That will be all,"

Major Dupont saluted before leaving his commander's office

"Well, this could be seen as good sign," suggested Renauld, lifting his hand from the receiver.

"What is it Colonel?"

"Our new Pope, Leo XIV, has put affairs of office and his own coronation to one side and asked me for an appointment to meet with him first thing tomorrow morning!"

Chapter Thirty-Two

The skies over Northern Africa

For Heather, the flight seemed interminable. Still bound by tape at the wrists and ankles, her body ached from the unnatural positions she had to assume to get in her vain attempts at getting comfortable. From listening to Conchos's intermittent conversations with the pilot during the last leg of the flight, she had gleaned that they were approaching their final destination. They were going to land somewhere near the port of Alexandria on Egypt's the Mediterranean coast.

The cabin light had been on most of time and despite the fact they had flown mostly during the night she had not managed much sleep. On route, they had landed briefly in Nassau to refuel. The sun had been setting as they took off again and now, looking out of the oval window, she could make out the orangey glow of dawn breaking through on the horizon.

Turning back she looked at the cruel, sinister face of Conchos who was sat on the seat facing her across the aisle. His eyes closed and head tilted back asleep.

They had barely spoken throughout the flight and when they did it was normally at her bequest – to ask for a drink of water or to fulfil nature's requirements. When they had landed a second time at Rabat she had tried to engage him conversation. She thought that if she could develop or nurture a relationship with him then maybe it could help. The attempt was flawed from the outset – Conchos was not interested and certainly had no intention of entering into any meaningless dialogue. He left her questions and comments unanswered and displayed no compassion whatsoever and she was left with the ghastly feeling that her situation was even worse than she could have imagined. He was devoid of any emotion.

With the light trickling into the cabin through the porthole-like windows, she continued to stare at the motionless figure of Conchos. The cabin was silent except for the constant purr of the engines.

"You know the Angel of Death is always beside you!" said Conchos coldly without moving or opening his eyes.

Heather's heart leapt and she screamed in fright as his eyes suddenly burst open, staring at her intensely.

"Your flight's nearly over," he continued and smiled he stood up from his seat and leant over the top of her face.

She convulsed with terror as she smelt his putrid breath close to her face.

"I've got special plans for you," he whispered softly and, brushing her blonde hair to one side, he kissed her on the cheek. Her body shook with fear, as he slowly pulled away. She felt as if she were being strangled, unable to breathe.

Standing up fully, he smiled at her, delighting in the fear and terror he could provoke with a click of his fingers. Her eyes glistening as they filled with tears she watched him pull open the cockpit door and step through to join the American pilot. The door clicked shut behind him.

Heather rolled her head against the cabin wall and sobbed. *Please let this nightmare end,* she begged silently. The hopelessness of her plight had removed what little fighting spirit she had left. *Where will Philip be now?* she wondered as she felt the plane lurch to one side as the pilot pointed the nose towards the ground for the final landing.

Fifteen minutes later, she could see the deep blue water of the Mediterranean Sea as they burst through the clouds. The plane banked one last time before landing at a barely used runway just outside the Egyptian City of Alexandria.

Ed Lehman steered them down the runway and they parked near some old disused hangars. There was a welcoming party. A black sedan sped out to greet the plane as they came to a halt.

Conchos opened the cabin door and let down the steps.

Heather watched in earnest as a round Egyptian face with a thick, bushy moustache appeared at the doorway. He was a large, rotund man clearly struggling with the exertion of climbing the three steps and sweating profusely in the heat of the day.

"Are we ready to go, Sami?" called Conchos. The tone of his voice left no doubt that a negative response would not be tolerated.

"Everything is taken care of," he answered with a grin. He was pleased with his own performance. In Egypt, if you had the right connections and money to spend you could make anything happen. It had cost more than he thought but Sami had used his influence to ensure that their flight would not receive any attention from the airport authorities and not be logged in any civil aviation records.

Conchos turned to Heather.

"This is the procedure – we need to walk quickly and quietly together to the car outside. Do you think you can manage that?" he asked.

Heather nodded her head in confirmation.

"Good, don't do anything stupid – I don't want to do something I'll regret… Do you understand?"

She nodded again.

"Right, let's take this off," he said, bending down and ripping away the tape that was binding her ankles together.

Grabbing her under the arm, he hauled her roughly to her feet. She stumbled as she felt the circulation returning to her legs.

"Ready?" asked Conchos.

Gritting her teeth she nodded again.

"I want you to walk down the steps. When you get to the bottom wait – I shall be just behind you. When I'm alongside, take my arm and together we'll walk across the runway and get into the back seat of the car."

Painfully, Heather edged herself out, lowering her head as she stepped through the cabin doorway. Immediately she felt the simmering heat and intense bright light of the Egyptian morning. Following his instructions carefully, she descended on to the tarmac. Waiting for him at the bottom, she squinted through the sunlight trying to survey the scene. There was not much to see, apart from the old hangars there was an administration building with a few cars parked next to it. *That must be it,* she thought. *He must be worried about the people behind those windows seeing me.* Any further notions she may have had disappeared completely as she felt Conchos's hand touch her shoulder.

Together, they walked across to the car whereupon the rotund Sami came scuttling across to open the back passenger door.

Conchos watched Heather get in and closed the door. He had unfinished business.

"Get ready to go – I'll be back in a minute," called Conchos to Sami before he turned and headed back up the steps of the plane to the cockpit.

"Be quick," replied Sami. "The shift is going to be changing very soon!"

Moments later he reappeared. Puzzled, Heather watched him push up the steps and lock the plane from outside. Speeding past the administration building towards the outer perimeter, they paused very briefly at the airport security gate where Sami handed over three entry passes and the guard duly obliged by lifting the barrier.

"We should get to the house in about forty minutes," smiled Sami over his shoulder as they roared off for the outskirts of Cairo down the deteriorating dual carriageway.

A few days later, alerted by the foul, disgusting smell, a couple of guards patrolling the airport broke into the chartered plane to discover the cause. Clutching handkerchiefs tightly to their noses and brushing the flies away, they found the unidentifiable body of the pilot, Ed Lehman. The skin on his face and neck had been peeled away, leaving a grotesque red mask. His eyelids had been removed and his head was fixed, pinned by a stiletto knife that had been stabbed through the tongue onto the dashboard in front of him.

Chapter Thirty-Three

Cairo, Egypt

Anna and Simon sat opposite each other in the coffee shop of the Hilton Hotel overlooking the River Nile while they finished their breakfast. The previous night's check-in had been relatively uneventful. Arriving around midnight, they had gone straight to Reception in the lobby and as suspected, had found that three rooms had been conveniently booked in their names. Simon had immediately suggested re-booking into a suite so they could be together but Philip was not keen on the idea.

"What if the kidnapper wants to get in touch with us?" he had argued. "We don't want miss any communication because we're in the wrong room or irritate him more than we have to!"

For a moment, Philip had awful visions of him taking out his anger on Heather.

Simon felt like saying that it was not important and that as long as they were in the correct hotel that's all that would matter to him but decided against it. He knew his brother too well; any objection would have provoked an unnecessary and irate confrontation. In the past he had witnessed Philip's volcanic rage when he was anxious and under duress and that was in less stressful circumstances than they were facing now. Anna felt tired as she silently watched the exchange. She was pleased Simon had not pushed the matter; all she wanted was her bed. Besides if he felt strongly about it he could take it up again the next day.

"No problem," Simon duly concurred that it was probably best to keep arrangements as they were.

Taking the lift up to their rooms on the eighth floor, they all unanimously agreed that sleep was the priority and that they would convene again at eight o'clock in the coffee shop on the ground floor where the hotel served a buffet breakfast.

It was now just after eight-thirty in the morning and Simon lifted the silver coffee pot to pour Anna and himself a second cup.

"Have you checked what time it opens?" she asked while buttering some toast.

She was excited about their next task. After breakfast, they would enter the world-famous Egyptian Museum and try to locate the third and final arkheynia. On the flight over, they had all studied the information folder Felix Bairstow had given them along with the original notes left by their grandfather, Sir Lawrence Trenchard.

"Nine o'clock is what the receptionist said – we've got a bit of time yet and, let's face it, we don't have to far to go, do we!" replied Simon, grinning as he checked his watch.

The Hilton Hotel was situated perfectly for the assignment they had in mind. In fact the coffee shop windows looked out directly towards the landmark museum's entrance. There was even had a separate exit to the street, allowing you to avoid the confusion of going back through the hotel lobby.

"Do you think Philip's going to be Ok?" she asked candidly after his earlier than expected departure from the breakfast table. She was genuinely concerned. *Impossible to imagine what he's going through, but it must be torture,* she thought.

Philip had joined them at eight for breakfast but had not stayed very long. He had eaten some of the buffet before deciding that he might as well get on with some of the jobs they had in hand, the first of which was to get the Judas Scroll and the map safely back into their possession. Rather than waiting for an appointment, he had decided that he would make a start now across the city to the Heliopolis district where the Cairo office of his investment bank was based. He knew they opened their doors at eight-thirty and he should arrive shortly after that.

"I'm not sure," replied Simon. "We're going to have to keep a careful eye on him. He seems to be thinking and acting rationally but I know what you mean – remember, all he cares about right now is getting Heather back. During the course of the next few days we're going to have to make some decisions that will need clear and unemotional thinking; we've got to be sure that when the time comes he makes the right choices because there won't be any second chances!"

"You're right," she agreed, nodding her head.

She liked the way Simon had phrased the last point. It gave her some hope for a difficult conversation she wanted to have with him later on but wanted to broach with him now. She thought if she could start the thought process then it would help later on.

"Simon... Imagine we find this third arkheynia and we use the maps to locate the hidden entrance to the labyrinth – what happens next?"

Simon looked at her blankly for a moment before responding.

"I guess we recover Heather and the Satanica finally get what they're looking for – the Book of Judas."

"Yes, but what does that mean exactly?" she repeated. She brushed a wisp of her black hair that had fallen across her face.

Simon studied her pensively as he took a sip of coffee. *She really is unimaginably beautiful,* he thought. When she stared at him like that she had an allure that captivated him.

"Simon..." she said, noticing the look in his eyes. They both smiled.

"Simon, take me seriously. I really think this is something we need to talk about," she repeated firmly but grinning all the same.

"Ok, Ok," he replied, smiling. He could see she was getting frustrated.

"I agree with you it's very important and I agree we have to discuss it in much more detail but let's talk about it later – right now it's time we headed off to the museum and found the third arkheynia."

Anna looked at him scornfully.

Simon waved his hand in the air at the waiter who recognised the signal and promptly brought the bill for him to sign.

"Need anything from your room before we go?" he asked.

"No, I've got everything," she replied, standing up.

"Come on then, let's go."

And together they walked to the glass swing door that opened into Tahrir Square and the prominent museum building across the street.

Anna looked up at the sandy coloured exterior of the museum. Although she had visited it on several occasions in the past she had never grown fond on the building itself. She always thought it was a bit one-dimensional and the neo-classical style was not as magnificent as it should have been considering the amazing treasures and artefacts that it housed. The building was constructed in 1897 during the reign of Khedive Abbass Helmi II and opened its doors to the public five years later in 1902. Despite being unimpressed by its grandeur, she still marvelled at its contents. With over a hundred exhibition halls, the first collection had been transferred at the turn of the century from the Boulaq Museum where the treasures had been assembled by the eminent French archaeologist August Mariette. The collection of rare and priceless artefacts had grown substantially since the initial construction, not least because of the awe-inspiring treasures found at the tomb of the boy Pharaoh, Tutankhamen. The discovery of an intact chamber in the Valley of the Kings by Howard Carter in 1922 catapulted the world's recognition of the museum to new heights. Pictures of the gold face-mask found covering his mummified remains in the sarcophagus adorned many magazines and books, capturing the public's imagination

294

on the fascinating and splendid history of Ancient Egypt. This interest had now manifested itself as more than one and half million tourists entering the museum's portals.

During Anna's apprenticeship days, when she had been on archaeological tours of Giza and Luxor, she had taken the opportunity while in Cairo to visit the museum on many occasions. The place always made her feel in awe of the brilliant ancient Egyptian civilisation that inhabited the region so many centuries ago. She loved this museum and had spent countless hours roaming the halls admiring the coins, papyrus, sarcophagi and scarabs that told the story of Egypt in the Old, Middle and Modern Kingdoms. Every time she spotted new artefacts that she had not seen before.

Stepping outside the coffee shop, they left the cool air-conditioned interior for the intense forty-degree heat of the early midsummer's day. As usual on the streets of Cairo, the traffic was congested and Simon grabbed Anna's hand tightly as they weaved between the speeding vehicles across Tahrir Square.

"You realise finding the third arkheynia would've been near impossible without your grandfather's directions," remarked Anna, doing her best to keep up. "There are over one hundred and fifty thousand artefacts stored and displayed here; if it's been moved from its location for any reason we're in big trouble!"

"Is that likely?" yelled Simon above the irate hooting of car horns.

"Well, they do change things about every now and then."

"In which case, keep your fingers crossed or else you're going to have to go through every room and every display till you find it," he said, smiling.

At the museum entrance there was a queue of chattering schoolchildren in their smart blue uniforms waiting while their teacher busily negotiated their entry with the attendant in the kiosk. One of the pretty seven-year-old girls looked up and grinned cheekily at Anna. She winked back.

"Whereabouts is the arkheynia?" asked Simon, pulling out the wad of Egyptian pounds he had been given by Philip earlier on.

"According to the notes, it is in the Great Hall of Rameses II, which is located on the first floor of the East Wing."

Simon took his change and they entered the main ground floor lobby of the museum where the imposing, towering statues of Amenhotep III and Queen Tiye sitting regally on their thrones became the immediate focus for all new visitors. The stone staircase ran up either side of the impressive figures that stared out across the atrium. Simon saw something else that fascinated him and walked over towards two smaller statues carved and painted out of limestone.

"Amazing," he said, moving closer to get a better look.

He looked down at the label and saw that the carving depicted a prince, possibly Rahotep the son of King Sneferu along with his wife Nofret.

"It was the convention in 2500BC and earlier to paint the man darker than the woman," said Anna as she watched Simon paying particular attention to the statue of Nofret.

The painted figurine was wearing a long sheath white dress with a mantle, a wide necklace with concentric rings and a black wig with a headband of rosette designs.

"She looks just as I imagined Cleopatra to look!" he said before he received a firm tug on his sleeve.

"Come on, we have work to do!" Anna scolded, tugging his arm in the direction of the staircase. Simon smiled and looked up around the hall. There was a balcony running around the entire perimeter of the upper floor.

Anna edged forward through the roaming groups of eager visitors. Although the museum had not been open long it was already a hive of activity with most of the tourists hovering around the displays or following the tour guides who were keenly demonstrating their abundant knowledge of the ancient artefacts by waxing lyrical about the treasures around the room. Reaching the top of the stairs, Anna strode purposefully down the wide stone corridor that she knew led to the Great Hall of Rameses II. Simon followed in her footsteps, making a mental note every now and again to come back and look at one of the exhibits in more detail when he had the luxury of more time.

There first objective was to locate the arkheynia's whereabouts but they also had some reconnaissance work to do. As they walked along Simon noticed one of the passageway doors was open. It was obviously not a thoroughfare for visitors so he paused to have a look inside. Anna, who was pacing on ahead, didn't even notice he had stopped. As he peeked in, a scruffily dressed Egyptian janitor clutching a broom suddenly approached him.

"Would you like to see the mummies?" he whispered hoarsely as if he was scared of being overheard.

"I can show you," he urged indicating through the door a room that was clearly cordoned off from the public.

Pausing to think for a moment, Simon suddenly nodded and took out a few Egyptian pound notes, which immediately made the old, unshaven janitor's eyes of light up. He took the money gratefully and opened the door wider.

"Follow me," the caretaker beckoned.

Forgetting Anna for a moment, he furtively followed him around the roped off area and through the door beyond. *This is clearly forbidden!* thought Simon but he threw caution to the wind. His first priority wasn't a keen interest in seeing the decaying remains of the mummies; he was sure that this was a regular financial scam run by the janitor for many unsuspecting tourists. His main objective was to establish if there were any new angles he could discover that might help them to enter the museum and capture the arkheynia later on.

"See," grinned the janitor, displaying a row of uneven, yellowing teeth and waving his arm at around the room. Simon entered. In coffin-like, glass cases one above another lay the remains of a dozen or more mummified Kings and Queens of Ancient Egypt.

The seedy grin quickly changed to puzzlement as the caretaker watched while Simon walked straight past the cases and onwards towards the door at the other end of the room.

"No, no – not over there!" he whispered loudly.

He was confused; did the Englishman not want to see the mummies? Besides he thought if he went through that second door then there was a strong possibility that he could get into real trouble.

Simon ignored him and quickly grabbed the handle. The old infrastructure of the building was well past its prime; with the wood decaying around the doorframe and the white paint peeling off, it was really showing its age.

"Stop, you can't go in there!" shouted the janitor, suddenly scared that his carefully laid plan to earn some extra money was going astray.

The door was stiff but Simon used his strength and jerked it open. Finding a potential avenue in and out of the museum was essential. If it meant he had to push deeper into the museum's out of bounds section he would not hesitate to do so. He had fully expected the door to lead to another room but what he saw came as a promising surprise. Pausing momentarily, he considered the old wooden staircase in front of him. *This could be my chance,* he thought hopefully.

Huffing, the scruffy janitor caught up with him and tugged his sleeve.

"Englishman, you can't go in there, it's forbidden – we'll both be in trouble, big trouble!"

Simon looked at him and fished in his pocket for his wallet. The man's eyes lit up again as he stared, mesmerised by the thick bundle of notes being pulled out.

"Where do these stairs lead?" asked Simon.

"They go to the basement... The store room in the basement," he confided, riveted to the money being waved in front of him.

"Now listen… You wait here, I would like a few minutes to go down these stairs, do you understand?" he said, raising his eyebrows and extending the thick bundle of notes.

"Ok Englishman, but you must be quick – the museum police pass this way all the time," he replied, reaching out to grab the ready money.

"No, when I get back," Simon commanded and pulled it away sharply.

The man scowled and reluctantly nodded his agreement.

"Just be quick!" he urged.

Quickly, he descended down the staircase. It was dark and dingy and he could tell from the dust and the musty smell that they were barely used. Passing the door that he assumed would lead to the ground floor, he continued until he reached the door at the bottom. Slowly turning the knob on the door and listening hard for any unusual sounds he peered out. There was silence as he saw a dark, sandy coloured passageway disappearing into the murkiness ahead of him. *Is it worth going any further?* he wondered, seeing a row of cement bags, pots of paint and other tools of the builders' trade lining up against the opposite wall. As his grandfather had highlighted in his notes, the underground chambers of the museum were vast and decrepit but as his grandfather's documents had also told them, it looked as if modernisation was finally catching up and there were some renovation plans afoot.

As he pondered his next move, he heard the constant sound of footsteps and was about to retreat back up the stairs when he realised that the noise was coming from above his head. He looked up and saw a metal grille that extended slightly beyond the building's foundations into the street pavement outside. *That's enough. It's not worth taking any more risks at this stage*, he thought and quickly retraced his steps back up to the first floor.

At the top, the museum janitor stood anxiously holding the door.

"Quick, Englishman!" he hissed as he heard him returning.

Pushing the door shut behind him, he held out his hand. He wanted his money.

"What's your name?" asked Simon as he pulled out his wallet and took out the bundle of notes.

"My name is Hareb, Englishman," he replied, gleefully snatching the money. Without waiting, he pushed the cash into his waistband and urged him back across the room.

"Come, we must be quick!"

Simon hurried past the glass cases with the mummified remains of ancient Egyptian royalty back to the main East Wing corridor of the museum.

Outside, Hareb eyed Simon quizzically. When he had disappeared down the staircase he had tried to work out what it was that the Englishman really wanted. With the roll of money safely stashed away he sensed there might be opportunities for further personal gain.

"What is it Englishman? What is it that you want?" he repeated with a frown.

Before Simon could reply he noticed the distraction in Hareb's eyes. Suddenly his face dropped as he stared over his shoulder.

"You must go!" he whispered abruptly, suddenly changing direction and trying to pretend he was engrossed in completing one of his regular janitor chores. Simon took his lead but looked back over his shoulder to see what caused the sudden state of consternation.

A museum guard, wearing his light green uniform, turned into their hallway. He caught sight of Hareb and immediately started stepping briskly towards them.

Fortunately for them the hallway was full of a large group of tourists admiring a rare "old kingdom" artefact housed in a rectangular glass case. The guide was eloquently pointing out that it was a rare, painted limestone statue of Kai, a high-ranking priest of Pharaoh Khufu dating back to 2575 BC that had been found on the Giza plateau as recently as three years earlier.

"What are you doing here? Get on with your work," grunted the guard menacingly at the cowering janitor. He was suspicious and fully aware of the little schemes that the museum's cleaners devised to supplement their income.

Simon, trying to blend into the background, watched as Hareb seemed to shrivel at the sound of the guard's words. Pretending to admire one of the display cabinets, he watched Hareb finally slip away. The zealous guard, satisfied that he had thoroughly admonished the janitor for his break in routine, continued ambling down the corridor.

As soon as he felt it was safe, Simon stopped inspecting the exhibit case in front of him and hurried in the direction of the departing janitor. He had established a useful contact now and maybe he could obtain some more information or even secure some inside assistance. Pushing through the crowd, he spotted him over the heads of some tourists. Racing on, he caught up with him just as he was about to enter the washroom. *Probably to count his booty,* thought Simon.

The janitor paused, looking around anxiously to make sure there was no sign of any guards.

"Can you meet outside later? I will make it worth your while," Simon urged.

Hareb looked at him suspiciously before answering.

"Ok, Englishman, where?"

"Can you meet me on the other side of Tahrir Square – there's a tea shop with a blue canopy over it. Do you know it?

"Yes, Al Sulayman's," he responded.

"Four o'clock?"

The janitor nodded and disappeared into the washroom.

Simon retraced his steps, walking slowly back down the corridor towards the Great Hall of the Pharaoh Rameses II. Privately, he wondered whether Hareb would actually turn up. *We'll have to wait and see,* he thought, suddenly remembering that Anna would be getting concerned about his whereabouts.

Entering the Great Hall, he saw her standing in front of an exhibition case. Anna turned with one hand on her hips as she saw him approaching.

"And where have you been?" she asked curiously.

"I'll tell you later. It might be something that can help us."

"Very mysterious," she said, shrugging. She felt mildly put out by his reluctance to tell her where he had been.

"Well, I've got some good news," she continued. "The third arkheynia is right where your grandfather said it would be – can you see it?" Anna pointed towards a table cabinet in front of them with a glass top containing a wide array of ancient relics and antiquities.

Simon eyes moved from one artefact to another as he tried to locate it. The pieces were all carefully pinned down on a foam base covered with an off-white cloth. Next to each fragment was a hand-written card giving all the known historical data surrounding each item. Scanning the contents it didn't take him long to pick out the unusual, distinctive shape of the final arkheynia.

"Read the card, it's fascinating," said Anna.

"This fragment of bone is believed to have originally come from the upper part of the human body. It was discovered in the late nineteenth century, around 1889 by French archaeologists investigating the remains of two bodies that were found in a cave along the West Bank of the Red Sea. Peculiarly, this section of bone did not come from the remains of either of the two bodies. Their cause of death remains unknown although there is some evidence to suggest that they had travelled from the North and came from an extreme Jewish society known as the Essenes. Theories have been put forward suggesting that they took shelter in the cave to protect and safeguard this fragment

302

of bone, which has been shaped and dyed 'blood red' at the round end. The purpose or use of this artefact remains a mystery but experts believe that it carries an unknown value and rare significance."

"Well the experts weren't wrong were they?"

"Amazing," agreed Anna. "They must have been travelling to place it in some far off location."

"Just sitting there… It's tempting isn't it? A shame we can't just reach in and grab it!"

"I know," replied Anna, "but look at the cabinet – it's locked solid from the side."

"Mind you the security in here doesn't seem to be that good does it?"

He looked around at the other visitors wandering around the displays. There were no CCTV cameras on the wall or any other obvious safety measures governing the defence of treasures that were considered to be priceless. In a way, he was not totally surprised, he had read a notice on the way in saying they were finally going to get round to installing a new air conditioning system in about six months' time. All the signs pointed to the fact that the museum was lacking strong financial investment.

"What we need is someone with access to these cabinets," muttered Simon, wondering whether his janitor friend might be able to help them.

"We might as well go back and give Philip the good news – at least we don't have to waste time trying to find it!" she suggested positively.

Twenty minutes later they strolled back into the lobby of the Hilton Hotel. Simon used the in-house phone to call his brother's room and was pleased to hear him pick up the receiver.

"Did everything go Ok at your firm's office?"

"Yes, no problems, I've got the Judas Scrolls back in our custody –

how about you?"

Simon was please to hear that he sounded considerably more upbeat than earlier on.

"Yes, we've found it – why don't you come down and we'll discuss our next step in the lounge?"

"I'll be down shortly," he replied. "I just want to make sure they've stored our Scrolls in a safe place."

"See you in a minute," said Simon who then looked up to see Anna window-shopping at a jewellery boutique across the other side of the foyer.

"See anything you like?" he whispered, grabbing her around the waist.

"Look at that!"

She pointed to a beautiful, intricate diamond necklace with a blue sapphire pendant and matching earrings.

"Yes, it's beautiful," he agreed. "Maybe I could buy it for you one day soon?"

"I'd like that," she replied softly and reached up to kiss him.

"Come on," he smiled. "I said we'd meet Philip in the lounge on the ground floor."

Entering the luxurious ornate room, Simon selected the most discreet table in the corner that would afford them the greatest degree of privacy. As they sat down in the plush, comfortable sofas it was difficult not to be riveted by the sight of River Nile in the background. The service at the hotel was exceptional and a waiter promptly stepped forward. Anna ordered for them and Philip as well.

A few moments later, he walked into the lounge and Anna's thoughts confirmed Simon's earlier assessment – he looked much more refreshed and back to his old self.

"So what did you find out?" asked Philip, joining them at the table.

"Well apart from finding the third key, I've got a meeting arranged with one of the museum's caretakers later this afternoon… We've planned to meet at one of the cafés on the square outside!"

"So that's what you were up to!" remarked Anna, as the waiter arrived with a tray of tea and coffee. He poured their drinks in silence, all of them waiting for him to finish before continuing.

"Any ideas on how we can get our hands on it? Any merit in Grandfather's suggestions?"

"I managed to get down into the basement briefly but there were signs that they've already started with the refurbishment work."

Their grandfather knew the risks and difficulties they would encounter trying to recover the final arkheynia so he had tried to pass on all the local knowledge he had. In his notes he had recommended that they investigate an entrance into the museum through the basement. Unfortunately, they all knew that the museum hierarchy had recently approved plans to renovate the basement by turning it into more exhibition halls, some lecture rooms and even a museum specifically for children.

"The workman have got to get in and out, though – what do you think?" asked Philip.

"It's worth following up. I can speak to this caretaker, providing he shows up of course – I get the impression he'd be prepared to answer any of my questions if the money's right... In fact he might even be able to help us!"

"That's good," replied Philip encouraged by the news. "It would be useful if he could give us any details on the security arrangements – how many guards are on duty and where... How often they patrol the rooms... What the nightshift pattern is..."

"Ok, I'll do my best to get as many details as possible."

"Let's say we manage to get in," interrupted Anna, listening intently. "How do we actually get the arkheynia out of its display case?"

"We've still got the replica we made in New York," noted Simon, "so we can replace it if necessary."

Philip nodded.

"I'd like to see the cabinet first but my view is we're going to have to cut the glass away – we simply don't have any choice I'm afraid."

He reached over for his cup of coffee.

"Later on this afternoon, I plan on buying the necessary equipment along with some items we can practice on – remember it's not just a question of removing the glass, we're also going to have to fit it back again – what do you think?"

"I agree it's the only way but how do we get inside with sufficient time to do it?" asked Anna not sounding totally convinced.

Simon nodded.

"So what's the plan?" she asked.

"I've got an idea but I need to go to the museum myself – Anna will you come with me this afternoon while Simon's meeting the caretaker to gather information on the internal security systems?"

"Sure," she replied, glancing at Simon. She had really hoped that she would be able to accompany him to the tea shop and help interrogate the janitor.

"I'm looking forward to hearing this plan," said Simon.

"We'll discuss it over dinner tonight," Philip replied.

Unbeknown to them, from the far end of the room they were being watched. A portly Egyptian gentleman with a thick, black moustache blew the smoke from his cigarette up into the air and popped in another stuffed olive from the table in front of him.

Chapter Thirty-Four

Vatican City, Rome

Cardinal Alphonso lifted his head as he heard the footsteps approaching. He was sitting on a wooden pew in front of the altar over the tomb of St. Peter in the magnificent Basilica. Tomorrow, this would be the scene of the first papal mass from the new Pope. He recalled the images of the last time he had attended such a service for his friend and mentor, Pope Paul XII. It was a very traditional service. The long, papal procession heading towards the altar, being halted three times on the way with the words, *"Pater sancte, sic transit gloria mundi"* – "Holy Father, this is how the glory of the world passes away", reminding him, amongst the pomp and splendour of the occasion that he is really a mortal man.

Sat alongside him was Cardinal Giacoma.

"Thank you for seeing me at such short notice," said Colonel Renauld, pausing in front of him. He was accompanied by Major Dupont who stood to attention a respectful distance behind his superior officer.

"What can I do for you, Colonel?" asked Cardinal Alphonso. He remained sitting in his scarlet robe with his hands resting in their familiar pose on his silver-headed, walking cane. The appointment request for a private audience from the Head of the Vatican's Swiss Guard was unexpected. At this sensitive time, with the coronation of the new Pope taking place tomorrow, he knew the Colonel's reasons must be strong for convening such an irregular meeting.

"It's a very grave matter, Your Grace; can I request that we speak alone?" he asked courteously.

The Cardinal nodded his agreement and glanced at Cardinal Giacoma who responded immediately He stood up and bowed respectfully to the elderly Senior Priest before departing towards the main atrium at the entrance of St. Paul's Basilica.

The Colonel also signalled to the Major to take up a position at the rear of the colossal hall's interior. He made his way to one of Bramante's modified columns, built in the sixteenth century to support the enormous dome that towered above them. Before Renauld sat down, he surveyed the scene around them one last time to make sure there was no one else within earshot. There was a party of labourers assisting with the arrangements for the next day's ceremony but this didn't seem to concern him unduly.

"It must be grave indeed… What is it, Colonel?" asked Alphonso once they were alone.

Renauld decided that if he was going to seek the counsel of Cardinal Alphonso then it was only reasonable that he gave him all the facts. For the next few minutes, he did all the talking and without interruption, the Cardinal Priest listened avidly, digesting all the Colonel's concerns and fears. He started off by explaining that from the time of Sir Lawrence Trenchard's death, he had suspected that sensitive information concerning the Book of Judas was being divulged to the Satanica. However, he was at pains to point out that it was only a hunch without any tangible evidence to support it.

Renauld then explained how he had decided to follow his instincts and give bogus information about the whereabouts of the entrance to the labyrinth to all six suspects, including Alphonso himself. Cardinal Alphonso gave a wry smile.

"I suspected as much," he remarked, shaking his head wisely before ushering him to continue.

Colonel Renauld reached the climax of his narration. He revealed the depth of the intrigue as he explained the faxed communication that had been transmitted from the administration offices of none other than Cardinal Camerlengo Fiore.

"I strongly believe that the Cardinal responsible for these leaks is one of the High Priests to whom I gave the bogus information – in short this evidence shows that one of the six most senior Cardinals in the Vatican is a member of the Satanica itself," stated Renauld, sitting back to await the Cardinal's reaction to such a damning statement.

"Amazing, truly incredible," said Alphonso, continuing to shake his head. "Such a web of deceit. What lies this man carries with him!" he muttered, lost in his own world of thought.

"What should I do, Your Grace?" he asked, gently trying to jog his mind back to the present and the matters at hand.

Renauld watched the thoughtful expression of Alphonso and proceeded to give him a further insight to emphasise the urgency of the matter.

"I have an appointment with our new Pope Leo the Fourteenth imminently and he will be seeking a full update on all matters that have passed since our last meeting – should I tell him what I've told you? Should I remain silent on the discovery? Although we know the fax communication left his office, we also know that all the others could have had access to the machine if they'd wished to use it!"

Cardinal Alphonso stared transfixed at the altar of St. Peter ahead of him with its tall, twisted pillars stretching up into the air above them to hold the canopy in place at the top. Methodically, he contemplated all the facts he had received and added them to some of the personal deductions he had made himself over the past fortnight.

Remaining silent for what seemed like an age to the Colonel, he finally roused himself from his trance and turned deliberately to face the military commander.

"You know Colonel our new Pope is a very clever and a very intelligent man," he remarked slowly.

Renauld appeared confused, struggling to fathom out what the priest was actually referring to.

"I'm not sure I understand your point," he replied, a little perplexed.

Cardinal Alphonso saw the look on his face and smiled.

"You made a decision that you could trust me didn't you?" he said, raising his eyebrows.

Colonel Renauld nodded.

"Well, maybe you should have the same faith in your new Pope?"

"You believe it was someone else then?" he asked quizzically.

"I believe that you are correct – as improbable and as inconceivable as it seems, I think that we do have senior member of the Satanica within our senior council. Suspicions… Yes, I have my own suspicions as to which Cardinal it might be but you must respect my silence on this matter for a bit longer – but, Colonel, let me ask you this, if you were to repeat the same conversation with Pope Leo XIV that you're having with me now, what do you think would be the outcome?"

Colonel Renauld himself was an intelligent man and he began to understand what Alphonso was driving at.

"How will he react? You must think about this and make sure that you understand the implications!"

Renauld looked over his shoulder at the sound of advancing footsteps.

"What is it, Major?" he asked.

"It's time, Sir,"

Renauld nodded. Observing his commander's acknowledgement, he marched back to his original post.

"Colonel, before you go, what are the latest developments in the Trenchards' quest for the Book of Judas? Are we controlling the situation?"

"Your Grace, we're rapidly getting closer to the time when the entrance to the labyrinth will be found – there have been some very important developments and I will strongly petition His Holiness that we should all meet, regardless of the informant amongst us, to decide the best way forward."

Cardinal Alphonso remained seated as Renauld stood up to leave.

"Thank you, Cardinal Alphonso, for your wise counsel – we will meet again soon."

His footsteps echoed around the atrium as he bid the elderly priest farewell and set off past the waiting Dupont. He immediately fell in line behind his superior officer.

"Ok, Major, you go back to the information centre and keep me abreast of any new developments – I want you to make sure that we keep a close eye on the movements of Cardinals Gregory, Giacoma, Weiss and Lefebvre, is that understood?" ordered Colonel Renauld before taking a different path and heading in the direction of the papal residence.

On the way he passed through the Pope's administration offices, which were a hive of activity with clerks anxiously concluding the last-minute touches to the next day's papal coronation.

The Colonel, stopping briefly to check his uniform in the mirror, climbed the stairs that led to the formal waiting room outside the Pope's private office. Within a couple of minutes of his arrival being announced, the door to his study was opened by the tall enigmatic figure of Pope Leo XIV himself. He was wearing the white cassock and traditional vestments of his new superior vocation.

"Come in, Colonel," he ushered, waving with his hand towards an elegant, antique Louis XIV seat in front of his magnificent desk. Stooping down low, the Colonel bowed and kissed the hand of the new Supreme Pontiff and Ruler of the Holy See. Amongst all his other new religious roles and titles he was now also the ultimate commander of the Swiss Guards.

Pope Leo XIV stepped around his ornate marble-topped desk to his chair while the Colonel sat facing him. The Pope's study was a large room and he quickly glanced around to check they were alone.

"You know, Colonel," he began. "All my life, since I was a small child, I have dreamed of nothing else other than fulfilling my blessed journey to become the next Pope – and now that the moment has finally arrived I will not let it count for nothing! I will not see our religion, our faith, our followers destroyed by the revelations that may spring from the Book of Judas – we must do everything in our power to stop the Satanica, *everything,*" he emphasised forcefully. "We have to destroy the Book of Judas once and for all, do you understand me?"

The words gave Renauld encouragement.

"I understand," he replied firmly.

"Now tell me," he asked in a softer tone, "what developments have there been?"

"Your Holiness, I will do so but I must first give you the grave news that we have an impostor within the most senior court of the Vatican. This infiltrator is delivering information directly into the hands of the Satanica – indeed it is likely that this Cardinal is also one of the Satanica's High Priests."

As he finished his statement, he searched Pope Leo XIV's eyes, looking for any tell-tale emotional sign or any outward trace of guilt that might give away his subversive nature. Renauld was pleased. He saw nothing to give him any cause for alarm; in fact to the contrary he felt his reaction supplied additional comfort to the earlier words of Cardinal Alphonso.

"Tell me everything – don't leave out any details," demanded the Pope angrily.

Again, Renauld recounted the story but this time was careful to omit the fact that he had already discussed the situation with Cardinal Alphonso earlier. It was something he would correct in the fullness of time.

"So the communication to the Satanica was transmitted from my office was it?" said Pope Leo XIV, thoughtfully rubbing his chin.

"I want you to issue an order to the Swiss Guard today informing Cardinal Alphonso, Cardinal Giacoma, Cardinal Gregory, Cardinal Weiss and Cardinal Lefebvre that they are no longer allowed outside the boundary walls of the Vatican City – please ensure that you inform each one of the priests that this instruction has been carried out under my seal and that I will meet with them after the papal coronation to give a full explanation of my the reasons."

"Very good, I'll see that this order is put in place immediately!"

"Colonel, I can imagine what must have been going through your mind since you obtained this news – rest assured that this is as great a shock to me as I'm sure it was to you when you discovered the truth. Together, we must find out which Cardinal's behind this but at the same time we must also bear in mind that the overriding objective is to destroy the Book of Judas… Nothing must compromise that objective, *nothing!*" he added. "If necessary exposing the impostor can come later – can you guarantee that no further communications will leave the Vatican?"

The Colonel nodded his agreement.

"Good. How close are we to locating the book?" he enquired, looking down and straightening the crucifix that hung on along chain around his neck.

"We've had a setback," said Renauld.

He knew the information he was about to divulge would be enormously valuable in the hands of the Satanica but, with the help of Cardinal Alphonso, he had already reached his decision to trust the new Pope on this matter. *Even so,* he thought privately to himself, *there are still pieces of the jigsaw that are best not discussed with any of the clergy at the moment.*

"The Satanica have kidnapped the fiancée of the elder brother, Philip Trenchard. We believe they're using her life as leverage. If they complete the quest to recover the keys of arkheynia and hand them over along with the scrolls they'll give her back alive – but once they have this they have the entrance to the labyrinth!"

"This is dreadful news," said the Pope, his voice rising in anger. "How much time do you believe we have?"

"I think we're only talking a few days now; my information tells me that the Trenchards are seeking the third and final arkheynia in Egypt. Once they've secured this the Satanica will be in touch to arrange the switch."

Pope Leo XIV looked troubled as he sat shaking his head.

"This is dreadful, where is Goran, is he…" His line of questioning was broken off by a loud knock on the door.

"Your Holiness, I'm very sorry to interrupt your meeting," said Cardinal Maurier, the newly appointed papal spokesman for foreign religious affairs and diplomatic affairs of office. "It's time for you to receive your royal guests from the Court of Spain."

Pope Leo XIV nodded and his papal assistant retreated closing the door behind him.

"I must go," said the Pope, turning his attention back to the Colonel.

"Will you organise a meeting at the first available opportunity after the coronation tomorrow – in the meantime I'll pray that that you'll be able to bring me better news!" he said, getting to his feet.

Colonel Renauld left the papal residence with a lot on his mind.

Chapter Thirty-Five

Cairo, Egypt

It was midday as Simon and Anna joined Philip in his bedroom to revisit their final preparations for the afternoon ahead. Together, they had decided the plan to obtain the third and final arkheynia. They all knew the risks but if they were to be successful it would require patience, skill and above all else, excellent timing.

Philip sat on the corner of the bed laying out his tools. He was pleased with the progress they had managed to achieve since he had retrieved the Judas Scrolls from his firm's offices the preceding day.

The previous afternoon's journey with Anna to the museum had been extremely useful. Together, without being to obvious to potential observers, they had examined the glass cabinet containing the arkheynia and decided that with a great deal of care and practice it would be possible to remove the glass panel from the side, slip a hand in through the gap, and gently remove the fragment of bone from its clasps. Once it was secured, the skill then lay in returning the cabinet to its original state. They would cover their tracks so that no one would ever know they had been there. The plan was to be executed during the night and it was a requirement that the burglary should remain undetected until at least the following morning. After removing the original, the fake arkheynia would be inserted in its place before the glass panel was refitted.

While Anna and Philip had completed their reconnaissance of the Great Hall of Rameses II and other areas of the museum, Simon had waited on an old, wooden seat outside Al Sulayman Café on the corner of Tahrir Square. He sat patiently for the old Egyptian janitor, Hareb to show his face. After twenty-five minutes had elapsed beyond the agreed meeting time, Simon reluctantly stood up to leave. Double-checking that he had the right venue, he stared up at the blue canopy and the dirty, deteriorating sign board with *Al Sulayman's* etched in black print across it. *He must have got cold feet,* he thought, wondering whether he should have been bolder with the financial incentive. Shrugging, he was about to set off back to the hotel when suddenly Hareb appeared from within the dingy café, gesturing him to come inside. *He must have arrived from the back,* thought Simon as he quickly followed the dishevelled caretaker inside. In front of him there was a long bar with stools fixed to the ground in front of it. Behind was a kitchen where some chefs were busy preparing orders. *It's a bit like an American diner,* he thought as they sat opposite each other in one of the cordoned-off booths in the corner.

"I'm glad you could make it," said Simon who then proceeded to watch Hareb's eyes pop out of his head as he took out his leather wallet and unfurled a large roll of American dollars.

"I thought you might prefer this currency," he added, smiling.

"What do you need?" he gasped and at the same time furtively looked around the room to make sure that they were not being watched.

Simon produced a notebook from his pocket. The first three pages were full of questions that Philip, Anna and he had thought of over lunch. Starting at the beginning he proceeded, one by one, to ask him for answers. Hareb was very forthcoming; he told him the pattern and the schedule of all the security patrols carried out by the guards throughout the night as well as detailing all the rooms and potential hiding places that could be of use to them.

Finally, only when he had given the answers to Simon's complete satisfaction, he was given the roll of bank notes, which he again he hastily stuffed into his grubby waistband.

"I must go now, Englishman," he said, cautiously looking around.

Simon nodded; he had all that he wanted. Closing the notebook, he pulled out some change from his trouser pocket and paid the attendant for the cups of tea they had ordered. Hareb wasted no time. He walked out under the canopy at the front and onto the pavement of the busy square. The light was fading and he was about to disappear into the crowd when curiosity got the better of him. He turned around and walked back in coming face to face with Simon again.

"What are you going to do, Englishman? Are you going to steal something," he asked in a voice lower enough that one could hear.

"No, I'm not going to steal anything – you have nothing to fear," Simon replied, trying to understand the janitor's line of questioning. Was the man who had just accepted over five hundred dollars feeling a pang of guilt or was he looking for a further source of income?

"The information you've given me's very useful – I work for an insurance company that provides cover for expensive works of art. It's my job to constantly make private enquiries and assessments on museums' security systems. You don't need to worry, everything you have told me will be confidential and no sources are ever named – I'll be leaving Cairo tonight so thank you again for your help," he continued.

Simon knew it wasn't a brilliant excuse but it was the best he could come up with in the heat of the moment. From the pleased expression on Hareb's face, he realised that his ploy seemed to have worked; it was exactly what he wanted to hear.

Visibly more relaxed, he turned and disappeared into the hustle and bustle of the metropolis outside.

While this was going on, Philip had set up the apparatus in his bedroom that would help him practice removing and replacing the glass panel. The bemused hotel porters helped carry the old furniture cabinet up to his room. He had acquired it from an antiques shop because of its marked similarities to the display cabinet in the museum and, with his newly purchased tools, he began practicing removing and refitting the side pane of glass.

As Philip worked away, with Anna watching on, Simon entered and gave them the news from his meeting with Hareb.

"You must be joking," said Philip exasperated as he heard the shift details of the nighttime patrols carried out by security through the Hall of Rameses II. To compound matters further, the glass panel he had just fitted fell inwards as he knelt in front of the cabinet.

"Damn," said Philip, trying to lift it out so he could start again.

"I'm afraid I pushed him on this issue several times and he always answered the same way, I'm afraid it's as regular as clockwork," Simon continued with a shake of the head.

"That means I have fifteen minutes to enter the room, take out the panel, remove the arkheynia and replace the glass before the scheduled stop of security patrol – I'll never do it!" he said desperately as the glass panel fell inwards again.

"Yes, you will," said Anna firmly. "From now on, we're going to recreate the same conditions as inside the hall of Rameses – you're going to practice against the clock, in the darkness, starting from outside the end of the corridor outside this room – you can do this Philip, I know you can!"

Exasperated, he rocked back on his knees.

"Thanks Anna, you're right, I've got to do this," he sighed while looking at his handiwork. "For Heather's sake, I've got to do this."

He threw himself back into his work and time after time Philip repeated the drill. Simon and Anna helped set up the environment so that it matched the conditions he would face the following night. This included drawing the curtains, blocking out the light and making his starting point in the hotel the same distance from his goal as they estimated he would encounter in the museum. On each practice run he dashed down the corridor of the hotel, occasionally passing startled guests, while Anna cheered him on, clutching a stopwatch. Entering the bedroom, he would run through the same procedure, panel out, arkheynia out, fake arkheynia in, panel back in and then sprint back to the hiding place before Anna's thumb came down on the stopwatch.

"It's no good, I'm never going to do it," he gasped with his hands on his hips.

Although his carpentry skills had improved dramatically, even on his best run, he could not manage a time below eighteen minutes and ten seconds.

"Come on let's leave it for tonight, we're very nearly there," suggested Simon.

They all agreed getting something to eat, having an early night and starting again first thing the next day was probably the best option.

It was now noon the following day and the time for practicing was over. Sitting on the bed in his room, Philip stared at the cabinet.

"It's going to be really tight," he said optimistically.

Anna looked at him quizzically. Even on that morning's best dry run he was still two minutes too slow.

"Is there any way we can take time off from the beginning or the end?" asked Simon.

"Yes," agreed Anna hopefully. "Maybe you have to hide in the Great Hall itself when the security guards conduct their scheduled round – that would cut off enough time for you to complete it."

Philip nodded his agreement. He was about to ask his brother to run through the locations he had been given by the janitor when the doorbell rang.

"That will be Room Service," said Simon, walking towards the door.

"A message for Mr. Philip Trenchard," said the bellboy, holding up an envelope with the hotel's crest on the outside.

Philip immediately jumped to his feet. *It must be from the Satanica,* he thought. He had been expecting them to get in contact soon.

"Thanks," said Simon, closing the door and handing the note over to Philip.

He wasted no time, ripping off the envelope and reading the typed contents.

> *"Be in your room at 2pm tomorrow afternoon. If you have done what I have asked you will be allowed to speak to her."*

Anna could see by the expression on Philip's face that it was just what he wanted to hear. He handed over the sheet of paper for them to read.

"I've got to do it in less than fifteen minutes. It's the only chance we have."

"Philip, do you want me to do it? Do you want me to go in your place?" asked Simon.

He had a good idea what his brother's reaction would be but he felt he had to offer all the same. After all he truly meant it – he felt desperate for his brother's situation and if necessary, he would have no qualms about battling against the odds to capture the final arkheynia.

"Thanks but you know I've got to do this – just wish me luck and be there as early as you can to get me out!" He leaned over and patted Simon gratefully on the shoulder.

"You know we should all be on our guard against any of the strangers around us," said Anna. The bellboy delivering the message suddenly reminded her that their movements were probably being watched.

"The kidnapper has the Satanica's accomplices working for him in Cairo – I suggest we make a mental note of anyone that we see for a second time. If we can work out who the watcher is without him realising then it could always offer us another potential avenue to find them!"

"Excellent idea," agreed Philip.

The doorbell went again and this time Room Service did appear with Anna's sandwich request.

"Right, well these should keep your energy levels up for the long night ahead," said Anna, carefully packing them into a small zipped bag along with some biscuits, fruit and drinks.

She had ordered plenty and together they finished the rest of the platter before Philip decided it was time they should go.

"One final check to make sure you have everything," said Anna, who grabbed the list she had made earlier. One by one she read out the items.

Philip nodded or patted the appropriate pocket for each item mentioned.

"Looks like I have everything," said Philip with a smile.

"Everything, except this!" said Anna as she stepped forward and gave him a big kiss on the cheek before wrapping her arms around him in a big embrace. "Good luck," she whispered. "I'll pray that everything goes according to plan," she added and her eyes welled up as she stood back.

"Yes, good luck," said Simon. "I know you'll be able to get under that time when it really matters!"

They had agreed earlier that there was no need for Simon to accompany them across to the museum. If he ended up bumping into the janitor Hareb again, it might arouse unnecessary attention that they could ill afford if their plan was to have any chance of success.

"How long do you think you'll be?" Simon asked Anna as he held the door for them.

"Not long – I should be back in twenty to thirty minutes," she replied.

"Ok – I'll wait for you here."

A few minutes later, Philip accompanied closely by Anna, crossed the busy street to the main doorway of the Cairo Museum. Philip paid their entrance fee and they entered the grand foyer where they immediately blended into the background of mingling tourists admiring the ancient treasures on display.

They followed the same route as the day before, entering the Great Hall of Rameses II to inspect the exhibition case housing the arkheynia one last time. They knew that it was extremely unlikely that it would have been moved, particularly as its position hadn't changed since the days of Sir Lawrence's visits but they had to double-check just to be on the safe side. Besides it would do no harm to check the Great Hall itself before Anna left Philip to complete the mission.

"There it is, exactly as we left it," said Anna, picking it out immediately.

The hall was full of activity and, careful not to attract attention, Philip again surreptitiously studied the glass panel that he would have to remove at the side of the case. He mentally tried to memorize the route his hand would have to follow in order to pick the arkheynia out from the other artefacts in the darkness of the night.

"Are you going to be Ok?" asked Anna, noticing the intensity on Philip's face as he ran his hand over the wooden coving holding the glass pane.

"Yes, yes – don't worry… I'm going to be fine," he muttered, trying to show some confidence despite the nervous, acidic feeling he felt in his stomach.

"Come on, it's time I built my nest," he said, gently guiding her back in the direction of the doorway.

Leaving the remarkable treasures of Rameses II behind, they followed the corridor back to the main staircase but instead of going down as before, they went up to the second and top story of the museum. The second floor was segregated into several further exhibition halls, including the most famous of Egypt's priceless relics, the treasures of Tutankhamen.

The landing at the top of the stairs was a hive of activity including a few security guards following their usual rounds. Looking as inconspicuous as possible, Philip checked his watch as they blended in with the tourist groups around them. Up to this point their timing had been deliberate and they paused, waiting for the signal that they knew would arrive any minute. Pretending to admire one of the half-man, half-lion limestone sphinx statues they heard the sound they had been waiting for. The Muslim call to prayer suddenly resonated above all the chatter in the hall. Outside on the edge of Tahrir Square was the Grand Mosque with its towering minarets. The voice of the Muezzin crying *allahu akbar* – "God is great" – into the microphone was projected across town through the enormous speakers attached to the Mosque's towers. Inside the museum, the sound went largely ignored by the visiting tourists but for Muslim security guards the call must be heeded even if for only a matter of minutes. Internally, the authorities and the guards had worked out a rota that allowed some to visit the museum's prayer room first whilst the rest attended after they had finished. From Anna and Philip's perspective, although this did not mean there would be no security guards on duty, it did mean that they could expect half as much attention as normal during the next few minutes.

Following the agreed plan, Philip glanced at Anna before walking briskly across the hallway into the gentlemen's toilets. In keeping with the century-old building, the room had a colonial, archaic presence with high old-fashioned ceramic urinals and old wooden closets. Looking up, he spied the skylight in the ceiling and after checking there was no one else inside the room, Philip opened the door to the hallway and gave Anna the signal. As the door gradually slipped closed on its hinges, he wasted no time in pushing his shoulder bag around his back and climbing up the toilet's doorframe. At the top, he held his balance while he jerked the skylight open. Outside, the light was beginning to fade with the onset of evening and he was grateful for the additional element of cover it would provide. Earlier, they had done their homework on the Museum's sandy-coloured rooftops and they had identified specific areas around the castle-style battlement and the interior that would present good hiding places.

Outside the washroom, one of the sightseers following a loud Egyptian tour guide along the passageway spotted the gentlemen's sign and peeled off in the direction of the toilet. Anna's brief was very simple, for the next few minutes she was to prevent anyone entering the washroom at any cost. Before he had reached the door, she had accosted him.

"Excuse me, Sir, I'm really sorry but would you mind using the other facilities, they're just down the corridor – unfortunately, we have a temporary maintenance problem, which we're doing our best to repair – we'll be putting up a sign in a minute."

Anna tried to sound as official as possible. She knew she might have to play this cameo role so had dressed herself in an outfit that closely resembled that of the museum staff.

Any thoughts the visitor had of objecting disappeared completely when he caught sight of Anna's face. The look in her eyes and the enchanting smile was sufficient to make any man say *yes*.

Meanwhile Philip completed the difficult physical manoeuvre. Using all his strength, he clutched onto the frame of the skylight and pulled himself up through the small gap and out onto the rooftop beyond. Quickly dropping it back in place but being careful not to wedge it too firmly shut, he darted behind the parapet.

As he surveyed his new temporary base he felt comfortable that it was shielded from all sides. His only Achilles heel was the unlikely scenario of someone flying a helicopter directly above him. He lifted his shoulder bag off and checked the time on his watch. *So far so good,* he thought and his mind drifted back to Heather as he settled down for the long night ahead.

That's long enough, judged Anna and she gave up her hallway vigil and commenced her way down the grand staircase and back towards the hotel room. *He may be all on his own now but at least we can still communicate with him in an emergency,* she thought, stepping across the marble floor of the hotel foyer. The previous day when Philip had been to his firm's associate office, he had been well received by the local senior partner. Apart from collecting the untouched scrolls, still in their identical packaging, he had also made one more special request. Philip asked the partner if he could organise three mobile phones with international roaming and texting facilities for a couple of weeks. The senior partner had been only too pleased to help and had sent a courier to the hotel with the new phones earlier that morning. The phones were taken under the company name so that the calls should to all intents and purposes remain anonymous to the Satanica.

Anna tapped the hotel door lightly and Simon opened it almost immediately.

"How did everything go?" he asked earnestly, closing it behind her.

"Ok, everything went as planned – we're through the easy part now so we'll just have to hope and pray that Philip makes it!"

"I'm not good at waiting," moaned Simon.

"I'm not very good either," she replied before her eyes suddenly lit up.

"However I do have an excellent idea. Rather than wait up here in the room why don't we go down and have a meal in that Italian restaurant. There's nothing to be served by waiting here. What do you think?"

"Great idea," replied Simon with a smile.

"Come and knock on my door – I'll take about thirty minutes to get ready."

"You've got twenty," said Simon playfully as he leant over to kiss her.

"I'll be as quick as I can," she said, smiling and pushing him away in mock indignation. She picked up a couple of her things that were scattered around the room and sailed back in the direction of the adjoining apartment, leaving Simon to get himself ready.

A short while later, after they had both showered and changed, they took the lift down to *San Lorenzo's* restaurant located on the upper terrace at the front of the building. Simon and Anna both took their new mobile phones with them. They were not expecting to hear from Philip until it was all over but they took them just in case he had any urgent need of contacting them.

As they followed the waiter through the Italian styled interior towards the balcony terrace, they were pleasantly surprised at how busy the restaurant was.

"The food must be good," said Anna, squeezing Simon's hand as they were shown to a round table in the corner of the terrace with a charming view over the River Nile.

"This looks perfect," said Anna as she was helped into her seat by the waiter who then lit the candle in the middle of the table. He politely handed them the menus before scurrying off to get their drinks order.

"Yes, excellent choice," he replied, staring out over the brightly lit cruise ships that were passing up and down in front of them. He had seen pictures of the Nile before but they had not done it justice. He had never realised the scale and magnitude of the river until he saw it from his hotel window on the first night.

Although it was humid, the evening temperature was perfect and the slight breeze whispering in off the riverbanks helped keep them cool. When the waiter returned a few minutes later, he came armed with an ice bucket and a cold bottle of Sancerre.

"Can I take your orders?" he requested as he filled the ample balloon glasses.

After scrutinizing the menu one last time and asking the waiter for his recommendations, they made their choices. Neither of them had eaten much during the day and both were now feeling hungry.

"To Philip! – let's hope he makes it," said Anna, lifting her wineglass.

"I'll drink to that," he replied as their glasses clinked together.

The momentary happiness passed quickly as Anna saw the expression that flashed across Simon's face. She recognised the tell-tale signs as she also had the same feelings.

Simon had suddenly felt a pang of guilt that he was enjoying the evening, drinking and laughing with Anna while his brother was stationed less than half a kilometre away on a rooftop about to undergo the most dangerous ordeal he had ever faced. If things backfired for Philip, the very least he could expect would be a rough journey to one of Cairo's notorious jails where money and reputations counted for nothing. Simon shook his head. He knew this would pale into insignificance for Philip if he thought that all hope of rescuing Heather had gone.

"He's going to make it, we have to be confident – Philip knows we'll be there for him and that we'll do whatever it takes!" she said and reached out to put her hand over his.

"It all hinges on tonight, if he doesn't make it we haven't got a back-up plan – we'd never be able to rescue him and there's probably little likelihood after an attempted robbery that we'd ever get close to the capturing the arkheynia again!"

"Listen," she said softly. "We have a few hours before he starts – let's enjoy the evening; it's going to be a long night."

Simon smiled.

"You're right, there's nothing we can do at the moment. Let's just be ready for when we're needed."

"Yes and let's hope that's picking up Philip tomorrow morning as planned," she added encouragingly.

Their moods brightened as the waiter appeared carrying their main course selections.

"That looks nice," said Anna as she cheekily helped herself to something off Simon's plate.

327

"Have you given any more thought to what we were talking about earlier?"

She knew this was an awkward topic to bring up but she had to try.

"You mean what will happen if the Book of Judas gets into the wrong hands?"

"That's right. I think we need to talk about it – if we end up completing this quest just to capture the final arkheynia and hand over the keys of the gate to the Satanica, what do you think it means?"

Since they had spoken earlier, Simon had been deliberating the consequences of the book falling into the wrong hands but the implications still confused him. Taking a momentary pause from enjoying the delicious cuisine in front of him, he looked up at her.

"Ok let's try and think this through – having listened to my grandfather, having seen and heard what I did when I visited Professor Palanski that day after the funeral, I have no doubt that the book exists – now if the book is discovered what happens? My understanding is that its contents question the very foundation upon which the Christian and Catholic religion are based – does that make sense to you so far?" he asked

"Simon, its worse than that, much worse than that," she replied, agitated that he had not grasped the true picture.

"The scrolls say that if the book is opened and the pagan ritual described within its pages are followed then the Devil, Lucifer, Satan, call him what you will – will be brought back to life in human form! According to the text wherever his evil shadow touches, it will bring immorality, wars, and plagues the likes of which have never been seen before! If the Devil's resurrected he will bring a holocaust that will challenge the race of men!"

"What makes you say this?" he asked, stunned at her sudden intensity.

"Because I know!" she replied. "It's written in the Scroll of Judas that I translated in Thailand – in fact according to the scrolls, Judas himself was the Son of Satan, brought to earth to face the Son of

God!"

Simon looked bewildered as he lifted his glass of wine and took a sip. "What are you saying?"

"Oh Simon," she replied. "I just don't know how to put this…"

"Try," he repeated firmly.

"If the Book of Judas ends up in the hands of the Satanica then I truly believe that mankind will witness death and atrocities on a scale never seen before! If we give them the keys to find this book then that's what we'll have unleashed on the world."

He rocked back in his seat and stared up into the midnight sky trying to come to terms with what he was hearing.

"Anna let me understand this – are you saying that we shouldn't give this killer the entrance to the labyrinth? That we should just let Heather die at the hands of this maniac?"

He clasped his hands behind his head. *What is Anna saying? That it's better for one woman to die to save so many?*

"I don't know what I'm saying," she sobbed, putting her head in her hands.

Simon shook his head in disbelief. He suddenly felt overwhelmed by the choice that faced them. Save Heather or save the lives of thousands, maybe hundreds of thousands! He stared at her as he tried to fathom out any solution to the problem but it was hopeless. How could they rescue Heather and stop the book from getting into the hands of the Satanica? It was just not possible.

"Why didn't you mention this before?"

"I wanted to," she said, fighting back the emotion. "But how could I mention this in front of Philip!"

He reached out and brushed the hair away from her face to reveal the tears trickling down her cheek. He took one of the unused table napkins and brushed them away.

"What are we going to do?" she pleaded.

"I don't know," he replied slowly. "I just don't know."

Just then the smartly attired waiter came through the balcony door.

"How was your meal, Sir?" he asked cheerfully before sensing the mood at the table.

"I think we'll have our coffee upstairs – do you mind just bringing us the bill?" asked Simon and the waiter nodded respectfully before picking up the plates and leaving.

"What time is it? It's getting cold," said Anna, shivering as she stood up from the table rubbing her hand up and down her bare arm.

Simon took off his jacket and slipped it around her shoulders as they walked back inside the restaurant.

"I hope Philip's Ok," she said as they stepped into the lift and pressed the button for the eighth floor.

"Do you want a coffee?" Simon asked as he fished in his pocket for the swipe card to the hotel room.

"I think I'll just freshen up a bit first," she replied. "Why don't you come to my room and we'll ask Room Service to bring some fresh coffee up? We've got a long night ahead!"

"Ok," he nodded, putting his card away and following down the corridor. It was the first time he had been in her room and he noticed immediately how much tidier it was than his own.

"Can you ring up Room Service?" she called as she closed the bathroom door behind her.

As he wandered towards the phone, he heard the shower being turned on. The bathrooms were luxurious with large walk-in showers.

Much tidier than my room, he thought, and grinned, looking around at the clothes laid out in neat piles along top of the dresser. Next to one pile was a folded newspaper. He walked over and gazed at the photograph taking up most of the front page. It was a picture of Pope Leo XIV waving from the balcony to the crowds below in St. Peter's Square. The article was circled in highlighter pen and he began to read it until he heard the fumbling of the bathroom doorknob behind him.

"Can you pass me the bathrobe?" asked Anna, peering through the gap. "It's lying on the bed I think."

Simon picked up the white towelling robe and took it to the bathroom door. As he reached out with the robe in one hand, she let the door swing open, revealing her glistening body, still wet from the shower. She looked up at him with widened eyes as she took the robe.

"You're so beautiful," he stuttered.

He suddenly felt all the passion and yearning of the past two weeks coming together at once. She continued to stare up at him invitingly, her smile tempting him to come forward. Water from her wet hair ran in tiny rivulets down her face. *She really is the most beautiful woman I've ever seen,* he thought.

"You know you could always take a shower with me?" she asked, willing him to move closer.

Smiling, Simon reached out, putting his arms around her and pulling her towards him. She let the towelling robe drop to the ground as he pressed her naked body to his and kissed her.

"Shall I put the Room Service on hold?" he grinned and started pulling off his shirt.

She didn't let him get very far as she walked into the shower, pulling him gently behind her. Fully clothed except for his shirt, he kissed her as the warm jet of water sprayed over them.

* * * *

On the roof of the museum, Philip looked down at the bag in front of him. He had eaten the sandwiches and fruit that Anna had arranged from the hotel earlier. It was dark but there was some light from the neon advertising signs that hung on buildings around Tahrir Square. Making sure no one could see the beam, he tested his torch to make sure it was in good working order. He found the waiting difficult. He had been there for over seven hours and he was really anxious to get started. Several times he had mentally pulled himself back from climbing down through the skylight but now the real time to begin had arrived.

He ran through one final check of the equipment and then swung the small backpack over his shoulder. Earlier he had folded his tourist clothes and changed into an all-black outfit for maximum camouflage effect. Opening the window, he put his head through and listened for any strange sounds. There was none. Quickly, he slid through the gap and hanging down with his arms outstretched, he jumped the final distance to the floor, trying to land as softly as he could. *Getting down is a lot quicker and a lot quieter than getting up,* he thought, moving to the door.

His eyes had become accustomed to the light and twisting the doorknob he peered outside, listening for any tell-tale signs. Checking his watch again, he stealthily crept across the passageway to the main staircase and peered through the darkness over the balustrade. *I don't believe it,* he thought irritably. He could see and hear one of the security guards below slowly walking along the passageway. The assignment was going to be hard enough without encountering problems at this stage. He knew he had to be in position at the Great Hall of Rameses II in exactly two minutes if he was going to have the maximum length of time, twenty minutes, to get the arkheynia out.

Thank God, he muttered as he looked over the balustrade again and saw him walking away down the steps towards the ground floor. Quickly, he descended down the staircase to the first floor and, being careful to remain in the shadows, he furtively made his way to the entrance of the Great Hall of Rameses II. Outside, he checked his watch again. The security patrol was due to enter at the other end of the hall in exactly forty-five seconds, he estimated. He crouched down behind one of the huge statues waiting for the moment to arrive.

Punctual as clockwork, he heard the door opening and the security guard armed with a flashlight wandered down the length of the hall. As the steps got closer Philip held his breath, praying that he passed without noticing anything out of the ordinary. *Thank God for the janitor's assistance,* he thought. The Head of Museum Security was a conscientious man who paid a lot of attention to detail. The routes followed by the guards around the entire museum had been tabulated in a well-organised, detailed plan. All across the museum the security officers were religiously following the network of paths to make sure the entire interior of the museum was covered. The next guard was due to appear in the Great Hall in fifteen minutes' time through the door at the far end.

This is it, thought Philip, his chest pounding in anticipation. He knew he needed to get off to the best possible start and this would mean timing his entrance into the Great Hall as finely as possible once the guard had passed. He was worried; in practice he hadn't managed to achieve a sub-fifteen minute time on any occasion. *It's now or never,* he thought.

The guard walked past, continuing on his round down the dark passageway. Philip waited a few seconds until it was clear and then raced into the hall, starting the stopwatch he had brought with him on the way. Kneeling down in front of the cabinet, the flashlight angled so that it gave him a shallow beam, he rapidly arranged the set of tools out on the floor. Keeping one eye on the stopwatch, he worked as quickly and as efficiently as possible. The glass panel finally slipped out and he laid it carefully alongside him on the floor. Reaching in, he felt his way along the path he had memorised earlier to locate the arkheynia. *Come on where is it?* he muttered to himself as he desperately searched with his fingers. Suddenly he felt it. The next step was intricate, he had to loosen the fastenings just enough to pull it free but with enough slack that he could put in the fake arkheynia and fix it into place again. A few more minutes slipped by as he worked away, using the tools to help him. Finally it broke free and he pulled it through the gap and pushed it into his bag.

He checked the stopwatch: he was falling behind schedule. He wanted to panic but knew that it would all be over if he lost his focus. Doing his best to remain calm, he quickly completed the last fastening and lifted up the glass panel to put it back into place. This was it, the last leg, if he could just get it fixed in time. He looked down at the clock again: only ninety seconds to go and he still had one corner to fix in place plus whatever time was needed to tidy up his tools and get out safely. *It doesn't matter,* he thought. *I've got no time left.* At least the glass panel was reasonably secure but he knew he had to leave. If the guard entered now it was all over. He heard footsteps in the background; quickly he grabbed his tools, brushed some of the residue away and rushed back towards the entrance. The door at the far end opened and immediately the guard's flashlight panned around the hall. *He suspects something,* thought Philip as he dived back into the hiding place he had used before. The next few moments seemed to take a lifetime as he tried to guess what the security guard was doing. *If he shines the torch on the cabinet from a distance maybe it'll be ok,* he thought, *but any closer inspection will definitely raise the alarm.* Holding his breath, the guard passed through the entrance and down the passageway towards the staircase. He let out a sigh of relief and dashed back into the hall to complete the work on the cabinet. Three minutes later it was fixed and all trace of his being there was removed.

His mood changed as he began to believe he could do it. Without wasting any more time, he crept back down the passageway and up the stairs towards his exit route to the roof. Checking the way was clear, he raced inside the washroom and climbed up the wooden frame and out through the skylight. As he rolled away behind the wall he felt relieved, and elated to be back in the sanctuary of his rooftop hideaway.

In the hotel, Simon sat on the edge of the bed and poured them both a strong cup of fresh coffee. It had just gone three o'clock in the morning and they both knew that, if everything had gone according to plan, Philip should be approaching the end of his exertions. Anna sat up in bed, pulling the sheet up in front of her. The pillows were lodged behind her back so she could sip her coffee without spilling it.

"Simon – how do you feel?" she asked with a mischievous grin.

"About what?" he replied.

"About us of course!"

"I feel great," he replied, smiling broadly as he reached out for her hand. "I think I'm falling in love with the most stunning woman in the world."

"No seriously," she said pulling her hand away. She wanted to hear something more meaningful, something more momentous.

"I *am* being serious, Anna," he said, reaching over and taking her hand back. "I feel so excited when I'm with you. I know these are unusual times that we're living in but you are that special person that I've always been hoping to find."

He gazed straight into her beautiful eyes as she clutched the sheet in front of her.

"Anna, I can't describe it…"

"Go on," she teased and threw a pillow at him.

"Well, despite all your bad points," he joked, "I love you, Miss Nikolaidis."

It was what she was desperate to hear. The white sheet fell away as she jumped forward to embrace him. Locked together, they held each other tightly. A few seconds passed before Anna could speak and when she did, her voice quivered as tears of happiness ran down her cheek.

"I'm so glad you said that, Simon Trenchard, because I'd already fallen in love with you," she said, squeezing him tightly again.

Before Simon could reply, the mobile phone on the side table beeped and he scrambled across the bed to reach it.

"Philip!"

"Simon, keep your voice down to an absolute minimum," he whispered earnestly.

"What happened?" he asked reducing his voice to whisper.

"I've got it – I didn't quite make it in the allotted time but I've got it. I'll tell you about it later," he added happily.

Simon punched the air.

"Fantastic – he's done it!" he whispered so Anna could hear.

"Are you Ok? Do you need anything?" he asked anxiously.

"No, just remember the change of clothes and get here as soon as you can."

The silence on the rooftop was absolute except for the odd car passing in the square below.

"Ok. We'll see you in the morning," said Simon and put the phone down.

"That's great news," said Anna, flinging her arms around his neck.

"Well we may as well get as much sleep as we can," he said, smiling and pulling her down alongside him on the bed.

For the rest of the night, their feelings for each other and the elation at hearing Philip's news allowed them to sleep happily. Thoughts of Heather's desperate situation would return soon enough in the morning.

On the rooftop, Philip had not managed to sleep at all and he stared up across the Cairo skyline as the morning sun began to rise bringing the city to life. The noise level gradually got louder. It started with the early morning chorus from the birds that lived in the square and then increased as the early morning traders started work and the traffic in the streets began to grow. *Not long to go now,* he thought and he began a few stretching exercises to limber himself up for the final exertion ahead. The final journey through the skylight would be carried out in broad daylight. It was going to be vital that he covered the ground as quick as possible.

In the hotel room the alarm went off and Anna pulled herself from Simon's grip and headed for the shower. The motion made Simon stir.

He stood up and, smiling, remembered the night with Anna before calling Room Service.

As he reached for the phone, he noticed something glisten under the glow of the side table lamp under Anna's pillow. He walked around and lifted the end and saw a tiny, golden crucifix on a chain. Thoughtfully, he lifted it in his fingers for a moment before putting it back in place.

Ten minutes later Room Service arrived with breakfast. Once they had both dressed and showered, they discussed the plan ahead while enjoying some Danish pastries and fresh, hot coffee.

"Ok, it's time to go," said Simon, who had been counting down the minutes. They were both keen to get Philip back and complete the final stage of their plan but there was nothing they could do until the museum opened at eight-thirty. It was still early but they knew visitors started queuing before opening time and they wanted to be the first in line. Fifteen minutes later they were negotiating the traffic across Tahrir Square.

After an interminable wait, the entrance doors were finally pulled open and they filed in after paying their entrance fee. Together they walked up the stairs to the first floor but then separated as planned. Anna walked down the wide corridor past the statues and treasures that Philip had negotiated his way around so stealthily a few hours earlier. She entered the Great Hall of Rameses II and made her way to the display cabinet to review his handiwork. If there was anything obviously out of place that she could correct, now was the time.

Simon continued upwards. He climbed up to the second floor and wandered along the rows of exhibits while texting a message to his brother to give him the all clear. There was a security officer patrolling the floor but thankfully he was taking more of an interest in a large group of German tourists who were being overly hands-on with one of the ancient statues.

Simon walked into the gentlemen's toilet and held the door shut as

Philip hastily opened the skylight, clambered through and dropped to the ground.

Without saying anything Philip held out his hand and his brother gave it a congratulatory slap.

He looks shattered, thought Simon as he handed him his bag of fresh clothes. In return, Philip handed him back the shoulder bag containing the final arkheynia. He then locked himself in one of the wooden cubicles where he changed clothing as quickly as he could.

"Ok?" asked Simon.

"Yes, go!" he replied.

Simon opened the door and without wavering from his course, set off for the museum exit.

A few minutes later Philip appeared looking better for the change of clothes. Anna was there on the second floor to greet him with a big smile.

"Absolutely fantastic," said Anna, gripping his hand tightly. "I've checked your handiwork and it looks perfect – only an expert would know!"

Philip smiled. He was very tired and was looking forward to eating something before getting a couple of hours of much-needed sleep. The journey back through the museum exit into the bright daylight passed without event.

"You've done it!" said Anna happily as they strolled back across the street, arms interlinked, to the hotel.

Back in the room, Simon embraced his brother as he came through the door.

"Behold! – we have the three keys of arkheynia!" said Simon, pointing towards the bed where he had laid out all the fragments across an empty pillowcase.

Chapter Thirty-Six

Vatican City, Rome

Sat behind his desk, Colonel Renauld felt mentally and physically tired. It had been a long, exhausting day controlling the tight security arrangements surrounding the papal coronation and the delivery of the new Pope's first Holy Mass. Around the world, people watched the colour and pageantry of the occasion as the live media reporting intruded beyond the bounds of any previous papal coverage. The placing of the traditional tiara, the symbolic crown of the Holy See, on the Pope's head had been watched live in more than a hundred countries.

Although the security arrangements had gone perfectly to plan the ceremony had been marred by the tragic death of Cardinal Gregory one hour before the event was due to begin. He had died of a sudden heart attack in his own quarters. It was generally known within the Vatican circles that he had not been in the best of health for some time and certainly since the announcement of the new Pope only a few days earlier the Vatican's physician had visited him on several occasions.

The news of his death had greatly disturbed Colonel Renauld. His immediate reaction was to request that the coronation be delayed until such time as he had properly examined the circumstances surrounding his death. To his annoyance, his appeal was dismissed by the new Pope, who sent Cardinal Bishop Lefebvre along to relay the instructions that the ceremony would proceed as planned.

As soon as practically possible, Colonel Renauld left the management of the coronation's security arrangements to his second-in-command in order to investigate the scene of Cardinal Gregory's death but he was too late to glean any useful knowledge. His body had already been moved away and any other clues that would have been helpful had been cleared away out of respect for the dead priest. Even so, as he walked out of Cardinal Gregory's quarters he felt that something was not right.

In Pope Leo XIV's Holy Mass he paid a special tribute to Cardinal Gregory. Cardinal Alphonso allowed himself a wry smile as he listened to the new Pope praise Cardinal Gregory to the rafters of St. Peter's Basilica. In glowing references, he glorified his brother's tireless devotion and lifelong dedication to the Catholic faith.

That was several hours earlier and now Colonel Renauld sat slumped in his chair, pondering the few facts he did have surrounding the death of Cardinal Gregory. The phone rang and he was suddenly awoken from his thoughts. Mustering his energy resources, he asked his secretary to put the call through.

"Goran, what news do you have for me?"

"Colonel, we're getting close to the moment of truth; my information tells me that all three keys of arkheynia are now in the hands of the Trenchard brothers – they now have the ability to locate the entrance to the ancient labyrinth."

"And the Satanica?" he asked gruffly.

"I'm afraid I've been unsuccessful in finding out any more information on their exact whereabouts – I'm sure they're present in Egypt and I also believe they've taken the kidnapped girl there with them!"

"What makes you say that?"

"There was an incident at an airport just outside Alexandria that wasn't reported in the papers – a mutilated body was found in the cockpit of the plane. Although it was difficult to get much reliable information, the bit that I did get suggested that the killing bore all the nice trademarks of the Satanica's executioner, this so-called 'Death Angel' killer."

"I see," said Renauld slowly. This was not good news.

"So the Satanica hold the strings – do as I say or I kill the girl? The killer's communicating with them and threatening to kill the girl unless they locate the labyrinth's entrance!"

Renauld sighed.

"And now," he continued, "they have all three keys of arkheynia. How do you feel Goran? Are you still feel confident we can destroy the Book of Judas before they secure it?" Renauld demanded.

Goran did not answer immediately. If he had been asked that question a day earlier he would have given an unequivocal confirmation that the book would be destroyed but the news he had received recently left him in doubt. In fact he was deeply disturbed by the recent developments.

"We will destroy it, Colonel, have no fear of that," he said, although he sensed his own voice lacked its normal confidence.

"I hope so, Goran, I really hope so – the consequences if we get this wrong are just unimaginable."

Renauld looked up at the clock on the wall; it was nearly time to go but he wanted to keep Goran in the picture on developments in the Vatican. He had already told him of his private meetings with Cardinal Alphonso in St. Paul's Basilica and the meeting with the new Pope in his papal apartments but the untimely death of Cardinal Gregory was a new revelation. Goran listened silently as he relayed all the information at his disposal. Like Renauld, he too expressed serious doubts about the true cause of the noble Cardinal's death.

Renauld checked his watch again.

"I have a meeting with His Holiness Pope Leo in a few minutes – he wants to discuss the latest progress we are making in destroying the book ahead of the Satanica. In fact, I believe he's requested that all the inner sanctum be present with the exception of the deceased Cardinal Gregory – and that means the Satanica's infiltrator will be there!"

"Be on your guard, Colonel," warned Goran. "The impostor's likely to become very dangerous if he believes he's about to be uncovered!"

"I know," he replied. "I'm not sure that I agree with the Pope's chosen course of action but I'm afraid he's made up his mind on this one!"

"Ok, I'll be back in touch with you as soon as I know what the Trenchards' next step is after Cairo."

"Will you be travelling, Goran?" asked Renauld.

"Yes, depending on developments I'm intending to take a flight out later on today – I'll keep you posted on my destination," he replied and signed off.

Renauld stood up and pulled down his colourful Swiss Guards tunic. He had never felt comfortable wearing it. Unlike his rank and file, he wasn't required to put it on every day but Vatican protocol dictated that he wore it for official ceremonies and they didn't come any more important than the Pope's coronation.

Right, its time for action, he thought and proceeded down the spiral staircase from his office and marched in the direction of the Sala Ducale. It was the chosen venue for the secret conclave by the Pope himself.

It was early evening as he walked across the square. All around him there were signs of the ceremony held earlier that day as workers continued dismantling some of the purpose-built wooden stands, which had been constructed for the enormous crowds that had converged from all parts of the globe for the historic occasion.

Renauld reached La Scala Regia, widely considered the most magnificent staircase in the world. It formed the principal entrance to the Vatican and connected it with the noble portico of St. Peter's. In his many years in charge, the grandeur of his surroundings never ceased to amaze Renauld and the staircase was no exception. At the base stood the impressive, equestrian statue of Constantine before it rose in four

342

majestic flights of marble steps. All the way up it was adorned with rows of Ionic pillars. At the top, it reached the threshold of the grand entrance hall known as the Sala Regia, which was covered with frescoes painted chiefly by the famous Vatican artist Vasari. One exception was the work of Salviati who produced the contentious image of Emperor Frederic I, lying prostrate, kissing the foot of the haughty Pontiff Alexander III.

Inside the hall, there were six grand folding doors, Renauld walked past the first one, which led into the Cappella Paolina. This enormous chamber was a grand church in its own right with a magnificent altar at one end being supported by pillars of costly porphyry.

Carrying on through the main hall of the Sala Regia, he took the last of the great folding doors on the left into Sistine Chapel. He smiled dryly to himself as he considered what had happened since the election of the new Pope in this very room only a few days earlier. Marching through, he opened the door at the far end and entered the Sala Ducale, which by contrast was large and simple.

The priests had already arrived and were sat on the wooden bench that ran along the side of the room. Colonel Renauld walked forward and he went up to each Cardinal one by one to pay his respects. Cardinal Alphonso was sitting patiently with Cardinal Giacoma at his side whilst Cardinal Weiss and Cardinal Lefebvre sat a bit further away.

Cardinal Bishop Lefebvre looks pleased with himself, thought Renauld. He was aware that one of the Pope's first administration matters had been to appoint a new deputy as Fiore himself had at one time been to Pope Paul. Cardinal Bishop Lefebvre had been the recipient of this accolade, the second highest appointment in the Catholic Church, namely the position of Cardinal Camerlengo to Pope Leo XIV. He sat stroking his dark goatee beard as he waited for proceedings to begin.

They didn't have to wait much longer. Pope Leo entered the Sala Ducale in his traditional white cassock and all those present immediately stood before him. He walked forward and sat in the wooden throne that was resting in front of them. They assumed their seats as he sat down.

"My brothers, I have gathered us here to discuss God's mission, the mission to destroy the Book of Judas," he said, his voice echoing around the chamber.

The room had been specially selected because of its intimacy. Once the doors were closed to the Sistine Chapel at one end and the Loggia di Raffaello at the other, then privacy could be assured. The intrigued priests looked on as the Pope made himself comfortable in the wooden throne. Around the perimeter of the dark room, tall white candles provided flickering light and the air was heavy with the flowery scent of burning incense.

"Your Holiness," said Cardinal Deacon Weiss, "is it true that you have decreed that we are no longer entitled to leave the Vatican?"

"Yes, Brother Weiss, you are correct – in fact I have some very serious and grave news that I'd like to share with you all that will explain my actions."

He paused to look into their faces.

"It would seem that one amongst us has fallen from the path of righteousness – within our midst we have an impostor... an impostor who serves the High Council of the Satanica amongst us."

Renauld also stared at their faces as Pope Leo XIV completed his startling announcement. He looked for any shifty movements or tell-tale signs of guilt. There was none. Their faces, with the exception of Cardinal Alphonso's, carried a seemingly genuine look of astonishment. Pope Leo XIV leaned over in his chair towards Renauld and asked him to explain the facts.

Starting with the planted story about the entrance of the labyrinth being close to Hom in Syria, he briefly explained his gut feeling and how it had been substantiated by the discovery of an external communication. He told them that it had been sent from the administrative offices of Pope Leo himself.

"Could the impostor not have been Cardinal Gregory?" asked Cardinal Lefebvre.

"The answer is yes, Your Grace, he could have been," replied Renauld, "but I have strong, private reasons to suspect that this is not the case."

Their faces continued to give away nothing but Renauld could not help thinking something was amiss, he couldn't quite put his finger on it but there was something that irked him about the way Cardinal Bishop Lefebvre reacted to the Pope's announcement. He continued focusing on him as the Pope carried on speaking.

"Now that's out in the open, you'll understand why no one is allowed outside the Vatican walls and why no further communication can take place – if any communication by whatever means is required it must be first approved by Colonel Renauld and the Swiss Guard – that applies to all of us and I include myself."

All but one of them sat in stunned silence on the wooden bench as they digested the news. The mind of one Cardinal was in angry turmoil.

"Colonel Renauld, can you now update us on proceedings?" asked the Pope grimly.

"I can inform you that all three of keys of arkheynia have been collected and are in the hands of the Trenchard brothers, but they've suffered a major setback," he said, pausing for a moment to register their facial expressions.

"The Satanica's agent has kidnapped the older brother's fiancée – the same member of the Satanica known as the 'Death Angel' and he is now controlling their every move. If they wish to see the girl alive they must find the entrance to the labyrinth and reveal it to the Satanica in exchange for her!"

"Is your top agent Goran no closer to locating them and the arkheynia than before?" demanded Cardinal Weiss.

"We're doing all we can, Cardinal Weiss... We know they're based in Cairo at the moment and we hope to report some positive progress soon," he replied.

"Frankly, *doing all we can*' isn't good enough, Colonel, don't you agree, Cardinal Alphonso?" asked Pope Leo. In stark contrast to their earlier conversation, he was annoyed to find out what little progress had been made.

"You know my feelings, Your Holiness," he replied, clutching the silver head of his walking cane.

"We are getting close to the end of the journey when our fate will finally be determined – we know the powers contained within the book and it's our heavy responsibility to do everything in our power to prevent this book from ever being opened, to prevent one page from being turned. If we can't be sure of finding the book first then we should destroy the tools that have been made to find it!"

The Cardinals alongside him nodded their heads in agreement.

"Colonel Renauld, do you understand?" said Pope Leo XIV. He had regained his earlier composure and spoke in a softer tone.

"If the keys of the arkheynia are destroyed… And everything and everyone associated with them, including the Judas Scrolls and those privy to the secret, the entrance to the labyrinth can never be found, can it?" he continued in a low whisper.

Renauld knew what he was being instructed to do. It had always been the Vatican's primary objective since the outset to destroy the Book of Judas itself. Only by doing this would they ever consider themselves truly safe from the holocaust of evil that had been foretold through the ages. However, if this couldn't be achieved the second best course of action was to prevent anyone else from ever finding it and this meant destroying the means of finding entrance to labyrinth.

"Is there anyone here who disagrees with the path we have chosen?" asked Pope Leo as he scanned their faces.

They all nodded their agreement.

"The lives of the living must not be allowed to destroy the lives of the future," he continued, addressing his words sternly to Colonel Renauld.

"You must find them and do your job now before it is too late."

"I understand, Your Holiness," he repeated respectfully.

Leaving the dark interior of the Sala Ducale, Renauld closed the door behind him; he stood alone at the end of the Sistine chapel. He looked up and wondered whether it was coincidental they he stood face to face with *The Last Judgement* by Michelangelo. The marvellous composition filled a vast space and he stared up at the image of Judas Iscariot, the disciple who betrayed Jesus Christ in his hour of need. He stopped for a moment to think through Pope Leo's words as his eyes remained fixed on the image of treachery. *Destroy the arkheynia and kill the Trenchard brothers. Very well,* he thought, *if that's the decision of the inner sanctum then that's what must be done. The question is do we have enough time? I need to speak to Goran as soon as possible,* he concluded and he turned on his heels and marched back towards his office.

Chapter Thirty-Seven

Cairo, Egypt

Simon and Anna had gathered in Philip's hotel room. It was rapidly approaching the time at which their unknown adversary had said he would call them in the note delivered by the bellboy.

Since returning from the museum earlier that morning, Philip had managed a couple of extra hours' sleep in bed but it was not really sufficient. After taking a shower and having something to eat he felt some of his energy return for the call ahead. Apart from the tiredness, he also felt the added pressure of knowing that he was going to have to be at the very top of his game if he was going to get Heather back. Taking a sip from his coffee cup as he stared out over the Nile from their eighth floor view, he considered the various questions that could arise. The thought of the phone ringing at any moment started the adrenaline pumping through his body again but it was mixed with a feeling of excitement at the thought of speaking with Heather.

For the past two hours Simon and Anna had helped Philip get mentally prepared for the call. They had discussed and considered every question or instruction that might arise and in turn what Philip's response should be. In essence they now had the keys to the labyrinth and the map to find it; they knew the Satanica's plan would be to deliver a set of instructions that would enable them to swap these in return for

Philip's beloved Heather. They all agreed that however the transfer was to take place it was vital that they released the arkheynia and the Scrolls only when they had Heather firmly in their sights. Mentally Philip felt much better equipped to handle the call after their pragmatic discussion.

"What ever happens, you have to remain calm," said Simon. He knew how annoyed he could become if things weren't going his way. "Remember, there's no point raising your voice, or shouting or demanding anything because you'll only put Heather at risk – we've no way of knowing how he might retaliate if he gets annoyed!"

Philip shook his head. He knew his brother was right.

Anna wasn't so sure.

"Philip, you've got something he wants, something that he'll do anything to get his hands on – you must realise he wants this as badly as you want Heather back! You can use this to your advantage," she urged.

"What do you mean?" asked Philip.

Listening to Anna's train of thought, Simon felt a sudden surge of panic deriving from the conversation the night before.

"I mean the kidnapper's going to make several demands of you and he's going to say that unless you do as he commands you'll never see Heather again – he knows that if he does anything to harm Heather before we hand over the arkheynia he'll never see them again! So maybe we should be asking him to deliver Heather and take the arkheynia from us according to *our* terms!"

"Are you saying we should say 'no' to his demands and risk Heather's life?" asked Philip, a little shocked by the direction the conversation was going. "Remember, he knows exactly where we are!"

"He's a killer, Philip – he'll kill anyone or anything that stands in his way when their use to him is finished!"

"I don't know," said Philip, staring at the phone. "We give him what he wants and he gives us back Heather – it should be as simple as that."

Simon glanced at Anna. She could tell straight away from his frosty expression that he didn't want her to pursue this line of reasoning any longer.

She stood up and walked over to the table where they had spread out the map and the Scroll of Judas. While Philip had been sleeping, Anna had been busy. With Simon looking on, she worked her way through the scroll's ancient text. As she translated a new line she would fiddle with the three arkheynia, trying to piece them together like an interlocking jigsaw. She knew that once they were connected in the right manner they would give away the secret location to the underground labyrinth.

The three fragments of bone seemed awkward and disjointed as she tried to connect them. Each arkheynia with its bright blood-red end had its own grooves and ridges but they seemed incompatible and Anna was getting frustrated. After several attempts, Anna struggled with them one last time. Holding them together in a formation she thought might work, she let go and they fell about the table again.

"It's no use," she said exasperated, "I can't do it!"

"Give them to me," said Simon, holding out his hand.

He fiddled with them for a few moments.

"I think they work like this," he said, and promptly snapped them together so that they made a triangular shape.

"Yes, that's it! Well done, Simon!" exclaimed Anna, taking them from him excitedly. "That's exactly how the scroll describes it!"

"What now?" he asked.

"Now we have to place the red ends, or feet as the scroll describes them, on the map at these specific coordinates," she said busily trying to align the triangle.

"I need a pencil or a pen," she said sharply and he jumped up to try and find one from the desk in the room.

"Ok, if I can start with this one to here," she muttered. "Simon I need you to hold this in place for me."

He held the three interlocking arkheynia on the map whilst Anna drew three straight lines from each angle of the triangle down at right angles to the perpendicular arkheynia.

"Ok, you can lift it off now – the entrance can be located at the point where all the three lines intersect each other," she said, as they both looked down to see what her craftsmanship had revealed.

"Bethsaida!" the both said at once.

"Do you know anything about the place?" asked Simon, trying to work out what modern-day country it was in from the scale of the map.

Anna sat shaking her head in disbelief.

"What is it? What's the matter?" he asked as he saw her distant expression.

"Nothing really I suppose, it just seems an unusual coincidence that all – as it happens I do know quite a lot about Bethsaida – I worked there for over six months on an excavation."

"Amazing – that's our good fortune!"

"It's a beautiful place, right next to the Sea of Gennesarath as it was called in the bible… It's better known to you and me as the Sea of Galilee – you might call it another coincidence," she said, picking up the interlocking arkheynia, "but modern day scholars call it the evangelical triangle because it is where Jesus carried out all his 'mighty works', his miracles… And where he laid down the foundations of what we now know as Christianity."

"Does the scroll say anything else?"

She screwed up her face as she ran her finger along the ancient language.

"Once we get there, it gives us some detailed instructions to find the entrance and some clues to help follow the way through the labyrinth – I just hope everything is as it was two thousand years ago!"

At that point, Philip had woken up and between them they related all the discoveries they had just made.

It was now fast approaching two o'clock and Philip took another sip of his coffee as they waited nervously for the phone to ring.

"Do you think Heather and the Satanica's killer are in Egypt?" asked Philip.

"I suspect he's definitely somewhere in the region. He wants to be in close proximity to the Book of Judas," replied Anna. "And he'll have Heather with him – he knows that he needs her present for the trade to take place."

The phone started ringing and Philip glanced up sharply at his brother.

"Be calm," Simon reiterated as watched him step over and pick up the receiver.

"This is Philip Trenchard," he said nervously.

"Very good," replied the steady, monotone voice of Conchos. "Have you got all three keys of the arkheynia?"

"Yes, we have them all safely in our possession – can I speak with Heather now?"

"Excellent," Conchos smiled privately to himself. "Yes, you may speak with the girl."

In the background, he could hear make out some noise like tape being ripped from skin followed by the sound of gasping as if a gag was being removed. It conjured up all kinds of visions in his mind.

Suddenly, he heard her cry.

"Philip, Philip," she sobbed uncontrollably into the phone

In a split second, his body went numb as the emotion surged through him.

"Heather, are you Ok? Listen I'm coming to get you, do you understand… I'm coming to get save you… Are you Ok?" he repeated. The sound of her sobbing voice was unbearable.

It was no good, she sounded as if she was having a breakdown. All he could hear amongst the moaning and the hysteria was "Philip" being repeated over and over again. Anna's eyes welled up and Simon desperately tried to keep control as they watched Philip's agonising contortions. They could see his suffering and his desperate attempt to remain in control.

"Heather," he called again, trying to get through to her.

"Philip, I love you!" she cried.

The next sound was a muffled, choking noise as Conchos replaced the tape over her mouth.

The excruciating pain of hearing Heather in distress brought Philip close to breaking point. He felt useless, unable to do anything to relieve her suffering. The intensity of his feelings transformed into uncontrollable anger as Conchos returned to the phone.

"Have you got the location of the labyrinth?" he asked calmly.

"Put her back on you murdering bastard!" he shouted down the phone. "If you harm her in any way I swear I'll kill you!"

Anna and Simon exchanged glances. They knew the agony Philip must be feeling as he vented his anger. At that point both of them would have done anything to help lessen his suffering. They watched as he lifted the phone from the desk and paced across the hotel bedroom floor. Anna had predicted this turn of events. Simon also knew how important it was that Philip remained in control otherwise who could predict the backlash that might follow. He caught his brother's eye and signalled with his hand for him to try and remain calm.

Gripping the receiver tightly Philip nodded to his brother. He stopped his outburst and listened for the voice of the "executioner" at the other end of the phone. It didn't arrive straight away. For several seconds there was silence and he anxiously wondered whether he was still on the line.

Suddenly, the cold, chilling voice of Conchos returned.

"Do you want to see her again alive?" said Conchos calmly. He had registered the words spoken in anger and he wouldn't forget them.

"Yes, of course I do!"

"Well, I want you to listen very carefully – do you understand?"

353

"Yes, I understand…" replied Philip. He had managed to bring himself back under control.

"Good, you will speak to her and you will see her again, but only if you do exactly as I say – do you understand?"

"I understand," he replied, nodding and sitting down again. Anna frowned as she sensed the way the conversation was going.

"Now that you have all the arkheynia," continued Conchos, "where does it say that the entrance to the labyrinth is located?"

Philip thought he could detect an accent. His pronunciation sounded slightly Germanic. *Maybe from the Low Countries,* he thought.

"By our calculations, the entrance is in a place called Bethsaida close to the Sea of Galilee," he replied. The torment of hearing Heather's distress was still coursing through him. *I'd do anything, absolutely anything to put this right.*

Without trying to disturb him, Anna moved closer to where Philip was sitting to try and glean more of the conversation. She could tell from the way the conversation was going that they had reached the point where the kidnapper would be issuing his fresh set of demands.

Philip could hear the rustling of papers in the background as he waited for his reply.

"Good, very good," Conchos muttered. "If you would like to see the girl again alive then these are your instructions – your brother will fly to Amman in Jordan. You and the girl will stay here. When I give the command you will go and pick up your friend; she is currently located within one hundred kilometres of your hotel – I will give you her exact location when your brother shows me the entrance to the labyrinth. Am I understood?"

"Yes, I understand," replied Philip.

That meant that all Simon had to do was direct him to the entrance. *Surely he can manage to do this within the next twenty-four hours,* he prayed hopefully.

"Remember I want no heroics. Your hotel is being watched – anything unusual and I will kill the girl – now, I have one final instruction," he commanded and the line went on hold.

"What's happening?" whispered Simon.

Philip was about to answer when Conchos's voice returned.

"There is a direct flight to Amman with Egypt Air at five-thirty. Your brother will take that flight and he will stay at the Marriott Hotel. I will communicate with him directly from there – do you understand?"

"Yes, I…" Philip began but was unable to finish.

The line went dead and Philip, his hand trembling slightly, slowly replaced the receiver and stared at the anxious faces of Anna and Simon. They waited apprehensively for the news. Listening intently, they nodded as he replayed the entire conversation word for word.

"That must have been just awful," said Anna.

Shaking her head, she got up and walked across the room to comfort Philip, putting his head in hands and rubbing his eyes as he reached the part where he told them how Heather had reacted when Conchos allowed her to speak.

Simon and Anna listened to the instructions he had agreed with the kidnapper.

"I had to agree… It's the only option!" he said, looking up for their approval.

"You mean I have to go alone!" said Simon in surprise. He wasn't even contemplating the personal danger – just his ability to do the job properly.

"How will I be able to find the entrance? I can't follow the instructions – they're in a totally different language!"

"It's Ok because I'm coming with you," said Anna stubbornly.

She knew that Philip wouldn't like it because it broke the protocols laid down by the Satanica but she had made her mind up – there was no way that she was going to stay in Cairo.

"Anna, he said that we should stay here – any deviation from his instructions and he said he'd kill Heather!"

"Philip, have you thought about the fact that her life will be in greater danger if Simon can't find the entrance!" she argued, her voice rising in frustration.

"Can't you just pass on the instructions to him? Can't you teach him?"

"It's just not as simple as that, the scrolls refer to things you have to see with your own eyes; the landscape may have changed, reference points may have become camouflaged... I've been to Bethsaida before and have good knowledge of the surrounding terrain – remember, Philip, we're talking about a labyrinth that was built over two thousand years ago!"

"*Damn,*" said Philip, cursing privately. *Why didn't I see this? Why didn't I explain it to him when I had the chance?* He knew in his heart that she was right. If they were ever going to get Heather back alive then Anna would have to accompany Simon.

"Ok, it makes sense," said Philip.

Simon breathed a sigh of relief and Anna smiled softly at him, realizing she had managed to win her case.

"How are we going to make it appear to these other Satanica henchmen that you're actually still here?" he asked.

Anna looked thoughtful for a second before answering.

"Just keep two rooms in both our names for the time being and stay out of sight, hopefully we don't need to disguise the situation for very long – we're going to be in Amman tonight and tomorrow morning we'll make the trip to Bethsaida – if everything goes according to plan we should be able to locate the entrance during the afternoon... in which case he should be contacting you tomorrow with Heather's location!"

"I think she's right," supported Simon.

"Are you going to take the same flight?" Philip asked, thinking through the possibilities.

"No, I think that's too risky – it's best if we travel separately," said Anna.

356

Simon wasted no time. He called the airport and made a reservation on the five-thirty flight as instructed before reserving a seat for Anna on the direct Jordanian Air flight that left one hour later.

"Ok, well I guess that leaves me waiting here," said Philip ruefully. "This is going to be difficult – I'm going to feel totally useless not being able to do anything – just promise me that you'll do everything you possibly can to get Heather back safely," he pleaded.

Simon looked at Anna, his mind recalling the conversation they had the night before.

"Trust me – we'll do everything we possibly can," answered Simon, putting his hand on his brother's shoulder.

"Go – you'd better get packed," he urged.

Twenty minutes later they made their farewells. Simon departed first, embracing his brother. An hour later, Anna departed the same way, promising to do everything she could to bring Heather back.

Chapter Thirty-Eight

Vatican City, Rome

The Cardinal stepped out of the shadows of the colonnade in St. Peter's Square and walked purposefully towards the entrance of the great Basilica. Still warm although the time was approaching nine o'clock, it had been a wonderful summer's day and the evening light was just beginning to fade.

Dressed in his elegant, scarlet robes of office, he quickly ascertained that the Square was empty except for the sentry from the Swiss Guard who stood to attention at the bottom of the Basilica steps. The guard, wearing his traditional, brightly collared tunic and metal helmet with the red plume of feathers, had been stationed there by Major Dupont. Remaining motionless he watched as the senior cleric crossed the square and begin climbing the steps at the furthest vantage point from his position. He was under strict instructions to observe but not to challenge.

The Cardinal strode past doing his best to avoid being identified. He put his hands up to his thick, velvet collar and pulled it up to avoid detection. The guard nodded in deference but in this light and wearing his robes of office, he knew the sentry would have little chance of identifying him from the multitude of Cardinals that would pass the same way.

Reaching the steps, he climbed up towards the impressive portico to St. Paul's Basilica. It was a path he frequently followed including the journey he had made earlier that day on his way to the Sala Ducale. As he scurried along, he thought about his impending rendezvous. His intimate knowledge of the Vatican and the movements of its senior clergy meant that at this time of the evening there were only three "likely" locations for the priest he was looking for. He had managed to rule out the first two possibilities from some discreet enquires from his own quarters – this left only the third location, the Clementine Chapel.

As he made his way through the magnificent archway, he could hear the melodious sound of the Cathedral choir as they practiced *Adeste Fidelis* in the Sistine Chapel.

Inside the enormous and cavernous hall of St. Paul's he passed close to the tomb of St. Peter with its famous bronze Baldacchino. It was empty now but only a short while earlier this area had been a hive of activity for the papal coronation of Pope Leo XIV. The Cardinal walked down the left hand aisle past the tomb towards the chapels that lined the perimeter of the great hall. He slowed down as he reached the Chapel of the Pieta, named after Michelangelo's famous marble sculpture made at the end of the fifteenth century. Being careful not to be observed, he paused for a moment to check the way was clear. It was as he had suspected, the chapel was empty except for a few burning candles.

Despite the sheer scale and magnificence of its interior, St. Paul's was a cold and dark place especially in the evening when it was so quiet with no natural sunlight. The abundance of flickering candles casting grey shadows along the edge of the hall added an eerie, mysterious feeling to the chill. Satisfied he was alone, he carried on walking along the perimeter, past the Chapel of Saint Sebastian containing Messina's monument to Pope Pius XII, until he reached the Gregorian Chapel. Again he stopped to check for any signs of life. The priest he was searching for was creature of habit. Without fail, he would normally travel every evening from his private quarters to the chapels in St. Paul's to pray before God.

Cautiously, he stepped inside the sixteenth century Gregorian Chapel, the work of Giacoma Della Porta, which was heavily decorated with mosaics and precious marbles. A quick scan of the interior told him all he wanted to know. The rows of pews were empty. *That leaves only one place,* he reflected as he silently turned to walk down the stone aisle along the perimeter of St. Paul's. Although he was dressed in his Cardinal's robes he wore cloth slippers below his cassock to minimise the sound against the hard, stone floor.

He passed the Colonna Chapel with its astounding marble altarpiece of Leo the Great halting the legendary Attila by Algardi. He checked it was deserted before continuing to his final destination, the Clementine Chapel. Outside in the shadows, he stood motionless, peering through an iron grille in the vestibule at the back of the church. The sacred chapel, renowned for housing the remains of St. Gregory the Great, was smaller and much more intimate than the others. Looking down the central aisle leading towards the magnificent altar, he saw the instantly recognizable hunched figure of the Cardinal deep in prayer. He quickly glanced around the rest of the pews and allowed himself a wry smile as he realized the priest was all alone.

Being careful not make to much noise, he made his way down the stone aisle while the choral singing floated through the chapel in the background. The bent figure, deep in mediation, was oblivious to anything or anyone.

Within a few feet of the hunched figure, he looked around the chamber one last time before he drew out a long thin blade from the sleeve of his robe. Taking two steps forward, he reached out and grabbed the Cardinal's hair, jerking his head upwards. The mortified priest looked up, shocked and surprised, as he recognized the twisted smile on his brutal killer's face. It was the last sight he would see. The assassin slit his throat and then drove the knife hard and deep into his chest, at the same time pulling his robe over his head yanking it tight to muffle any choking noises that might alert passers-by. The Cardinal died quickly.

Listening hard for any unusual sounds, he heard none. Without wasting any time he pushed the lifeless body back into the hunched praying position before calmly standing up to depart.

Taking one step back to admire his work, he spotted the dead Cardinal's walking cane lying on the floor. He picked it up and rested it against the limp body before leaving.

Chapter Thirty-Nine

Amman, Jordan

The scheduled flight from Cairo to Amman in Jordan was a short one. Simon breathed a sigh of relief as the plane took off on time. At one point, when he was stuck in the commuter jam leaving central Cairo, the dismal outlook for getting to the airport on time had caused him some distress but a combination of some strong words and a financial incentive had spurred the driver into action. Although Simon was in a rush to check-in, he had also made up his mind to be vigilant and watch out for the other passengers in the terminal. For all he knew, Heather's kidnapper or maybe one of his henchmen could be on his flight to observe his movements and confirm that he had boarded the plane.

After the earlier call, Philip had mentioned that the accent on the telephone had been Dutch or German, so he kept his ears and eyes open for any suspicious looking Caucasian European males travelling alone. In his hurry to make the flight, he raced through the departure lounge to the boarding gate but no one caught his attention. As he took his seat in business class he checked the passengers around him but they were predominantly local Arabs. The three white males he did see looked totally harmless as far as he was concerned.

The flight landed at Amman airport and he quickly proceeded

through immigration carrying just hand luggage. Reaching the taxi rank outside, he hailed a cab and instructed the driver to take him to the Marriott Hotel.

"How long will it take?"

"Maybe half an hour, maybe a bit more," replied the Jordanian taxi driver casually.

Simon pulled out his new mobile phone and called Philip to let him know that he had arrived safely and according to plan. The car journey took about forty minutes in the end. The building occupied a prominent location on the side of a hill rising in the middle of the city and along the rim of its rooftop was a bright red neon sign that announced the *Marriott* logo from some distance away.

When he checked in with Reception, he discovered that a room had already been reserved in his name. *He likes to know what room you're in,* he thought as he signed the hotel's papers. The idea that such a cold, emotionless killer who had inflicted such atrocities on Professor Palanski knew exactly where to find him was frightening. *As long as I've got the means of locating the entrance I'm safe,* he reminded himself before settling down in the room to wait for Anna's arrival.

It was approaching ten o'clock by the time Anna finally knocked on his door. Simon pulled her inside and kissed her on the cheek.

"Everything Ok?" he asked.

"Yes, fine," she replied, although the expression on her face told him that not all was well. She looked concerned. She looked as if she was carrying a great burden that she couldn't share with anyone else.

"You were longer than I thought – did the flight land on time?" asked Simon.

"Yes," she replied. "I wanted to make sure that no one would see me in the hotel so I called to get your room number and waited downstairs until I was sure it was safe... I didn't want to take any chances."

That made sense, Simon thought.

"What is it then?" he said appealing to her. "There's something on your mind that you're not sharing with me isn't there?"

She turned her head away.

"I know there is," he added.

Anna knew he was right. She had been wondering how she would break the news to him ever since she had walked out of Philip's hotel room a few hours earlier. *If he takes this the wrong way I know our relationship will be over before it's really had a chance to begin,* she mused.

"Can I have a drink?"

"Of course, what would you like?"

"Just a glass of wine," she replied and Simon opened the door to the mini-bar and uncorked a bottle of white wine. He poured them both a drink and he sat down on the edge of the bed while she sat in the easy chair next to the coffee table.

"What is it, Anna? You know there's nothing that can come between us now."

There's only one way I can deal with this, she thought. *I've got to be straight and honest with him.*

"Simon, do you remember our conversation last night when we were waiting to hear from Philip?"

"How could I forget it," he said, smiling.

"Seriously, I don't ever want you to forget how much I believe it," she said earnestly. "I love you and when you hear what I've got to say, I want you to remember that."

He had a sudden feeling of in trepidation as he realized she was being serious.

"What is it, Anna?" he repeated eyeing her curiously.

She looked up at him.

"Simon, I work for the Vatican!"

He sat there frozen for a second trying to comprehend what she had just said. *How on earth can this be true?*

"What?" he stuttered, shaking his head in dismay. "I don't believe it."

"I was recruited by a man called Goran, a Vatican agent, several years ago," she continued despondently in a voice riddled with guilt.

"I don't understand – are you really Anna Nikolaidis? Is that your name?" he questioned, looking up at her in puzzled astonishment.

"Yes, I am – I am Anna Nikolaidis," she answered positively and stared at him with her eyes wide open.

"You need to explain this to me, Anna. I don't understand," said Simon, suddenly feeling hurt that he had discovered a part of her life that he never knew existed.

"One day a long time ago I met a man called Goran who told me that he worked for the Vatican. At the time I thought the meeting was by chance but I've subsequently learnt that it was all prearranged. He knew about my background and asked me whether I would be interested in working in the museums where the treasures of the Vatican are stored – it was a very exciting offer for a young archaeologist, particularly with my strong Roman Catholic upbringing."

She paused and took a sip from her glass of wine.

"After two months of working in the museum helping to put uncatalogued items into chronological order, I was told, very much to my surprise, that I was to have an audience alone with the Pope – That was Pope Paul the Twelfth… The Pope who recently passed away," she added.

"I remember the meeting well, he was such an imposing and impressive figure. He was a very kindly man although he was getting on in years… I think he was in his early eighties. Anyway, he told me one day I was very special, that I would be called upon to do God's work and that I should do all that I could over the coming years to prepare for it – I gladly accepted this was the case and over the coming months with Goran as my tutor, I learnt all about the history of the Satanica and their sinful and immoral ways."

Simon sat silently listening intently to every word. He could barely believe the story that was unfolding.

"While under Goran, I was educated and trained in many skills, almost like a soldier, so that when the time came I could fight against the evil. The training was rigorous. I spent months learning armed combat, how to use tactical weapons, how to prepare and detonate explosives! They tested me by simulating various conceivable situations that they thought might arise so that when the time came I would be ready – however, they never actually told me what my calling would be and at the end they returned me to my home in Greece where they told me to wait patiently until the day came."

"I don't believe it," Simon burst out. "You were *expecting* me when I came to your excavation site just outside Athens!"

"That's right Simon, I was." She looked up. "I had been contacted a few days earlier by Goran and summoned back to the Vatican – I was given a private audience with Pope Paul the Twelfth again and he told me the full story of the Book of Judas and what it would mean if it were ever to fall into the hands of the Satanica. The Pope told me I would be accompanying you on a quest for the book and, with Goran's help, I was to do all I could to destroy it."

She looked up, trying to read Simon's expression.

"Go on," he urged.

"Goran told me that only the Pope and he would be aware of my existence and that I was to communicate everything directly through him – so yes… I was expecting you to visit that day," she muttered sadly. "But you must be believe me I never expected this outcome."

"So you've been in contact with the Vatican the whole time?"

Sat on the edge of the bed she clasped her hands.

"Yes, that's right," she answered. She almost felt resigned to Simon's reaction and stared up blankly at the wall in the silence that followed.

"Simon believe me, I never knew it would turn out this way," she said,

366

pleading with him to understand. "When we started I was prepared to do anything to destroy the book, I was even trained to kill if necessary!"

He shook his head in amazement.

"And what are your Vatican orders now?" he asked, shaking his head.

"I was told in Cairo to destroy the arkheynia and…"

Simon looked up at her face as she paused.

"And to kill both of you!" she continued.

He stood up and walked towards the window running his hand through his hair.

"And now what?" he said loudly. "What are you planning to do now?" he added with a sarcastic undertone.

"Don't do this, Simon," she pleaded again.

He put his hands on his hips and stared out of the window across the streetlights running down the hill into the centre of Amman. Anna watched him, silently hoping and praying that he would be able to see the truth.

His mind ran over all the events they had shared during their journey together across the world. Despite his initial anger and the shock at hearing her astonishing revelation he knew deep down that he still meant every word he had said to her Cairo. Thoughts raced through his mind as he recounted their conversations but underneath it all he could see she was being genuine now and that ultimately what really mattered was the fact that he loved her.

He turned around from the window and when she saw the expression on his face, her hopes were raised.

"Anna… What are we going to do now?" he asked softly and held out his open arms.

Smiling with relief, she jumped up and rushed forward into his embrace. For a moment, they just held each other tightly.

"What are we going to do?" Simon whispered again.

"We're going to do our best to save Heather – that's what we're going to do," she replied defiantly.

"We can do it! I *know* we can do it," she repeated, squeezing his hands.

"Do you have a plan in mind?" he asked, looking down at the huge smile across her pretty face.

"I have the beginnings of one but I'm afraid it's going to be a late night," she warned.

"What do you mean?" asked Simon curiously.

She opened her bag and produced a photocopied section of the Judas Scrolls. He looked at the ancient writing and wondered how on earth she could make sense of it.

"This is the part of the scroll that deals with finding the entrance once you're in the town of Bethsaida – I need to make sure that you understand every single aspect of this section… You need to know where to start your search and you need to know what you're looking for as you follow the instructions because I won't be with you!"

"Where are you going to be?" he asked, slightly taken back. He had hoped they would be able to work together but now he suddenly had distressing visions of being alone with the "executioner" who so grotesquely killed Professor Palanski.

"I'll be nearby in Bethsaida, don't worry," she said as they heard a knock on the door.

"It's late," he whispered curiously and walked towards the door.

"Who is it?" he asked.

"Message for Mr. Trenchard," answered the delivery boy. He opened the door and took the envelope.

Pulling it open, he read the contents and handed it on to Anna.

"A Mercedes and a driver have been arranged for your departure from the hotel at 8am. The driver will take you across the Israeli border and into Bethsaida. Once you find the entrance I shall give you the location of the girl."

"Can we trust him to deliver his side?" asked Simon.

"No, we can't trust him at all but this is the only option open to us if we're going to try and save Heather – remember, he's going to be watching you very closely as you follow the clues that will lead you to the labyrinth's entrance… Whatever happens you must be careful not to give it away before we have the information we need!"

"Where will you be?" he asked again.

"I know Bethsaida very well. It's a small place but I'll be watching – once we have the information we need, I intend to finish this assignment one way or another!"

"I'll help you," said Simon. "Just tell me what to do?"

"Ok, it's going to be a long night – the first thing I need you to understand is the terrain. You're going to have to recognise the topography of the landscape as you travel through it!"

He nodded and rang Room Service for some fresh coffee. They were both exhausted from the long night before but they knew they had to keep going.

The strong coffee duly arrived and Anna began lecturing Simon on all the contents of the scroll. Bit by bit he built a picture in his mind of the landscape he would face and the path he must follow to find the entrance. Over two hours later, after running through every possibility, every likely scenario, they decided that he had captured all the knowledge required for the mission ahead. He sat back in his chair, confident that he knew her plan inside out.

"Ok, let's hope it works!" he said finally, checking his watch.

The strategy was both dangerous and risky but under the circumstances they knew they would have to take chances. It relied on events unfolding in a sequence that she had predicted. If anything happened to alter one of the chain's links it could have a disastrous effect on the outcome and indeed the safety of Simon's life. He knew he was in a vulnerable position but there was too much at stake. He cast his mind back to what seemed an age ago – the vision of Philip, frozen with despair as he listened to the distressing sound of Heather's hysterical and muffled screams. There was no doubt in his mind; he was prepared to go to any necessary lengths. If it meant putting his life at risk he would gladly do so if it meant getting her back in one piece.

"You must get some sleep," said Anna interrupting his thoughts. She cleared up the coffee table in front of them, ripped up their scribbled workings and threw them into the wastepaper bin.

"And what are you doing?" he replied.

"I'm afraid I've got to go."

"What do you mean?" he asked, watching her stand up.

"I'm travelling to Bethsaida now; I can't wait to travel until after you've set off can I?" she said, smiling bravely although the thought of another sleepless night was appalling.

She saw Simon's worried expression.

"Don't worry," she said. "I know the area well – I'll be there ready for when you arrive tomorrow morning."

For several minutes, they stood holding each other tightly at the bedroom door.

"I love you," said Simon as Anna twisted the door handle open.

She kissed him one last time before she slipped out into the corridor and then into the dark night beyond.

Chapter Forty

Vatican City, Rome

Colonel Renauld was angry. He was angry with his subordinates, he was angry with Major Dupont and above all he was angry with himself. *How could I have allowed this to happen?* he reflected. Since the body had been discovered in the Clementine Chapel along the perimeter of St. Paul's Basilica he had taken it upon himself to shoulder most of the blame. He certainly felt guilty that his security arrangements had not been sufficient to prevent the tragic cold-blooded murder of Cardinal Alphonso.

It was now seven-thirty in the morning as he made his way back to his office from the mortuary. Along with Major Dupont, he had been up all night since the body was discovered shortly after ten o'clock the previous evening. Fortunately, from a containment point of view, Renauld had been the third person to arrive at the scene of the crime after the body was discovered by two choristers returning to their quarters.

He had been walking in the papal gardens at the rear of St. Paul's Basilica when the murderous encounter took place. He had been using the solitude to think matters through. The beautifully tended garden, with its tall Cyprus trees and carefully pruned hedges lining the gravel paths, was a place where he often sought refuge when he had a lot on his mind. Early on in his walk as he approached the Basilica's rear entrance he had been alerted by the panic and commotion within the Clementine

Chapel. The choristers had walked up to speak to the Cardinal and found him dead in his pew. Later on in his investigation, when he had enquired of the boys what they were doing entering the chapel, he discovered that they regularly stopped to pay their respects and chat with Cardinal Alphonso on their way home after singing practice.

On witnessing the blood stained corpse, his instant reaction had been to call Major Dupont and issue a "state of alert" warning and an urgent curfew order. No one was to be allowed out of their quarters until his command had been rescinded.

At the scene of the crime, the two choristers, crying inconsolably, were collected by his armed guard and whisked away to an administration block where the Swiss Guards' medical officers looked after them – Renauld wanted to ensure that the two shell-shocked young boys remained in the medical corps' custody until he was in a position to interview them later on.

After calling Major Dupont, he had looked more closely at the body. Despite the blood around his face and on his robes, he was still instantly recognizable as Cardinal Alphonso. He cursed himself when he realized who it was. He felt they had developed a special bond together, a special relationship that spanned many years. When the discovery of the impostor had been confirmed by the faxed communication, it was Cardinal Alphonso to whom he turned. Renauld knew he could depend on Alphonso, the wise man of the Vatican. In his long role as a statesman, he had seen many of the crucial events that had beset the church over the modern era – indeed he was one of the senior priests who sat on the ecumenical council when it had first debated the authority and existence of the Judas Scrolls.

Lifting the Cardinal's head, he saw the neat slit that had been made across his throat. The expression on his face was one of shock and horror. *I wonder if you saw the killer,* he muttered to himself.

Casting his eyes down further, he saw the hilt of the razor sharp blade still protruding from the bloody wound on his chest. *What clues can this give us?* he pondered, wondering whether or not to retract the knife so that he could get a better look. He decided against it. *Probably wise to leave it for the time being,* he thought – the doctor in charge of the post mortem might glean some additional knowledge that he couldn't otherwise.

He was about to let the dead Cardinal's head fall forward again when he suddenly noticed something on his neck. Squinting, he leaned down to get a closer look, pulling the velvet ruff of the Cardinal's collar to one side to get a better view. Renauld shook his head in dismay when he recognized the markings. Scratched into the side of his neck were the letters "MM". A trickle of dried blood ran down from the last point of the second "M" but it was still clearly identifiable. *We're dealing with an extremely cool customer here,* thought Renauld as the anger raged inside him once again.

Moments later, as the elite, trustworthy soldiers from his regimental guard arrived as requisitioned earlier, he sadly let go of Alphonso's head and it again fell forward towards the wooden pew. They were also accompanied by two of the medical orderlies who quickly and professionally set about the job in hand.

Renauld looked up at Major Dupont, who was standing at the front of the four-man deposition.

"Did you check with the sentry looking after the private quarters?" he asked irritably. "I want to see that man later," he added.

Colonel Renauld had not placed the Cardinals Weiss, Giacoma and Lefebvre under house arrest or attempted to restrict their movements but he had requested radically improved surveillance measures.

"I'm afraid they've all left their quarters tonight at some time or another," replied Dupont.

"What about the sentry in St. Peter's Square?" he barked back.

"He remembers seeing one of the Cardinals crossing the square and entering the Basilica not long ago but he couldn't recognize him," he answered bleakly.

"Where are the three Cardinals now?"

"They're all in their own private quarters with guards on the doors."

"Ok, that's how it should remain from now on," Renauld pronounced abruptly.

He looked down at the Cardinal's lifeless body again.

"I want this to be handled entirely in-house. I want you to escort the medical team with the body back to the mortuary – this information, this event, is classified top secret. Do you understand?"

He paused for a moment, looking them directly in the eye. He didn't have to wait long to receive the chorus of agreement from his dependable second in command and his troop of armed personnel. He knew these soldiers and the orderlies personally; they had all been under his command for several years and he was confident that he could trust them implicitly.

"Whatever happens I do not want this leaked to the outside world. Major, you're to keep those who know what's going on here to an absolute minimum – right, let's get moving!" he ordered.

The old, decrepit corpse of Cardinal Alphonse was lifted up and put into a plastic body bag, his large gold crucifix glinting in the chapel's candlelight as the orderly zipped it up.

Renauld stood motionless with hands clasped behind his back as they hurriedly lifted the body and exited the chapel in the direction of the mortuary where the body of Cardinal Gregory was also lying on one of the slabs. The senior medical orderly stayed behind a few minutes longer to make sure there was no trace of the murder scene on the floor or around the wooden pews.

Left alone in the Clementine Chapel, Renauld looked down at the spot where Alphonso had been murdered and saw that his walking cane had been left behind beneath one of the pews. Picking it up, he looked around the dark corners of the church and saw the place where the remains of St Gregory the Great were housed near the entrance of the modern sacristy. *Maybe you too will be canonized one day,* he reflected. *You certainly deserve it with the dedication and loyalty you've shown this church.* He tapped the silver head of the cane and turned to follow his men across the back routes around St. Peter's Square.

During the night he had conducted interviews with anyone who might have been able to shed some light on what actually happened. Extremely shrewd with his questions, he was very careful not to broaden the band of people already privy to the tragic and monstrous killing. Unfortunately, he gleaned very little of any use from the process. As the facts stood his best lead was the Cardinal who had been observed leaving the cloisters and crossing St. Peter's square only minutes before he had ventured on the scene. The Vatican pathologist who had been allowed into the closely guarded secret had calculated that the approximate time of death was consistent with this Cardinal's presence in the square.

Discreet enquiries into the movements of Cardinals Weiss, Lefebvre and Giacoma also led to blind alleys. When he cross-questioned them individually, they all had robust, sensible alibis, although for one reason or another they could not be substantiated by third parties to the extent that he would have liked. Renauld prided himself on being able to read a man's face and mannerisms but the interviews had revealed nothing. They all showed what seemed to be genuine horror at the appalling news of the Cardinal's death and their sorrowful demeanour afterwards made it almost impossible to glean anything new. Certainly, Cardinal Giacoma's distress shown for the man he had faithfully served since he first arrived at the Vatican was touching in its sincerity.

However, he knew that one of them had to be the murderer and whoever it was they had been cool enough to act undercover in the Vatican for a long time. The question was which one of them was it? His instincts told him that Cardinal Lefebvre was sometimes a little too quick with his responses and he made a mental note to try and find all their travel records over the past few months.

The investigation had taken all night and he knew there would be little chance to catch up on sleep over the next few days.

Tired and exhausted, he trudged back to his office as the sun was rising across the square; his anger had still not completely subsided. He knew that he had allowed himself to become so preoccupied with events taking place in Cairo that he had taken his eye off important safety measures at home. He privately wondered whether the preparations and security arrangements he had orchestrated at the papal coronation had dulled his ability protect the Vatican's clergy in the aftermath. Either way, he thought, now was not the time for recriminations; the killer was still very much in their midst and his over-riding concern must be for the future security of the new Pope and the other Cardinals whose lives may also be in danger.

He climbed the spiral staircase up the tower and into his office. The news he had received from the Vatican pathologist was weighing heavily on his mind. Once the doctor had completed the post mortem on Cardinal Alphonso he asked if he could have a quiet word with Renauld in private. The Colonel had agreed. He then listened with concern as he learnt that the death of Cardinal Gregory had not been through natural causes as it had seemed at first. He too had been murdered but not in such an overt, brutal manner. The pathologist had run several tests on his vital organs and found traces of "phytotoxins" in his blood stream. Fortunately, he was well versed in this area of medical analysis. This poison, he announced, could typically be found in certain plants like the *abrus precatorius,* or rosary pea and if administered in sufficient quantities as would appear to be the case, it would have caused Cardinal Gregory to die through an anaphylactic shock as if the blood had been infected by a deadly foreign protein.

Why is the murderer doing this? wondered Renauld as he sat down wearily behind his desk. *Does he think he can save himself by eliminating the other Cardinals? Or is he, like the killer from the Satanica, someone who enjoys cold-blooded execution? Maybe he's looking to remove the Vatican's chain of command, its decision-making capability in the final run up to locating the Book of Judas...* This was Renauld's preferred option. If the news of the killing were leaked to the outside world the Vatican would be turned into a highly pressurised, media circus that would hamper their ability to act.

The thoughts continued to pile up in his mind as the phone on his desk rang.

"I received your message, Colonel, what's happened?" asked Goran. He too had been up most of the night.

Renauld rubbed his eyes, and talked him through the whole murderous affair. He spared none of the details as he described the disturbing and harrowing sight of Cardinal Alphonso lying motionless, stabbed in the Clementine Chapel during the late evening.

"Would you like me to return to Rome?" asked Goran.

He knew that would not be the best use of his resource but he had a tremendous admiration and respect for the Colonel. Fortunately, Renauld also knew where Goran's best uses lay. He thanked him for the gesture but assured him that they would be able to handle matters.

In truth Goran was shocked to hear the news. In his many years working as an undercover agent in the Catholic Church he had witnessed some very strange episodes, particularly around the time of the papal elections but this event was extraordinary. To kill a senior priest such as Cardinal Alphonso in cold blood in the most holy of Catholic shrines was simply unbelievable. If this revelation were ever allowed to spill out into public domain then the backlash from governments and the world media would be devastating.

Goran discussed this important point at length with the Colonel. He could understand straight away why Renauld was so determined to keep the lid on it. They both realised that the news of Cardinal Alphonso's death would have to be announced shortly but the manner of his death should remain secret. Timing was crucial. They were within hours of understanding whether the Book of Judas had been found or destroyed and at this sensitive juncture they could do without any time consuming side issues.

"Goran – I'm going to see Pope Leo XIV in thirty minutes or so. I could really use some good news to give him at this difficult time! Did you manage to speak to her in time?" he asked hopefully.

"Yes I did, I caught her as she was travelling out of Cairo."

"Where was she going?" he queried.

"I'm afraid she wouldn't tell me at that point," he replied. Renauld could tell from the sound of his voice that there was a problem.

"What do you mean she wouldn't tell you?" he asked anxiously. "What's going on?"

Renauld was staggered by the news. Since the very first day she had been introduced into the Vatican, Anna Nikolaidis had been the model of a strong and dependable agent. Her performance during the months of hard training was exemplary and although chosen originally for who she was, in the end she had proven herself to be an agent of the very highest calibre. They were delighted with her progress. As the months rolled by both of them realised that she had the skills and expertise necessary to complete the assignment. She was trustworthy, reliable and had the ability to remain calm under pressure.

Renauld waited for Goran's response, praying that they had not made a mistake. Her final months had seen her undertake some of Goran's most rigorous tests and she had passed them with flying colours. Finally they were convinced she could stand up against the evil cunning of the Satanica. This was unquestionably the most important assignment ever undertaken in the battle-scarred history of the Vatican.

"I've had my concerns for a while now but it appears she's become emotionally attached to the younger Trenchard brother," Goran replied.

Renauld sniffed. This was not an eventuality they had expected or foreseen. They had been too focused on ensuring her survival against the Satanica.

"What does this mean now? Is she still going to complete the mission as planned?" he asked abruptly.

"I passed on your orders that she was to destroy the arkheynia and kill the Trenchard brothers but she was not prepared to do it – she thinks she can complete the original mission and destroy the Book of Judas before the Satanica get it!"

"Am I correct? She has the final arkheynia now doesn't she? So she knows exactly where the Book of Judas is located!"

Renauld was beginning to appreciate the situation.

"Yes, she told me she knows where it is," he answered flatly.

"I don't understand – why won't she tell you where she's going?" he said, slightly confused.

"She knows that if she does I'll be right behind her; she can't risk me jeopardizing her plan. When we last spoke she said she was going to try and save the girl held by the Satanica."

He knew this was foolhardy. It played straight into the Satanica's hands.

"She also led me to believe that the younger Trenchard had gone on ahead at the request of the Satanica – the older brother's remaining in Cairo for news of his girlfriend's whereabouts when they complete the exchange!"

"I see," muttered Renauld pensively.

"I did everything I could to persuade her against making this decision but she wouldn't listen," he continued. "I think she knows it's wrong to put the life of this girl ahead of the consequences of the book but her feelings for the brother have clouded her judgment!"

"So what do we do?" asked Renauld despairingly.

"I sincerely believe she'll be in touch with me again shortly – she knows she needs me but she won't get in contact along as I can pre-empt her plan. Believe me, she'll be in touch very soon," he added confidently.

"I don't like it," Renauld replied gruffly. "It's too risky. We hope that either her plan, whatever that is, succeeds or that she contacts you with sufficient time to destroy the book! Either way we've lost the initiative… We were in control of the situation but now…"

Goran interrupted.

"Colonel, she may have deviated from our instructions but right now, she's the best hope we have and despite everything, I still believe in her… I still believe she won't risk the catastrophe of the book reaching the hands of the Satanica."

"I wish I could share your confidence," he answered with a hint of despair. Just as he finished, the door to his office opened and his personal assistant marched in and placed a fresh cup of coffee on his desk. She nodded politely before turning to leave.

"At least we know, even with the change of plan, that she's capable of doing the job," Goran suggested positively. He felt responsible for what had happened. He knew they had their backs to the wall.

Renauld checked his watch. It was time he broke the news of the Cardinal Alphonso's untimely death to the new Supreme Pontiff.

"Where are you now, Goran?" he enquired.

"I'm in Beirut – Anna's only clue was to mention the fact that they had discovered the entrance to the labyrinth in the Levant. I'm trying to use my connections at the moment to discover what flights they took from Cairo Airport."

"Ok, Goran, well let's pray that you're right and that she calls you very soon – it seems that today will be the day when they start looking, or even find, the entrance."

"I'll call you as soon as I have any more news," he concluded and signed off.

380

Renauld spoke to his Personal Assistant to confirm the timing of his appointment with His Holiness. The Pope's private secretary had understood the urgency of the matter had quickly moved other official appointments to later in the day.

"The meeting's confirmed," said the Colonel's assistant promptly.

On hearing the news, he lifted the coffee cup and drained the last remnants. He had given orders that the curfew was to be lifted from eight o'clock that morning and people were to go about their business as normal. The only exception he made was informing Cardinals Weiss, Lefebvre and Giacoma that they had to be accompanied by a member of the Swiss Guard whenever they ventured outside their private quarters. This had met with some resistance to begin with. Weiss commented that it felt as if he was being singled out, accused of being the impostor, but when they were informed that it was being applied consistently to all of them and it was for their own protection as much as anything else, they became much more amenable to the constant intrusion.

The sun shone brightly as Renauld paced across the square and up the steps towards the papal apartments. *I wonder how he'll react to the news of Alphonso,* he thought as he greeted the Pope's private secretary.

"Please go straight in," he ushered. "He's expecting you."

The tall, dark haired figure of Pope Leo was sitting behind his long, gilt-edged desk in the corner of his office. As Renauld explained the tragic circumstances surrounding the brutal slaying of Cardinal Alphonso's brutal death, he thought he took the news rather strangely. His first reaction was one of genuine shock but from then on he completed the story in silence as the Pope starred coldly out of his office window. Occasionally the silence was broken as he shook his head and muttered something inaudible under his breath.

When he had finally finished narrating the sequence of events, including the new revelation that had been delivered to him by the pathologist at the mortuary, he paused and waited for his response.

A further minute of silence passed before Pope Leo XIV spoke.

"You know he was a great friend, Colonel, not just a worthy adversary as a lot of people within these walls would like to think," said the Pope sadly.

For a brief moment, the Commander of the Swiss Guards was caught in two minds as he tried to gauge his emotional sincerity. *Are his feelings authentic? Is there something strange about his behaviour?* he thought. He had expected a more animated reaction but maybe he was simply misinterpreting his lacklustre response, particularly after all they had been through over the past few weeks. *I won't prejudge him,* he thought privately.

Suddenly, the Pope's silent stare was replaced by a look of anger. In the next moment, Renauld's initial feelings were consigned to the past as Pope Leo XIV exploded with rage. His voice was trembling with passion at the injustice of Cardinal Alphonso and Cardinal Gregory's death.

"I want whoever did this," he shouted. "Do you understand me, Commander? You are to do whatever it takes to find out which one of them is the murderous, evil priest of Satanica that would do such a thing!"

Saddened at his own words, he paused and took out a handkerchief to rub his tired eyes.

"Do you have a plan?" he asked abruptly.

Colonel Renauld could see by the look on the Pope's face that he was estimating how much responsibility for the deaths should be placed at his door.

He paused for a few seconds before responding. Privately, he was still seething at the paucity of information they had accumulated on the impostor within their midst. He knew it reflected badly on him. *A plan? Yes, I have a plan that might redeem my credibility and return some of my lost pride within the inner sanctum... but will it be acceptable?* During the very early hours of the morning, he had thought of a scheme, a cunning scheme that would unlock the truth behind the three remaining Cardinals but the associated risks of failure were also high.

"I have considered the components of a strategy, Your Holiness, but unfortunately I fear that it carries grave danger, particularly for you if anything should go wrong."

"Go on, I'd like to hear more," he insisted, his curiosity was aroused and fuelled by his overriding concern to wheedle out the truth and bring the trail of death from the impostor to an end.

"I can't advocate a plan that might put your own life at risk," he reiterated stubbornly but the words fell on deaf ears.

"Enough," said Pope Leo sharply. "Tell me your scheme!"

Reluctantly, Colonel Renauld outlined the ingenious plan he had crafted during the early hours of the morning. He would have liked time to discuss it with Goran but that was no longer possible. Every now and then he stopped at the Pope's behest to answer a query or add weight to a minor point. As he concluded he could tell that the Supreme Pontiff approved by the excited look on his face.

"It's perfect," he answered with a smug smile of satisfaction. Personally, Pope Leo felt nothing but bitterness and deep resentment towards the Satanica for what they had done.

Up to this point the conversation had centred mainly on Cardinal Alphonso's death. Colonel Renauld decided now was the time to reveal more information surrounding the untimely death of his rival for the papal throne, Cardinal Gregory. Pope Leo listened attentively as he informed him of the pathologist's findings and the deadly toxins found in his bloodstream.

"I don't believe it," he gasped, outraged.

The news added to his indignation. Silently, he wanted revenge. Although he may have had his differences with each Cardinal over the years, they were on the side of moral righteousness and they should be avenged. The Commander watched the fury burn deep within his eyes.

If the Pope had been wavering in his decision to go ahead with Renauld's strategy the story of Cardinal Gregory's death would have tipped him over the edge.

"We'll go ahead with your plan – please make ready the necessary preparations right away," the Pope urged him categorically.

Again, the Colonel nodded his agreement, privately pleased with the outcome. He would make sure that no stone was left unturned in order to find the killer and redeem his reputation.

"We must also ensure that the news of these tragic deaths is kept within these four walls," he added.

"You're quite correct," remarked Pope Leo. "It's absolutely critical that the truth behind these deaths is kept concealed – are you satisfied that you can do that?"

"I am for the time being," he answered. "My men are loyal but there are also third parties not under my long term control involved here."

"I appreciate that, Colonel but you must control it," he said forcefully. "The world must learn that the heart of the Vatican is suffering, they must know that we're currently in a deep state of mourning at the tragic and dreadful coincidence of two Senior Cardinals dying prematurely… They died of heart attacks only a few days apart!"

Colonel Renauld nodded his head. In this instance it would fall to him to control all the media exposure. He felt distinctly uncomfortable with the thought of lying to the press particularly when the truth would probably come out later. He preferred to think of it as "deliberately misleading" but he knew, and accepted, that in the circumstances it was a necessary evil.

Pope Leo XIV wanted to move on – he concluded the discussion by stating they would organise a joint remembrance ceremony in St. Paul's in a few days' time. He listened patiently to the measures Renauld had taken to ensure the protection and security over the next few days and nodded his general agreement. As he informed the Pope of the guards placed on Cardinals Weiss, Giacoma and Lefebvre Renauld noticed his wry smile before he was pressing him on to other matters.

"Please tell me how we're getting on with my instructions to destroy the arkheynia," he asked pointedly.

In that instant, Renauld made the decision to inform the Pope of their undercover agent. He told him about Anna and how they had placed her with the two brothers from the very start. He realised there would be a backlash for having kept him in the dark for so long but the news that they had someone close to the action might soften the blow.

Over the past few days, he had been mulling over whether or not he should break the news to the new Pontiff. The decision to tell him broke all the rules of the campaign as laid down by himself and Goran at the start but it was a calculated move. If the Pope himself was actually a High Priest of the Satanica then he knew their cause was lost anyway.

As an extra security precaution he had made secret and discreet enquires into the whereabouts of the Supreme Pontiff on the night of Cardinal Alphonso's death. Unlike his results of his investigations into the movements of his fellow cardinals, the findings were conclusive. The Pope had been hosting a private ceremony attended by many international and local dignitaries who could and did testify to his constant presence throughout the evening. He felt relieved when his second in command had passed on the news.

As Renauld revealed the story of Anna Nikolaidis, Pope Leo's jaw dropped in amazement as he learned how his predecessor Pope Paul XII had coordinated and sanctioned the plan. As predicted, his shock turned to fury as he questioned why he had not been kept in the loop as the Pope's trusted "Cardinal Camerlengo". The rage was short-lived. Renauld used the very real example of the Satanica impostor in their midst as an obvious reason for keeping the knowledge secret and limited to only a few people. In case this wasn't sufficient for Pope Leo, he added that Pope Paul XII had also insisted that for Anna's protection her whereabouts and existence was to remain hidden from all but the select few.

Pope Leo XIV smiled as he warmed to the fact that they had someone so close to the heart of the matter whom his own army commander trusted and believed was competent enough to complete the assignment,

His expression wavered slightly as the Colonel brought him up to date with the latest facts. Nothing was left out. The options ahead of them to destroy the book were now fixed. Either Anna had to succeed with whatever plan she had devised, or Goran needed to be given sufficient time to complete the task.

Pope Leo XIV nodded his head in acknowledgement.

"So the time has finally arrived!" he whispered with a bemused smile. Perturbed for a moment, Renauld thought he noticed a disturbing glint in his eye.

"Where's Goran?" asked the Pope.

"Beirut. He's waiting to hear from Anna, Your Holiness," Renauld replied candidly.

"Much rests on this young woman's shoulders. I shall pray for her – our future and our deliverance from evil rests in her hands."

Renauld nodded.

"Colonel, I shall ensure that I'm here with no commitments from this point forward. I want to be kept abreast of every development... And I mean every development!"

Renauld could see that the meeting was over and he stood up to go. Bowing low before the Pope, he turned and walked to the door.

"Colonel!" said the Pope in a loud whisper.

Holding the door, he paused and looked back.

"You look very tired," he said, shaking his head. "I know the job you're doing for us and I won't forget it... I shall be praying for you."

"I appreciate that, Holy Father," he replied with genuine sincerity and set off in the direction of St. Peter's Square and his office.

Chapter Forty-One

Amman, Jordan

The telephone rang at six o'clock in the morning. Arranging the call with the hotel operator had been Simon's last act before going to bed. It had been a restless night and despite his tiredness, it had taken him some time to finally get to sleep. His mind was too full of thoughts. The revelation about Anna working for the Vatican, the anticipation of finding the labyrinth entrance and the prospect of saving Heather were all buzzing around in his head. Once he had finally dozed off, he slept deeply. The events over the past few days had been both physically and emotionally draining.

Reaching over, he cancelled the alarm and then picked up the receiver to order from room service. After showering, he used his mobile phone to call the Hilton Hotel in Cairo. Moments later he was put through and Philip answered the phone eagerly, already awake and dressed despite the early time.

After the initial greeting, Simon wasted no time in explaining the latest bombshell to his brother. Philip was also amazed and confounded at the news. He couldn't believe that all this time since they had picked her up in Greece that she had really been working for her puppet masters in the Vatican.

"That's one twist our grandfather would never have foreseen," commented Philip wryly on hearing of her special training to combat the threat of the Satanica.

When he considered her athleticism and some of the combative traits she had shown in her personality over the past few weeks it seemed totally plausible. In fact the more he thought about it, the more it made sense. He recalled her coolness under pressure in the Theodore Grainger's mansion and some of the quiet, persuasive suggestions she had discreetly put forward to solve some of their critical problems.

"Incredible," remarked Philip again. "Where is she now?"

"She's already moved across the border into Bethsaida – she wanted to get prepared ahead of our arrival today," he answered.

"You really care for her, don't you?" said Philip.

Simon paused, contemplating the scornful intonation in his choice of words. *Is he being disparaging?* he thought but then shrugged it off. He knew his elder brother too well. The comment wasn't meant cynically. It was simply the fact that he was anxious and desperate to save Heather from the Satanica. Simon could imagine the thought process going on in his brother's mind. Was his younger brother more concerned with Anna's safety of Anna? The younger brother sensed the irritation. Simon knew he was expected to share the same single-minded dedication and commitment to Heather's safe return.

"Yes I do," Simon replied. "And don't let's forget that Anna's assignment could have ended in Cairo – she was ordered to destroy the arkheynia once and for all. If she'd carried out that command we know only too well what the consequences would have been!"

"You're absolutely right, I'm sorry," he apologized quickly. "I know she's on our side… It's just so frustrating sitting here not being able to do anything to help!"

Simon could understand the way he was feeling. He would be the same if it were the other way around.

"Right, I've got some last minutes things to sort out before the driver comes to collect me. I'll keep you informed the best way I can," he concluded.

Philip signed off by wishing him luck and added that he would remain glued to his mobile and the hotel phone in the event of any news coming through.

Simon finished off his breakfast and checked his bags again. He knew he still had some time left so, sitting down at the coffee table, he mentally replayed all the intricate details he had been taught by Anna the night before. Using a pencil and the hotel notepad, he jotted down the series of directions from the Judas Scroll in the sequence that Anna had explained. Nervously, he glanced at his watch again and took a deep breath. It was time.

After quickly settling the room bill, he walked through the foyer to the main hotel entrance. As instructed he stepped through the sliding glass doors at exactly eight o'clock. Immediately he heard the sound of a car engine starting up. Moments later an old navy blue Mercedes pulled up in front of him and the hotel doorman promptly stepped forward to open the back passenger door.

Simon bent down to peer through the gap and see who was sitting at the steering wheel.

"Please get in, Mr. Trenchard," said the wide-eyed driver with an intimidating sneer on his face. He waved his arm, ushering Simon to sit down in the back of the car.

Simon threw his canvas bag across the back and got in as the hotel doorkeeper slammed the rear door shut behind him.

The driver turned back to the front and the blue Mercedes exited the hotel grounds and set off along the dual carriageway to the north. The car, with its gear lever mounted on the steering column, must have been at least ten years old, he thought, but it was still reasonably comfortable. The rear window had dark curtains that could be pulled across for added privacy and the air-conditioning system seemed to be struggling to keep pace with the hot climate. Outside the temperature was already approaching the mid-thirties so any cooling relief was gratefully received.

Simon stared at the back of the driver's head. He estimated that he was a good few inches shorter than himself; about five foot ten with a thin, wiry build. He had slick, jet-black hair, parted on one side with a matching, thick moustache. His face was narrow and Simon noticed from the occasional, furtive glances he received in the rear view mirror that he had unusually high cheekbones and deep-sunken, weasel-like eyes that instantly made you distrust him. Simon placed him at around forty-five years old.

At the start of their journey, as they drove through the downtown Amman traffic, he tried to engage him in general conversation but it was futile. His questions went unanswered and even when he became more persistent, the driver continued to focus silently on the road ahead. After a while, he gave up and stared out of the window as they passed through the outer suburbs of the capital.

After forty minutes on the same road they reached Jerash, famous for having the most complete and extended set of ancient Roman ruins outside of Rome itself. Built in the second century BC, the city was a thriving commercial centre in the ancient Decapolis and the gradual decline only started in the eighth century after a series of traumatic earthquakes rocked the region. As they wound their way along the dusty road, he watched the tall, leaning pillars that led to the Temple of Zeus disappear into the background as his thoughts turned to Anna and the present. Staring out, he silently wondered whether she had already made the journey to Bethsaida safely.

As they left Jerash they continued north on the main road to Damascus until they reached a fork in the road signposted to Irbid. They took the north-westerly fork and thirty minutes later were passing through some of the most fertile territory in Jordan fed by the Yarmuk River. Driving through the centre of the town, he realised it was bigger than he had imagined, largely as a consequence of all the Palestinian refugees who had fled across the border over the years from the West Bank. He recalled

Anna the night before mentioning that he would have to pass through a town called "Beth Arbel" in the biblical times, now much better known as "Irbid".

As they left town, the driver spoke for the first time.

"We will be reaching the Israeli border post in about twenty minutes – please make sure you have passport ready," he instructed.

Conchos had been thorough.

Once he had been informed that the entrance to the labyrinth was located in Bethsaida, he had wasted no time in secretly communicating the news to the Satanica High Council in Amsterdam. Much to his perverted sense of satisfaction, they were delighted with his progress. They too could now see the long wait was almost over for the Book of Judas; very soon it would be within their grasp.

Conchos was also very pleased with the way everything was progressing although he felt some discomfort with his immediate surroundings. Normally he could expect to have to have a strong network of contacts in the major centres where he usually plied his executioner's trade. From this perspective, the Near East was not a familiar territory. Reluctantly, he had to accept that he required more assistance from the High Council than he had originally intended. It was important that every detail and every imaginable outcome was considered now that the latter stages of his plan were being enacted. The Council had advised him of a trusted and loyal member who would go to any lengths, and indeed had in the past, to serve their evil requirements. His name was Hassan and he had been given the task of driving the younger Trenchard brother to Bethsaida from the Jordanian capital. Conchos had been given his contact numbers and he had called him directly. Step by step, he explained to Hassan his responsibilities, leaving him in no doubt as to the importance of his undertaking.

Finally, Conchos was satisfied with his arrangements but he was aware that the journey held one further complexity that must be overcome –

the border crossing. Knowing how difficult it was to cross from Jordan, he had entered Israel through Tel Aviv on the coast of the Mediterranean and worked his way northwards to Bethsaida. For this part of the operation, the help of the Satanica's network had proved invaluable. They had used their considerable underground influence within the Israeli administration to ensure that the blue Mercedes would have a trouble-free and uneventful crossing.

Hassan, the silent driver, was making good time. Simon could see the checkpoint ahead as they began their descent down into the canyon of the Jordan valley. In fact from the top of the ridge the view was amazing. In the distance, he could see the small town of Bethsaida etched out against the vast expanse of water in the background that was the Sea of Galilee.

Simon felt his ears popping as the car made the steep descent down the winding roads that had been cut out of the rock face towards the valley floor. A kilometre away from the border post the road began to taper into an ever-narrowing channel. Black and white barriers on either side helped funnel the sparse traffic into one lane.

"Have your passport ready," hissed Hassan.

He hurriedly wound down the window in line with the wishes of the gesticulating Israeli sentry who was brandishing a machine gun menacingly from his waist. The car slowed down to a halt before a thick, red and white striped metal pole that served as a barrier.

Taking stock of his surroundings, Simon was surprised at the number of soldiers on duty, all of them dressed in their full combat uniforms. Peering beyond the white cabin kiosk fitted with reflective glass, he spotted a flat, sandy-collared building, which he guessed must be the platoon's garrison.

The soldier, clutching his machine gun with one hand, grabbed their passports with the other and handed them to an officer standing behind him. Opening the documents, he stepped forward to get a better look at their faces, eyeing them suspiciously through his dark sunglasses. Simon remembered reading some articles recently about the heightened tension in the West Bank following some brutal Israeli repercussions after a spate of Palestinian suicide bombings. Only two days earlier, three young Israeli cadets had been killed while on patrol in the Golan Heights to the North and revenge had been exacted with characteristic speed and brutality.

"Purpose of your visit?" the officer barked at the driver.

"Tourist," replied the driver grinning inanely. "The British gentleman wants to see the remains of the Holy Lands," he added, casting his eyes over his shoulders at Simon.

The army officer turned his attention to the passenger in the back seat but only very briefly. It almost seemed as if he was going through the motions, thought Simon, rather than with any particular interest in the true purpose of their visit.

A few minutes later and the army officer yelled at a subordinate standing near the barrier. As it rose for them to proceed, he noticed the Israeli officer whisper something inaudible to the driver out of the corner of his mouth. *Astonishing – they're in collusion!* he thought instantly. *The Satanica have a long reach,* he thought, shaking his head with surprise. Moments later they passed under the metal pole and through the gateway to Israel.

They drove along the dusty track for another fifteen minutes before Simon noticed the first sign announcing their impending arrival in the biblical town of Bethsaida. He recounted Anna's comment that the town was allegedly the birthplace of three of the disciples including, rather curiously, the Apostle named Philip. *I hope that's a good omen,* he thought as the small village came into view. The few low-level buildings that constituted the centre of town were spread out across the mound-like hill just as Anna had described it. The fact that he had been given some sense of familiarity with his surroundings inspired him with confidence particularly as he began to notice parts of the landscape she had described earlier.

He looked in the rear view mirror and saw the weasel's beady eyes focused on him. *This is it, we're getting close to the end of the journey,* he thought and checked his watch. It was approaching ten o'clock and he silently prayed that Anna had made it safely across the border. She had mentioned that she could not afford to take any chances with the border crossing so had deliberately used the cover of darkness to negotiate the mountain peaks lower down the valley.

The car began to slow down and Simon looked up.

"What's happening?" he asked the mute driver. He didn't expect a response and he didn't receive one.

They came to a halt just outside a disused shed on the edge of the village. *Strange, no sign of life anywhere,* concluded Simon staring out of the window at the rundown shack. Suddenly the opposite passenger door burst open and a man climbed in alongside him slamming the door shut loudly.

Startled, he momentarily froze as he sensed who it was. He shuddered and felt the hairs on the back of his neck stand on end as he looked into the callous face of his adversary. Without needing to be told, he knew this was the murderer who had so appallingly butchered Professor Palanski and countless others through his immoral, depraved labours for the Satanica.

The driver began to edge the car forward again as Conchos's cold, heartless eyes pierced right through him.

"Tell the driver where we're going," he said impersonally without any trace of emotion.

Simon heard the Germanic accent in his voice as Philip had described in Cairo.

"Where's Heather?" he uttered although his insides were churning as he attempted the brave show of defiance.

"Simon Trenchard…" Conchos responded dryly, a thin, contemptuous smile appearing across his face.

"We have an arrangement don't we?" he questioned rhetorically.

His confident poise and demeanour contrasted fully with Simon's personal discomfort and shrivelled sense of well being.

"Show me where the entrance is and I'll give you the address of the girl," he continued. The tone of his voice never wavered but remained calm and constant endorsing his power to control the situation.

Simon stared at him, contemplating what to say.

"I don't see you carrying any of the scrolls or the map," he said, looking down at his small bag of belongings.

"It's all in my head," Simon responded.

"Yes, of course it is," he murmured, his twisted smile reappearing across his face.

"Very wise – very wise indeed," he repeated again slowly. "Now which direction should we go?"

Simon looked out of the front windscreen.

"Drive to the road that runs south along the seashore," he instructed the driver.

Hassan looked at Conchos who nodded his agreement. The Mercedes speeded up down the track that ran around the bottom of the hill on the outskirts of Bethsaida. Peering out, Simon concentrated hard to keep his mental bearings correct. The town had a small population of local inhabitants and most of the visitors to the area were on tours or holidays to see the modern-day sites of the biblical lands. Bethsaida, forming one of the corners of the evangelical triangle as it had become known was a popular staging post. Peering out of the window to his right, he looked up at the barren, rocky hillside with low-level, square-shaped white houses built sporadically up to the top of the knoll

The driver reached a junction in the road. Instead of turning right into the winding lane that ran up the hillside into the centre of Bethsaida, he took the left fork towards the coast.

Conchos also made a mental note of the route they were taking because he knew he would be following it again later that day. The previous evening, after arriving in Tel Aviv, he had been busy making arrangements for the impending arrival of the three High Priests of the Satanica's ruling Council. All of them were travelling alone through different entry points and on different itineraries, but they knew their paths would be fused together later that afternoon when they congregated at the Lebanese Resthouse. The small hotel was situated close to the shores of the Sea of Galilee, near a town called Tiberius. This venue would become immortalized in their long and distinguished history, he thought. The records would show that the final meeting of the Satanica Overlords took place here before the legendary Conchos completed his final labour and led them to the entrance of the labyrinth. He smiled. This point would mark the zenith; the culmination of centuries of worshipful reverence to the Dark Lord and his embodiment in Judas.

As the car continued down the sandy track towards the seashore the environment began to change. The barren, sandy track contrasted with the greener, darker alluvial features of the lowlands as the sporadic bushes and vegetation became denser.

"Which way?" hissed the driver over his shoulder.

"Just keep going straight until I tell you when to stop," replied Simon, trying to sound confident.

Conchos calmly studied Simon's anxious face. *Does he really have the knowledge? Does he really know where we're going?* he wondered, watching his furtive glances out of the window as they travelled beside the placid waters of the Sea of Galilee.

Simon could feel the expectation and pressure mounting as he scanned the terrain looking for a clue that would tell him they were on the right track. *Come on, you've got to be there,* he urged silently but he was worried.

The Judas Scroll and the papyrus map dated back approximately two thousand years; the landscape could have changed enormously during that period of time.

He turned his attention to the great expanse of water on his right. According to the Bible, this was the scene of Peter the disciple's great moment of triumph when he miraculously walked on the water. *That's what I need,* he thought, shuffling his legs in discomfort, *a miracle.*

What was it that Anna had mentioned he should do if he couldn't find it? He strained hard to recollect her words from the night before. Suddenly it didn't matter, a wave of relief flowed through him as the tell-tale sign on the landscape told him he had found the place he was looking for.

"Slow down, driver," he said sharply.

Excitedly, he double-checked to make sure but he knew in his heart that this was the right place.

"Stop the car over there," he instructed, pointing towards a decrepit old bridge that spanned the road ahead of them.

They all stepped out of the car. Simon wandered on to the old bridge to inspect their surroundings. Below them was a wide, empty riverbed, known to the local population as Wadi Ibri. Although the rainfall was infrequent in these parts, when it did arrive, it arrived in a torrent and the droplets would hit the rocky mountainsides where the trickles would merge to become streams and the streams would merge to become ever-growing rivers. Although this new river was always short lived, when the combined torrent flowed its force was unstoppable and, over the centuries, it had cut an ever deeper ravine into the softer part of the rock below them.

Simon felt relieved as he looked directly down at the dry wadi bed some fifty feet or so below him. Slowly he followed the line of the gorge as it disappeared between two high, rocky peaks in the distance. *Amazing,* thought Simon as he stared up at them because it was the unusual shape of the peaks that had drawn him to that location. The higher summit on the left immediately caught the eye. It rose majestically above the surrounding hillside and then gradually began to taper until it became more and more needle-like. *Like a witch's hat,* he thought. On the other side of the valley, the size of the mountain also stood out – only the shape of its crowning glory was the exact antithesis of the other. It was perfectly flat as if someone had taken a saw and sliced the top off. The extraordinary contrasting summits were a remarkable feature of the scenery and the first clue that Anna had described to him.

"And where do we go from here?" prompted Conchos.

Simon looked down.

"This way – we walk," he replied.

Conchos wandered back towards Hassan and gave him some instructions. He was to remain beside the car and wait there until he returned. The driver nodded dutifully and turned back towards the stationary vehicle.

Simon checked his own pocket and made sure he had his mobile with him. *It's pretty remote,* he thought. *Let's hope you can get a signal in these hills.*

His next observation reminded him of the severity of his situation. Conchos removed his jacket and threw it onto the back seat but not before he had pulled out an automatic from the pocket and shoved it into the waistband of his trousers.

"Let's hope I don't need this," he said, spying the look on Simon's face but somehow the tone of his voice failed to convey any sense of reassurance. He knew too much about Conchos to be taken in by any false pledges of safety.

Getting down to the stony ridges of the wadi floor wasn't as straightforward as it had initially seemed. The sides of the ravine were far too steep to climb down so they had to come up with an alternative plan. They walked back down to the coast and along the shore until the point where the dry riverbed flowed into the Sea of Galilee. From there they turned inland and walked back up the ravine, the walls getting higher and higher as they marched upward. Under the bridge where they had parked there were a few old, rusty cans and bottles splayed around that passers-by had obviously thrown down from the bridge above their heads. The temperature was scorching in the midday sun but the shade offered by the deep, narrow valley gave them some respite.

"Do you know how far we have to go up this ravine?" asked Conchos, being careful to walk a couple of paces behind Simon.

"Can you tell me where you have hidden Heather?" he replied belligerently.

"You know it's best not to annoy me," he pointed out with an implication that was not difficult to understand.

Simon felt confident that even if the gruesome being accompanying him on this journey was an insane, psychopathic killer, he would still not touch him until he delivered his golden prize.

"I reckon it'll take us twenty minutes or so," he responded grudgingly.

Although the walk up the stony track was constantly uphill on a fairly even gradient it was not a difficult one. Over the years the various flash floods had eroded deep rock pools full of transparently clear, fresh water in the bed of the river. Around the pools were tall palm trees that had grown tall with the plentiful supply of water and nutrients.

After walking for fifteen minutes along the wadi, Simon intensified his focus on the steep rock faces that ran alongside them. As Anna had informed him, the scrolls had revealed a way he could gauge his current location relative to the entrance to the labyrinth as he travelled up the deep ravine. If he looked up towards the pinnacle of the mountain on his left, he saw the extraordinary conical rock that towered into the air. By judging the position of the sun in relation to the uppermost point he could determine his bearings: he would expect to find the entrance when the sun came directly in line with the needle. He was getting very close and he kept his eyes focused on the geological protrusions of the ravine walls above their heads.

As he skipped across a shallow pool of water, he saw that the ravine ahead began to channel around in a gentle arc to the right. Running all the way along the left hand edge of the river bed against the sheer wall face was a deep water pool with rushes growing through the shale and pebbles along the fringe. Checking his watch, he looked up at the sun and realized that he had found the place. Pausing for a moment, he scoured the bend of the canyon wall running above his head, the different colours of the rock jammed together highlighting seismic upheavals over thousands and thousands of years.

It's got to be around here somewhere, he muttered to himself and trained his eye on a ledge running the length of the rock wall twenty feet above them. Above it was another thirty feet of sheer rock wall before it reached a fairly inaccessible wider ridge at the base of the mountain. *There it is!* he thought. He knew Conchos had his eyes focused on him so he was careful to disguise his line of vision.

"We can stop here," he said, turning around in front of the rock pool.

"Where is it?" asked Conchos sharply, looking around the ravine.

"I think you need to give me some information, don't you?" Simon said coyly.

He tried to sound confident despite the nerves he felt buzzing around inside. On their climb up the dried riverbed, apart from looking for clues to find the entrance to the labyrinth he had also kept an eager eye out for the places where he thought Anna might be hiding. So far he had seen nothing to give him any extra comfort – no signs that indicated where she could be and now he was at the crossroads of exchanging the final clues that could save Heather's life. *Where can she be?* he wondered, cursing her quietly under his breath. Surely she must have found this location ahead of him – after all he had followed her directions.

"Very well," replied Conchos, slightly bemused. "As a sign of good faith I'm prepared to give you the information you're looking for – your brother needs to take the main northern road out of Cairo signposted to Alexandria. If he stays on this road for half an hour he'll find the girl in a small town called Ashmun. Now, where's the entrance?" he said impatiently.

"You know that isn't enough for him to find her – what's the exact location?" demanded Simon, stubbornly refusing to be intimidated. This was the moment that Simon had been dreading.

Conchos smiled.

"Ok, I'll tell you," he said calmly, "but first, point me in the right direction."

Conchos knew that he didn't need to employ any rough hand tactics because he controlled all the master cards in the deck. If Simon was lying or if he suddenly determined that he would not reveal the entrance then Conchos would make sure the information on Heather's location would never reach his brother.

"You see that ridge," said Simon, pointing upwards with his hand. "You need to get on it and walk along until you are above the centre of the rock pool."

Conchos turned around and scanned the rock face for possible routes up to the ledge. There was no obvious path – the only way was to use the various natural footholds in the ravine wall and climb up the equivalent of a two-storey house to the narrow shelf above them.

Checking his pack, he swung it around his back and made sure that his gun was firmly pushed into his waistband.

"You will wait here. You're not to move," he commanded fiercely as he walked back down the ravine to a section of the wall that offered more in the way of assistance to the climber.

As Conchos commenced his ascent, Simon trained his eyes back on the ravine wall and at the tell-tale carvings that had been etched out of the stone above his head. Only a trained eye would be able to spot the signs that marked out a five-pointed star in the rock face. If you looked at the points individually they looked like normally eroded, weathered features of the gorge but when you allowed the mind to see the entire picture, to encompass all five points, the centre of the pentagon was clearly revealed above the wider part of the ridge standing over the deep pool of water in front of him.

What a truly incredible feat of human engineering, thought Simon as he began to perceive what he was truly looking at. In between the hard, muddy red limestone rock at the floor of the wadi bed and the start of the mountain above them, was a compressed lighter-coloured layer of softer, more pliable sandstone. If his calculations were right the ancient architects who had built the labyrinth had seen this fault and tunnelled down through the softer sandstone layer into the base of the mountain.

Simon could see that Conchos was a strong physical athlete. He needed to be to scale the sheer face of the wall, pulling up with his hands as he drew his feet up to the next crevice beneath him. After ten hard minutes he finally hauled himself up onto the ledge. He turned to look down at Simon before running his eye along the length of the narrow shelf high above the ground up the narrow canyon.

"Along this ledge?" queried Conchos, his voicing echoing around the cavern.

"Until you're directly above the centre of the rock pool," replied Simon, continuing to scan the summit of the narrow gorge above his head as he wondered where Anna could be hiding. He saw the gun sticking out from Conchos's waistband. If he needed cover later he was out of luck. The wadi bed area around the rock pool was completely exposed from the ledge above his head.

Conchos began the balancing act. In places he could walk naturally but in other sections he was forced to slow down and edge his way carefully, sideways on with his back pinned to the rock face.

Gradually, he edged around the bend, above the pool of crystal clear water to the point that he estimated was halfway. Taking it step by step, his normally calm exterior lit up as he spied the entrance. There was no mistaking it.

Simon recognized the signs and realized the moment of truth was upon him. If Anna was not there he would be a dead man. In fact, if she wasn't there then it was not only the end for him but also for their extraordinary quest to secure the Book of Judas. Their mission would be over. The book would fall into the hands of the Satanica and the world would sit and wait for the holocaust of evil that would follow.

"You've got what you're looking for; I've fulfilled my part of the bargain – what's the rest of the address," he shouted loudly from the canyon below.

Conchos ignored him. He had reached a perfectly round hole, the size of a large tyre cut into the ledge. He brushed away some bushes from the edge and then peered down into the darkness. There was a flat floor below about eight feet down. Conchos looked back at the route he had just followed; he knew that he would need to come up with a plan to make the entrance more accessible to the Zoroastrian High Priests when they entered the labyrinth later that day.

"Well, what are the details?" repeated Simon boldly. He had to have faith that Anna was somewhere nearby. The Satanica's executioner had what he wanted and in the next few seconds he could turn around and kill him stone dead.

Conchos suddenly diverted his attention back to his next hapless victim below and the twisted sardonic smile reappeared across his face.

"Very well," he said, pleased with way his strategy was developing.

"When the road enters Ashmun, he must go right at the second roundabout; she's in the Sanna Building, Apartment 106 on the ground floor, which is located on the left hand side of the Mosque."

Simon made a quick mental note of the details, hoping he would get the chance to pass them on to his distraught elder brother.

"The only problem is," said Conchos, slowly looking down from the ledge above his head, "is that you're not going to live to pass on that information!"

He smiled cynically as he reached down and pulled the gun from his waistband.

This is it! thought Simon as Conchos raised the pistol. He then calmly attached an additional silencer barrel attached to the end and pointed it down at Simon's chest.

Where are you Anna? he mumbled, desperately praying she would appear in time.

Conchos took aim, his finger on the trigger… The noise of the shot echoed around the barren canyon but it was not from Conchos's gun. The bullet missed Conchos by inches, ricocheting into the rock face.

Startled, Conchos quickly stared down at the blood seeping from his hand; the same hand that was holding his gun. The bullet had chipped the rock and the razor sharp stone splinters had pierced his hand. He looked down at Simon who dived to his left as Conchos tried to steady his aim, the pain in his hand preventing him from applying pressure to the trigger. With one desperate last gasp effort he fired at Simon who made a muted noise as he fell, rolling into the edge of the rock pool. Unable to cling onto the pistol, he dropped it and it clattered and splashed into the crystal clear water below.

Quickly he looked up at the ridge of the canyon opposite him and saw the face of his female assailant. Anna was again steadying herself as she carefully took aim.

You! thought Conchos angrily, before he dropped down into the dark hole and the entrance to the labyrinth below.

Anna stared after him, frustrated and furious with herself that she had missed with her first attempt – in that moment she could have accomplished her mission. She knew the shot was going to be difficult with a pistol over such a long distance but that was the only weapon that

Goran could provide her with at such short notice. The moment for a second shot had passed.

"Simon," she screamed as she realised he was lying motionless by the pool on the canyon floor. As fast as she could she pushed herself backwards from her prone vantage point on the top of the ridge. *Simon, please be ok!* she gasped, racing along the side until she reached a point where she knew from earlier experience that she could climb down the steep rock face to the wadi below. In her desperation to get to Simon's side she slid down the last ten feet of shale, jarring her ankle as she landed in the shingle and pebbles at the bottom. Fortunately she wasn't badly hurt and, picking herself up, she dashed over to his prostrate body.

Thank God he's moving, she thought as she hurriedly kneeled down beside him. Face down on the bank, he lay with legs outstretched in the rock pool's shallow waters. Inspecting his body, she immediately saw the cloudy bloodstained water lapping around his legs and, grabbing below his arms, she hauled him up on to dry land.

"Are you Ok?" she exclaimed as she stopped, surveying his body and looked into his eyes. Simon's attempted smile brought a wave of relief through her body.

"Yes, I'm fine," he said, wincing as he clutched the top of his leg.

Moving his hand she saw the source of the bleeding. The bullet from Conchos's gun had entered the top of his thigh, exposing the raw flesh. *He's been lucky,* she thought, pulling the sleeve off her shirt to make a tourniquet.

"What kept you?" he said, smiling.

She raised her eyebrows in dismay, angry with herself that she had so come so close to losing the man she loved. The whole experience had shaken her but she knew that she still had a job to do.

"I'm afraid I only got here a few moments before you – I had to get in position quickly when I saw you coming up the wadi and I just couldn't hear what you were saying from up there on the ridge."

She indicated her position with a glance of the head.

"Did you get him?" he asked hopefully.

"No – he dropped down into the labyrinth before I could get another shot off. His gun fell into the middle of this pool."

Kneeling alongside him, she suddenly perched herself more upright and stared into his eyes.

"This may hurt a little," she warned and then turned the tourniquet sharply.

He groaned as she fastened it as tightly as she could.

"What about the address? Did you get it?" she asked as she helped him walk to some shade at the edge of the narrow canyon beneath a palm tree.

"Yes, I've got it," he responded, suddenly remembering what Conchos had said.

"Thank God!" she answered, relieved that something good had been achieved from their near catastrophe.

"Have you got your phone?" she continued as he propped his back against the bark of the tree.

Simon felt in his pocket and pulled out his damaged phone.

She rumbled around in the small rucksack she was carrying and pulled out the mobile phone that Philip had given her in Cairo.

"Take this and call Philip. I don't think I'll be needing it! I'm going to have to follow him inside. I can't let him get too far ahead."

The expression on Simon's face told her everything.

"I'm sorry, no choice – I've got to do it," she added firmly.

He nodded reluctantly.

"Then I'm coming with you," he said, trying to push himself up with his palms.

"No, Simon," she said putting her finger on his lip. "Please – I think you've put yourself in the firing range enough for one day," she said with a comforting smile.

He looked upset.

"Really, I'll be Ok," she added reassuringly. "I'll also be able to move much quicker without you."

"Ok," he said, gritting his teeth in discomfort as he rested back down again.

"Will you be Ok here until I get back?" she enquired.

"I'll be fine – I can move… just not very quickly," he grinned.

"That's good. I think you may have to move in order to get a signal – I could get one from the top of the ravine."

He could sense she was eager to get started.

"Go, Anna," he said, looking up into her excited, glimmering eyes.

"I love you," she whispered and leant over to kiss him.

"Just make sure you come back," he called as she threw the backpack over her shoulder and got herself mentally prepared for the ordeal ahead.

Standing up, she nodded back at Simon before running past the palm trees and around the rock pool to the ravine wall. She chose the exact same section that Conchos had identified and managed to negotiate only fifteen minutes earlier.

Sitting as comfortably as he could with his back to the tree, Simon watched her progress, amazed at her strength and agility. A few minutes later she had completed the climb and edged her way along to the entrance. She paused briefly above the hole and turned back to look at Simon. He saw the look of intense concentration in her eyes and smiled.

She smiled back before disappearing down into the labyrinth below leaving him to ponder the strength of the signal on her mobile phone. It was too weak to make a call so he lifted himself up and started making his way back down the wadi towards the Sea of Galilee. All the way he constantly studied the lithium crystal display for any improvement to the phone's reception.

The pain was excruciating, bursting upwards every time he put pressure on it. He searched around in the undergrowth around the tree looking for something that might help take some of the weight off his bad leg. He was in luck. He found a solid branch from an Acacia tree that was just the right length to act as a crutch. Simon was familiar with the tree from his time working in the UN relief agency in some of the more inhospitable terrains of the African continent. He recalled having been told once that it was the wood of the Acacia tree that had been used by the Israelites to build the Ark of the Covenant and he smiled at the analogy.

Resting the branch under his armpit, he put his weight on it and was pleased with the results. Anxious to pass on the news of Heather's address to his brother, he hobbled as fast as he could through the pain barrier, his mind continually slipping back to the dangers that must be lying in wait for Anna.

Please God, she's got to make it out safely, he thought, taking a deep breath as he forced himself on down the dry wadi.

Chapter Forty-Two

Cairo, Egypt

Since the phone call from his brother earlier that morning, Philip had been busying himself getting ready for the breaking news. Being alone made it harder but he refused to feel sorry for himself. It was a struggle but he forced the negative demons out of his head, thinking only positive thoughts about Simon and Anna's predicament and Heather's chances of survival. Rather than sitting still in his room feeling down and melancholy, he started organising himself for a successful phone call and a potential onward journey ahead.

First of all he made arrangements so that he could make a quick exit from the hotel if needed. He packed away all his belongings and then paid the room bill in advance of his impending check-out. After that he spoke with the concierge, explaining that he needed to hire a driver and car for the day. To make sure the concierge fully understood the importance of his request, he pulled out a sheaf of crisp Egyptian pound notes from his wallet and placed them on the counter in front of him. His automatically eyes lit up.

"This car and driver need to be fast and he needs to have an expert knowledge of Cairo and the surrounding area – do you understand what I mean?" he enquired hopefully.

The concierge needed no further encouragement.

"Immediately, Sir," he replied willingly and flashed his sincere, well-rehearsed smile.

Twenty minutes later there was a driver standing beside his vehicle in the hotel car park waiting for his next set of instructions. He had been told by the concierge in no uncertain terms that he was working on a priority assignment and that he must not leave the vicinity of the car on any account.

Once he had organized the transportation, Philip crossed the foyer into the hotel's business centre where he studied all his onward travel options. He checked all the different routes that would get them both to northern Israel and the corresponding flight schedules. He found the young Egyptian lady on reception in the Business Centre extremely helpful.

At the end of his research he concluded that the quickest and most logical point of entry into Israel would be through the coastal airport of Haifa. He cursed the fact that there were no direct flights from Cairo to any Israeli destination; the most logical route he could find was a connecting flight through Larnaca in Cyprus. The obliging girl gave him a print out of the take-off and landing times. Philip was taking no chances; he reserved several seats on all the flights going out that day and booked an open ticket for two. One of the attendants working for the hotel concierge who had become used to Philip's generous tips duly obliged by collecting the tickets from a local travel agency and delivering them to his hotel room.

It was approaching midday and the long insufferable wait in his hotel room was beginning to play more keenly on his already frail nerves. Checking his watch for the hundredth time, he stood up and paced across the room wondering if there were any other arrangements he could put in to place. He knew that anything he could do now to save time later was a bonus. There was nothing else he could think of and he looked around the room until his gaze fixed on the phone sitting next to the bed. The temptation to pick it up and call Simon or Anna was enormous but it would be breaking the agreement they had made. He quickly dismissed the thought.

Is there anything else I can be prepared for? he wondered but he knew that he had gone through everything in minute detail. In fact he had even left the hotel briefly that morning to locate a pharmacy to purchase an assortment of remedies. He had no idea what state Heather would be in when he found her and he wanted to be ready for any eventuality.

Sitting on the edge of the bed with his hands clasped together, he stared at the mobile phone plugged into its battery charger on the coffee table. He felt annoyed and guilty that he could not be contributing in some larger way to saving the life of his beloved fiancée. Relying so heavily on Anna and Simon didn't rest easily with him. All his life, both in his career and the social circles he moved in, he was used to being in control, used to being in charge of his own destiny.

The mobile phone rang and he sprang to his feet, jumped towards the coffee table and snatched it up.

"Yes," he said.

At the other end Simon, who had finally located a strong signal, knew better than to entertain thoughts of any discussion other than delivering Heather's exact location.

"She is in a town called 'Ashmun' just to the north of Cairo – " said Simon, still out of breath from the strenuous exertion of dragging his injured body down the wadi bed in the blazing heat of the afternoon sun.

Thank God, they've made it! thought Philip as he heard Simon's voice. Breathing deeply, he grabbed the pencil he had organized to take down directions.

"…You must take the road out of town to Alexandria. Once you reach Ashmun you'll take the right hand exit at the second roundabout where you'll see a local Mosque," he gasped and readjusted the uncomfortable wooden crutch under his arm. "Next to the Mosque you'll find an apartment block called the Sanna Building. She's in Room 106, it's on the ground floor – go Philip and I pray everything's Ok!"

"Simon, I'm going… I'll call you back when I'm on the road," he replied swiftly and hung up. He felt high with a mixture of elation and relief running through his body. At last he could get into action.

Grabbing his pack, he looked around the room one last time before dashing out of the door towards the waiting car downstairs. Minutes later he was cursing the normal Cairo traffic congestion and urging the driver to speed up as they passed through the suburb of Heliopolis on route to the main carriageway to the north.

Once, and only once, Philip was convinced that his driver fully understood the directions he relaxed back in his seat for a moment. He double-checked the detailed road map resting on his knee and satisfied himself that they were taking the quickest route to Ashmun. Outside, the traffic was beginning to ease as they approached the outer suburbs. Philip picked up the mobile sitting alongside him and called Simon.

He listened silently as Simon recounted his frightening liaison with the killer from the Satanica and his extraordinary brush with death. Despite Philip's exhilaration at the prospect of being reunited with Heather, he felt a massive wave of emotion towards his brother sweep over him as he began to realise the position he had put himself in to save the life of his fiancée. In his heart he knew he would never be able to thank his brother enough. As Simon continued to recount the story telling him how Anna had dragged him out of the rock pool before going on to enter the labyrinth, he also realised the importance of the part she had played. Philip forgave her for any earlier subterfuge; her words and actions had shown her true character. He too just like Simon made a silent wish that she would return unscathed from the labyrinth and then he grinned to himself at the thought of Heather and Anna being in the same room again when the curse of Judas was finally over.

In his excitement, Philip kept interrupting his younger brother's flow, bombarding him with questions until he got the answers he was looking for. Finally he felt as if he was up to date. He knew what had happened, he knew where Simon was located and he knew what condition he was in. The only question he posed where he had an unsatisfactory response was with regard to the new mission Anna had embarked on. It was an answer they were both going to have to wait for. Sensing the emotion in Simon's voice, he felt a desperate urge to be there helping him. *As soon as I get Heather,* he thought to himself.

"We've got to do something to help her," muttered Philip into the phone.

"Then just get Heather and get here as soon as you can – with your help I think I can climb up to the entrance."

"I've organized the flights; we'll be there as soon as we can."

"It might be better not to bring Heather," suggested Simon.

Philip thought about the comment for a second.

"Maybe," he replied. "Let's see what condition she's in. I'm not sure I want to leave her alone again."

"Ok, I'm going to ring off," said Simon. "I want to save as much power in this battery as possible – call me when you're on the way."

"Will do," replied Philip. "Don't worry we'll be there as soon as we can!"

While on the phone he had missed the change of scenery that was going on around him. Gone were the built-up, crowded streets and in came the sandy, barren expanse of the countryside intermittently broken up by small villages along the wayside.

"How much further to Ashmun?" he shouted from the back. The Egyptian driver had given up with the ineffectual air conditioning and lowered his window. The warm breeze whistled around the car as it sped along.

"A couple of kilometres that's all," the driver responded without taking his foot off the floor.

They passed the first sign for the town of Ashmun and Philip started to imagine the moment when he would be reunited with Heather. He thought of all the things that he desperately wanted to tell her. *Never again am I going to leave you alone,* he told himself.

The car sped straight across the first roundabout. Philip leant forward, resting his arms on the back of the front passenger seats as he eagerly began directing the driver's movements.

"Take this right," he instructed as the second roundabout came into view.

"Over there, park over there," he cried, seeing the distinctive dome-shaped white Mosque with its two minaret towers. The murky, rundown building next to it had a large sign on the top announcing its name in big red letters – *Sanna Apartments.*

"Quickly," he urged the driver, pointing to a space.

At the front, along the bottom of the apartment block was a row of shops. *It must be on the ground floor behind them*, he thought and clambered out of the car as it came to a halt on the sandy gravel at the front.

"Wait here," he shouted, leaving the car door open as the perplexed driver watched him race down the side of the decaying building.

Luckily he had chosen the correct side and, spotting the dirty, decrepit entrance he bounded up the steps outside and burst in through the swing door. Apart from the noise of a child crying in the background there was little sign of life down the corridor in front of him.

The building was only about thirty years old but it was totally rundown. It was inhabited by labourers, their families and other less skilled members of Egypt's vast population caught in the poverty trap whose struggle to make a living left them with little respect for their surroundings. Stepping inside, Philip grimaced as he saw the accumulation of dirt and broken tiles on the floor.

He quickly took in his environment. In front of him was a long, dark corridor and next to him on the wall, which was daubed with black graffiti, was a broken plastic sign indicating the direction to apartments 101 to 109. Philip followed the direction of the black arrow.

What sort of state will she be in? he wondered. Heart pounding, he rushed forward down the corridor counting down the room numbers. Halfway down he reached the door to apartment 106. As he was about to try the handle he froze. *What if someone else is inside?* he thought, stopping to consider his options? He put his ear to the door and listened hard but he heard nothing.

Breathing quickly, his overriding thought was to get in as quickly as possible. For all he knew every second counted. Standing back, he studied the door – he knew one good, solid kick would break it down.

Using the wall behind him for added support, he raised his leg and brought the heel crashing down on an area close to the lock. With a loud crack the door burst open fracturing off its hinges.

He rushed inside. The small room was dark and empty with barely any furnishings to speak of – just a wooden table and a few cheap-looking chairs. The dirty, stained curtains were pulled across the windows.

"Heather," he called, panic beginning to set in. This was not how he had planned it.

Set back on his left was a tiny filthy kitchenette with an old kettle on the side next to the sink surrounded by dirty cups. The room only had one door, which he realized must lead to the bedroom.

He twisted the handle and pushed the door open.

The apparition in front of him brought Philip's world crashing down around him as he sank choking to his knees, his body sagging as all hope drained out of him.

Heather, the woman he lived for, was dead.

In the middle of the windowless, empty room she sat strapped to a chair, naked from the waist upwards. Her eyes were pinned open and screamed of the agony and torment she must have faced before she finally slid into oblivion. Tears filling his eyes and streaming down his cheeks, he could barely bring himself to look at her frozen, disfigured body.

"What kind of person could do this?" he cried. The top of her head was bald where the sadistic, psychotic killer had cut off her long blonde hair and then bizarrely reattached it to various parts of her body. Out of her mouth flowed a long clump of her blonde hair and all around her body the sadistic cruelty had been repeated. On her back, on her chest and on her shoulders the killer had taken a knife and dug several deep holes into her flesh before draping more clutches of her hair from the open wounds. The effect was repulsive and startling. *What kind of human being could do this?* he thought, recoiling as he struggled to look at her face.

Coughing and spluttering, Philip retched on the floor as he imagined the pain she must have gone through at the hands of this madman. A feeling of light-headedness overcame him and he too for a moment felt a numbness as though he was slipping away to another dimension.

Aided by the wall, Philip mustered the courage to stand up and approach her lifeless body. He wanted to hold her and talk to her but the mutilations were so abhorrent, he couldn't bring himself to do it. This was not his Heather.

Distraught, he felt his body tremble as he pictured how the killer must have enjoyed terrifying his victim before dispensing his brutal torture. The emotion changed to anger and resentment. It surged up inside him. At that moment he desperately wanted to vent his fury on the thing that had done this. He looked down at her hands and saw the bright green emerald ring he had given her on the day he had proposed. Reaching down, he slipped it off her finger and kissed the back of her hand.

In a slow trance he walked to the door and back down the passageway although inside he was really bursting with despair, fuelled by the futility and unfairness of it all.

Outside he used his mobile phone to call the local hospital and police before asking the driver to park across the street in a hidden lane. They arrived quickly. From a distance, he watched as her body was carried out of the building encircled by police cars and placed into the waiting ambulance.

"Cairo Airport," he said to the driver.

Chapter Forty-Three

Vatican City, Rome

There's no point in delaying, thought Colonel Renauld; after all, the Pope himself had sanctioned the strategy. He stretched back in his chair, a study of concentration, contemplating the finer points of his master plan while rolling a pencil between his fingers. The only unsatisfactory aspect of the scheme was the risk to the life of the Supreme Pontiff. He mulled over whether he could dress up a decoy – but he knew if he was going to draw out the impostor then it would have to be convincing.

His quiet reflection was disturbed by a forceful rap on his office door. Sitting upright, he casually tossed the pencil on to the top of his desk.

"Come in, Major," he beckoned loudly. He knew who it was; he had been patiently waiting for the arrival of his loyal deputy.

Major Dupont, like the Colonel, had been up all night assisting with the investigation into Cardinal Alphonso's bold and tragic murder. The fatigue showed on his face.

"Take a seat," said the superior officer, gesturing towards one of the two comfortable chairs set at an angle in front of his desk.

Dupont sat down.

"Major, together, you and I are going to run a plan to smoke out this murderer in our midst before he's responsible for any more bloodshed!"

Renauld scowled before continuing on – he still found the concept of a sleeping assassin posing as Cardinal for so many years quite extraordinary.

"We need to find out which one of them's the bogus priest and whichever one of them it is, he's an extremely cool and deceptive customer! Anyone who can sit amongst us all these years, lying dormant, waiting to strike must be both devoted and fanatical... And now we know he's also prepared to kill and probably to die for the cause!"

The Major, listening to the Colonel, sat attentively as he slowly explained his train of thought. The Commander held his Deputy in very high regard; he was an astute, intelligent officer whom he had used on a number of important occasions as a sounding board for top-level executive decisions. If he had any doubts, or if he suspected there were any flaws in the plan then he knew he could rely on the Major's meticulous and pragmatic nature to give him an educated "no-frills" response.

"Where are the Cardinals at the moment?" he asked

"They're being encouraged to remain within their private quarters unless there's an extreme emergency – I have guards posted on their doors."

"Fine – well the first thing we have to do is arrange a bit of clever subterfuge – we need to stage-manage the capture of Cardinal Alphonso's killer," he said smiling matter-of-factly.

"I don't understand?" replied the Major with a puzzled expression.

"I want the three Cardinals to believe that we've caught the killer – afterwards I want to be able to address them together in the same conclave and apologise profusely for the actions of the Swiss Guard. I want to apologise for the ignominy they've suffered by being considered a suspect for such a treacherous and diabolical act, I want to apologise for the inconvenience and hardship caused to them during the course of the investigation – If my plan is to have any chance of success, it is essential that they no longer feel they're under my direct suspicion!"

"Understood," said the Major, nodding curiously, intrigued to know what the Colonel had up his sleeve.

"After that comes the difficult bit. I need to stage a situation where they overhear our conversation – I want each one of them to know what the latest progress is with regard to the Book of Judas. Do you have any ideas?" he questioned his junior officer.

Major Dupont thought for a moment before answering.

"Well, if we need to use a place where the acoustics would make our voice travel then I would recommend our discussion takes place in the Sala Ducale; the hall is such that a whisper below the dome can travel across the length of the room. I could then arrange for the three Cardinals to be in the adjacent library where the sound would be magnified!"

"Excellent, Major," he replied nodding slowly and imagining the scene they were setting.

"Alternatively, I could draft a confidential memo to you that contained the information you wanted to pass on and then arrange for it to accidentally get into their possession."

The Colonel pursed his lips, pondering the suggestion for a moment.

"No, I don't like it," he answered. "Let's stick with your first suggestion; I think that would be more plausible."

The Colonel, satisfied that Dupont had helped him establish an important link in his plan, then went on to explain his strategy in full. For several minutes, the Major listened attentively, grasping all the finer details and contemplating the potential pitfalls that might lie ahead. Finally, as the Colonel drew to the plan's finale, he uttered the concluding words and sat back in his chair and waited expectantly for his subordinate's response.

The Major's face was a picture of studiousness as he paused to think through the ramifications of such a cunning scheme. All along his gut feeling had been behind the idea but when the stakes were so high the concept had to be foolproof.

"It's good, Colonel, very good – I'd suggest we need to use only our most elite and specially trained officers for such a clinical assignment. The need for precision timing will be critical."

"Agreed, Major," replied Renauld, pleased with the reaction. His confidence was buoyed by the support.

"And am I right in thinking this plan's been fully sanctioned and endorsed by Pope Leo XIV?"

"You're quite correct, Pope Leo's given the plan his approval," he answered promptly.

Colonel Renauld knew that it was politically correct for the Major to ask such a question. He also knew that his loyal subordinate would take his own word as being satisfactory evidence but to reinforce the point he held up a single sheet of paper signed by Pope Leo himself. It was sealed with the Ring of Fishermen from the Pope's own hand, authorising the Colonel to proceed.

Between them, they spent the next few minutes identifying the key officers and soldiers capable of delivering and executing such a plan. Finally, the Colonel scanned the shortlist of men they had drafted.

"Excellent, Major, but remember we have very little time – I want you to brief these soldiers immediately and then set up the rendezvous so that we can commence our strategy in exactly one hour's time. Do you think we can be organised within that timescale?"

"I'll see to it," he replied.

The Major stood up, saluted and left the room, leaving the Colonel to contemplate his own cameo role in the grand scheme of things.

One hour later the elite and trusted officers of the Swiss Guard had been selected and briefed by Major Dupont. Following his instructions closely, they entered the private apartments of the three suspected priests – Cardinal Deacon Weiss, Cardinal Bishop Lefebvre – and finally the quarters of the deceased Cardinal Alphonso's close aide and confidante, Cardinal Giacoma. The officers carried out their orders, being careful to make sure that the priests were treated with the utmost consideration and respect. Firstly, they apologised profusely for the inconvenience but stated that Colonel Renauld had requested an immediate conclave in

421

the Vatican library so that they could be informed of a very important development. The officers, with subtly guarded optimism, pointed out that from the little information they possessed at that time, it would appear that the priests' attendance at the meeting would be very much in their best interests. Without exception each Cardinal expressed a willingness and eagerness to attend. They were all curious at what the latest revelation could possibly be. Adding to the priests' bemusement, the guards also insisted on accompanying them straight away to the Sala Ducale, insisting that Colonel Renauld was keen to brief them at the earliest opportunity.

From a window high up in the Swiss Guard's tower, the two senior officers, Colonel Renauld and Major Dupont looked down on the priests' steady procession as they crossed St. Peter's Square and headed up towards the portico leading to the Sala Regia. The Lieutenant, commanding the three handpicked soldiers, had already been shown the exact location where the Cardinals were to be seated in anticipation of Renauld's imminent arrival.

"Well, now is the time – Are you ready, Major?" asked Renauld, raising his eyebrows.

"Yes, Sir," he replied confidently and together they descended the stone spiral stairs and crossed the square, following the priests into the heart of the Vatican.

Inside the Vatican, the Lieutenant, wearing his colourful harlequin tunic, led them up the famous staircase and across the hallowed hallways to the Sala Ducale. With a friendly, relaxed manner, he politely requested that they wait in the small library connected to the room. Surrounded by bookcases in every direction, the library had a magnificent high ceiling and the walls were covered in ancient manuscripts and treasures accumulated by the church over the centuries since the Roman Empire and earlier.

"Your Graces – Colonel Renauld will be with you very shortly," announced the Lieutenant. "Please be good enough to wait here."

The officer ushered them to a wooden bench alongside the open arched entrance through which they had just passed. The position had been set up by Major Dupont earlier when he had tested the acoustics coming from the Sala Ducale. The Lieutenant knew that they might choose to stand or to sit elsewhere but the closer their locations to the wooden bench the better it would be.

"I don't understand," said Lefebvre, looking perplexed. "This isn't the usual venue for meetings with Colonel Renauld!"

"Your Grace, I did suggest alternative rooms but I am afraid the regular places for a conclave were already in use – Colonel Renauld stated that the important priority of holding the meeting early greatly outweighed waiting for one of the usual rooms to become available."

The Lieutenant's well-rehearsed answer not only appeased the surly priests' inquisitiveness but also served to build up their curiosity and reinforce the intrigue surrounding the Colonel's arrival.

"Please, Your Graces" he repeated, "make yourself comfortable, he will be with you very shortly."

All of the priests, dressed in their long, scarlet robes and birettas, sat down in a line on the bench waiting patiently for his arrival. The Lieutenant was privately pleased with his work.

After a few minutes' silence, Cardinal Giacoma started a conversation but it was short-lived. They heard the slam of the heavy double doors of the Sala Ducale and the distant noise of footsteps, slowly pacing forward along the wooden floorboards towards their chamber.

"Have you managed to speak to Goran?" asked Major Dupont, knowing that the pitch of his voice was loud enough to carry the entire length of the room and beyond the adjoining archway to where the Cardinals would be sitting.

"Yes – I'm pleased to say that the position's improved considerably. In fact I'd say we clearly hold the upper hand over the treacherous Satanica now."

Cardinal Bishop Lefebvre raised his eyebrows as the barely audible words carried through.

The three priests were alone. The Lieutenant and his three trusted armed guards had been instructed to take up sentry duty outside the far end of the library once there crucial assignment had been completed to their satisfaction. Colonel Renauld wanted to create an impression that the shackles were off.

"The destruction of the Book of Judas now lies firmly in the hands of Pope Leo the fourteenth – it's his decision and his alone…" continued Renauld. "Our agent's now situated at the entrance to the labyrinth waiting for the Holy Father's final approval before going in and completing the mission."

The commanding officers continued walking slowly across the floor of the Sala Ducale, their heavy shoes making their footsteps echo around the great chamber. The fact that it was bereft of any furniture only compounded the resonance around the walls.

"I don't understand," queried Dupont. "After all these years, why is His Holiness not giving the instructions immediately? It doesn't make sense!"

"I understand your sentiment, Major, but we can't question his authority in this matter – he had instructed that the decision to destroy the book will be made between him and the Almighty Holy Father. He instructed me that he wishes to speak with God, he will pray alone in the Clementine Colonna Chapel for one hour before communicating his final decision."

"Do we have that much time?" asked the Major promptly.

"No – I'm afraid it's not all good news. Goran believes the High Priests of the Satanica and their agent are already very close to the labyrinth's entrance, so timing will be crucial."

"Colonel, do you think we should override this ridiculous situation and communicate the order to Goran directly," voiced the Major, adding a subtle hint of desperation to his tone.

The three Cardinals sat in total silence on the bench straining their ears to catch every last word of the officers' cunning conversation. Cardinal Giacoma, his shoulders hunched stared at the ground and shook his head.

"Unfortunately that option's no longer available to us; the Pope has arranged the communication channels in such a way as that only he can give the order for Goran to enter the labyrinth."

"I don't believe it," replied the Major instinctively. He had really taken to his new acting role.

The officers had covered half the length of the Sala Ducale and Renauld gestured to Dupont by raising his arm that this was far enough. The echoing sound of their footsteps ceased.

"What is it, Colonel?" he asked on cue.

The seated Cardinals heard the sound of their hurried footsteps start again only this time they were walking in the opposite direction.

"I'm afraid there's one final issue I need to agree with His Holiness before he goes to the Colonna Chapel; he's insisted that he wants to be alone and I've agreed to respect those wishes. I'll be five to ten minutes that's all… And besides it would appear that the Lieutenant has not yet arrived with Cardinal Weiss, Lefebvre and Giacoma – he is aware that we are meeting in the Sala Ducale isn't he?" questioned Renauld rhetorically.

"I'll check on their progress," answered Dupont dutifully.

The three Cardinals heard the large doors swing open and slam shut behind them.

Almost like clockwork, thirty seconds later the Lieutenant marched back into the library to apologise for the delay.

"I can't understand it. They were supposed to have set off several minutes ago," he commented ruefully.

"They did," answered Cardinal Deacon Weiss, looking furtively at the faces of the Cardinal Lefebvre and Giacoma as he spoke.

"They briefly entered the Sala Ducale before turning back again," he informed the officer.

"Please be patient. I'll try and find out what is going on," responded the Lieutenant who retreated back through the library door, pulling it closed behind him, to where his soldiers were standing on guard.

Outside the Sala Ducale in the Sala Regia, Colonel Renauld expressed his delight with the way their performance had gone.

"Well done, Major," he said, congratulating his number two.

"How long shall we give them, Sir?" asked Dupont.

"Another five minutes should be sufficient," he replied with a grin. "I think we've given our impostor something to think about."

After the allotted time, they both recommenced their journey back to the dark and less salubrious Sala Ducale. However this time when they entered the double doors at the far end, slamming them shut behind them, they could see the three Cardinals waiting at the far end for their imminent arrival. While they had been out, the Lieutenant had followed their instructions and politely requested that the Cardinals move back in to the chamber next door. The priests, now slightly confused about the original location for the meeting, had willingly obliged

"Your Graces, I am very sorry for keeping you waiting like this," said Renauld cordially as he approached.

"What is it? Why do you want to see us?" asked Cardinal Lefebvre sharply, waving his hand at both Cardinal Weiss and Giacoma in an animated fashion to emphasise the "us" in his question.

"You're right, I owe you an immediate explanation," he replied, staring directly into Lefebvre's eyes.

There was something about the priests' demeanour that he found objectionable. If had to say which Cardinal topped the bill as the most likely candidate, Lefebvre was the first name that sprang to his mind. *Can he be a High Priest in the Satanica?* he wondered privately. Unfortunately there was nothing to support his hunch – neither any information dug up on his past nor any circumstantial evidence to link him with the present-day cult.

"Very well, let me get straight to the point – I'm very pleased to inform you that we've caught the brutal murderer of Cardinal Alphonso and that he's openly confessed to his crimes."

Renauld stopped and observed their facial expressions for any tell-tale signs but it was difficult. They all expressed a look of bewilderment at the news but anything more was impossible to read. Whichever priest it was that worked for the Satanica, apart from being an accomplished executioner, he was an extremely good actor.

"Who did it?" asked Cardinal Giacoma. "Who was capable of carrying out such an appalling atrocity to the man loved throughout the Vatican City?" Tears of emotion welled up in his eyes. *He is convincing,* thought Renauld.

"I am ashamed to say that I must take some of the blame, Cardinal Giacoma," he answered. "It was a soldier, a new recruit who joined the Swiss Guards only six months ago – we always observe an extremely robust and rigorous investigation into any new faces but on this occasion he got through the net. We're grilling him hard to find out if there's a link with the Satanica but nothing so far." His voice sounded resigned to the circumstances.

"What would make a man do such a thing?" asked Cardinal Giacoma.

"I believe we will eventually establish a link with the Satanica," replied Renauld optimistically. "The man's clearly deranged and preliminary research into his past indicates he has a history of violent and disturbed behaviour – of course I accept responsibility as the commanding officer and in due course I'll instigate a full investigation into how such a criminal could enter the Swiss Guards!"

Cardinal Deacon Weiss with his carefully groomed black, goatee beard stood up and shook his head in dismay.

"This really is a terrible business… Terrible," he repeated.

"I would like to thank you for your understanding since his murder was discovered, I know that the armed guard has been intrusive and the restrictions imposed have been unnecessarily harsh but we couldn't afford to take any chances," added Renauld responsibly.

"You're now free to go wherever you want; you may even leave the Vatican if you wish – of course I'd appreciate it if you'd inform me where you were going but this is not mandatory."

He smiled pleasantly.

"I am also pleased to tell Your Graces that there'll be no further Swiss Guard security attached to you unless you'd like my officers to remain with you for your own added protection."

He watched their faces relax at the declaration of freedom.

"That's all I wanted to say," he concluded.

The three Cardinals all expressed their surprise and pleasure at the new developments.

They unanimously congratulated him on his exceptionally quick resolution of the heinous crime and promised to let him know if they were leaving Rome.

Colonel Renauld and Dupont watched as the Cardinals walked out of the room.

"Have we done enough to catch our fish?" wondered the Commanding Officer quizzically as the doors closed behind the last priest.

"We'll know very soon," replied Dupont thoughtfully.

"Ok, let's get to work – we need to lay our trap," said the Colonel, springing into action. "I'll go and inform His Holiness that the time has arrived."

Chapter Forty-Four

The Labyrinth of Judas, Bethsaida

Anna let herself down through the opening to the labyrinth by hanging onto the rim and dropping down the final few feet to the cave floor. It was pitch black except for the light filtering through from the gap above her.

Her first impulse was to crouch quietly and listen for any unexpected sounds. She knew the Satanica's serial killer was in there somewhere and he would be expecting her arrival. She waited a couple of minutes to be on the safe side but there were no strange noises – just an eerie stillness. *The calm before the storm*, she thought.

Her eyes began to become more accustomed to the darkness and she suddenly became more aware of the structures around her. Squinting, she could vaguely see a perfectly flat wall up ahead that seemed to bear some strange markings. Anna considered the Satanica's agent again. Even after she had fired the first shot, she remembered the calm way he had looked up at her on top of the ridge. Most people would have jumped for cover but he didn't panic. The thought made her remain crouched a few minutes longer. Despite the fact she knew he would be keen to get to the centre first, she had to be sure he wasn't lying in wait around the corner. Finally deciding that he was not in the vicinity, she quickly fished around in her pack and pulled out a flashlight, shining it on the wall ahead.

The beam lit up a large flat wall covered from top to bottom in a language that Anna recognised. It was the same as that used in the Judas Scroll. Superimposed on the background was an enormous Pentecostal, five-pointed star cut deeply into the flat rock face. This finding alone was simply amazing and the archaeologist in her desperately wanted to stay and study the wall in great depth. The five-pointed star, which also marked the labyrinth's entrance from the ravine, had long been closely associated with satanic worship.

She flashed the light up to the top of the writing and worked out a very literal translation of the first few words:

"You have entered the House of the Devil, unless you worship the Black Lord without compromise in all his darkest forms then the passages ahead will show you torment and suffering beyond the limits of your imagination and endurance of human kind..."

She found some of the words difficult to make out but using a bit of poetic license she managed to make sense of the translation. Skipping the next bit, she moved the light down the wall to a prominent section that stood out from the rest. The script was larger and the carving around it was more elaborate:

"The Devil's House holds the power to reveal the Black Lord, the Book of Judas, sacred satanic words of the living death that will descend upon men..."

The words made a tingle run down her the length of her spine. *Incredible, what on earth is out there?* she wondered. She moved the torch all the way around her and saw that a well-defined, man-made passageway, about twelve feet high by ten feet wide, ran away on a gradual incline into the bowels of the mountain. The construction was technically perfect, each line and corner was perfectly carved into the rock.

Despite the warnings of impending doom, she was spellbound by the enormity of the position she currently found herself in. This site had remained dormant, undiscovered by any mortal for over two thousand years and now that its dark secret had been unlocked, the awesome responsibility of saving Christianity and mankind had fallen to her.

She shone the light at the ground. There was an abundance of dirt and dust that covered the floor and she immediately spotted the fresh tracks of the agent who had started the journey ahead of her. *I must get going,* she prompted herself. *I can't afford to let the gap get too big.* Judging by the length of space between each footprint she could read that he was travelling quickly.

Holding the flashlight up, she started jogging down the stone passageway. At regular intervals she noticed the five-pointed Pentecostal star engraved into the wall. She knew something about labyrinths. During her time in college and to a certain extent in some of her fieldwork she had often been required to study their ancient forms and she knew that their close association with religious tradition dated back over four thousand years and that there were three principal designs, the "seven circuit", the "eleven circuit" and the "twelve circuit" labyrinth. The most common of these was the "seven circuit". It was said that as you meandered through a labyrinth, turning 180 degrees every time you enter a different circuit, or loop, it balanced the mind, inducing receptive states of consciousness. In everyday life, many people made the mistake of imagining that a maze and a labyrinth were the same thing but this was a common foible. A maze has dead ends and many trick turns whereas a labyrinth has one path leading to the centre and then back out again. There are no dead ends and no trick turns. The labyrinth was a truly sacred place that was alleged to have supernatural powers. As she jogged down the passage she could sense the power and the evilness of its inherently powerful design pulling her towards the core.

The tracks continued ahead of her and every time she saw herself approaching a turn she switched off her flashlight and listened for any unusual sounds. As she continued along the path with all the twists and turns, she knew that she had totally lost all sense of direction. Occasionally, slowing down, she would turn a corner and the subsequent passageway, always on gradual incline, would be much shorter leading her to conclude the centre was nearby. Her anxiety and anticipation levels increased dramatically as she neared each corner – before the notion was dispelled as she rounded it and her torchlight again revealed a longer section of the labyrinth.

She had been moving for over fifteen minutes when she reached another U-turn in the smooth rock face. Taking her normal precautions, she switched off the torch and, listening intently, she slowly put her head around to make sure the pathway ahead was clear. There were no unusual sounds and no glimmers from any flashlights in the distance. Suspecting that the route was clear, she stepped out and put the torch back on concealing the full beam with her hand.

The sight that greeted her made her jump in shock. All around her the immediate passageway was decorated with the remains of human skeletons embedded into the fabric of the walls. She removed her hand and shone the light across them. They were everywhere, even covering the ceiling of the tunnel. On the ground, smashed skulls littered the way and the air had become cold with a heavy, musty smell. She took a deep breath and continued down the passage being careful with her footing but it was almost impossible not to make a noise on the ancient brittle bones cracking beneath her feet. Moving slowly, she convinced herself that the killer was not lurking around the corner as she gradually recovered her composure.

What was it that Simon said? she wondered, trying to recall their conversation. He had mentioned something in relation to the building of the labyrinth after his meeting with Professor Palanski. She suddenly recalled Simon's words. He had mentioned that during the times of Christ, the treacherous evil followers of Judas had infiltrated the bizarre religious sect known as the Essenes and tricked them into helping with this monumental construction. After it was finished they had all been brutally and ruthlessly massacred. *These must be the tortured, mortal remains of that sect,* she surmised as she carefully stepped around a thin pole holding numerous pierced skulls crushed one on top of another. *So this was their reward for building the Temple to the Devil!* she thought and again began to pick up the pace on the way down the murky passageway.

After a few more minutes she noticed that the spaces between the footprints of the killer were getting shorter and shorter. *He's slowing down!* she thought and did the same. Placing her hand over the end of the torch again, she reduced the beam's exposure to just the immediate vicinity and carefully edged her way forward.

She sensed she was getting near the centre. As she turned the next bend she froze. The walls of the passageway had disappeared. She quickly jumped backwards but realised if he was out there waiting for her that he must have already seen the glow from the flashlight.

Anna could tell by the change in the acoustics that the room around the corner was substantial, quite probably the main central chamber, she thought. Feeling around inside her pack, she switched off her torch and pulled out her gun. Unless he was carrying a second, this was the one distinct advantage she held over the agent of the Satanica after his weapon had fallen into the rock pool outside.

With her back to the wall, listening intently for any unusual sounds, she rapidly tried to assess all the various options. She knew that if she went in with the torch on she would be a sitting target. As it was she had probably given away her position and any element of surprise when she had mistakenly turned the corner. Alternatively she could enter the chamber carefully without the flashlight turned on but this would also be extremely difficult. Without any light the room was pitch black and even when her eyesight became accustomed to the darkness, the clarity and scope of vision was very limited. None of the options were very appealing but whatever the circumstances she knew she had no choice but to go in.

Ok, she thought, making her mind up. *I'll go in armed with the torch on in one hand and the gun in the other. He'll know exactly where I am but if I keep my back to the wall and concentrate on any new sounds I should be able to track him down.*

She was now totally alone. Nobody who could help knew where she was and nobody was ever going to come to her rescue until it was too late. This battle would decide the future rights over the Book of Judas. It was good versus evil. Her cunning and guile versus the most malevolent, potent force in the Satanica and the battleground was – she stopped to think. *How did the tablet of stone at the entrance put it? Yes,* she remembered, *the battleground will be in the House of the Devil.*

With her heart beating fast, the tension rose inside her as she stepped out and declared her hand. She flicked the on-switch; the powerful beam from the torch pierced the darkness. This time she made no effort to disguise its force and with her hand out but with her back pressed firmly against the wall she edged around the bend into the great chamber of the labyrinth.

Quickly she flashed the torch around the room, concentrating her focus on anything that might shift sharply in her immediate vicinity but there was no movement. Her nerves were tingling with each step. As she slowly moved forward she became more confident that he was not about to pounce on her from some nearby hiding place. It would be difficult because of the vast open space in front of her and the wall of the chamber against her back. In the darkness she quickly turned her attention to assimilating as much information about her surroundings as possible. The size of the great hall under the mountain was mind-boggling – even with the full beam, the light dissipated before it reached the other side. Keeping her back firmly pressed against the wall, she shone the light upwards and around the arched, smooth rock walls. The chamber appeared to be circular with a curved, dome-shaped roof spanning its entire diameter. She estimated that it must be about sixty metres to the other side from where she was standing. Shining the torch down, she saw that the ground slid away below the ridge she was standing on. The entire base of the chamber was bowl-shaped, mirroring exactly the concave ceiling. Straining her eyes she pointed the torch towards the centre and saw a large, elevated square stage like a chessboard in the middle with four staircases spaced equidistantly around the central stage. The steps had no railings or means of support but ran down the entire length of the slope before levelling out for about ten metres. At the end of this walkway the steps rose up sharply to meet the edge of the square platform. Carved with precision out of the rock, the stone steps were like bridges, about two metres wide and on either side they fell away into darkness.

Anna marvelled at the construction. Had the labyrinth been known to mankind it surely would have qualified as one of the wonders of the world. The precise coordination of the geometric shapes and meticulousness of the design was evident even from her limited scope of vision. The openness of the great chamber added to her confidence and she moved away from the wall towards the top of one of the four staircases leading down to the centre. Pausing, she looked down the descent at the elevated platform below her. Tall pedestals with tulip-like heads stood at each of the four corners and she assumed that these could be used to provide light. In the middle of the marble platform was a raised stone altar table standing on four thick columns with the five-pointed, Pentecostal star engraved into its surface.

Despite the apprehension that the Satanica's assassin was in the chamber with her, her curiosity to see actual Book of Judas, the object of their arduous voyage around the globe, was intense. A new thought crept into her head: maybe she should concentrate on getting to the book first rather than play cat and mouse with the merciless serial killer. The idea grew on her. If she got to the book first she could destroy it. Taking this course of action was sure to attract him and when he showed himself she would be ready.

As she cautiously trod down the first two stone steps, her ears straining for any new sounds, she looked back over her shoulder at the way she had come in. The torchlight lit up on the wall and she gasped as she registered the unbelievable intricacy and detail that had gone into the chamber's decoration. The ancient script, announcing the House of the Black Lord, had been painted painstakingly around the wall's entire circumference.

Suddenly she heard a noise and span around, flashing the light as quickly as she could across the periphery of her vision. It sounded like a stone or a pebble bouncing down the steps, the noise of the ricochet amplified by the silence and shape of the dome above her head.

Panic setting in, she could feel he was somewhere close as the eerie stillness returned, only to be shattered as another stone started bouncing further down the steps in front of her. Twisting sharply, she spun around with the flashlight, pointing it in the direction of the sound but in that split instant she new that she had been tricked. Terrified and realising her mistake, she tried to turn and point the gun at her assailant. It was too late. The full force of the heavy object in Conchos's hands crashed against her temple and she crumpled unconscious in a heap on the hard stone steps.

Barefooted, Conchos smiled; he was pleased with the way he'd carried out his plan to silently stalk his female victim. After dropping the gun and descending through the entrance, he had realised that she would be coming after him. The damage to his hand from the chipped rock face had given him a lot of pain to start off. It had severed the tendons but the constant aching had finally begun to ease. He flexed his fingers. *I can use them if I have to,* he thought.

Knowing that he had to get to the book first, he didn't stop to admire the scenery but raced through the passageways, determined to get to the centre first. In the end, sweating from the exertion, he had arrived in the great chamber fifteen minutes ahead of her arrival, which had only given him enough time to explore his environment and set his trap.

Picking up her gun and flashlight, he quickly checked to make sure she was unconscious before striding down the steps towards the large square stage with the grey stone slab in the middle. Using the torch, he collected the rucksack that he had hidden earlier on and found the means of spreading more light. One by one he went around the four corners of the podium setting fire to the dry material in the open metal cups at the top of each of the finely crafted pedestals. As the flames began to burn brightly in each receptacle, the light spread around the chamber revealing more and more of the satanic verses inscribed in the outer walls along with brutal, demonic carvings and portrayals of grotesque, mythical horned creatures that purported to be the earthly form of the Black Lord.

The raised platform, connected to the outer wall by the four stone staircases was made of dark, flecked marble. Conchos stood on one side and looked down into the dark pit that fell away from the sheer edge. Puzzled, he had only one thing on his mind: where was the Book of Judas. He had expected to find it sitting on the grey, stone altar that commanded the centre of the square.

He looked up and saw Anna's body lying motionless, prostrate on the steps. *I'll be with you shortly,* he thought, as he continued scanning the great domed hall. Finally, he saw something that broke its constant geometric lines. Helped by the light cast by the flames, he could see the opening to another passageway exactly one hundred and eighty degrees from the entrance he and Anna had used when they entered. Taking the torch, he hurriedly climbed the flight of steps and entered the short passageway, which led into a much smaller antechamber with an open doorway at the far end. Treading carefully, he shone the light up and saw the archaic text inscribed in bold letters around the curve of the low, arched portal. Excited, he bent down to squeeze through the diminutive gateway; he realised how close he was to claiming the ultimate prize. Inside, it felt as if the temperature had dropped by ten degrees. He was accustomed to fear and danger but he sensed an immortal evil in the air beyond anything he had experienced before. He shone the torch around him and then felt a chilling wind pass through him as his eyes fixed on the tomb of Judas Iscariot. His biblical name, "Loudas Iscarios", was carved in deep, bold italic lettering engraved on the side of the crypt. The strange wind sensation made him cough and splutter as he walked up to the thick stone casing. *Now is the moment of truth!* he thought. Putting the torch in a position where the light could assist him, he leant down and started to push the thick stone slab that sealed the coffin. It required a tremendous effort to begin with but once he had some momentum it scraped and jarred its way along the serrated seam. With a last heave, the lid opened sufficiently for him to see the contents and he grabbed the torch to see inside. The first thing he saw was the mortal remains of his skeleton, which was scattered along the length of the tomb, but then his eyes lit up. All he cared about was resting in the centre with the remains of a human hand on the cover. He had found the mythical Book of Judas, the crinkled pages in a thick, black binding covered in a layer of dust. Conchos could tell from the positions of the bones that Judas must have been clutching the book to his chest when the lid was closed over two thousand years ago.

Incredible! he thought as he carefully leaned over the edge to pick up the sacred manuscript. Again, just as before, he shivered as he though he felt a stiff breeze blow against him. It was an odd sensation in a sealed burial chamber with no contact with the outside world.

Being extremely careful, he brushed away the dirt and lifted the book. Now that he held his prize, his mind began to race ahead to the next series of tasks that lay ahead of him. He knew time was of the essence and he grabbed the torch with one hand and stooped as he carried the manuscript back through the archway and into the antechamber beyond. The flames' flickering light returned as he left the burial crypt, walked down the steps back to the elevated platform and delicately laid the book down on the stone table. Its condition was remarkable – like the scrolls themselves, the pages had been treated with a unique plant extract to preserve the paper. Considering the centuries over which the book had remained in an atmosphere with little moisture, it had worked perfectly. The pages were not totally pliable but they were not brittle either.

Conchos went back to his small rucksack and pulled out a state-of-the-art miniature digital camera. In line with the instructions of the Daimones and the High Priests of Zorastri, he opened the cover and proceeded rapidly to photograph the pages of pictures and black lettering that made up the ancient language. It was meaningless to Conchos – to him it looked like Egyptian hieroglyphics – but to the High Priests who could decipher the Dark Lord's tongue, the pages contained the satanic ritual to unlock the power and glory of the devil upon mankind. It was the key to unlock a holocaust of evil.

Moving as fast he could, Conchos took five minutes more to use the camera to scan every page. When he had completed the task he put the silver device back into his pack and turned his attention back to the woman's body, still lying prostrate on the stone steps.

Lifting her up, he carried the deadweight back down to the platform and roughly laid her out across the stone slab of the altar table. The side of her face and her forehead were dark purple with the bruising and congealed trickles of blood ran in long lines from the gash in her head down her face and neck.

In normal circumstances he would have had no qualms in taking his knife and mutilating her skin and body beyond physical recognition. *After the pain I've suffered in my hand I'd especially enjoy going to work on her body!* he thought, grinning dementedly at the prospect. The feeling of anticipation at carving up her body surged through him but he knew now was not the time. *No, the circumstances have saved you for a little time longer,* he thought, trying to suppress his sadistic instincts a bit longer. Unknowingly, she had helped him complete one of the labours given to him by the High Priests of the Zorastri. They knew that in order to complete the devil's reincarnation, they had to sacrifice a human of pure spirit before commencing the dark, satanic ritual as decreed by the Book of Judas. He smiled; the High Priests would be pleased. The bloody and brutal sacrifice of Anna Nikolaidis would be perfect.

Looking around for inspiration, he quickly pondered how he could secure her arms and legs. He would have to leave the labyrinth for a short period to collect the High Priests and he certainly couldn't afford to take any chances that she would regain consciousness while he was away. He didn't have any rope or tape in his pack. All of a sudden a malevolent smile appeared on his face. He had an idea – a macabre idea that appealed to his evil, sadistic nature.

Lifting up her body, he climbed down the steps from the platform and carried her back up the wide stone steps towards the antechamber. Inside, he wasted no time dragging her through the small portal and into Judas's burial crypt. Getting his arms beneath her and being careful not to inflict any pain on his damaged hand, he lifted her up and shoved her through the open gap into the. Her head fell awkwardly on the bones before hitting the stone coffin floor. Quickly walking around the vault, he lowered his shoulder and used all his strength to push the huge stone slab back into its position. Dusting his hands together, he picked up the torch and headed back into the main chamber, checking his watch on the way.

I need to get moving – they'll be waiting for me, he thought, considering whether or not he needed to take his pack with him. He looked at the bound manuscript on the centre of the table, unsure whether or not to take it with him. He rapidly came to the conclusion that it was already in one the safest locations known to mankind and the sooner he could get back the better.

Conchos climbed the steps to the entrance and looked back one last time at the glimmering light from the four burning fires that lit the stage. The Book of Judas glimmered in the centre of the sacred, satanic altar table. Pleased with his work, he turned, and holding the torch out in front of him, he started jogging his way back out of the labyrinth.

Knowing what to expect as he turned the one hundred and eighty degree corners helped him cover the distance in a much shorter time. Finally, he reached the shaft of light pouring in through the ceiling that meant he had reached the outside world. In order to climb back up though the opening, Conchos knew he had to jump up and grab the edge of the rock and use all his strength to haul himself up. Normally this would not have posed a problem but he cursed as the pain shot through his injured hand. Gritting his teeth, he used all his upper body strength to get through the hole and onto the ledge. Out on the ledge, he shielded his eyes from the afternoon sunlight's intense glare as he looked below him for the body of the Simon Trenchard. He was sure that his shot had hit the target before he dropped into the darkness. Whether he had or not, the body was gone and that gave him cause for concern. He wondered whether he should go back for the book... but he knew perfectly well that if he hurried he could be back within thirty to forty minutes. Sweat dripping off his face from the exertion, he clambered down the rock face, falling the last few feet before again starting to jog down the dry wadi bed.

In his hurry to get back to the waiting High Priests of the Satanic cult, he failed to notice the probing eyes watching him from behind the large green leaves of several bushes growing tightly together.

The sight of Conchos climbing down from the ridge and running down the ravine filled Simon with shock and horror. *What does this mean? Is there any possibility other than that Conchos has killed her?* The answers to his own questions filled him with dread. *I've got to get in there,* he thought but he knew he could not do it alone. *Where's Philip?* he wondered desperately/ *I should have heard from him by now.* He pulled out the mobile phone and dialled his brother's number. His phone was switched off. *He must be on the way here,* he thought.

As he sat wondering what to do next he began playing around with Anna's phone. An idea suddenly struck him. *Maybe I can find the number of the Vatican agent that Anna had mentioned last night,* he thought, scrolling through the menu.

He checked the recently dialled numbers on the phone. He didn't recognise the number of the last call she had made before handing it over. The international dialling code didn't give him any clues – he knew it wasn't Egypt.

He decided he had nothing to lose and called the number.

After a couple of rings a young lady answered in a friendly sing-song voice.

"Hallo, Airport Hotel, how can I help you?"

Damn, it's a hotel, he thought. He desperately tried to recollect the name Anna had called the agent.

"Hallo," said the girl, again checking if anyone was on the line.

"Sorry, do you have anyone at the hotel called Coran or Goran, or something like that?" he enquired, not expecting to get very far. If she asked him for his surname or his room number he knew he would be lost.

"What was that name, Sir? Did you say Goran?" she repeated.

"Yes, I'm afraid that's all the information I have," he replied, realising it was not a lot to go on.

"A gentlemen named Goran Kradowicz checked in this morning – could that be the man?" she answered obligingly.

"Could be," he said hopefully. "Can you put me through?"

"Certainly, Sir, and thanks for calling," she answered and he heard the click of the line being re-directed then the ring tone at the other end.

"Hallo?" answered Goran. Only Colonel Renauld and Anna knew he was on this number and he prayed it was she.

"My name's Simon Trenchard – do you know me?" he asked.

Goran was shocked to hear the voice at the other end; he had been patiently waiting all day for a call or a message to arrive from Anna but this was unexpected.

"Yes, I know you," he stuttered, trying to gather his thoughts. *What can have happened?*

Simon gave an audible sigh of relief; he had found him.

"Where's Anna?" asked Goran insistently. He was not a patient man at the best of times and the exasperation had been mounting up all morning.

"I'm at the entrance of the labyrinth. Anna's inside – I think she's in real trouble," he moaned. "She went in after the Satanica agent but she hasn't come out again!"

Simon went on to brief Goran on his own condition and the fact that the killer had reappeared from the labyrinth entrance alone.

"Where are you? Be precise and be clear," he demanded abruptly.

Simon understood. As succinctly as possible, he explained how to get there step by step.

"Excellent, I'm on my way – I want you stay hidden and observe anything that happens. Don't do anything till I get there, Ok?" he asked before ringing off.

Simon put the phone down and stared up at the ridge leading to the entrance. *Please be all right,* he begged.

Conchos wasted no time. Once he was back with the vehicle he had the driver take them to the Lebanese Resthouse close to the shore of the Sea of Galilee. The three High Priests of Zorastri were waiting patiently. Their malevolent, carnal dreams of unlocking the Devil's soul were about to be fulfilled.

As the car halted, Conchos stepped out and obsequiously bowed his head down low before them. Without showing any reciprocal acknowledgement or even a flicker of emotion, the High Priests climbed into the car seats, each carrying a similar black leather holdall. Conchos disappeared briefly into the Resthouse for ten minutes and when he returned he carried a much larger kitbag. He needed additional resources because he knew he was going to have to make the entrance accessible to men considerably older than himself. Getting them up to the ridge was a major problem but he had the solution.

Taking the wheel of the car, Conchos ordered the driver to stay at the Resthouse and wait there until they returned. He was pleased with the progress they were making although he still felt a little disconcerted at the mysterious disappearance of Trenchard's body from the rock pool where he had fallen.

Stopping the car alongside the bridge, he noted that it had taken longer than he had planned. The priests followed Conchos up the dry riverbed.

"You have done well," said the Daimones, the Lord High Priest.

Through his myriad of warped values Conchos felt elated; he thrived on the praise he received from his master.

Simon saw them pass within a few feet of his vantage point. *Who on earth are they?* he wondered, peering out through the leaves as they carried on up the rocky ravine in single file. He carried on watching as Conchos, with the bag around his back, climbed up the rock face to the ledge. He was close enough to make out the pained expression every time he had to rely on his bad hand for support. Once on the ridge, he opened his bag, took out some tools and began hammering metal supports into the rock similar to the ones used by professional climbers. After ten minutes he threw down a rope ladder, which he secured safely in place.

One by one, the Zoroastrian priests climbed up the steep face and negotiated their way along the ledge to the labyrinth entrance. Simon checked his watch as he observed them disappear inside.

As soon as he felt it was safe, he pulled out the mobile phone. He cursed as he saw the amount of battery power remaining. *Philip, please be there,* he mumbled, dialling his mobile again.

It rang a couple of times before Philip picked up.

"Where are you?" shouted Simon. "I need you here now!"

"I'll be there very shortly," he stated quietly without any life.

The manner and style of his brother's monotone response made him freeze. He knew instantly that something was wrong. In his anxiety and concern for Anna he realised it hadn't even occurred to him to enquire about Heather.

"Philip how's Heather? Is she Ok?" he asked uneasily.

"She's dead," he replied.

Chapter Forty-Five

Vatican City, Rome

Colonel Renauld entered the papal quarters of Pope Leo XIV. He had left Major Dupont in charge of orchestrating the final touches to their plan in St. Paul's Basilica.

The atmosphere in the Pope's administration department had changed dramatically for the better in the days after his official coronation. Even though the staff that looked after his affairs were principally males in a male-dominated environment, his new personal secretary, a highly influential member of his team, was an intelligent young lady. Renauld had become aware of her growing reputation in the short days since her groundbreaking appointment had been made.

"Good afternoon, Colonel Renauld," she said cordially as he approached her reception desk. "His Holiness has made it clear that you're free to enter at any time," she continued, waving him up the short flight of steps that led to his study and common meeting room.

He nodded curtly and proceeded up the steps and through the door. Inside, the Pope and Ruler of the Holy See was silently meditating behind his ornate marble-topped writing desk. His eyes were closed and his hands pressed together as if he were praying but in truth he was in deep contemplation. His mind was analysing and re-assessing all the information surrounding their progress to rid the world of the evil Book of Judas and its alleged macabre revelations. He realised that they weren't just fighting the Satanica; time was also their enemy as it slowly began to slip away from them. He turned his thoughts to the murders of Cardinals Alphonso and Gregory. These were grave matters indeed and they would surely cause a stir when the truth surfaced in the outside world but right now their significance was low. Shaking his head, he wondered what else could be done at this late stage to improve their chances.

Renauld observed the Pope's study of concentration and after gently closing the door behind him, coughed respectfully to signify his presence. Waking from his trance, the Pope's eyes burst open, startled for a moment, although his hands remained clasped together.

"Colonel Renauld, apologies, please come in and sit down. I was trying to find some ray of hope, something to fix onto in our hour of need – I've prayed for the young girl. I hope she doesn't realise the weight of expectation that rests on her shoulders or she will surely fail," he added while his hands parted from their prayer and descended to straighten some of the ruffles on his regal white cassock.

Obeying the Pope's wishes, Renauld stepped forward from the door and sat in the comfortable Louis XIV chair facing his long desk.

"Your Holiness, the time has arrived – as we discussed, I have carefully laid the groundwork for our plan. Each Cardinal now believes we've caught the murderer in our midst and that they're no longer viewed as potential suspects. Their guards have been removed and they're at liberty to travel freely as they wish… It's now time to spring the trap!"

The Pope shook his head sadly. He seemed tired and drained of colour, the normal, powerful aura of self-confidence and energy was absent.

"Where are they now?" he asked in a subdued voice. Renauld thought he also detected a note of despair in his voice.

Pope Leo's faith in human nature and in his ability to distinguish good from evil had been severely tested by one of these so-called men of the church. The subterfuge, the cowardly acts of murder and the enormous sense of betrayal would all carry a heavy price for the future of their faith. When he stopped to think about each Cardinal individually, the sense of betrayal just grew stronger and stronger. Over many difficult and trying years they had worked together, forming a strong relationship based on trust and mutual respect. *How can one of these priests, one of my closest allies and friends, possibly be a member of the Satanica?* he wondered despondently. It just didn't seem possible.

"According to my last report, they're all still in the vicinity of St. Paul's," the Colonel reported.

An expression of melancholic disdain appeared across the Pope's face as he reflected on the latest news.

"Your Holiness, are you still comfortable with our arrangements?" asked Renauld with a feeling of concern. "You know you don't have to go through with this if you don't want to – in fact I still recommend that you reconsider," he continued.

"Enough," replied Pope Leo loudly, holding up his hand at the same time. "I trust you implicitly, Colonel, and I want this matter sorted out once and for all!"

He paused and took a deep breath before continuing on a more passive tone.

"I'm sorry, Colonel. Please don't take my vagueness as indifference… I have a lot on my mind. Our focus has to be on the events surrounding the Book of Judas – have you heard anything more from Goran?"

Renauld's confidence was quickly restored. He could see from the Pope's manner and body language that he was determined to see the plan through to the end.

"Unfortunately, I have no news at this point in time, Your Holiness – I share your concern. I too feel uncomfortable with the fact that we can do nothing from here but we need to be patient for just a little bit longer."

Renauld wondered how much confidence he had in his own words.

"Maybe, Colonel, we should have given the instruction to destroy the arkheynia from the outset... Maybe we should have just stopped the Satanica from finding the entrance when we had the chance," reflected the Pope solemnly.

Renauld nodded. He had been an outspoken advocate for completing the mission in its entirety. He had argued that the security of the Vatican would never be fully re-established until the book was done away with once and for all.

"All I can tell you is that if I had to choose two people to fight my cause," said Renauld assuredly, "I have no doubt that I'd choose Goran and Anna for that assignment."

The Pope looked across at him and smiled.

"Yes – we do have some hope don't we?" he replied a little more eagerly. "In times like this we must have faith in the greatest redeemer of all – our Lord God will surely provide the way."

There was knock on the door and the Supreme Pontiff's private secretary popped her head around the corner.

"I am very sorry to disturb you but there's an extremely urgent call from Goran for you, Colonel!" she said hastily.

Immediately, Renauld stood up to follow her out of the room.

"I can transfer the call in here if you like," she suggested.

The Colonel looked at Pope Leo for his instructions. He nodded his approval to his secretary and she rapidly disappeared to finish the task.

Seconds later, the phone rang on the corner of his ornate desk and the Pope beckoned him to take the call.

"Goran, this is Colonel Renauld," he stated promptly and listened to the excited voice speaking at the other end.

"It's Goran," said Renauld seriously, briefly holding his hand over the mouthpiece to re-confirm the caller to Pope Leo.

The Pope also felt a renewed sense of hope as he observed the positive mannerisms being displayed by Colonel Renauld. He watched him listening, nodding vigorously at the information he was receiving. The call lasted just a couple of minutes before he brought it to an end.

"Call as soon as you're there, do you understand?" he demanded urgently before hanging up the phone.

Pope Leo waited expectantly for the news.

"There have been some important developments," he said sternly. "Your Holiness, the Satanica have found the entrance to the labyrinth – Anna's also inside but her condition's unknown. Goran has the exact location of the entrance and has secured helicopter transport... He estimates that he can be at the site within forty-five minutes – possibly sooner!" he said positively.

Pope Leo XIV sat back in his chair and took a deep breath as he stared upwards to the heavens.

"We're better off than we were before," he summarised. "Let's hope this is an auspicious day and I will pray that our Lord will show them the right path to follow."

Renauld acknowledged his words with a nod. One way or another, they both knew that the time of reckoning had finally arrived. After enduring the interminable wait, everything had quickly turned and the last act of the play was gathering an unstoppable momentum.

The Colonel suddenly checked his watch. He recalled the time he had indicated to the three Cardinals that the Pope would be praying when he had crossed the floor of the Sala Ducale. *We need to get moving,* he thought privately. He had been in the Pope's office longer than planned and if there was still going to be a chance of this working then he needed to instil a new sense of urgency into proceedings.

He turned to address the Pope. The issue of Goran's reaching the labyrinth would have to wait for now. They were going to have to get moving if their trap was going to be sprung.

"Your Holiness, are you sure you want to go ahead with our plan?" he asked again for the final time.

"Yes, Colonel Renauld, I'm perfectly sure, and I can see by your face that you're getting anxious. I'll make my way to the 'Altar of the Chair' immediately," he answered.

"Your Holiness, do you remember the location and the exact position you must adopt when you get there?" he asked double-checking.

Earlier that day, he had walked with the Pope through St. Paul's to the small chapel beyond the tomb of St. Peter to make sure he was fully comfortable with how the plan would work in practice.

"I remember it perfectly," he responded, reassuring him with a warm smile as his tall frame rose from his seat.

"Anyway, Colonel, I'm not afraid because I know you'll be there to protect me," he added with confidence.

Together they walked out of his office and down the stairs of the papal apartments until they reached the doorway leading out into St. Peter's Square. Following the plan to the letter, they talked together until they reached the foot of the steps leading up to the main portico to St. Paul's Basilica. It was a point that could be observed from nearly every building that surrounded the great ceremonial square. His tall stature and his unique white cassock made his identity unmistakeable for anyone who might be observing.

After a few more minutes of discussion, Colonel Renauld bowed humbly before the Supreme Pontiff and turned to walk away from the steps towards his office tower beyond the pillars of the colonnade at the opposite end of Bernini's piazza. At the same time, His Holiness, Pope Leo the fourteenth, Ruler of the Holy See climbed the grey stone steps that led into the Catholicism's most famous house of worship.

On his way, the Pope looked up at the façade of the Basilica with its rich decoration of images depicting Christ and the Apostles. Modern-day public opinion on the beauty of the Vatican's exterior architecture varied between both extremes. In the past it had almost become a requirement that every new Pope should add a new building or change some of its features. In fact each addition had added to the overall effect, which had become one of consolidation. It was a far cry from the initial dreams of Raphael and Michelangelo in the fourteenth century. Pope Leo XIV was himself a critic of the exterior but inside, he knew there was no other place in the world like it – it was a magnificent setting for the abundant treasures and works of art held by the Catholic Church.

Considering the mission he was undertaking, he felt surprisingly calm as he strolled into the atrium with its ornate pine-cone shaped fountain. Inside the Basilica, the nave, which had been designed by Carlo Maderno, was approaching ninety metres in length; it had originally been Michelangelo's intention to build the great dome above four equal sized naves in the shape of a Greek cross but his plans changed over time. The Pope's mind reverted to the task at hand. An attendant of the church, surprised by the sudden appearance of none other than the Holy Father, quickly bowed his head in deference as the Pope marched purposefully past him.

Colonel Renauld had been particularly clever with his choice of venue. The "Altar of the Chair" was enclosed right at the far end of the nave beyond the altar of St. Peter. It was a well-known tradition in the Vatican amongst the Roman Catholic clergy that this chapel was the private and religious domain of the Supreme Pontiff.

Occasionally, the Ecumenical Council looking after the general affairs of the Church would announce that it was open to a wider circle for an extended period but that was not case at this point in time. Renauld knew when he chose the "Altar of the Chair" that it had all the traits that would make an assailant comfortable with his task. He would have privacy, time and an escape route that would ensure his getaway was unobserved.

Continuing down the main central aisle of the long nave, he wasted no time in getting to the restricted chapel. Inside, he pulled the thick velvet purple curtain along its rails indicating that the chapel was being used by the Pontiff, who wished to pray in solitude.

Inside the church was the Chair of St. Peter, which gave the room its name. Its wooden frame had been repeatedly restored over the years and it was inset with carvings depicting the pagan myth of the Labours of Hercules. Romantically it was considered as the Episcopal throne of St. Peter but in reality historians pointed out that it was more likely to have belonged to Charles the Bald, who ruled in the ninth century.

As instructed, Pope Leo XIV stepped forward and sat down on a pew near the elevated platform upon which the Altar of the Chair was placed.

On his right were the tombs of Pope Urban VIII and Pope Paul III. The latter had a statue of the enthroned Pope above it with two female figures representing Prudence and Justice in front of the stone sarcophagus. He looked around him and then settled into the agreed position to recite his prayers.

In the meantime, Colonel Renauld was hurriedly getting himself into position. The "Altar of the Chair" differed from the other chapels in that it had two very different modes of entry. The first was through the main portico, through which Pope Leo had entered and the second was through a small door leading to the Vatican gardens at the rear. This entrance was kept locked and could only be opened from the inside. He knew his other elite officers were already in place. Furtively, he entered through the rear door and quickly took up the position that he had earmarked for himself behind a large wall tapestry. He looked at the Pope; his eyes were closed deep in prayer but his lips moved as he gently rocked backwards and forwards reciting the Latin verse. *Ok, the trap has been laid; now to see if it works,* thought Renauld.

Earlier Major Dupont had debated with Colonel Renauld over whether or not they should station some of the soldiers in "out of sight" locations within the heart of St. Paul's. Dupont was more risk-averse and had reasoned that it could provide them with excellent information in advance of the impostor's entry to the "Altar of the Chair" chapel. The Colonel had given the prudent suggestion the consideration it deserved but in the end had decided against it. When the Cardinals had left the Sala Ducale earlier on that afternoon he had given specific instructions that apart from posting the normal sentries on duty the Cardinals were not to encounter or see another soldier from the Swiss Guards within the Vatican. He was adamant about this point and felt it was still important if this assignment was to succeed. If the impostor became aware that he was being observed or if he noticed too many guards in the vicinity he might feel the risk was too great.

The decision was a brave one. Between the chapel and the entrance to St. Paul's there were no Swiss guards on duty.

From his dark, shaded position behind the tapestry, Renauld could only observe the Pope deep in prayer. Unfortunately from this vantage point he could not see the velvet curtain that spanned the entrance. After standing on the spot motionless for fifteen minutes, he began to wonder whether the whole thing was a waste of time and whether or not his time would be better served elsewhere. After another ten minutes, he was on the verge of pulling back the heavy, woven tapestry and cancelling the plan when his body froze.

He had the distinctive feeling there were other watching eyes in the room. Silently he cursed his poor scope of vision and strained to listen for any unusual sounds or movements. He suddenly felt nervous; this was not how he had planned it. He had anticipated being able to hear anyone entering but whoever was out there, if anyone was out there, had removed their shoes and anything else that would cause a sound.

In this position they would be able to get within ten feet of the Pope before he could see them. From this distance with speed they could make a lunge that would be unstoppable. *I can't risk it*, he thought. *I must step out and confront whoever the assailant is before it's too late.*

At that moment, the stillness was broken and he heard the sound of feet gathering momentum on the stone floor. *Oh my God he's attacking!* Without thinking, Renauld ripped the tapestry away. In that instant, he saw the billowing purple robes of the assailant who was launching himself on the last stage of his murderous attack at the hunched white figure of the praying Pope. The attacker clutched a long, thin blade in his hand similar to the one used against Cardinal Alphonso. In the same moment, one of the elite guards appeared from a small niche behind the large stone tomb of Pope Urban VIII, and he too sprang forward with all the force and energy he could muster at the lunging Cardinal.

Colonel Renauld arrived at the scene too late but the soldier didn't. In that moment, Renauld froze in surprise and panic; there was nothing he could do. He saw the contorted, manic face of the killer. His eyes were bulging and every sinew on his body was stretched with his final effort. The Cardinal was off the ground with his knife stretched out in front of him as the elite guard smashed his shoulder into the side of his torso knocking him off course. The Cardinal's head jarred against the wooden pews as the force of the heavy guard crushed him into the stone floor. His crumpled body lay awkwardly on the ground. The noise of the collision echoed around the chamber as the pews went down like dominoes and crashed around the tiled floor. The sudden impact had knocked the weapon from the Cardinal's hand and the shiny blade made a tinkling sound against the stone floor as it bounced along the empty aisle.

Renauld didn't stop to watch the rest of the action but grabbed the confused Pope and bundled him to a recess at the side of the chapel. In that moment, the velvet cover swung back and Major Dupont arrived with reinforcements. Two guards raced to the Pope and unceremoniously pushed him against the wall as they took a defensive position in front of him.

The guard whose vigilance had saved the life of the Pope jumped up ready for the next attack from the assailant but it didn't happen. The attacker groaned. In his excited fervour to complete the job, the soldier hit the motionless figure one more time before realising the fight was over. The prone body writhed in agony as a small trickle of red blood flowed out from below the scarlet robe covering the evil assailant's face. Standing up, the guard quickly went over and picked up the weapon, handing it over to his Commanding Officer. Colonel Renauld nodded respectfully at the soldier. He would speak to him in private later to commend him for his actions but now was not the time.

"Who is the criminal? Whose black heart wants to kill the Head of the Catholic Church?" shouted the Pope angrily, pushing his way past the two guards who were desperately trying to protect him.

His voice quivered with nervous excitement. The near fatal experience had shaken him; he had come much closer to death than he had ever imagined.

Colonel Renauld stepped over an upturned chair as he looked at the unknown Cardinal writhing in agony on the floor. He was more eager than anyone else in the chapel to reveal the Satanica assassin responsible for the death of Alphonso and Gregory.

With all the eyes staring down at the figure, Colonel Renauld bent over and jerked away the scarlet robes covering his face.

The bloody face of Cardinal Bishop Lefebvre with his black goatee beard sneered up at him.

"Lefebvre!" the Pope gasped out aloud.

As the realisation set in, he shuddered at the thought of all the sensitive and confidential information they had discussed over the years. Lefebvre had been his closest confidant and most trusted aide.

"How could you do this?" he asked hopelessly.

Shaking his head, Renauld stared down at the Cardinal lying at his feet, shocked to the core by the sheer evil of the sneer on his face.

Lefebvre used his sleeve to wipe away some of the blood around his mouth before speaking.

"You may have me," he derided with a maniacal twisted smile, "but your time will come very soon. The Book of Judas will be ours and when it is the world will know the power of the Black Lord!"

"Get him out of here," shouted Renauld at two of his guards as he turned his attention back to Pope Leo XIV who was still trembling with shock.

"Your Holiness, we have work to do here. I'm going to instruct my men to escort you back to your apartments," he said, trying to sound as calm as possible. He felt back in control but it had been a close call, too close for comfort.

"I'm fine," he replied, gazing forlornly at the robed figure being roughly manhandled by the guards. The disappointment at learning the truth about Lefebvre was etched on his face.

"Major," Renauld shouted again, "take His Holiness back to his apartments immediately and arrange for his physician to attend."

"I'm fine, I can manage," the Pope repeated in a subdued voice as Major Dupont gently urged him forward. Before he left the chapel, he paused and delivered an intense, withering stare, full of disgust at Cardinal Lefebvre who was held tightly by two armed guards.

A few moments later Pope Leo XVI had left the room and Colonel Renauld gave instructions for three additional guards to accompany the heavily restrained Cardinal Lefebvre out of St. Paul's via the back door to the papal gardens. He wanted to keep the incident out of the public eye as much as possible.

After the procession escorting Lefebvre had left, Renauld watched while the remaining guards put the scene back into place, making sure all traces of what had happened were erased.

He saluted his loyal soldiers as they left the chapel promising to deliver a debriefing session early the following morning.

Alone in the chapel he sighed with relief as he realised how close to catastrophe they had come. His plan had worked though, he thought, pleased with his own performance. In the aftermath, if the Book of Judas was destroyed, then this moment would go a long way towards re-establishing his authority and reputation.

Renauld wandered back down the main nave of St. Paul's and out into the fading afternoon sunlight. As he descended down the steps and marched across the square he wondered whether or not to call Goran on his mobile phone.

He felt exhausted and decided to wait until he was back in the comfort of his own office. As he approached the tower at the end of the square something suddenly caught his eye. In front of him, he saw his young Lieutenant come out of the door at the bottom of his office tower and start running towards him.

"What is it?" cried Renauld, puzzled, as the officer got closer. The look on his face gave him a distinctly uneasy feeling.

"I think you need to see this, Sir," he answered and handed over a blue folder.

Renauld opened it sharply and quickly scanned the contents of the printed sheet inside.

"Oh my God," he said out loud.

In the next instant he dropped the folder and began running as fast as he could back up the square towards the papal apartments. As the sweat began to run down his forehead from the exertion all he could think about was the contents of the sheet of paper. He had to find the Pope.

Inside the Vatican he raced up the staircase that led to his apartments. There was no time to observe the usual pleasantries as he shoved open the door to his papal quarters. Bursting into the Pope's administration chambers he ran up the connecting stairs to his Private Secretary's office.

The secretary was nowhere to be seen but the prostrate body of Major Dupont was sprawled across the three steps that led up to the Pope's study. The sight that greeted him was shocking. Major Dupont was barely conscious. A large silver dagger was sticking out from below his right shoulder blade with blood oozing down his uniform.

"In there," gasped Dupont, his face contorted with pain as he tried to point to the study door.

Drawing his revolver from its holster, Renauld raced up the steps and flung the door wide open.

"Welcome Colonel," said the calm voice of Cardinal Giacoma as if he had been expecting his arrival.

He was standing behind the hunched, terrified figure of Pope Leo XIV who was sat at his desk. In his hand he held a small pistol, which he was pointing directly at the Pope's head.

"Surprised, Colonel?" he chided. "Why don't you step forward and put your gun down on the floor?"

Renauld took a few seconds to consider his options. The look of abject defeat in Pope Leo's eyes made him curse his own failings.

"Ok," he said slowly, holding his gun loosely in the air before kneeling down slowly and placing the revolver on the floor. What choice did he have?

Giacoma indicated with a nonchalant flick of the barrel for him to raise his arms back above his head where he could see them.

"Judging by your last-minute entry, I guess you know who I am?" said Giacoma with a smile on his face.

"You bastard," said Renauld, registering the expression of fear on Pope Leo XIV's pale face. "Why don't you kill me instead of the Pope. There's nothing to be gained by murdering him."

"Ah, but there is," replied Giacoma confidently, the smile broadening as he sensed victory. He brought the gun up closer to his head about to pull the trigger.

"Stop!" shouted Renauld loudly.

Giacoma looked up and relaxed his stance for a moment.

"What is it Colonel? Do you have something to say because we haven't got very long have we? I know your troops will be with us any second now," he said, glancing towards the door while calmly keeping a firm grip of the Pope's head.

"You see, Colonel, I've always been prepared to die," he added with a cynical smile.

"What I said earlier, in the Sala Ducale," gasped Renauld. "That was rubbish, I made it up to lure you out – the Pope doesn't hold the key to finding the book at all."

Giacoma stared at him blankly for a moment.

"Not good enough Colonel – you will both die," he snarled and raised the gun up to the Pope's head, about to pull the trigger.

At that moment the Colonel winced sharply as a loud bang went off. When he opened his eyes and looked up he saw a red dot on Giacoma's stunned face where the bullet had entered just above his eyebrow. For a second, he stood there frozen, his eyes wide-open, like a waxwork dummy before he crumpled and fell to the floor.

The Colonel looked behind him; the outstretched hand of Major Dupont was trembling, holding a gun out in front of him.

He jumped up and rushed around to the crumpled figure of the Pope lying across the surface of his desk. Before moving him, he double-checked that Giacoma was dead. The Pope was numb with terror from the traumatic encounter.

"Your Holiness, it's over!" he said putting his hand on Pope Leo's shoulder.

The Pope stared up at him and nodded. *He'll survive!* thought Renauld.

Leaving him, he walked back over to the open door where the dead body of Major Dupont lay outstretched across the steps still clutching the gun. He sat down next to his body just as the private secretary and the papal physician came running into the office. There faces were aghast at the carnage and seconds later they were closely followed by a band of soldiers commanded by his trusty young Lieutenant.

"In there – quickly," ordered Renauld with a glance of the head.

As they hurriedly passed by up the steps he knelt down despondently and took his deputy's hand.

"We owe you so much," he muttered quietly.

Letting go of his hand and laying it across his chest he made himself a promise. He would make sure that this act was never forgotten if it was the last thing he ever did. The courage he had shown in foiling the Satanica with his last mortal act would remain an everlasting memory for all those that would come to serve within the sacred walls of the Vatican City.

Standing up he walked back into the room where the doctor was busily fussing around the Pope.

"Is that it, Colonel?" stuttered the Pope. "I don't think the House of God can survive any more death and bloodshed on its doorsteps!"

The Colonel nodded. He felt mentally, physically and emotionally exhausted.

"Your Holiness, we still have one final bridge to cross," he answered, his mind turning to the struggle that must be facing Goran.

"What made you suspect there was someone else?" asked the Pope tiredly. He too was drained of energy.

"One of my officers presented me with a report I'd been waiting for – it detailed all the international movements of Cardinal Weiss, Giacoma and Lefebvre. The report told me that Lefebvre and Giacoma had travelled to Amsterdam together on several occasions prior to Lawrence Trenchard's death... Remarkably enough, they even travelled together after the meeting where we briefed Goran on the mission ahead!"

"Incredible, simply incredible," he replied before succumbing to the doctor's repeated requests for him to remain still.

"All these years, the Satanica have been busily getting their dormant moles in place for just this occasion – do you know that it was my constant badgering of Pope Paul VII that finally persuaded him to make Lefebvre a Cardinal," he sighed ironically, shaking his head in dismay.

"Your Holiness, I will try and speak to Goran and return with news as soon as I have it."

"The last bridge," nodded the Pope hopefully. "I will pray that we can cross it."

Chapter Forty-Six

The Labyrinth of Judas, Bethsaida

Simon tried to stand up. Using the Acacia tree's hard but narrow trunk, he pulled with his arms while taking the weight on his good leg. He winced with pain. The tourniquet on his leg had been pulled tight and although it had stemmed the bleeding, his thigh had become very stiff and sore. *I can do this,* he thought, gritting his teeth. *I did it earlier and I'll do it again.* He pushed the branch he had found earlier beneath the crook of his arm and tested its strength again. The movement caused him a lot of discomfort but that wasn't going to stop him now. As he took his first step he recalled Goran telling him to stay where he was. *That's all very well,* he thought, but who could say whether Anna had the luxury of time.

As he slowly stumbled his way back up the ravine, he tried to ascertain his options. On top of everything else, he was still in a state of shock after hearing the devastating news of Heather's gruesome death. He tried to imagine how his brother must be feeling. After contacting Goran he had managed to speak to Philip again but his response had only worried him more about his brother's state of mind. Gritting his teeth from the pain running through his leg, he continued to hobble up the wadi bed towards the labyrinth entrance. At that moment he would gladly have done anything to turn back the clock to that evening in New York when they set off to Theodore Grainger's mansion – only this time he would have taken Heather with them. Shaking his head, he knew the time for mourning would come; his efforts now had to be for the living, for Anna.

Simon could feel the salty beads of sweat stinging his eyes from the exertion. Although it was now late afternoon with the sun beginning to fade, the weather was still hot and humid. To make the conditions more bearable he tried to keep in the shade of the ravine.

Only ten minutes earlier, from his vantage point behind the bushes, he had seen the Satanica's executioner enter the labyrinth followed by the three strange figures. They had used a rope ladder that was still hanging down from the ledge up the rock face. Now Simon steered himself towards it, determined to try and save Anna by hauling himself up. He refused to accept that she could be dead but even his most optimistic thoughts predicted that she must be in grave danger.

Clutching hold of the ladder, he climbed up. Heaving hard, he pulled up two rungs using his strong forearms and his good leg as an anchor on the bottom rung while taking the pressure off his bad leg by letting it swing free. Grimacing, he held on tightly, looking up the ladder to the ledge about fifteen feet above his head. He felt reasonably confident that he could climb the ladder but how could he possibly perch on the narrow ledge and keep his balance to navigate his way along to the entrance.

Reluctantly, he let himself down again to rethink his plan. *It's hopeless!* he thought. Even if he managed to work his way along the rock face and climb down the entrance hole, how was he ever going to see where he was going? He didn't have a torch with him. He knew there was no chance he could do this alone – he needed help. Letting himself back down to the ground gently, he resigned himself to waiting.

Leaning against the rock face, he pulled out the mobile phone Anna had given him from his pocket. There was no signal and no battery power. He threw it angrily on the ground in disgust – it seemed that his only option was to wait for his brother's arrival but what state was he going to be in.

After Philip had told him that Heather was dead, Simon had called him back. He was in a hire car about thirty minutes away from the Sea of Galilee. Although the conversation was stilted and monosyllabic, Simon had passed on the final location details and told him to stop and get certain provisions.

Frustrated by his limited ability to move, he sat down next to the rock pool and waited impatiently for his arrival.

He didn't have to wait long. Only ten minutes had passed when Philip appeared on the horizon down the wadi bed. He was running at a brisk pace, Simon noticed. As he got closer, Simon could see the grief etched all over his face. With his shirt drenched with sweat and his body glistening from the sun, he finally reached the rock face where Simon was standing. Tears welled up in Simon's eyes as he reached out emotionally to his brother. They embraced for a moment.

"I'm really sorry, I just can't imagine it!" muttered Simon under his breath.

As they released one another, Simon looked into Philip's eyes and he could see that he was lost in a self-contained world of his own; his vacant look said all he needed to know. This was a problem for Simon. He knew his brother well enough to recognise the signs from their childhood. If the level of suffering became too unbearable for Philip he rebelled. His defence mechanism was to expel emotion by becoming obsessively aggressive with the cause of the problem. In this case Simon could read the signs. Philip wanted revenge and he would not stop until he had found Heather's killer.

"Where's the entrance?" gasped the older brother, still dripping with perspiration.

Simon stared at his brother for a moment before answering. This was a dilemma he hadn't envisaged. On the one hand he was desperate to get inside and save Anna. He knew the only way he could do this was with his brother's help. On the other hand he knew that letting his brother enter the labyrinth in this state of mind was madness.

"Where is it?" repeated Philip impatiently.

Simon thought quickly. He knew that if he was going to enter there was no way he could prevent Philip from following, besides he would need his help. He made up his mind to keep a careful eye on his older brother.

"Up there," said Simon, pointing to the shelf above the rock pool. "We can get up using that rope ladder – I can just about climb the ladder but I'm going to need your help getting along the ledge with this leg."

"Ok, I'll go first," suggested his older brother. "Let's go."

"Wait a minute," said Simon. "I've got an idea – if we're going in there we need a weapon – there's a gun in the rock pool. The kidnapper dropped it when Anna fired at him."

"Whereabouts?" asked Philip, staring into the clear water and pulling off his shirt.

Simon recalled the moment when Conchos stood above on the ledge taking aim with his gun.

"It would have landed over there somewhere," replied Simon, pointing.

Philip wasted no time. He plunged into the pool and swam down, keeping his eyes open. At the bottom it was dark and he rubbed his hand along the rock, being careful not to cloud the water with the silt. A flash of silver metal suddenly caught Philip's eye and he stretched out to reach it. Watching from above, Simon saw him swim to the surface clutching the revolver; the silencer was still attached to the end.

"Well done," yelled Simon.

Philip trudged out of the pool, tossed the wet gun to his brother and received his dry shirt back in return.

"It will still work won't it?" Simon asked, drying it on his clothes.

His experience with firearms was fairly limited but he knew that if the fit between the projectile and the casing of the cartridge was tight then the water would not have been able to affect the gunpowder at the base.

"Try it," Philip suggested

Simon screwed the silencer back on, aimed and fired at a tree down the ravine. The gun made a short, controlled hiss before hitting the tree truck.

"Ok – let's get inside the labyrinth," urged Simon, limping towards the ladder.

"You go first," said Philip, his clothes sticking to his wet skin.

Simon grabbed the rope ladder and started hauling himself up. Each rung was difficult but he was determined to make it and with his brother's added encouragement he reached the top. Philip knew the next bit would be difficult. He helped Simon to turn and perch on the ledge while he climbed up after him. Once Philip was in position, he offered his hand and helped Simon to his feet. His brother grimaced with pain as he struggled up.

"Can you go on?" asked Philip, watching Simon pause to catch his breath.

"I'm Ok," he gasped, looking down at the ground twenty feet below. He had never felt comfortable with heights at the best of times and when he looked along the narrow ledge he wondered if he could make it.

"I'm going to need your help over the next bit," he added, indicating with a nod of the head the section where the shelf narrowed.

Using Philip as an anchor, he clawed his way along the sheer rock wall, his face pressed against the side in places. With every sideways shuffle he breathed in sharply from the pain as he was forced to put his weight onto his injured leg. Edging his way through the narrowest section, he knew there was no going back now. With Philip's strong support he ignored the constant ache and throbbing, determined that he was going to make it.

"Just a few more steps," said Philip as he spotted the entrance hole. Checking his brother's progress, he allowed himself a quick glance down at the sapphire blue waters of the rock pool below.

Simon suddenly groaned as his leg missed its footing.

"Philip!" he screamed as he began to topple backwards.

It felt as if everything was suddenly moving in slow motion as he hovered for a few seconds desperately trying to cling to the wall but it wasn't working.

Instantly, his brother shot out his hand and grabbed the front of Simon's shirt, pulling it tightly. With his hand on a secure rock, he hauled his brother back to the ledge as they heard the falling rocks splashing into the deep pool below them.

"Thanks, that was close!" said Simon gratefully once he had regained his balance.

"Just a bit further to go," said Philip, relaxing his grip and allowing Simon to use his extended arm as a means of support.

The ledge became a little wider in the last few steps and he felt a wave of relief as he carefully sat down, perching on the edge of the hole.

"Ok, I'm going in – can you let yourself down?" Philip asked, anxious to keep the pace up.

Simon nodded and Philip lowered himself in first, dropping the last few feet to the stone floor. He pulled out the flashlight that he had organised earlier after Simon's instructions and quickly scanned the beam around him. The light highlighted the ancient text that Anna had discovered earlier. Philip had no idea what the script said but the gory and obscene illustrations painted around the dark chamber told him all he needed to know. Shining the torch in a three hundred and sixty degree turn, he knew he didn't have time to dwell on the satanic imagery. His main concern was establishing that the coast was clear and sorting out which route they should follow.

He saw the passageway immediately and when he lowered the beam to the floor, he noticed all the human tracks left in the dust and the dirt.

"Ok, you can come down when you're ready," he whispered up to his brother.

Simon wriggled around so that his legs dangled through the entrance hole before gradually lowering himself down. His body dangled into the dark cavern while he firmly held onto the rocks around the rim with his outstretched arms. Philip knew this was going to hurt but he had to do it quickly. If Simon was to let himself fall the final few feet it might injure his leg further and make walking totally impossible. He quickly reached up and grabbed around the top of his legs, being as careful as possible not to pressurize the wound. Then, as Philip took Simon's weight, his brother let go, and he gingerly cushioned his descent to the cavern floor.

At last, we're in the labyrinth, thought Simon as his eyes began to get accustomed to the dark. Philip handed him a torch.

"What's our plan?" asked Simon furtively.

"We're going to find Anna and then I'm going to kill him the same way he killed Heather!" replied Philip.

Simon looked at his brother. His face was devoid of emotion other than an intensity burning deep within his eyes he was channelling all his pent up rage into revenge. Simon shook his head. This was dangerous; he could see that his brother had lost some of his own will to live.

"Whatever happens down these corridors," he muttered, "I must make sure I can protect him from himself."

"Let's get moving," said Philip.

Simon nodded.

"Goran should be here any minute now," he added.

They had both been concentrating so hard on gaining access that they hadn't really considered his arrival. They assumed that he would catch up sooner or later. *I just hope it's before the final confrontation,* thought Simon.

"Let's get to the centre as quickly as we can," said Philip. "If he makes it in time it's a bonus!"

"Agreed," he answered and with the older brother taking the lead they started off through the twisting, turning corridors of the labyrinth.

* * * *

Deep inside the mountain, Anna slowly came back to her senses. Raising her hand to her head, her face contorted as the sharp pain burst through her temples above her eyebrows. Clumsily, her hand rubbed the wound where she had received the full force of the blow. It was dark and she felt boxed in as the ache continued to throb relentlessly.

Where on earth am I? she wondered, trying to stretch out her arms and legs in the darkness. She quickly sensed she was in a small, confined space as her senses of touch and hearing had become magnified – she could even hear the sound of her own breathing.

She sniffed the air; it had a rotten, putrid smell. Frightened, Anna continued to reach out with her hands feeling the cold stone edges as she tried to work out where she was. Turning to one side with her head pounding, she bumped into something that scrapped against the stone base. She reached out for the object and felt it with her fingers. She froze in shock. It was a skull! In that split second she realised where she was – she convulsed with terror.

Filled with horror, she desperately scrabbled around, panicking in the confined space as she tried with all her strength to push the stone slab above her head. It was futile.

After thirty seconds, she realised it was hopeless and stopped banging her fists on the unyielding lid. Sobbing with frustration and fear, her body sagged, as she recognised the utter hopelessness of her position. Recalling the moment when she had been attacked in the labyrinth's main chamber she cursed her own incompetence as the unbearable and terrifying thoughts continued to compound in her head. *Is the coffin buried below the ground? How long will the air last? What's happened to Simon?*

Whichever way she looked it was useless. She was trapped, buried alive in a suffocating, claustrophobic stone tomb and it was highly probable that she would die there!

* * * *

Goran was in a hurry. The pilot of the helicopter had not landed but was hovering above the bridge allowing his passenger to descend quickly by rope. It had been difficult to find a helicopter with a pilot prepared to travel through Israeli airspace but with the lure of substantial sums of money, half of which was transferred in advance, he had found someone prepared to make the dangerous journey.

They flew low at top speed through the mountain ranges to avoid detection by radar. As the helicopter burst through a low pass and out across the waters of the Sea of Galilee, he knew they were close. Grabbing the pilot by the shoulder, he pointed to the bridge in the distance. Seconds later he was hovering above the point as Goran threw out the rope and started scrambling out the side. Jumping the last few feet, he hit the ground running. The pilot acknowledged his wave before turning in an arc to head back towards his base just south of Beirut.

Goran was a professional. In his early career he had been a member of the Polish Army before being seconded to serve with a UK Special Forces unit that worked behind the lines in Yugoslavia during the traumatic times of Milosevic's ethnic cleansing. Now was the time to justify all those hours of hard training, he thought as he began jogging up the wadi bed. He was pleased to finally be in action and knowing time was crucial he pushed himself to the limit.

His first objective was to locate the entrance. The Simon's instructions had been clear and concise and he felt confident from his surroundings that he was moving in the right direction. Gazing up to the horizon, it was easy to spot the unusual needle-like summit rising up on the left hand-side of the ravine.

Jumping over obstacles in his way, he hurried up the ravine in the fast-fading afternoon light. After ten minutes he looked up ahead and recognized the shape of the canyon as it came into his field of vision. Moments later his hopes were raised. The rope ladder was still hanging down from the side of the ledge.

He paused for a moment.

"Simon," he called, looking around him but there was no movement.

He called again but then noticed the mobile phone on the wadi bed floor. Picking it up, he walked over to the ladder. There was a patch of crimson blood on the rope.

He's gone inside, he thought, angry that he had disobeyed his orders but also slightly puzzled. How had he managed to enter if his injuries were as bad as he had told him on the phone? *Can his brother be here,* he wondered.

He touched the blood with his finger; it was still wet. *They must be in there,* he thought. *I've got to catch up with them.* He had hoped that the element of surprise would be on his side. Moving as fast as he could, he climbed the ladder and rapidly paced along the narrow ridge to the entrance.

He paused, peering into the darkness below before swiftly peeling off his rucksack and lowering it with a rope to the stone floor below. He had to be careful; it contained some highly volatile and dangerous explosives. Dropping down next to the pack, he pulled out the powerful camping lamp and began concentrating on wiring up the secondary explosives.

He eased them gently out of their case – the rectangular, light-yellow blocks of Tetrytol were small but devastatingly effective. On detonation, an explosion would travel at the rate of twenty-four thousand feet per second, demolishing the immediate area with the same effect as ten times the amount of TNT.

Goran worked quickly, he was well practised in the art of explosives. After a few minutes he sat back and admired his handiwork. He had used enough detonating power to bring down the entire side of the mountain. Satisfied that everything was in place, he primed the explosives and set the timer for forty minutes.

"Whatever happens now," he muttered to himself, "I've made sure that the Book of Judas and its contents never see the light of day."

He watched as the clock started its countdown and quickly synchronised the stopwatch on his wrist. *That's it,* he thought. *I've got forty minutes to complete the mission otherwise we're all dead!*

He pushed two revolvers into his waistband and shoved an extra clip into his back pocket. Pulling the torch out of his pack, he bravely set off without knowing whether he had enough time to negotiate his way through the labyrinth passages before the detonation time was up. He only had one thing on his mind and that was his mission to destroy the Book of Judas. If he could remove the world of the Satanica, save the lives of Anna and the Trenchards, as well as himself, then it would be a bonus but the book must be destroyed first.

* * * *

Inside the great chamber at the end of the labyrinth, the High Priests of Zorastri, commanded by their mortal master, Daimones, were making their final preparations for the satanic ritual

The four fires burned brightly in the metal cauldrons sitting on their pedestals in each corner of the elevated square platform. Around the voluminous chamber's deep perimeter Conchos had lit a series of wax candles to further illuminate the proceedings.

Daimones stood in the centre of the stage, flanked on either side by his fellow Zoroastrian High Priests, all dressed in the same black hooded robes. The sleeves bore the red initials "MM" in remembrance of the fallen Vatican priest who had been recruited by the Devil to dispense evil amongst mortal men. It was his chilling words, warning about the Book of Judas, that had caused the Satanica's potent force to grow ever stronger.

The marble platform floor had been swept clean to reveal the stark lines and markings that had been covered by centuries of amassed dirt.

When they had first entered the chamber, Daimones had hurried down the steps to examine the Book of Judas resting on the stone altar table. Filled with wonderment at the sight of the sacred black treasure, he had kissed the cover before examining its mystical and powerful contents. He was also no stranger to the ancient text, the same as used in the Judas Scrolls that Sir Lawrence had discovered at Qumran. While his fellow priests set the stage, he carefully turned each page, translating the black rites that would unlock the reincarnation of the devil.

When he had finished he turned to Conchos and nodded. The time to begin the ceremony had arrived. Daimones placed the large symbolic silver chalice alongside the Book of Judas.

The discovery of the chalice had mystified Conchos earlier. After finishing the first section of the book, Daimones had requested that he be taken to the tomb of Judas. He had entered alone and returned moments later with the chalice. Conchos was left with a puzzled expression. He had investigated the crypt fully and he knew there was nowhere the chalice could have been hidden.

They had returned to the platform, where Daimones continued to study the ancient text. The chalice was needed to drink the blood of the

Devil, mirroring the Catholic Holy Mass in which the "Blood of Christ" is consumed. However, in this case the chalice was not be filled with Communion wine but with the actual blood from the sacrifice of a pure human being. The ritual was brutal and macabre; it was the antithesis of the Communion service. Instead of bread representing the "Body of Christ", the "body of Satan" was represented by the human flesh of the victim.

"You may fetch the girl," commanded Daimones, his voice echoing around the chamber.

Conchos, patiently awaiting his next instructions, turned and strode off the platform and up the steps towards Judas's crypt at the other end of the chamber. The path along the grey stone steps to the antechamber of the vault had been marked with tall candles whose guttering flames enhanced the evil and sinister ambience. As Conchos stooped through the tomb's entrance the flickering light fell upon the gruesome portrayals of bloody sacrifices and horned, demonic beasts on the labyrinth's walls.

Conchos was secretly looking forward to seeing his victim's mental state. It would be his role to sacrifice and mutilate the girl, a job he would relish even more than usual in her case. He leaned down against the sarcophagus lid and began to push the heavy stone tablet to one side. Inside the dark, claustrophobic tomb, Anna was lying perfectly still, imagining her imminent slow death. The noise made her jump. The sound of stone grating on stone was the first thing she had heard since regaining consciousness. She wanted to burst into tears.

As the tomb cover slid further over to one side she wanted to sit up and fight just in case it was Conchos, who might lock her in again for eternity but she couldn't; her body was rigid. Sobbing with relief, she prayed that it was someone who wanted to save her.

Hope disappeared in that instant when she recognised Conchos' malicious staring eyes peering in. Her body quivered; it felt as if rigor mortis had set in except for the occasional uncontrollable muscle spasms.

Petrified, her eyes fixed on his blank, emotionless face as he reached in and violently dragged his victim out the tomb. Heaving her body over the side, he let her go and she fell head first onto the hard stone floor. Stunned by the impact, her eyes rolled as if she were about to pass out. Blood trickled down her face as her teeth pierced her bottom lip.

Conchos pulled out some black tape from his pocket; he knew by the state she was in that she was not going to put up a struggle but he wasn't taking any chances. Her courage and nerve could return at a later point during the ritual. He quickly bound the tape tightly around her wrists and ankles before placing a final strip across her mouth. He looked into her eyes and smiled. She tried to focus but then felt her head jerk backwards as he callously dragged her body through the low, arched gateway out of the crypt.

Outside the room, without showing any respect, he slung her like a carcass over his shoulder and carried her down the candlelit steps of the immense, dark chamber. Anxious to please his Daimones, he swiftly reached the elevated stage where the High Priests of Zorastri were fervently awaiting their sacrifice's arrival. Conchos dropped Anna roughly across the breadth of the white stone-slab altar before respectfully lowering his head and retreating several paces. As he took up his position at the on the edge of the platform, he felt the blade of his knife in his pocket. He gloated as he began to imagine the next job he had to do.

Daimones, his eyes burning with a maniacal passion, raised his arms in the air to begin the appalling and macabre ritual. The Book of Judas lay open on a small lectern and his fellow High Priests, the top half of their fanatical faces hidden by their black hoods, stood motionless facing their master, Daimones.

In a loud, thunderous voice that reverberated around the great chamber, Daimones began to read the "sacred" black text from the Book of Judas. At the same time the two priests started a low rhythmic chant that was repeated over and over again.

Anna partially opened her swollen eyes as she heard the booming voice of Daimones and the repetitive mantra – she recognised the strange and sinister pronunciation of the language used in the text of the Judas Scrolls. Their words invoked the coming of Satan, asking him to rise up once again into the House of the Black Lord and reveal his mortal presence. As her mind gradually attuned to her surroundings, she suddenly realised that *she* was the human sacrifice that Daimones was offering to the devil. She wanted to scream but the tape made it futile. She turned her head to the side and saw Conchos with his knife in one hand. With a ruthless glint in his eye, he smiled back as he slowly dragged his finger along the blade.

* * * *

Goran turned the corner and almost ran into the pillar covered with the deformed skulls of human labourers mercilessly beaten to death on the labyrinth's completion. Without flinching, he pushed it to one side and continued sprinting down the passageway in his race against time. Single-mindedly, he ignored the bones beneath his feet and the gruesome illustrations on the walls. He knew that if he could get to the centre quickly, it might give him some valuable additional time. Goran was devoted to the Vatican and the Church. He was prepared to sacrifice his life – to martyr himself – to accomplish this mission but he didn't want to die just yet and his will to survive speeded him on all the faster. Moments later, as he turned the next bend he heard the low, menacing chant of the Zoroastrian High Priests. *I'm nearly there,* he thought slowing down rapidly. He rounded the corner carefully, his senses alert to any dangers.

Shining the torch in front of him, he raised his gun as it illuminated the wide-eyed, expectant faces of both Trenchard brothers. They had heard the distant sound of running getting closer and had assumed it was going to be the friendly spectre of Goran.

Goran dropped his gun and dimmed the beam of the torch as soon as he recognised them and edged silently forward to where they were crouching. He had noticed that one of them was carrying a nasty leg wound.

In the background the sound from the ritual worked up to a crescendo, Daimones' voice could be heard echoing around the chamber as the mantra reached fever pitch

Simon was inspired with a sudden burst of confidence at Goran's arrival. Just one look at the way the agent moved and the kit he was carrying told you that he was a professional.

"Just around that bend the passageway opens into an enormous underground temple," whispered Simon, urgently pointing with his finger.

The brothers had only just reached the end of the labyrinth themselves and being extremely careful not to make any sound, had managed to sneak up close enough to see what was happening.

"We need to be fast," said Goran, checking his watch. "I've set explosives to detonate in just over twenty-five minutes – I want both of you to get moving back to the entrance now, as quick as you can – do you understand?"

Philip and Simon exchanged glances while the background chanting persisted. The resonant voice of Daimones amplified by the spherical, domed ceiling.

"Go – quickly!" he hissed angrily.

Neither brother moved.

"Ok, we don't have time for this… I'm going in now," he continued, pulling his revolver out of his waistband as he brushed past Philip.

Simon grabbed his arm forcefully.

"We're going in too – do you have another gun?"

Philip quickly added his agreement. He had seen Conchos standing on the edge of the platform brandishing the knife. He remembered how he had found Heather and the anger surged. He wanted to kill him as slowly and as painfully as possible.

Pausing for a second as he passed Philip, Goran glared intensely into their faces before looking out across the chamber at the pagan ritual going on below. There wasn't time to argue; he could see the ceremony was reaching its zenith. He pulled out a gun and tossed it to Simon.

"Stay behind me and aim your first shot at the Satanica's executioner – he's the one without the black robe on," he whispered and ushered them behind him with his hand.

Goran crept forward to the opening of the great chamber. Philip followed him while Simon, ignoring the pain, limped behind them at the rear.

Arms aloft, Daimones boomed out in his sonorous voice and he signalled to Conchos to step forward and carry out the callous, cold-blooded sacrifice. He stepped forward clutching the knife, relishing the part he was about to play. Anna squirmed as he approached but it was useless – she was about to die and she knew it. The chanting stopped and in the silence that followed Conchos raised the knife above her chest.

In that instant, Goran burst around the corner, rushed down the first five steps of the chamber, stopped, and balanced himself with both arms outstretched as trained one eye down the sight of his gun.

Arms still aloft, Daimones' trance was broken as he suddenly looked up to see where the noise was coming from. It was last thing he saw as the bullet pierced his skull, his corpse crumpling forward across Anna's writhing body. Surprised by the speed of the attack, Conchos saw the bullet hit Daimones and leapt, landing face-down on the marble floor.

Philip ran onto the ridge at the top of the stairs just behind Goran and immediately took aim at Conchos, now rolling across the platform for cover. The shot missed, sending sparks flying up off the marble floor. Conchos had reacted quickly and he reached out for his pack.

Simon, desperate to reach Anna, didn't bother to take a shot. He passed Goran down the steps moving as fast as his pain-racked body would let him. His heart had jumped when he saw the state she was in, prone in the middle of the altar table. All he wanted to do was get there as quickly as he could. In his anxiety, he ignored the pain.

The two black-robed priests of Zorastri were bewildered. The first thing they heard after Goran's dramatic entrance was the sharp whipcrack as the bullet smashed Daimone's cranium. Turning and realising what was happening, they raced to the edge of the platform. Too late – Goran's second shot hit one of the cloaked priests in the back and he fell, splayed across the floor while the other leapt into the black void below. There was no way up from there.

In the deadly confusion, time stood still for a moment as the horrifying realisation of what was happening suddenly dawned on Philip. Simon and Conchos were on a deadly collision course.

From his vantage point he saw Conchos on his belly behind the stone slab table, readying his gun just as Simon began to climb the steps up to the platform.

The next few seconds passed in slow motion. Philip sprinted down the stairs and charged the gangway headlong. Just as he caught up with Simon, Conchos raised the muzzle, training it coolly on Simon's heart… Without thinking, Philip launched himself through the air, slamming into Simon as Conchos squeezed the trigger, the shot rang out and the two brothers tumbled in a heap onto the stage.

Another shot was fired but this time from Goran's revolver. Philip's race to the platform had provided him with the just the cover and time he needed to set up his position. The bullet made a sharp thud as it hit Conchos's chest and the force pushed him back along the slippery, marble surface.

In the eerie stillness that followed, Simon and Philip lay motionless in a tight embrace, staring into each other's face.

"Philip?" mouthed Simon as the tears welled up and started rolling down his cheeks.

Goran raced up onto to the platform to find the Book of Judas.

"Philip!" he cried again as his brother's eyes flickered one last time before closing forever.

Simon's head sank down onto his dead brother's chest.

"There's no time – he's dead," shouted Goran.

He had seen the bullet enter the base of Philip's skull. He grabbed Simon's shoulder and shook it hard but he didn't move.

"Get Anna... Quickly!"

Goran hurriedly stepped over him and rushed to the stone table. Anna's battered, bruised face pleaded with him to release her.

"For Christ's sake, get Anna will you," he shouted loudly again. Goran was desperate to help Anna but he knew he had work that needed to be finished off first.

Simon suddenly came back to his senses with the mention of Anna's name. Choking back the tears, he peeled himself away from his brother's embrace. He knew that bullet had been meant for him.

Simon ignored the pain; he heaved himself up and covered the last few paces to the altar table. He knew he could save her. The Daimones' dead body was still sprawled across her. Grabbing his black robe, he pulled him off roughly so that his dead weight fell to the floor. Simon looked down searchingly into Anna's face. She was in a dreadful state.

A few steps away, Goran had reached the Book of Judas, which was resting on the lectern. Quickly, he carried it towards one of the fires burning on top of the pedestals.

Simon put his gun down and first tore the strip of tape strip from her mouth as tears of relief began to fall down her cheek and began fumbling frantically at the bindings on her hands and feet.

"We have to get out fast – Goran's planted explosives that will detonate soon!"

Anna nodded while Simon continued unravelling the tape around her wrists and ankles. It didn't take him long and he finally sat her upright on the edge of the altar table.

"Can you move by yourself?" he asked, wondering what the options were if she couldn't.

Behind him he suddenly heard a groan and he saw Anna's eyes fix on something over his shoulder. It was Conchos; still alive and trying to reach his gun on the edge of the marble platform. Simon could tell he had been hit badly – he could barely move and there was little chance of his reaching the pistol.

Anna slid down from the table and picked up Simon's gun. Clutching her side in pain, she lurched towards Conchos, her face a mask of utter revulsion and loathing. Filled with hatred and barely able to carry the heavy gun, she pushed Simon out of the way as he tried to help her. Conchos saw her coming and his shuffling movements became more frantic but it was useless.

Standing back a few paces, she pulled back the catch on the gun, wanting him to feel the same fear that he instilled in others – that morbid dread that consumes you when you know your life is about to end. She looked into his eyes, hoping to see that terror, but she was disappointed. Emotionless and without remorse to the very end, he stared up at her vacantly before a thin smile spread across his lips.

From point blank range Anna pulled the trigger and the crack echoed around the cavern.

Goran saw the bullet hit Conchos, killing him outright. He looked down at the Book of Judas in his hands and paused for a second before throwing it into the fire of the metal cauldron. He watched as the flames began to engulf the pages of the manuscript.

481

"Move!" shouted Goran, checking his watch. "The explosives will detonate in about sixteen minutes!"

Anna stood rigid over the body of Conchos but was jerked back to the present as Simon grabbed her arm and pulled her in the direction of the stairs. Being dragged along, she screamed in horror as she saw the dead body of Philip lying across the marble floor.

"Come on – he'd want us to do this," said Simon persistently, pushing her hard to keep going moving.

Goran stayed on the platform a few moments longer watching the flames devour last few pages. His mission was complete as the book finally disintegrated and he set off following them out of the chamber. He caught up with them quickly. Despite his own condition, Anna was using Simon for support. Goran realised they would never make it at this rate – and the explosive detonator he had set was irreversible.

"Move!" he urged Simon gruffly and hoisted Anna over his shoulder.

Together they began sprinting to the exit, Simon doing his best to keep up. Goran checked his watch again and cursed whoever had designed the intricate labyrinth. Again and again a corridor would suddenly give them hope that they were reaching the outer limits before again it turned back towards the centre.

"Are you Ok?" shouted Goran over his shoulder.

"Keep going, don't stop," yelled Simon. The pain in his leg was all but unbearable.

Goran pushed ahead. He knew he would have a problem getting them out of the labyrinth at the other end. Finally, he turned the corner and saw the welcome shaft of light at the end. Running to the end, he lowered Anna to the ground and checked the explosives' timer: seven minutes and counting...

"Please help him," gasped Anna.

Goran knew there were sufficient explosives to blow half the mountain away. If he went back they might never get far enough away. He saw the look on her face and set off quickly back down the passageway.

"Where are you?" he shouted as he turned another corner. He heard the reply – faint but not too faint. He was close.

"Come on, let's move" said Goran when he finally reached him and wedged his shoulder under his arm.

Together they climbed back through the tunnels until they reached Anna. Simon could tell from the fading light that afternoon was turning to early evening.

"Ok you first," shouted Goran to Simon. "When you're out, help pull Anna up and then jump into the pool below – have you got it?"

"Got it," gasped Simon.

Using all his strength, Goran pushed Simon upwards until he could reach the outer perimeter of the rock around the hole. Earlier, Simon had managed to tighten his tourniquet but it had fallen loose and blood was flowing freely from the wound. Pulling up with his arms while being pushed from below, he made it. Balancing precariously on the ledge, he reached down to take Anna's hand. Her light frame made it easy for them to lift her and seconds later she was next to him.

"Jump, both of you!" shouted Goran aggressively from below.

Simon looked down at the rock pool for an instant, steeled himself, grabbed Anna and pushed her over the edge. Arms flailing, she plunged into the centre of the pool before bobbing back up to the surface. Simon quickly followed as Goran's head and shoulders appeared through the entrance hole behind him.

"We've got to keep going – get as far away as possible," shouted Goran before launching himself after them.

At different speeds, they clambered out of the water. Goran immediately went to assist Anna but she put her hand up.

"I can do it – please help Simon!" she cried.

483

He stared at her for a second; he was determined to make sure his protégé survived.

"Really!" she repeated earnestly.

"Go then," he shouted and she mustered her strength to try and run down the wadi bed towards the Sea of Galilee.

Goran turned around and saw Simon stumbling in the shallow water.

"Come on then," he said offering his shoulder again and they began chasing Anna down the rocky slope.

"Faster," shouted Goran, almost dragging Simon's body along.

He checked his watch – thirty seconds to go.

"Over there, Anna," he yelled, letting go of Simon briefly to point towards a stone outcrop that offered shelter.

The noise of the explosion was deafening as its ferocity ripped through the side of the mountain, sending rocks and debris flying through the air in every direction. Simon and Goran hurled themselves under the outcrop as the shockwaves shuddered down the ravine. The force made the ground shake as rocks broke free and fell down the canyon walls.

Finally, after a few minutes, the noise stopped and they sensed it was safe to stand up again. The after-effects of the explosion continued as occasional rock falls ran down the mountainside and blinding dust clogged the air.

Anna, emotionally and physically scarred, felt the cuts and swelling on her once-beautiful face. Tears filling her eyes, she walked over to Simon and slipped her arms around his waist as they both gazed up the ravine to where the entrance had once stood. They were both thinking of Philip.

Goran sat exhausted on a rock and pulled out his phone to see if there was a signal. It was weak but he tried dialling.

Colonel Renauld picked up the receiver in Rome's Holy City; he was in Pope Leo XIV's study waiting for the news to arrive.

"The book has been destroyed!" Goran rasped, still gasping for air.

Goran gave an abridged version of events before asking for their help in making a suitable escape from Israeli territory. He knew it would only be a matter of time before troops appeared on the scene.

Colonel Renauld was delighted to pass the news on to the Pope. The mission had been successful. They had destroyed the Book of Judas and it would never again raise its ugly head to threaten the existence of mankind.

Chapter Forty-Seven

...Sixteen months later

The Israeli Government classified the explosion as confidential and did their best to play down any approaches or questions on the subject from concerned foreign governments. Instead, they entered into protracted discussions with the Vatican to ascertain what had really happened on the shores of the Sea of Galilee. Both parties had cooperated well together during the fifties when the ancient Qumran Scrolls were first discovered but for some reason the Israelis never felt that they received a satisfactory explanation for the unusual explosion in the middle of some barren mountains.

Over time, the powerbrokers within the Vatican ensured that all the loose ends were not so much tied up but gradually eliminated. For the first six months of Pope Leo's reign in office the media had a field day. They suggested lies, deceit and power struggles within the Vatican walls were responsible for the unusual deaths of so many high-ranking Cardinals in such a short space of time. The media even offered its own conspiracy theories about Pope Leo XIV's accession to the papacy. The damage caused to the image and reputation of the Roman Catholic Church was extensive but only a handful of people knew how much worse it might have been.

After thirteen months, the Israelis decided the only way to get to the truth was to excavate the site of the explosion. It took weeks to clear even the superficial debris but they soon realised that below the rubble was an ancient burial site and they called in a team of archaeological experts from Jerusalem University to mastermind the project. The Vatican watched proceedings from the outside. They even requested permission to attend the excavation but the Israeli government flatly refused. In fact their initial findings persuaded them that the site should not only be confidential from the eyes of the Vatican but that it should also be out of bounds to the media and general public as well.

Many more weeks passed before they reached the labyrinth and its maze of passageways that led deeper into the base of the mountain. They found human remains. Many that were centuries old but some were much more recent. The findings only added to the intrigue surrounding the explosion.

The large team of professionals worked on the site each day, with a new team taking over for the nightshift. Many of the experts were driven on by their intense curiosity about what was slowly being revealed below the piles of rubble. With the night-lights on, they worked tirelessly within the perimeter of the huge scaffolding blocks that were covered with tarpaulin to make sure no outside eyes could see what was going on. After more weeks of hard work they finally revealed the raised marble platform that had once stood in the middle of the great chamber and the smaller antechamber that led to the crypt of Judas.

Sixteen months after the explosion, a young trainee archaeologist was walking along the perimeter of the square during the nightshift. He shone his torch along the edge as he reviewed the day's completed work – the light caught something and he ran his fingers along the surface...

The dirt felt soft and he scooped away a few handfuls to reveal a small, hollow crevice in the wall. Pointing the torch, he peered in, his excitement growing as the object glinted again in the light. He pushed his arm in and felt a hard object wrapped in a canvas-like material – he pulled it back through the gap. For a split second, he considered sharing his find but quickly decided against it. Why should he? His superiors would only claim the glory for themselves...

Unfolding the fabric, he peered in before quickly stuffing the contents into his shirt and making his way hastily back to his lodgings. Once in his room with the door firmly locked shut, he opened it again...

Inside was a small, silver digital camera – quickly, he dimmed the lights and switched on his computer. He had the necessary leads and connected the camera to download...

He sat back, staring in awe as the waves of information flooded down onto his computer screen. *Incredible, simply incredible,* he thought as he scrolled down through page after page of ancient text littered with grotesque illustrations.

He paused, wondering what to do next...

Slowly and deliberately, he leant forward and pressed the mouse – his computer began dialling the outside world to share his discovery...

Printed in Great Britain
by Amazon

17408175R00283